THE HIGH IMPEDANCE OF MAGIC

"The task is simple," master magician Rosimar said. "Just remove the weights from the scale in the order indicated when I signal."

As Rosimar hurried to the doorway, Jemidon studied the scale. An array of springs and switches clustered around the balancing arm, from which ropes, pipes, and pulleys led to other apparatus of magic.

Jemidon saw Rosimar wave an arm to begin and took a step, extending his arm to remove the top weight from one pan of the scale. But as he did, he tripped and stumbled. His hand crashed into the weights, sending them all to the floor. His feet tangled in the ropes and levers. With snaps and twangs, they jerked free of the moorings. He heard a sharp crack as the ballista released its charge. In a moment, the place was a chaos of wreckage and wild confusion.

Once again, Jemidon had failed abjectly at the simplest practice of magic. The great experiment was ruined. And now there would be no way to save Augusta and himself from the slave collars of Trocolar!

Secret of the Sixth Magic

LYNDON HARDY

A Del Rey Book

BALLANTINE BOOKS • NEW YORK

To my mother, Zella

CONTENTS

PART ONE: *Robe of the Master*

PART TWO: *The Postulate of Invariance*

PART THREE: *The Axiom of Least Contradiction*

PART FOUR: *The Verity of Exclusion*

THAUMATURGY

The Principle of Sympathy ——— like produces like
The Principle of Contagion——— once together, always
together

ALCHEMY

The Doctrine of Signatures ——— the attributes without mirror
the powers within

MAGIC

The Maxim of Persistence ——— perfection is eternal

SORCERY

The Rule of Three ——— thrice spoken, once fulfilled

WIZARDRY

The Law of Ubiquity ——— flame permeates all
The Law of Dichotomy ——— dominance or submission

Secret of the Sixth Magic

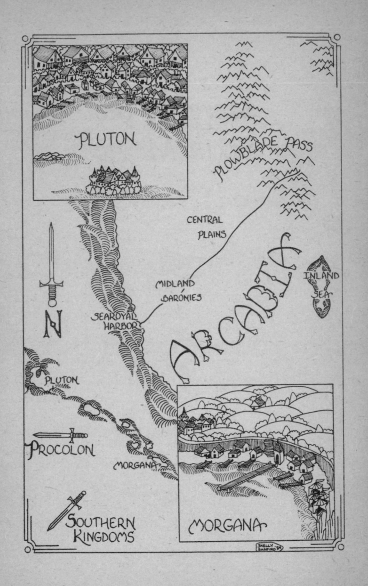

PLUTON

PLOWBLADE PASS

CENTRAL PLAINS

INLAND SEA

MIDLAND BARONIES

ARCADIA

SEAROYAL HARBOR

N

PLUTON

PROCOLON

MORGANA

SOUTHERN KINGDOMS

MORGANA

SHELLY SHAPIRO '83

PART ONE

Robe of the Master

CHAPTER ONE

A Matter of Style

JEMIDON'S pulse quickened as he stepped from the creaking gangplank onto the firmness of the pier. Finally, he had arrived at Morgana, the isle of sorcery. He must have scanned a hundred scrolls to make ready, but he felt as uncomfortable as if he were totally unprepared. And this time, unprepared he dared not be.

As the other passengers disembarked from the skiff and jostled past, Jemidon drew his scholar's cape tight against the onshore breeze. His hair was raven-black, combed back straight above a square and unlined face. With deep-set green eyes, he scrutinized whatever he saw, seeming to bore beneath the surface to discover the secret of what lay within. He had the broad shoulders of a smith, but pale skin and smooth palms marked him as one who did not toil in the sun. Although the purse at his belt bulged with a respectable thickness, his brown jerkin and leggings were threadbare and plain. Around his neck on a leather thong hung a smooth disk of gold, the features of the old king long since worn away.

At the end of the planking, Jemidon saw a brightly painted gatehouse, guarded by two men-at-arms who collected a copper from each one who passed. On either side, all around the small harbor, rough-beamed buildings crowded the shoreline and extended precariously over the water on makeshift piers. Warehouses and property barns, canvas mills and costume shops, tackle forges and mirror silveries, and all the services for both the sea and the inland mingled in disarray.

In the bay, three ships lay at anchor; from each, a procession of small boats shuttled men and cargo to the shore. The land rose sharply behind the harbor, first to a wide ledge and then into a jumble of heavily vegetated hills and valleys that Jemidon knew hid the lairs of the sorcerers. He dug into his purse for a coin. With a mixture of reluctance and anticipation, he joined the end of the line paying the landing fee.

"Which path to the hut of Farnel the master?" he asked the guards as he dropped his coppper into the pot. "I see there are many trails up into the interior, and he is the one whom I must find."

The guard on the left shook out of his bored lethargy. "All visitors are confined to the shorelands," he said, "lord and bondsman alike. Stay among the houses of the harbor or on the path that runs from the bazaar to the keep. The hills are for the masters and tyros only." He paused and stared at Jemidon. "For your own protection, they are forbidden."

Jemidon frowned back and clutched at the coin around his neck, running his thumb and fingers over the smooth surfaces. Too much was at stake to be impeded by petty restrictions. Too many years already had been wasted.

"Then how does one meet a master?" he asked carefully, trying to remove all emotion from his voice. Somehow it was important that no one else knew the significance of what he sought. If, by some unthinkable chance, he failed once again, failed for the final time, he wanted no mocking smiles and whispered sniggers when he returned to the harbor to sail away. "How do I engage Farnel in conversation? Talk to him long enough so that I might present a proposition that is to our mutual benefit?"

The second guard looked up from his tally sheet and laughed. "To come eye to eye with a sorcerer other than in the presentation hall is not something that most would wish."

Jemidon tightened the grip on his coin. "Nevertheless, I must," he said.

"Then wait near the entrance to the hall." The guard shrugged. "Wait in the hope that Farnel decides to come out of the hills this year and give a performance. He is less likely than most, but it would be your only chance

4

with safety. Along the shore, all of the masters have sworn to cast their illusions from the stage and nowhere else."

"But it is for the very fact that he has stopped entering the competitions that I have chosen Farnel," Jemidon said. "If he presents alone, then he might have no need for what I can offer as a tyro."

Another skiff banged into the pier, and the guards' faces warped in annoyance. One returned his attention to completing the tally sheet and the other motioned Jemidon on through the gate before the onset of the next arrivals.

Jemidon started to ask more, but then thought better of it. He turned to follow the rest of his landing party through the gatehouse and onto the beach. In a slow-moving queue, he crossed the narrow stretch of sand and climbed the wooden steps placed in the hillside. Several tedious minutes later, he reached the broad ledge, some ten times the height of a man above the level of the sea.

The native rock of the ledge was covered with a bed of crushed white stone that led away in two directions. To the south, the path angled around the bend of the island to where Jemidon knew the keep and presentation hall for the lords stood. To the north, the trail ended abruptly against a cliff of granite that thrust into the still waters of the bay.

On the beach at its foot stood the bondsman bazaar. Two wavy rows of tents stretched across the sand. Some were grandiose and gaudy with panels of bright colors supported by three or four poles, but others were no more than awnings covering rough podiums, counters, and simple frames. The path between the tents was deserted and the cries of the hawkers silent. Nightfall was still six hours away. In the distance, beyond the bazaar, the hazy outline of mainland Arcadia could just barely be seen.

After looking about for a moment to get their bearings, most of the landing party headed south, carrying goods and trinkets. The rest soon disappeared around the curve to the north, chattering excitedly about last year's glamours and what had caught the fancy of the high prince. Jemidon paused for a moment, deciding which way to go, then finally started in the direction of the presentation hall, but more slowly than those who preceded him.

The advice of the guard was not at all what he had wanted to hear. Waiting for Farnel could take the rest of the season, if the man came down from the hills at all. Convincing the sorcerer to accept him as tyro immediately had been what Jemidon had hoped to accomplish.

As tyro to a sorcerer, he would study cantrips and enchantments rather than incantations, formulas, ritual, or flame. And then, when the instruction was complete, he would become at last a master, to fulfill what had to be his destiny, to make amends to his dead sister, and finally to cleanse away his guilt—to end at last the quest that had started almost as far back as he could remember.

Jemidon's thoughts tumbled as the rock crunched beneath his tread with a hypnotic cadence. He had been precocious as a child, solver of riddles, puzzle maker, and lightning-fast at sums. He would have a choice of crafts, his father had boasted, possibly even give the archmage a challenge or two. He was the gleam of hope for the family, the way out from the oppressive toil of the wheatlands to lives of their own.

But when the time for testing had come, he had failed at thaumaturgy, the most straightforward and least complex of the arts. And the less remembered about his trials the better.

Then, four years later, when a traveling apothecary came through the village, he had a chance to see if alchemy was his match. For thirty-two months he toiled, scrubbing glassware, digging roots, and grinding powders, just for the chance to try a simple formula from a common grimoire.

There was always an element of chance with alchemy, as everyone knew. No activation could be expected to succeed at each and every attempt. But after a dozen failures with a formula that usually worked nine times out of ten, he was booted out in a shower of hard words about wasted materials and improper preparation.

For two years more he wandered the inland seas, finally taking up a neophyte position at a small magic guild.

The precision and symbolism of magic ritual appealed to the bent of his mind. But after he tripped over a tripod and hit a gong one time too many, the masters shunned his aid in the costly and time-consuming rituals that provided the guild its wealth. Without the practice, he languished while others moved with certainty into the deeper mysteries of the art.

He ventured to the south, hunting for a wizard and the secrets that held sprites and devils in thrall. But after a year of defocusing his eyes on a flame, trying to penetrate a barrier that was tissue-thin, he gave up in disgust.

For each of the arts he had tried, he had been sure that he had the aptitude. He had been quick to learn and he found the theory easy, easier than to many others who had started much earlier than he. Each time, hope had blossomed anew that he had at last attained his craft. But somehow the practice escaped him; when it came time to perform the spells, to implement what he had learned, he had been strangely clumsy and unsure. With a string of mumbled incantations, formulas that went awry, imprecise rituals, and missed connections through the flame, he found he could not exercise any of the four crafts. For none was he suited.

And now he sought to try sorcery, the craft that required the greatest understanding of one's inherent capabilities and limitations. Sorcery was the only art that was left—his last chance to become a master.

If one wanted to study sorcery, then Morgana was obviously where he should come. Nowhere else was the craft of illusion practiced so freely. Nowhere else could Jemidon receive so much instruction in so little time. And by looking through the popular broadsides as well as the arcane scrolls, he had deduced which master more than any other would need what he had to offer—if only he could get to Farnel before it was too late to prepare for this year's competition.

Jemidon stopped his slow pacing. The pathway was totally quiet. Those up ahead were not to be seen. Evidently all of the skiffload behind him had gone to the bazaar. No one else was on the trail, and the flanks of

7

the hills cut the gatehouse from his line of sight. He looked at the beckoning dirt path directly to the left of where he had stopped, a path that wandered away from the bed of crushed stone up into the notch between two cliffs.

"Without risk, there is little reward," he muttered aloud as he made up his mind. "Master Farnel will have a visitor, even if he chooses to spend the entire season away from the hall." Without looking back, he clambered up the path.

The stubby shadows of midday grew into the slender spires of evening while Jemidon followed the random patchwork of paths through the hills. He encountered no one, and the signposts were few and well weathered. It took him many hours to find the one that pointed in the direction of Farnel's hut.

The sun slid toward the jagged horizon as Jemidon climbed the last few lengths to his goal. As he did, he gradually became aware of angry voices from some point farther up the trail. His view in front was blocked by a boulder tumbled onto the path and resting in a litter of smaller stones and snapped branches. The scruffy underbrush on the hill face to the left bore a slashing vertical scar that marked the huge rock's passage. The rise on the right was not nearly as steep, but the vegetation was sparser, with stunted trunks and tiny leaves growing from fissures in a monolithic slab of rock.

Cautiously, Jemidon approached the barrier and squeezed between the dislodged boulder and the adjacent hillside. As he peeked up the trail, he saw a group of youths surrounding two older and taller men who alternately waved their arms and pounded their fists to emphasize the words they were hurling at each other.

The encircling band all wore simple robes of brown, the mark of the tyro, and the two they surrounded were dressed in master's black. On one of the masters, the logo of the sorcerer's eye was old and faded. The other's emblem sparkled with embroidered gold. Behind them all stood a small structure of rough-hewn planks. Thin sheets of mica filled lopsided window frames, and a curl of smoke snaked from the top of a mud-brick chimney on the side.

Farnel's hut, Jemidon thought excitedly, and the master is probably one of the two who are arguing in front. He had done far better than waiting at the hall. Slowly he crept closer to determine the best moment to speak out. As he did, the others paid him no heed; they were totally engrossed in the loud conversation.

The more plainly dressed master growled with a husky voice. His face was rough and deeply wrinkled, like crumpled paper. A fringe of white circled his bald crown. Age should have bent his back and stooped his shoulders, but he stood straight as a lance, refusing to yield as a matter of principle.

"Simple thrills and no more," he snorted. "Pockmarked monsters, bared bosoms, spurting gore. Your productions are all alike, Gerilac. A moment of sudden shock and then they are done. Hardly anything of substance to add to the legacy of the craft."

"Like your renditions, I suppose," Gerilac answered. "With colors so mute that even the tyros fall asleep." He stroked his precisely trimmed goatee and smoothed his shoulder-length hair into place. On the mainland he could have walked in the company of the lords and none would have noticed. "By the laws, Farnel, it is well that the rest pay your antiquated theories only polite notice. If all were to follow your lead, the rich purses from the mainland would have stopped coming long ago. No one chooses to pay a sorcerer who is a bore."

"But it is not art," Farnel shot back. "We do only cartoons of what was performed a decade ago. In another, stick figures jerking around the hall will capture the accolade."

"And how valuable is this art of yours?" Gerilac fingered Farnel's robe. "Sewing your own mends. Rationing your meals between the private charms in the off season and the charities of your peers. Compare that with the elegance of my chambers and the number of tyros at my beck and call. I have won the supreme accolade for the last three years running, while you enter no productions at all. Is it because you choose not to compete, or perhaps because you cannot, even if you tried?"

9

"I was first among the masters of Morgana long before you earned your robe," Farnel growled. "If you doubt it, look me in the eye. I will stand with you in the chanting well in any season."

"Strike out again and Canthor and his men-at-arms will see that you spend more than a single night in the keep." Gerilac hastily flung his arm across his face. "You know the agreement among the masters. And lack of control is bad for the reputation of the island and the traffic from the mainland that rides with it."

"Drop your arm, Gerilac. Another few nights on a cold slab just might be worth it."

"Farnel, Master Farnel!" Jemidon called out suddenly. "You are the one I seek."

The sorcerers stopped abruptly. All eyes turned to see who was responsible for the interruption. One of the tyros, older than the rest, tugged another on the sleeve.

"Get Canthor," he said.

The second nodded and bolted from the circle. In an instant, he disappeared around the next bend in the trail. Jemidon watched him go, pushing away the upwelling of last-minute doubt. He set his jaw and stepped forward boldly. Speaking to Farnel without a large audience would have been better, but he must seize the opportunity when it presented itself.

For a moment the others watched him advance. Then the ring of brown robes dissolved and regrouped in a line between him and the sorcerers.

"I am Erid, lead tyro of master Gerilac." The one in the center pointed a thumb to his chest. "And my master does not take kindly to interruption." He paused for a moment and then leered a crooked smile. "For my own part, however, I welcome the opportunity, before the bailiff comes to snatch you away."

"My dealings are with master Farnel," Jemidon said. "A tyro will not do."

"You should have heeded the warnings and stayed within the confines of the harbor," Erid said. "Here in the hills, we practice glamours of our own choosing." His smile broadened. "Even if you have a taste for art, you

10

might find the experience somewhat, shall we say, disconcerting."

Laughter raced across the line, and menacing smiles settled on the tyros' faces. Jemidon squared his shoulders and straightened to full height. He was five years older than any of the youths, but several stood a full head higher.

"My intent is not to provoke," he said slowly. "And I did not come to be the subject of your experimentation."

"Then your prowess is remarkable indeed," another of the tyros said. "Tell us how you plan not to look one of us in the eye or keep your ears always protected against a whisper."

"Enough. Leave him be," Farnel cut in. "You do your master no credit and waste what is most precious besides. Your talent should be channeled toward pleasing the moneyed lord, not baiting a bondsman who wanders away from the bazaar."

"I am no bondsman," Jemidon said. "I am free to study what I choose. And my knowledge of the lore of Arcadia, the sagas of Procolon across the sea, and the chants of the savage northmen can be of great value to you. Let me speak more of my merit and you will be convinced."

"I am indeed the master you seek," Farnel said. "But I see not merit but folly in one who wanders here alone. It is true that all the masters of Morgana strive to dispel the reputation of fear that sorcery enjoys elsewhere. Indeed, the livelihood of our small island depends upon it. The lords of the mainland would not come and pay good gold for our entertainments if there was a hint of greater risk involved. But our craft must be experimentally manipulated as well. Only near the harbor have we forsworn all glamours; only in the presentation hall do we enchant with consent. Here in our private retreats, one can rely only on the good judgment of whomever he encounters. The tyros cannot be kept under constant watch to ensure that they stay within the bounds of prudence.

"And your luck today was not the best." Farnel turned and cast a frown back at his peer. "You may be noted for your prizes, Gerilac, but your students in particular set no standards by their conduct."

11

"An easy thought for one who has no tyros of his own." Gerilac flicked some dust from his rich velvet. "Although with no accolades in a decade, not even a minor mark of merit, one can understand why there would be none."

Farnel ignored Gerilac's reply and turned back to Jemidon. "Come, I will escort you to the harbor. It would not do you well to be found by one of Canthor's patrols."

"I have a proposition for you," Jemidon insisted.

"Not now." Farnel waved down the path. "Let us get to the harbor without delay. Gerilac has babbled at me all afternoon, and I do not care to hear more of his plans to bedazzle the high prince."

"Discussion of the relative value of your skills and mine does bring discomfort," Gerilac said. "Go ahead, take advantage of your excuse while you have it. Further conversation will not change your worth in the eyes of the other masters."

Farnel's face clouded. He whipped back to stare at Gerilac without saying a word. Gerilac flung his arm across his face; then, after a moment, he slowly lowered it to return the stare. Warily, the two sorcerers closed upon each other, the first words of enchantment rumbling from their lips.

As the masters engaged, Jemidon saw Erid and the other tyros exchanging hurried glances. With a sudden movement, Erid spun his way, but Jemidon guessed the intent. Quickly he stepped aside to avoid the push that would send him sprawling.

Erid staggered to a stop and waved the others to his side. "This one talks of dealing only with a master, but now we will see how well he likes the skill of a tyro."

Jemidon looked at Farnel and Gerilac circling one another, arms across their eyes and loudly shouting to drown out each other's charm. He would have to cope with the tyros himself. He took a half step backward; then, without warning, he reversed direction and drove his head into Erid's midsection. They crashed to the ground and began to roll down the trail in a tumble. He heard Erid gasp for breath as he locked arms around the tyro's back and began to squeeze. The sky and the ground rotated by in alter-

12

nating streaks, but Jemidon kept his hold. Gritting his teeth, he ignored the sharp jabs from the small rocks that lay in their path.

One stone scraped against Jemidon's cheek; another scratched a ragged line along his bare arm. Then, with a jarring thud, his head cracked against the large boulder that blocked the path. Jemidon's eyes blurred. Involuntarily he loosened his grip.

Erid tore himself free. He grabbed for the branches of a scraggly bush and pulled himself to his feet. Jemidon groggily flung his arms out, trying to reestablish his hold, but Erid avoided the snares and pushed Jemidon to the ground. "And now the enchantment," he slowly panted. "Perhaps one that will engender a little more respect."

The other tyros ran down the slope and seized Jemidon by the arms as he struggled to stand. He shook his head, but they grabbed his ears and forced him to look in Erid's direction.

"As to the fee—" Erid pointed at Jemidon's chest. "The bauble of gold will do."

Jemidon struggled to free himself, but the tyros held him fast. His senses reeled. Erid's image danced in duplicate. "Seize the coin at your peril," he managed to gasp. "For fifteen years have I carried it, and even though I would have to track you to the northern wastes, I will have it back."

Erid looked into Jemidon's eyes and hesitated. The fire that smoldered there was not to be dismissed lightly. "Perhaps not worth the trouble of taking," he mumbled. "But if truly it carries with it the memories of when you were a boy, it will make the enchantment all the easier. Yes, that is it. Think of the coin, hapless one, while you look into my face."

Jemidon immediately slammed shut his eyes, but the tyros held him steady and forced his lids back open. Unable to avoid Erid's stare, he heard the beginnings of the sonorous chant that dulled his consciousness.

Jemidon tried to defocus Erid's face into the blur of sky behind, but his thoughts became sluggish and lumbered away on their own. Erid's eyes loomed larger and

13

larger until they blotted out everything behind, finally engulfing Jemidon's will and swallowing it whole. He felt the events of the morning wash into indistinct nothingness and then the day and the week before. With accelerating quickness, all his travels folded and were tucked into small compartments of his mind that he could no longer reach. He was a youth of twenty, fifteen, and finally ten.

Jemidon felt the constraints which held him fall away and he took a step forward. The hillside shimmered and was gone . . .

He found himself in a dimly lighted hovel, still hot from the blazing sun and choking in slowly settling dust. He heard the weak cough from the cot and saw the strained look on his mother's face as she gently placed her palm on his sister's forehead.

Hesitantly he offered the coin in his hand back to his father. "But this brandel will pay for the alchemist's potion," Jemidon heard himself say. "It will make her well. I can take the examination next month or even next year, if need be."

"The next month or the next year we will still be here, Jemidon." His father waved an arm around the small room. "And no more sure of a coin of gold then than now. Take the payment for the testing. Even master Milton says you have a head for it; he remembers no one else in the village with your quickness." The old man's eyes widened and he looked off in the distance. "An apprentice thaumaturge. It is the first step to becoming a master. And then, after Milton passes on, you will be the one who nurtures the crops for lord Kenton and ensures his harvest. You will sit in honor at his table.

"And when you wear that robe, this will be but a memory for us all. There will be pursefuls of coins—why, even tokens from the islands! Go, Jemidon; your sister wishes it as fervently as I."

Jemidon looked to the cot and grimaced. His sister did not care about apprenticeships and fees of the master. She was too young to know. All she wanted was to get well, to play tag again, or to ride on his back and laugh. He was taking away the one sure chance she had for a

14

cure, leaving her and gambling that the fever might break on its own accord.

But more important, when he finally succeeded, could he ever truly pay her back? Even as a master, could he compensate enough for the weeks of chills yet to come—or worse, the atrophied limbs that might result when it was all over? Was a robe of black worth so much that the choice was as easy as his father made it?

"Go, Jemidon. Milton gathers the applicants in the square before the sun passes its zenith. Being late is not an auspicious beginning."

Jemidon felt the upwelling doubt; but looking in his father's eyes, he could not find the courage to speak again. He clutched the coin, nodded silently, and turned for the door.

Then the imagery of the glamour blurred. Days passed in a heartbeat. No sooner had he left the hut than he seemed to have returned.

He was back outside his doorway, staring at the rough cloth which covered the entrance. How long he stood there he could not recall; the sun had set, and even the lights in the other shacks were long since extinguished.

"Jemidon, is that you?" His father's hand pushed aside the drapery and motioned him inside. "The four days of testing are done. You were to have returned by noon. Your mother could stand it no longer, and I was just going to look."

Reluctantly Jemidon entered the hut. A single candle cast slowly dancing shadows on the rough walls. He saw the rumpled covers and the empty cot, but felt no surprise. He had heard at noon, after Milton had discharged him in the square. Shyly he looked at his mother, kneading her hands in an endless pattern and staring into the darkness.

Jemidon's father followed his gaze and lowered his own eyes. "It was for the best," he said huskily. "For the rest of us all, in the long run, it was for the best."

Jemidon opened his mouth to speak, but his throat was dry. Numbly he followed the sweep of his father's hand to the small stool near the table.

"But do not dwell on that now," he heard his father say. "There will be time enough for tears. Tell us of your test. To which journeyman will you be assigned? Was it Aramac? They say he is the swiftest. Certainly Milton would pair the best with the best."

Jemidon shook his head and slowly unclenched his fist. He bit his lip as he looked down at the gold coin sparkling innocently in his palm. He saw his father's eyes widen in amazement and felt the beginnings of the sobs that would rack his body for many hours to come...

"Canthor. It is Canthor!"

The yell cut through Jemidon's spelled memories. The image of glinting mail and stern faces suddenly mixed with the receding dark shadows of his father's hut.

"To the keep, take the intruder to the keep!" a voice bellowed above the rest.

Jemidon strained to separate the confusion, but he could not escape the charm. The last he remembered before collapsing into oblivion was choking the painful words to his father: "They collect no fee from those who fail."

The first rays of the rising sun slanted through the high window. Jemidon frowned and shielded his eyes. He rolled slowly on his side and stretched awake. The thin layer of straw had done little to soften the hard stone floor, and it seemed each muscle in his back protested the movement. Except for the one shaft of light, everything was in soft darkness. It took several minutes for him to see his surroundings.

The room was shaped like a piece of pie with the central tip bitten off. The gently curved outer wall contained the only window. Descending sunlight illuminated dancing motes of dust and splashed on the rough flagstones of the floor that was held together by crumbling mortar. An iron grating prevented exit to a corridor to the interior. In the dark shadow beyond was the outline of a spiral staircase that led to other levels of the keep. Across the cell, hands resting on intertwined legs, sat the master sorcerer Farnel.

"Any enchantment broken in the middle can produce undesired effects," the sorcerer said. "Even one that tries

16

to make you act as you once were. I decided to come and watch you through the night to see that you recovered well."

Jemidon shook his head to clear it of the cobwebs of memory. He rose to sitting and centered the coin on his chest. Grimly he pushed the old images away, back to where they had been safely hidden. He did not need their vividness to remind him of the debt he had to pay. For one gold brandel, somehow, he yet would become a master.

Jemidon turned his attention to Farnel, who was patiently watching. With a final deep sigh, he focused his thoughts on the present and what he had to do.

"Perhaps it is just as well that events transpired as they did," he said. "Your attention is what I sought, and now it looks as if I might have it."

"Do not bore me with your proposition, whatever it is." Farnel raised his hand. "I am content with my surroundings. I do not care for some reckless adventure for a lord from across the sea, regardless of the number of tokens dangled my way."

"Yet you have not won any prize in the competition for a decade," Jemidon said, "nor even bothered to enter in the last three."

"A worthless exercise," Farnel snorted. "A mere shadow of what it once meant. Before the high prince assumed his regency, the supreme accolade and the rest of the prizes were decided on merit, artistic merit. The old king may have ruled with too light a hand, but he could distinguish between a vision of true depth and a shallow thrill."

"The high prince is not the only judge," Jemidon said. "Do not all the master sorcerers vote on the compositions of their peers as well?"

"Swayed by the easy coin, every one," Farnel said. "Once the visits of twenty lords were enough. They appreciated the images that we placed in their minds and paid fairly for the entertainments we gave them. It was not much, but we lived in adequate style."

Farnel rose to his feet and began to pace slowly about

17

the cell. "But then, on some idle thought, the high prince and his followers came one year to see what transpired in this corner of the kingdom and left in one visit more gold than we received from all the rest combined. And with his bulging purse, he placed in our heads images as sharp as any of us could have formed with our craft: robes of smooth linen; soft beds; and not one tyro, but a dozen to do our bidding. Now none has the strength to vote his conscience. They all fear what would happen if this one small group were displeasured. The lesser lords, the bondsmen who accompany them, the principles of artistic composition—they do not matter as long as the high prince continues to add hundreds of tokens to the prize sack for the supreme accolade."

Jemidon nodded and chose his next words carefully. "The works of Farnel have remained cast in the traditional forms; this is well known," he said. "But is it because of this steadfastness alone that they are now held in such low esteem?"

Farnel stopped and scowled at Jemidon. "You have received an ample portion of my good nature. Do not presume it gives you license to judge."

"But I do know something of sorcery and the artistic images you make with your craft," Jemidon said. "The Antique Pastoral, Calm Sea in Winter, Mountain Sunlight, and many more."

Farnel stared at Jemidon. "My works of a decade ago," he said slowly. "I see you have not sought me out unprepared."

The sorcerer closed his eyes and ran his tongue across his lips, savoring the memories. For a moment there was silence, but then Farnel snapped back and waved the thoughts away. "But they won no prizes. The drift to shallow forms and empty expression had already begun."

"I know also of what the others said of your works," Jemidon rushed on. "Bold in principle and mood, but flawed in historical or geographic fact. Incorrect costuming of the period, a jutting sandbar in the wrong place, reflections from an impossible direction."

18

"Excuses, all of them," Farnel said. "The works of Gerilac were the new sensation in the eyes of the prince."

"But had yours not been built on error, what then?" Jemidon persisted. "Without the nagging irritants, how might the artistic education of the high prince have proceeded? And who now might wear the robe of velvet?"

"Your tongue is glib. I grant you that," Farnel said, "but the sands have already been cast. What is done is done. It is a matter of style, and our craft suffers because of it."

"I am a scholar," Jemidon said. "Between my attempts for what I must achieve, I have earned my bread in the libraries of the lords and the great cities, reading the old scrolls, tracking down obscure facts, finding the answer to ancient riddles so that one baron can show the power of his intellect to another. And in the course of all of this, I have learned many things that can serve you well."

Jemidon paused for a moment, then rushed on. "Two centuries ago, the capes of the lords hung only to their waists and their faces were clean-shaven. The sandbar in the Bay of Cloves is covered by the high tide. In the morning, when one is looking down into the valley beyond Plowblade Pass, the shadows are on the left."

Farnel looked at Jemidon in silence for a long while. He ran his hand over the back of his neck but said nothing.

"Knowledge," Jemidon said, breaking the silence at last. "Knowledge to remove the inconsistencies from your works, the imperfections that seem to bother the other masters so. All that I have learned in my wanderings I will share." He touched the coin on his chest. "That and one brandel more if you take me as your tyro and lead me to mastership of sorcery."

"And so it is as simple as that." Farnel laughed. "But one must start with a young mind, smooth and pliable, not a mind already filled with the lessons that gave one his manhood. If you must dabble in the arts, seek some other, such as thaumaturgy. You are too old to begin any other."

"No!" Jemidon shouted. "It is to be sorcery." He stopped suddenly, embarrassed by the outburst that echoed

19

off the stone walls. "I am aware of the difficulties," he continued after a moment in a softer tone. "That is why I have come to you. I know that none of the other masters would choose to take me because of my age. But then, none of the others might feel so keenly about winning the supreme accolade in order to reestablish the standards for the art."

"And the one gold brandel?" Farnel asked.

Jemidon breathed deeply, almost choking on the words. "It is the most important of all. You see it around my neck on a simple loop, but somehow it is more intricately intertwined with my innermost being. It is for no ordinary barter; I can give it up only when the debt it was meant for has been fully paid."

Jemidon started to say more, but the jangle of a key in the lock distracted Farnel's attention.

"Canthor, you come half a day early," the master said, rising to his feet. "I thought the penalty for wandering in the hills ran at least from sun to sun."

Jemidon slowed the rush of his thoughts and looked at the figure swinging open the grating. The bailiff wore leggings and a sleeveless tunic. The skin of his arms was smooth and taut. Short bristles of hair, struggling back from a daily shaving, covered a shiny head. Only his face showed any aging; his eyes swam in a sea of wrinkles from a perpetual squint.

"The crude pranks of Gerilac's tyros are punishment for any man." Canthor laughed. "I dare wager that this lad will no longer take our warnings so lightly. No, now is the time to depart. Before Erid and the others think of coming here and sneaking in more practice."

He waved Jemidon to the corridor with one hand and grabbed Farnel by the arm with the other. "And as for you, my rough and unbending friend, far less bother would there be for me in the first place if the masters set decent examples for the tyros to follow. Gerilac told me of what you were attempting when I was summoned."

Farnel shrugged. "If what he built had some merit, it would not matter."

"A soldier is measured by his most recent battle," Canthor said, "no matter how glorious were the ones that came before. If you wish to challenge Gerilac's ascendancy, it must be in the presentation hall, not with hot words shouted outside its walls."

"Sage advice from one who has not raised a sword in true anger in many a year!" Farnel snorted. "If that is so, why are you here instead of taking a side in the growing unrest in the northern plateau of the mainland? The high prince has need of men-at-arms."

"The difference is that I am content with my lot," Canthor replied. "As long as there is sufficient bread on my table and pulling masters apart does not occur too often, I do not care what the others may say behind my back."

Farnel frowned and began to pace the room. "It is too late in the season," he muttered, "and for too long have I not dabbled with the themes and forms."

"Spend time in the bazaar," Canthor said. "Listen to the bondsmen prattle about their lords' latest fancies. You know that pandering to the popular tastes is how Gerilac achieves his successes. You could learn in a few nights what Gerilac guesses at for the entire year."

"Yes, yes, I have thought of that idea often enough myself. But masters do not thread their way among the hawkers and imitation delights," Farnel said. "That is a job for a tyro, and there is none who would care to accept my tutorage."

The master stopped suddenly and his eyes narrowed in thought. He looked at Jemidon and shrugged. "I suppose an alchemist would say that some of the random factors have aligned," he said. "Very well; as Canthor says, it would be better than mouthing more words of protest that the others pay attention to less and less. I accept your proposition. I will begin your instruction as you desire. In exchange, you will spend part of each day in the bazaar, befriending the bondsmen and learning the latest gossips and popularities of the mainland. We will work together for a presentation to the high prince."

Jemidon felt some of the pent-up emotion dissolve away. For once, things were going well. Perhaps this time there finally would be success. "And after the prize is awarded, how long then until I can have my own robe with the logo of the staring eye?"

Farnel placed a hand on Jemidon's shoulder. "The agreement is that I will teach. I can promise no more. It is up to you to marshal the talents within that will make you a master."

CHAPTER TWO

Test for the Tyro

JEMIDON slumped down on the stool in Farnel's hut. The last few months had been a blur. He had worked from sunrise far into the night, following Farnel's instruction, gathering information in the bazaar, and helping to prepare their audition. He was tired, yet at the same time mentally exhilarated. After four months, Farnel still accepted him as a tyro.

"A battle scene." Farnel shook his head as he jotted a final note and tore the full sheet from the easel. "Who would have thought that I would dabble in something so explicit and mundane?"

"But the whispers in the bazaar point consistently and clearly," Jemidon said. "Once you piece them all together, a pattern emerges. The high prince is troubled about the unrest in the wheatlands, and the crushing of the rebellion at Plowblade Pass three generations ago would be an excellent salve."

He scooped up the outline as it fluttered to the floor and pinned it in line with the others already filling the walls in Farnel's small hut. A bed of straw, hearth of smoke-blackened brick, and bowl-cluttered table were at the far end. The coarse blankets under which Jemidon slept on the floor were pushed into a corner. On the longest wall, thin planking supported by tiers of stone sagged

22

under the weight of bound parchment and furled scrolls. The rest of the space was a jumble of wadded paper and stacks of properties used in illusion making—model dragons, silks and furs, cameos of billowing clouds and stormy seas, glass trinkets, and sun-bleached bones.

"Yes, yes, I know." Farnel slid from his high stool and stepped over the pile of swords, axes, helmets, and other weapons lent by Canthor to aid in the suggestions. "Your sojourns to the bazaar indeed provided the focus for the path we should take. And your knowledge of the historical event has been most complete. The agony of the commander before ordering his followers to their death gives me sufficient scope to project something of a deeper meaning.

"Still, I am uneasy. We started so very late, compared with the others. They have had time to polish their presentations to a high luster, while we are not quite done with a complete structure from end to end. Had we been, I would have shown a rough outline to the other masters in the hall this evening. Already they are deciding which to reject and which to keep for presentation to the prince. And when the high prince comes, there will be no time left for more auditions. He is here for about a week only. If one is not ready for him, there is no point in continuing further."

The master scratched the back of his neck. "Yet there are signs of hope. Even Gerilac must have some concern that I am competing again. He was almost civil as he sat next to me at the council meeting when we had our morning meal."

"Perhaps he begins to wonder what profit comes from my evenings in the bazaar," Jemidon said. "I have noticed Erid and the others cautiously following me from time to time. But it will do them little good. Tonight will be the last. I have only one more tent to visit, that of a trader named Drandor, at the end of the row."

Jemidon paused and wrinkled his brow. "He is a rather peculiar sort, to hear the others talk, not connected in any way with the affairs of the prince. But they also say

23

the trip is worth it, just to see his pretty assistant, if nothing else."

"I admit the value of your trips," Farnel said, "but sometimes I wonder if so many have been necessary to achieve the same result. Ordinarily a tyro's evening is spent practicing the charms his master has taught him during the day."

"I have been studying," Jemidon protested. "And if there were more time, I would try to expand your outline into more detail and select the charmlets that will be used. Then we would feel more confident about the final impact that our presentation will have. Rote and repetition can come later. I have memorized well. I am sure of it."

"Why, most of this outline is explicit enough." Farnel frowned and looked at the jottings covering the walls. "The basic idea is not to use a fine brush when a mop will do. The sorcerer should only suggest; the viewer will fill in a much more vivid scene with his own imagination."

"But why risk the random thoughts that might come into their minds when you can direct the precise image with certainty?"

"You already know enough to answer that," Farnel said. "What is the basic law of sorcery?"

"The Rule of Three," Jemidom said, "or 'thrice repeated, once fulfilled.' Each charm must be spoken in its entirety three times without the slightest error, or it will come to naught."

"And the more detailed the illusion?"

"The longer and more difficult the glamour." Jemidon paused for a moment. "Ah, yes, I see the connection. In Procolon across the sea, where sorcery is a sinister weapon of state, the length of the charm does not matter. But in a presentation hall, under the lightest of glamours, the words must be swift, or else the lords will hoot and ask for the next production."

"It works for the benefit of the master as well." Farnel began to scrutinize the last sheet of the outline, cramming cryptic notes into the margins of what was already there. "Each charm robs something of the life force of the sorcerer; there is only so much power within him. And the

24

simpler he can make his glamours, the longer will he prosper. Why, it is for that very reason that the sorcerers of Arcadia forswore the deeper cantrips ages ago and retired to Morgana to deal in nothing more than simple pleasures.

"But enough of that. I want to run through the broad outlines before we go. There will be sufficient time to select the details, once we have been chosen for the final program."

The sorcerer turned to the first sheet and studied its contents. "Let me see, the high cliff walls that define the pass, the hint of storm in the morning, and the last meal in the camps. Perhaps Alaraic's Foreboding, followed by Magneton's Walls of Closure and then Aroma of the Hunters. Yes, they should be sufficiently close."

"Would not Dark Clouds and Clinton's Granite Spires be more to the point?" Jemidon asked.

Farnel cast Jemidon an appraising glance. "You learn fast, tyro, but in this case, the combination will not work. When Dark Clouds is connected with the opening, it finishes on too low a syllable to connect onto Clinton's charmlet smoothly. I am a practiced master, but even I would not risk mouthing such a transition."

"A small Hint of Curiosity sandwiched between the two lines them up perfectly." Jemidon moved to the easel and grabbed the pen. "As I said, I have been studying. See, I think of all these charmlets as little squiggles on the paper. They can be joined together only if their endpoints and slopes smoothly align. Making the grand glamour consists of splicing the curves together so that they move in the general direction you want."

Farnel frowned and studied the sketches as Jemidon rapidly filled the easel. He stroked his chin and rolled his eyes upward in thought. "An interesting way of looking at it," he said at last. "But in the end, it comes to the same thing. The sorcerer must piece together the words for the charm he wishes to achieve."

"But by visualizing the curves, you can slide them around like a puzzle and discover new combinations without risking a self-induced trance to envision them fully formed."

25

"And have you tried this theory of yours?" Farnel asked. "Even with the simpler charms for which I have given you the words? How many of them have you linked together?"

"Well, none," Jemidon said. "I have not had the time. The manipulation of the charmlets on the easel seemed much more interesting. I have always had an interest in finding the underlying patterns of things. And sometimes I have succeeded when others have overlooked them. Who knows, it might lead to some new principle."

"Nevertheless, a master sorcerer is known by the charms he executes, Jemidon, no matter how well he can recite the theory. Believe me, the first time you misspeak, and one goes awry, the sickness that follows will make you wish you had doubled your practice."

"But the rote is so boring. It is just a matter of putting in the effort to do it."

"Exactly so," Farnel said. "Exactly so. There is more to success than making a fuzzy plan that leads in the general direction of the goal. At some point, each step finally must be executed to the finest detail."

Jemidon frowned. He did not like the way the conversation was going. Soon Farnel would be insisting he pass up exploring the last tent and spend the evening endlessly running through simple recitals. And surely he could do that easily enough. The time would be as good as wasted.

His frown deepened as other thoughts tried to bubble to the surface. Determinedly, he thrust them away. Work the simple charms—of course he could. There was no need even to try. And he might learn something of value in the last tent, some additional fact to merge into the whole and make their presentation even better.

"The sun is setting," he said quickly, "and it might be better if I visit this Drandor soon, before the bazaar gets too crowded. The traders are more willing to talk if their tents are not filled with customers."

Farnel looked outside at the growing dimness and then back at Jemidon. "In sorcery, a master can only suggest," he said after a moment. "It is the tyro who ultimately must force himself to attempt the tests. Yes, yes, go on. I see in your eyes how much you want to investigate this last tent. I will dabble with what we have and perhaps even be ready for a first trial when you return."

Jemidon stepped onto the bazaar pathway and jostled the crowd already starting to build. He had walked the distance from the hills to the shoreline in under an hour. Here he could lose his concerns in a myriad of distractions. It felt good to be away from Farnel's hut and the sorcerer's all-too-accurate observations. To Jemidon's left, a hawker in a tunic of gaudy red and green touted sketches that leaped from their canvases. On the right, he heard the moan of a faraway whistle under a sign promising to conjure up rare creatures of legend. Down the path were the other displays, multifaceted mirrors, rotating checkered boards, and vaults of total darkness, where one sealed his ears with wax and dipped his hands in a numbing salve before entering. The cries of the pitchmen, music from adjacent rows, and noises of the crowd mingled into a meaningless hubbub.

Besides the usual taverns and stalls, the bazaar was crammed with peddlers of cheap illusions. They had nothing to do with real sorcery; that was banned in the harbor area by decree of the masters. But with their lords traipsing off to the presentation hall to fill their minds with the artfully constructed images, the bondsmen hungered for a taste of the same thrills. So they paid their coppers for the risqué sketches, the touch in darkness of the slimy tentacle, and the dizzy heads from spinning in the small cages hung from a rope.

Jemidon meandered down the pathway, watching the reveling bondsmen and listening for interesting snatches of conversation. Nothing was worth stopping for, and finally he reached the end of the row. He looked over a medium-sized tent, set apart from the rest; this was Drandor's, the last to check. Jemidon saw that the pavilion was made from three smaller ones, inexpertly sewn together, with excess fabric hanging in disarray where they joined. The colors had long since faded. No pennants flew from the poletops, nor did any peddler challenge the passerby to come inside.

Jemidon ducked to enter the low opening. It was dark inside, illuminated only by two small candles, their flames unprotected by any sort of bowl. "What do you sell?" Jemidon asked, as the slight figure behind the high counter began to take on detail. "Your brothers in the other tents are much more boastful of their wares."

"Exercises for the mind," a melodious voice responded. "Journey with these and you can create illusions of your own making."

Jemidon's eyes widened as they adjusted to the flickering light. He saw a young woman with curls of golden hair and sparkling eyes that revealed their bright blue, even in the dimness. Her features were delicately drawn with the deftness of a sculptor; if not for the tension in her face that pulled the skin tight and wrinkled the corners of her eyes, she would have been judged most fair. From a loop around her neck cascaded a free-flowing gown that sparkled in a subtle iridescence. On her left arm was wound a thin band of dull iron, the emblem of the indentured servant. The counter in front of her supported a scatter of small works of metal, twinkling in the candlelight, webs of intertwined wires, tessellated polyhedra, and burnished flatwares intricately pieced together.

"Your tent has been placed in the wrong position." Jemidon appraised the woman's beauty. "The more traditional entertainments are closer to the entrance by the harbor."

"It is as I have said," the woman responded, after a quick look over her shoulder to the curtain which partitioned the tent. "Entertainments for the mind. Please, buy one. It will help me a great deal."

Again Jemidon marveled at the voice, tinkling softly like a chime in a light wind. "My name is Jemidon," he said without thinking. "What is yours?"

"Delia," she replied. "But that is unimportant. Please examine what I have to offer."

Jemidon looked down at the countertop and grabbed at the tangle of wire that was closest. "Ah, you mean

28

puzzles," he said as he recognized the objects. "I am afraid you will find that few of the pages and runners will care for such things. But with me, you are in luck. I have played with such baubles for years. Unlike my experience in the arts, I seem to have some knack with them. Watch how quickly this one can be undone."

Jemidon closed his eyes for a second to recall the sequence of moves. He grunted in satisfaction that the memory was still there. Then he deftly whirled the wires through a blurring pattern and, with a dramatic flourish, dropped the puzzle onto the counter. The wires tingled dully but remained in a tangle.

"Let me see that again," he said in disbelief. "I must have made a wrong move. It has been some time since I worked this one in particular."

Jemidon picked up the puzzle and closely scrutinized the bends and runs. "Yes, there is a difference here. The outer loop on the larger wire whirls to the left rather than to the right. That means..."

His voice trailed off as he shut his eyes and ran through the sequences again. "Very clever." He opened them with a grin a moment later. "It makes the ending the mirror image of what one would expect."

With a rush only slightly slower than the first time, he completed the altered moves and tossed the decoupled pieces back onto the counter. "Most unusual. Do you have any more like that? I thought I had tried all there was to be found in Arcadia."

"Have him pay or make room for the next." A deep voice sounded from behind the partition. "Your job, girl, is to sell the merchandise, not bat eyelashes at the patrons. Melizar wants a filled purse in a fortnight. No less will do."

The curtain swept aside and a short, dark-haired man entered to stand beside Delia. Bushy eyebrows and mustache framed eyes dark as coals. The lips pulled up in a wide grin, revealing yellow, stained teeth and whitish gums. He grasped her bare arm in a viselike grip: although the flesh paled from the pressure, she bit her lip and did not speak.

"This evening we must do better, Delia," he said. "On the other islands, they were poor and a token was hard to pry loose. But here we have the jangle of copper and silver from the mainland. Why, even this gentleman carries a coin of gold. Tonight there will be no excuse. Fill the purse as you have been directed, or else you will learn more of my pastimes in the room behind."

Jemidon looked at Delia's suddenly frozen expression and impulsively he wrestled with his pouch to produce a coin. "Here, let her go. She has served her purpose well. And know that it is because of her that I buy one of these trinkets. From you, there would have been no sale."

"I am Drandor the trader," the small man said, stretching his smile even further as he released his grip. "And I see you are a gentleman of discerning taste. Perhaps some other item from far away would pique your interest as well." He swept his arm in a large arc while making a bow. "Here in the back are the better items that cannot be bartered for less than true gold or tokens of the islands."

Jemidon looked at Delia rubbing her arm, her lips still set firm. "You have no cause," he said. "It is not her fault that your tent is not abuzz with gawkers like the others. Raise up a flap or two. Add some light and sound."

"My partner, Melizar, wants buyers, not ones who only look and then go their way," Drandor said. "And do not waste any thoughts on the girl. She is not a bondsman with rights and privileges, but fully indentured, no different from a lute, a painted vase, or any other item I have to sell. I can do with her what I will."

Drandor followed Jemidon's eyes back to Delia and grunted. "Unless, of course, the gentleman is sufficiently smitten to bargain for her as well. Although I warn you, the price will be dear. She cost no less than fifteen tokens in the exchanges at Pluton. And it would take much more to compensate for my lost pleasures, if she were to go."

Delia reached out her hand and placed it on Jemidon's, which was resting on the counter, her eyes opening wide in sudden expectancy. He looked into their deepness and sucked in his breath. If he had a purse of gold, impul-

30

sively, he knew how he would spend it. Only with a determined effort was he able to will his faltering attention back to Drandor.

"You mentioned items from faraway lands," he said quickly. "Perhaps there will be something more to my liking."

Drandor grunted and pulled aside the curtain. Jemidon rounded the counter and stepped into the rear portion of the tent. Bolts of cloth, stacked precariously, towered on one side of the entrance. Cases of spices, their aromas competing for attention, framed the other. Huge bottles filled with dense green swamp gas lined the far wall in front of another tentflap that must lead to a final compartment beyond. A small furnace with coals still smoldering stood beneath a large wooden frame, from which hung a collection of shackles, spikes, and chains. Pokers and tongs, their tips thrust into the cooling sand, still glowed a dull cherry red. Scattered about were sketches of terrified women straining against their bonds to avoid the touch of searing iron. One was draped carelessly over the body of a small rodent, its limbs bound to a small wooden frame by tightly turned loops of thin wire and its crushed skull lying in a pool of blood. Near the center of the tent, stringed instruments and long, hollow reeds lay in a jumble on top of a pile of small drums, their heads pulled tight by tiny weights spaced around their rims.

From a cage in a far corner, cloaked in shadow, Jemidon heard a canine growl, followed by another deeper than the first. Instinctively, he froze and held his breath. He had encountered large mastiffs before, but somehow these guttural rolls touched a primitive nerve. It had been a warning, and he knew he would not be given another.

"Not now, my pretties," Drandor said. "This is for business."

A single paw thudded against the framework in defiant protest, and then there was silence. Jemidon slowly let out his breath. He peered into the pen, trying to see what could shake a crate so large and stoutly built; but except for four burning eyes, there was only blackness. He

31

smoothed the short hairs on the back of his neck and glanced over the other stacks and containers.

"And what is that?" he asked with forced casualness, pointing at a lattice of wires and beads that stood waist-high to his left. "Another puzzle that I have not seen before?"

Part of the structure resembled a model scaffolding, with struts at right angles methodically outlining an array of touching cubes. But other lines of differing colors radiated from the vertices at odd angles, creating amorphous bulges and isolated tendrils that snaked into the air. Some of the nodes where many lines came together were encased in intricately carved and brightly colored beads. Even from a distance, Jemidon saw that with the proper twist a bead could be decoupled and slid along one of the wires to the next vertex down the line.

He reached to touch the curious structure, but a high-pitched voice cut him short. "Property of my master, property of Melizer," it said. "I am a guardian, and you must not touch."

Jemidon looked upward and saw that the light from one of the lamps was not produced by a flame, but by the incandescence of a tiny imp, flittering brightly in a glass prison. Its large head was in grotesque proportion to the delicate limbs and gossamer wings. One eye seemed swollen shut from a wart that covered most of one jowl and sprouted three coarse black hairs as thick as nails.

"An imp in a bottle," Jemidon wondered aloud. "Why, after the archmage battled the demon prince years ago, I thought all wizards abandoned such indiscretions. You deal in marvels indeed."

"Like the lattice, there are a few items not for sale," Drandor said quickly. He glanced at the flap leading to the third compartment and then spoke as if he were on a stage, enunciating each word so that everyone listening could hear. "The imp and the drums are the private property of my partner. He merely stores them here while— while he rests. The pets are a gift from him to me."

Drandor paused, watching the tentflap, apparently awaiting a reaction. The canvas rippled slightly and a wave of cold air sluggishly rolled underneath the gap above the floor rugs, but nothing else happened. Drandor let out his breath and turned his attention back to Jemidon.

"But no matter. What else, what else?" he suggested. "State your pleasure. I can satisfy a prince with what I have in stock today."

Jemidon watched the flap a moment more as the cold coiled about his ankles. But the canvas hung straight. Except for the gentle breathing of the mastiffs, he heard nothing. With a shrug, he turned back to what had originally attracted his interest.

"I have only copper," he said absently as he studied first the imp and then the lattice underneath. "The gold around my neck I will not part with for any of this."

"Only copper!" Drandor exclaimed. "Copper and no gold! I am to show these choice wares only to those willing to pay, and in a discreet manner besides. Melizar wills it so. Take your imposturing to another tent, where they are more gullible and less prudent with their precious time."

Drandor grabbed Jemidon by the arm, but he shrugged the trader off. "A moment, just a moment more. There is some pattern about the way the struts leave the central cube at an angle. See, with a few more cross bracings, they would form another symmetry there."

"Begone, I say." Drandor reached for Jemidon a second time but then stopped as a blast of trumpets suddenly pierced the air.

A muted cry soaked through the heavy canvas of the tent. "The high prince. The high prince. He disembarks in an hour for the first night of illusions at the hall. Bondsmen of the prince and his retinue, attend unto your lords."

Farnel and his sorceries popped back into Jemidon's mind, and he knew that time enough had been spent at the bazaar. Despite his reluctance, he must immediately return. There would be little time left now in which to prepare. He looked at Drandor's scowl and again at the cage in the corner. With an irritated wave, he indicated that he was going.

"I will return, Drandor," he called as he passed through

33

the front tent. "There is much here that interests me."
He cast one glance back at Delia, standing like a statue
behind the counter. "Yes, much more that I would like
to understand exceedingly well."

Farnel's reaction upon Jemidon's return was an energetic one. "Tonight," the master said. "We must present
what we have tonight. My peers will determine the final
list at the end of the audition session that is taking place
now. They will make the selection and be done with it,
so that the winners have time to prepare."

"But as you have said, we are not quite ready," Jemidon replied. "Only the barest of sketches with no substance behind any of them."

"It cannot be helped." Farnel waved away the words.
"Get the stool and observe what I have put together. Note
the jumpy transitions and any other major flaws. If it holds
together well enough, we will go to the hall immediately
and demand to be heard."

Jemidon climbed up on the stool. Farnel stood at the
opposite side of the room, adjusted his robe, and then,
without preamble, rattled off the glamour. With surprising
quickness, the sketch on the first sheet seemed to spring
to life; the mountain felt real, the distant thunder fore-
warned of the approaching storm. Jemidon saw the blur
of troops and heard the oration on horseback and the yell
as the two seas of men poured toward each other. In rapid
succession, the images flitted by, each indistinct and lack-
ing in detail, but somehow capturing the depth of feeling
that ultimately would be there.

And through it all, Jemidon was keenly aware of his
real surroundings. The hard stool was uncomfortable; the
smells of yesterday's meal still hung in the air. In the
periphery of his vision, the disarray of the hut had not
gone away. He felt the freedom to engage or ignore the
images as he chose. Idly, he broke focus and sought out
Farnel to see how he gestured as he ran through the charm.
Once Jemidon concentrated on looking, the sorcerer sprang
into view. His eyes wide and staring, Farnel continued
mouthing the charm.

Then, without warning, the master's eyes bulged even further. He grabbed at his throat, and a dry rasp escaped, instead of a sonorous tone. In an instant the spell was broken. The mountains, the lightning, the cavalry, all vanished in a flash. Jemidon saw only Farnel in his hut, the master falling to his knees and emitting retching sounds as he sagged.

Jemidon sprang from the stool and ran to where the sorcerer had collapsed into a tight ball, clutching his throat with one hand and holding his other arm tightly to his stomach.

"Farnel, Farnel, what happened?" Jemidon yelled. "Why did you lose control?"

The sorcerer's eyes twitched rapidly from left to right. He lolled his head to the side. "Gerilac," he croaked. "The reason for the restraint at the meeting. I should have known. A few drops of some depressant in the wine would have done it. Enough for me to lose my voice and falter. He knew the prince would come today and that it would be our very last chance to audition."

Jemidon stepped back, giving the sorcerer room, and then helped him struggle up on one elbow. "He fears my entry into the competition," Farnel said. "He fears it! Now more than ever, I must go on."

The master rose to sitting, and Jemidon offered an arm to pull him up. The sorcerer wavered a moment and then lowered himself back to the floor with a groan. "It is not done yet," he said weakly. "I can feel the backlash stirring in my head. It will be several days before I can attempt another spell."

"But the selection," Jemidon said. "You told me we must hurry or be too late to be considered."

"You will have to cast the glamours. Gather up the outline. I will accompany as best I can."

"The glamours! I do not know a tenth of what is needed and none had I practiced, for them to go well."

"You said you had practiced," Farnel growled.

"Studied, yes," Jemidon said. "Studied but not practiced. It is an entirely different thing." The feeling of what suddenly was being asked of him began to brew inside.

Of course he knew he finally must prove his capabilities to Farnel, but not like this, not until he was truly ready.

"It is only a quick skim-through," Farnel insisted. "Just set up the stage and cast a light Power of Suggestion. It is the first one that I taught you. The masters have seen many such outlines. They will be able to extrapolate to the quality that is there."

Jemidon started to say more; but, from the look in Farnel's eyes, he knew that further argument was useless. Reluctantly, he gathered up the sheets and bound them to an easelboard. "Rest on my shoulder as we go," he said. "Perhaps your strength will return enough so you can cast the charm yourself."

Farnel coughed and waved Jemidon to the door. The sorcerer grabbed a torch and teetered after with a shuffling step. Without speaking, they started on the path.

After half an hour of stumbles and rest stops, they arrived at the wooden building that was illuminated by a ring of torchlight at the end of the trail. It was the largest structure on the island, larger even than Canthor's stone keep. Weathered cedar covered the exterior, a quilt of planks running in different directions, as new extensions were hastily added to accommodate the increased entourage that the high prince brought with him each year. Originally a two-storey rectangle of modest size, the hall sprawled in an ungainly array of annexes, corridors, and lofts. Jemidon and Farnel entered through the low door cut in the rear and ascended the half-flight of stairs that led to the stage. Behind the first few rows, the seats were not arrayed in a regular pattern. Instead, they clumped in groups of twos and threes, some with tables and lounges close at hand. Between each group, threading back and forth across the upslope, ran a confusion of partitions that blocked the view of one group from another, while not obscuring the stage.

"The Maze of Partitions," Farnel croaked as he waved at the sprawl of paneling. "Getting to a seat from the entrance in the front of the hall is like one of those puzzles you are always babbling about."

Jemidon ignored the master's frustrations at the turn

of events. He looked at the muted tapestries on the outer walls that absorbed even the echoes of midday to produce an unnatural silence. From a well at the foot of the stage, an almost painful light leaped up to hit the array of faceted mirrors overhead. Beams of white blankness reflected throughout the theater, into the recesses off the luxury boxes along the walls, and through the corridors to the more private suites branching in random directions. Besides the wellbeams, the hall glowed from a scatter of candles and oil lamps tucked into odd crannies, the ones closest to the tapestries above buckets of sand or water, in case they should catch fire. One stretch of paneling was streaked with smoky black from an apparent accident long ago. Others danced with frescoes and mosaics, pale reminders of popular glamours cast over the years.

Except for the masters sitting in the first row, the auditorium was empty. But Jemidon found himself imagining the scene on the night of the judging for the supreme accolade—what it might be like, once he wore the robe of the master . . .

In his mind, a buzzing chatter filled the air, despite the heavy wall hangings. From unseen alcoves, coy giggles danced above the general drone. Silks and satins paraded through the maze, and rare perfumes mingled with the heat-laden air produced by the smoking torches. Smooth-faced pages glided between the boxes, offering sweetmeats and wine, stoically ignoring the teasing caresses of the noble ladies.

When his face finally appeared in the multifaceted mirror, the voices abruptly stopped in all the small cubicles. Perhaps from backstage, the lilt of a simple melody radiated into the hall, deliberately soft so that everyone strained to hear. In synchronism with the rising curtain, he began his glamour, a roll of warm words that gently compelled and embellished the dimly lighted shadows on the stage. The reflections of his eyes permeated everywhere, seemingly attentive to each individual who was there.

From simple beginnings, the hints of form transmuted into bright images. Sounds and smells blended with the

37

rest. Like the impossible union of a masterful composition of music, a stunning work of art, culinary delights, and innermost euphorias and fears, they all swirled together in an integrated whole.

Gasps of pleasure, cries of surprise, and screams of simulated pain poured forth from the enraptured audience as the spell wrapped them in its grasp. With a rising crescendo, the emotional intensity of the imagery reached its climax, and then, with an abrupt transition back to reality, it was done. There was a moment of stunned silence, a timid clap, and finally a roar of applause. Jemidon, they would call, Jemidon, master of sorcery, master of the arcane art. Choose his work for the supreme accolade! Choose it as the best for the prince...

"And so from this dozen we must choose the four to present to the prince."

Jemidon jarred his thoughts back to why he was there as he felt Farnel's elbow in his ribs. He blinked and quickly looked about. He had heard one of the masters addressing the others.

"As usual, a difficult choice; they all have merit. But we cannot expect the lords to sit through more than four and still retain their good humor."

"There is yet another." Jemidon shook himself fully alert. "Master Farnel breaks his long absence with a submission for consideration by his peers."

"It is growing late." Gerilac rose and looked at Farnel. "Besides, the master does not look all that well. Perhaps he has decided at the last minute to withdraw after all."

"For this selection, I will cast the glamour." Jemidon forced out the words, trying to ignore the queasy feeling building in his stomach. If he were going to be a master, then performing a simple charm for a single row should be of no concern at all. Despite the lack of practice, he knew the words well enough. "Master Farnel will observe with the rest of you, in order to gain a better critique of the results."

"A tyro—and one who has received instruction for less than a year. Most unacceptable," Gerilac said.

"But Farnel's coming out of his withdrawal should be

encouraged," another replied. "Have with it, tyro. I am curious as to what your master has to offer."

Jemidon nodded and quickly relayed the instructions to the runners for which properties to fetch and position. A few minutes later, the stage was alive with activity. While the fabric boulders and mountain skyline were pushed into place, Jemidon descended into the chanting well. He placed his sandals in the footprints painted on the floor, as Farnel had instructed, and slid his forearms into the rests.

Jemidon blinked at the strong light and turned his head slightly, so that the glare was not directly in his eyes. In the proper position, an image of his face reflected up onto the mirrors overhead and then was projected to all the recesses of the hall.

The curtain closed. After a moment, the final scrapes and thumps behind it halted. In the silence that immediately followed, the churning in Jemidon's stomach intensified. Why hadn't he spent more time learning the words to the simple charms? At the time it had appeared so easy. He should at least have gone through them once to cement them in his memory. Now, instead of the studied calm that Farnel said was so necessary, visions of hurried flight streaked through his mind. He tried to concentrate on utter blackness and to push the thoughts away; but, like minnows swimming through a large net, they passed through his barriers with ease.

The curtain rose. In a mounting panic, Jemidon grabbed for the first word of the charm. He opened his mouth to speak, but then hesitated and frowned. Somehow the way it formed on his tongue was not quite correct. If he spoke, something subtle would be wrong. He strained to recall the proper enunciation, as Farnel had taught it to him, but the sharp edges that made all the difference blurred. He raced forward to the second word, hoping by association to recover the first, but it, too, dissolved into a meaningless garble. With a feeling of sudden helplessness, he tore through the first stanza, searching for some phrase that remained firm and solid; but as he did, it all slipped away, until not a single syllable remained.

"Well," he heard Gerilac boom down from above, "we are waiting for the effect. At least something to cover the seams and rips in the properties. They are meant only to be a hint. The glamour is to carry the burden of it all."

"The first scene is morning in Plowblade Pass," Jemidon called back. "From the west come the lightning flashes of a storm."

"Ah, opening with a riveting display," someone said. "Eye-burning bolts of yellow, claps of thunder that hurt the ears. It seems that Farnel has come around at last."

Jemidon tried a final time to recall the glamour, but it was totally gone. There was no point in trying further. His mind was blank.

"Come, come, the lightning," the voice persisted.

"No, that is not the main effect," Jemidon called up. "You see, master Farnel intended to focus on the commanders." Quickly he shuffled through the easel sheets. "Here, I will show you the outline. It begins in the second scene."

"But the thrill of the storm."

"It is not directly in view." Jemidon raced up the stairs in a flapping of papers. "Just muted rolls and brief flashes at the periphery of vision. More of an ominous foreboding, to set the mood. It is later that the principle theme is brought forth."

"The prince will not sit still for such empty art!" Gerilac exclaimed. "There are three or four here with much more interest and impact."

"If you could see the effects and how they mix together, you would better understand," Jemidon said weakly.

"Understand, understand!" Gerilac shot back. "It is for you to understand, tyro. We pick the four to present to the prince on the merit of what we see here and now. No credit is given for hasty preparation and promise of improvement later on."

Jemidon looked down the row of solemn masters, their faces all stern and one or two nodding agreement. "Master Gerilac is right," one of them said. "It would be unfair to the others to judge on scribbled notes alone. At the very least, there should be some Power of Suggestion. Why, even a tyro of a week should know it well. Return with your master. There is nothing more here that you can do."

Farnel pushed forward, but then staggered, clutching his stomach. For a moment, he strained to launch a protest of his own, but no words could he force out. No one spoke. After a long silence, the master's shoulders slumped. With a deep sigh, he grabbed Jemidon's arm and turned for the stage door, a look of bitter disappointment clouding his face. Jemidon pulled himself free but did not protest further. In a daze, he slowly followed the master out of the hall.

Like a drowning man, he reached out for the blur of explanations whirling in his mind, trying to grab a reason as it spun past, a reason besides the one he shunned for why he had failed again.

He had been rushed, or perhaps he had not studied as diligently as he should have. The chanting well was unfamiliar and threw off his composure. Farnel had said to use the Power of Suggestion when, deep inside, he had thought Shimmering Mirrors would have been better. Or maybe it merely was a matter of luck. Even the best of the masters did not complete every charm they attempted. A single slip of the tongue in the beginning was all that it would take. A random slur, or a moment's forgetfulness, and the spell would be broken.

For a long while, the two walked the path of white stones in silence, Jemidon's thoughts tumbling, and Farnel with his hands clamped in a tight knot behind his back.

"Gerilac and the supreme accolade," the master whispered as they finally approached the hut, the deepness of his voice beginning to return. "Again it is a possibility."

He grabbed at a branch that poked onto the trailway and snapped it in two with a savage twist, hurling the free piece up the hillside. "Gerilac knew the prince would come today and acted accordingly. And incapacitating my voice for a few hours was enough. I should have been more alert during the instruction. The signs were there, but I was distracted by the preparations. You absorb a lot quickly, Jemidon, but not once did I see you try even the simplest of charms. Yes, your mind is quick, but somehow, deep inside, you rebelled against sorcery."

"No!" Jemidon exclaimed, breaking out of his reverie. "I will do better. We have an agreement. My help in a production in exchange for your instruction." He felt drained from the disappointment in the hall and did not like where Farnel's thoughts were leading.

"The opportunity of this year's production has been lost." Farnel shrugged grimly. "It again will be Gerilac or some other bragging at the feasting when it is done. But that is not any different from what it has been so many years before. Somehow I shall find the will to endure it. I will go and raise my tankard with the rest and look them all in the eye, if they dare to return my stare."

Farnel paused for a moment in thought. His eyes narrowed as he studied Jemidon before him. "But as for you, trust the experience of the master. The end-of-season celebration should be avoided. Aye, not for you the celebration, and perhaps not even sorcery. I think, Jemidon, that one of the other arts might be better to your liking."

"I know something of them all," Jemidon said. "But now sorcery is my only choice."

Farnel's brows contracted, and Jemidon rushed on before the sorcerer could speak.

"Yes, I know of thaumaturgy with not one law but two: the Principle of Sympathy, or 'like produces like'; and the Principle of Contagion, 'once together, always together.' The craft is much used to fertilize the crops and increase the yields in the wheatlands where I was born.

"And I know some of alchemy with its Doctrine of Signatures: how 'the attributes without mirror the powers within' to guide the formula maker concocting his potions, salves, and the sweetbalms which close the deepest wounds.

"And I also know of magic and the Maxim of Persistence, which states that 'perfection is eternal.' Even you must have some notion of the craft. The indestructible tokens of Pluton come from the guild there that performs its rituals for the trading houses and monetary exchanges.

"And finally, I know of wizardry with two laws of its own: the Law of Ubiquity, which states that 'flame permeates all' and is the channel to the domains of the demons, entire worlds totally different from our own and filled with the likes of great djinns, flittering imps, rockbubblers, and ticklesprites; and the Law of Dichotomy, 'dominance or submission,' which tells that one must totally control the devil he calls or submit to its will instead.

"Yes, I know all the laws which define and guide the arts—the principles from which all else follows."

"Then select one and gain its mastery," Farnel said. "Sorcery is but one of many from which to choose."

"I have chosen!" Jemidon exclaimed. "I have chosen them all! There are none left to sample. Why do you think I come to you at such an age? Because I have struggled with each of the other arts for several years before. And for each, the result has been the same. Somehow, somehow when it has come to the first test, the first chance to prove my worth, I have failed. I have failed at them all—thaumaturgy, alchemy, magic, and the lore of the wizard. For them all have I labored to no avail. Sorcery is my last chance to become a master."

"I should have known all of this before we made our agreement," Farnel said.

"Evidently a few months were not enough," Jemidon protested. "I guess I did not concentrate on the fundamentals." He licked his lips, straining for the right words. "But now we have a whole year. And we will be on guard for petty tricks besides. Yes, the next year will be different, and I will be well on my way to becoming a master."

"And does the robe mean so very much?" Farnel asked.

"So very much?" Jemidon choked. "So very much?" The vision of his dying sister, the look he saw in the eyes of others when Milton passed by, the riches, the power, the prestige, all danced in his thoughts. "There is no question of how much," he said. "It means everything. Everything! Besides the robe of the master, there is nothing else at all."

43

For a moment, Farnel did not speak. Finally he turned back in the direction of his hut. "You can stay until after the end-of-season festivities in a week," he said. "With you still about, Gerilac might wonder if there is some scheme of my own that is hatching. The uncertainty is the least I can repay." He glanced a final time at Jemidon. "And after that, we will see, we will see if there is any profit in instructing you further."

CHAPTER THREE

Stormflight

JEMIDON pulled his arms tighter around his knees to shut out the onshore breeze. The wind whipping up and over the granite cliff seemed to whisper dark secrets as it sped by. The moon was full, shining in a gap in a cloud-filled sky. Its cold and sterile light cast pale shadows among the dark buildings of the harbor below. The lights were all out; the ships of the prince had left hours before.

Only in the presentation hall, Jemidon knew, was there any activity. The masters and tyros celebrated the end of the season with an all-night revelry that lasted until the award of the supreme accolade at Canthor's keep the next day. Even Farnel was attending the festivities. He would not sulk and planned to be as merry as the others to prove that he did not really care. But he had sent Jemidon away. After a few bottles of ale, the sorcerer could no longer count on eyes sharp enough to keep his tyro from trouble with Erid and the others. And after what had happened at the preliminary selection, it was doubtful that Jemidon could hold his own.

The week after the failure in the chanting well had been a total numbness. Farnel had said no more about the future. It was clear enough that Jemidon would have to prove he could at least cast simple charms if he were to stay. And since Farnel was no longer preparing a presentation, there had been ample opportunity to try. But each time Jemidon had found an excuse and shrunk away from the test. The possibility that the master was right and he had no skill was too frightening to face. And he had acted like a child as it was, pouring out his past in a babble and pleading for another chance. How could the master give him even the smallest portion of the respect he hoped to have when he finally won the right to wear a robe?

Jemidon looked down to the beach at the base of the cliff. He had had no interest in watching the flurry of tent striking during the afternoon as the hawkers hurried to depart for the next market. With the sailing of the nobility, Morgana was transformed in a single day to a moribund isolation that would not be shaken until the beginning of the season the next year.

Jemidon shrugged and hurled a small stone into the air, trying to follow its descent into the gently lapping water below, his eyes sweeping over the deserted bazaar. All but a few of the attractions were furled and stowed away on ships bound for other islands. As the rock fell, a spark of light grabbed his attention. He looked closer, to see Drandor's oddly shaped tent still standing in almost perfect isolation on the sandy beach.

As Jemidon watched, a sudden movement focused his attention more. He saw the trader pull a heavy roll of fabric from the opening and drag it with short jerks across the sand to a scaffolding newly erected nearby. Drandor grabbed one corner and stepped on a short stool, uncoiling what looked like some sort of rug or tapestry. Then he paused, uncertain, and looked back in the direction of the tent. One of the flaps was rolled up, and Jemidon thought he saw fleeting motions in the dimness within. The gusty breeze carried hints of garbled whispers, lilting phrases that he could not quite understand.

Drandor appeared to be listening as well. Several moments passed before he turned his attention back to his burden. Then, straining to full height, he looped one corner onto the edge of the framework and moved to the other end to do the same. After some struggle, a large panorama, five times the length of a man and easily as tall, was boldly displayed to the grounds of the bazaar.

Drandor brushed his hands and started for his tent, when a sudden gust of wind toppled the scaffolding onto its side. Faint curses drifted up to Jemidon on the cliff. A cloud dimmed the moon and a few warning drops started to fall.

Jemidon pulled his cape around him and started for cover. But then he stopped as he wondered why Drandor did not do the same. In the quickening wind, the trader struggled to right the tapestry and ignored the coming storm. With ropes anchored to some large boulders, he steadied the mural in the proper position and, with two quick incisions, created rifts to spill the wind.

A gentle sprinkle began to fall as Drandor pulled a large oil lamp, backed by a reflector, from the tent. For several minutes, he struggled to get it lighted. Finally a circle of light beamed to the tapestry flapping in the wind. The scene was an unfamiliar one, a rock-strewn foreground set against a reddish sky. Strange beasts grazed and hunted in splayed grasses and tangled briars.

Drandor lugged forward a large box and pried off the lid, just as the first sheet of heavy rain crashed from the sky. Jemidon felt the water quickly soak through his clothing, but he wiped his face dry and followed the action below. Again Drandor appeared uncertain and looked to the tent. Finally he nodded and reached into the box, pulling out a panel of paper stretched across a light frame. He held it up for inspection, but the falling rain immediately shredded it to ribbons. Shrugging, the trader brought forth a second. Careful to keep it vertical, he placed it in front of the lantern. The lamplight shone through the paper onto the mural and another beast appeared, grazing among the others. Drandor quickly threw the panel aside and reached for a third. The same beast was projected again, although in a slightly different orientation than before. Quickly the trader ran through a fourth, a fifth, and then many more. Jemidon saw that the set of figures was in a sequence, each one showing the next posture as the animal extended his neck to reach for a fruit dangling from a low branch.

As the scenario unfolded, more figures came into view. Meteorlike rocks streaked across the sky. One swooped low, almost touching the plant tops, and men with grayish skin and wearing loincloths descended among the beasts. While some stalked the animals with nets, others used picks and shovels to pry into the boulder-strewn ground. The soaring stone that had dropped them to the surface reappeared over the horizon. Pieces of discovered crystal were dumped onto the net-ensnarled beasts, and then the tangles of rock, animals, men, and nets lifted back into the sky. Like swords drawn to a lodestone, they were attracted to the flying monolith as it sped away.

As he watched, Jemidon felt the numbness of the past week dissolve away. The trader's actions were somehow a tantalizing fascination that kept him watching, even though he was getting soaked to the skin. He felt buoyant, a sense of chains being snapped, of being cast adrift and sailing away. He listened harder to the wind whistling past his ears, ran his tongue over his lips to taste drops of rain, and rubbed the wet sharpness of the coin about his neck, using all his senses to experience what was happening. But the drifting was somehow internal as well, an irresistible tug that snapped anchorages hidden far away and started huge monoliths lumbering free to seek other resting places.

For a long moment, Jemidon puzzled about the strange feeling, but then a movement on the path that led up the face of the cliff distracted his attention. Golden curls, plastered down by the rain, bobbed above the edge. He recognized Delia struggling upward on the slippery stones, tripping over the tatters of her soaked gown.

"Jemidon!" she cried. "A stroke of luck in my favor! You must help me. Drandor is distracted, and now is my chance."

Jemidon's eyes ran over Delia's wet gown that followed closely the curves of her body, but she ignored the stare. She ran forward and grabbed his arm.

47

"Quickly," she said, "quickly, before he releases them to come after. I must get to the harbor. I plan to sail with the flotilla of the high prince."

"They left with the tide hours ago." Jemidon felt the sense of drifting fade and then vanish altogether. All was rock-solid, as it had always been before. Her closeness eclipsed the attraction that had pulled his attention to the trader. For the second time, she was asking for his help. To know her better might produce sweet rewards.

But she was indentured. Drandor probably could produce some document of sale. And Canthor would not care about the apprehension in her eyes. Maintaining the reputation of Morgana to the traveler would be his only concern. For Jemidon to get involved would mean risking expulsion, being forced to leave before Farnel could teach a single thing more.

"To gamble in the token markets of Pluton was foolish. Yes, I admit it." Delia filled the silence. "But many others have I seen rise from the streets to manor houses on the seacliffs. And even those who lost and had to sell their freedom to pay their debts did not fare so badly, if their masters were kind.

"My first acted with discreetness." She lowered her eyes. "And the whip of the second was easy enough to avoid, if you made no errors in totaling the sums in his countinghouse. But when his own fortunes crashed and he could not choose to whom his properites would go, it was Drandor who carried me away.

"And from the first, he has licked his lips in anticipation. Nightly he heats his tongs and pinchers and oils his chains. He leaves crude sketches of my scarred face and maimed limbs for me to find in the morning.

"With him, it is a game. Evidently his partner, Melizar, prevents him from acting rashly with their joint property without due cause. And so he hints, threatens, and tells me his fantasy a bit at a time. Then he waits, waits for my reaction, for some protest, a falter in carrying out a command—any shadow of an excuse for him to justify feeding his desires."

48

Delia stopped and shuddered. "And by the laws, it has worked. I can stand it no longer. I must be away."

Jemidon reached for Delia's hand, but then dropped it as his thoughts tumbled. How could he help? Save for the harbor area, he was as defenseless on Morgana as she. To whom else could they turn? Farnel would not want to get involved with a complication that had nothing to do with his art. And any other master or tyro would be interested in them only as the recipients of some degrading spell.

"You are legally bound," he said, but then stopped when he heard a low growl that carried to the cliff top, despite the wind and rain.

"They are free for the hunt!" Delia exclaimed. "He has discovered my absence far sooner than I thought."

The short hairs on Jemidon's neck bristled. "Come," he said in sudden decision. "We will go down the slope, back the way I came."

"Wait, there is more." Delia did not pause to thank Jemidon for his aid. Instead, she ran to the cliff edge and dipped back over the rim. A moment later she returned, struggling with the lattice and the imp bottle that Jemidon had seen in the tent a few days before. "My passage from the island. Any captain will gladly trade a berth for items that can fetch a goodly sum elsewhere."

"They are not yours to take." Jemidon hesitated. "And they will only slow you down."

"Then I will carry them myself." Delia juggled the bottle under one arm and tried to swing the lattice across her shoulder. "If Drandor must face his partner's wrath for their loss, then so much the better."

A second growl rolled through the air and then another. Jemidon shrugged, rushed to the lattice, and flung it across his back. He grabbed Delia's hand and jerked her about to follow him across the cliff top. She took a cautious step, and immediately they both fell in a splatter; the rain had given the granite a treacherous slickness.

"The imp!" Jemidon shouted. "Shake the bottle and disturb his sleep! His light will guide the way."

Delia rattled the jar, and a weak flickering pulsed from

its interior. "Patience, master," a thin voice called. "In a moment, I will be ready to do your bidding."

Jemidon ignored the imp's babbling and peered into the darkness. Like the bow of a great ship, the monolithic plug of granite on which they stood pushed defiantly into the sea. On the side adjacent to the bazaar, the wall was steep, although generations of patient hammering had pounded a path to the broad and gently rolling top. The other side was more sheer still, and a descent at night carried too much risk.

"Yes, the way I came," Jemidon said. "The cliff top slopes back into the interior of the island. We will pass close to the dwellings of many of the masters and tyros; but with all of them at the presentation hall, it probably will not matter."

Jemidon climbed to his feet and started out at a fast walk, one arm over his shoulder holding the lattice and the other guiding Delia to follow. He heard Drandor's voice closer than before and barks of excitement. He began to trot and then, jumping over a large crack, broke into a run. In a moment, they were racing down the slope, dodging jagged ledges as best they could and skirting boulders too large to vault.

The wind tore at Jemidon's cape, and he squinted away the rain which dashed into his eyes. He felt the cold chill of the water, despite the exertion. Behind, he heard the gasps of Delia's breath as she struggled to keep pace and the flail of her feet when she tripped and scrambled for balance.

The time ticked away. It had taken a small part of an hour for Jemidon's leisurely ascent, but the return seemed far longer. He wanted to charge forward even faster, to sprint at top speed until they could reach some cover. But the small slips and stumbles impeded their progress. The race through the blowing rain progressed in agonizing slowness.

Finally the way leveled off, and the soggy crunch of pebbles underfoot indicated that they had intersected a path used by the sorcerers. Jemidon slowed, but Delia plunged onward, the change in terrain catching her by surprise. Her feet skittered on the wet stones, and she fell, pulling Jemidon with her. They collapsed in a tumble of arms and legs. The lattice clanged loose, and the imp bottle squirted free to roll down the road.

The rain diminished for a moment. The full moon shone through. Arms around each other, the two panted deeply, trying to regain their breath. Jemidon looked back to the cliff top and choked in surprise. There, framed in the moonlight, were three silhouettes. If he had not recognized one as a man, he would not have believed the scale. Drandor had been small, but even so, a dog on all fours should come no higher than his waist, not halfway to his shoulder. The mastiffs' limbs were not long and spindly like a racing hound's, but muscled and full. Their heads were all snout beneath slight ridges that marked the eyes and ears. Jemidon saw the trader point in his direction, probably at the imp light, and then let go of the rein. The larger mastiff howled. With a surge of strength, it jerked its huge body to charge down the hill. The other answered and quickly followed behind.

Jemidon pulled Delia to her feet and randomly selected which direction to flee down the trail. They sprinted by the lattice, and Delia bent to scoop up the imp bottle as they passed.

"Not that!" Jemidon shouted. "The rain is washing away all of the scent. When the moon clouds over again, that light is all they will have to track us by."

He looked back over his shoulder to gauge how much time they had to find a place to hide, and his heart sank. The dogs seemed to skim down the slope in great bounding strides. They had already covered half the distance between them, while he and Delia had moved hardly at all. Jemidon ran for another few steps and then halted, shaking his head.

"It will be to no use," he gasped. "They will run us to ground in the end. Whatever we do, it may as well be here."

"But what?" Delia's eyes widened. "I have seen what has been left of the carcasses from the times before." She pointed back to the cliff top. "See, Drandor is following so that he can savor what they will do."

For a moment, Jemidon watched the shadowy rushing hounds and the trader moving more slowly behind. He saw them disappear into blackness as the moon again winked out and he shook himself into action. He ripped off his cape and began to wrap it in a thick bundle about his left forearm. He felt a small, hard lump in one of the pockets; with a grunt of recognition, he removed the metal puzzle he had purchased from Delia a few days before.

"Your hem," he said in sudden inspiration. "Tear me a strip and then get low to the ground."

Delia opened her mouth to speak, but Jemidon motioned her to silence. In a brief moment, the mastiffs came rushing up to the bottle, howling at their discovery.

The sky was now totally black. Only the glow of the imp cast any light. The chorus of clicks and pops of the rain against the pebbles of the path masked the noise as Delia ripped her gown. Together, she and Jemidon crouched to the earth and held their breath, watching.

The dogs circled the bottle, and one gave it a push with its snout. The imp's incandescence flickered brighter, bathing the heads of the hounds in a ruddy glow. Jemidon saw lips pulled back to expose long rows of ghost-white teeth, the canines slender and pointed, extending to the chin. Tiny eyes darted to and fro, cruel searchlights scanning for their prey. Clouds of steamy breath pumped from their nostrils into the humid air. The larger mastiff growled in frustration. It pushed at the imp bottle a second time and then put its nose to the ground, slowly sniffing the trail that led in the other direction.

Jemidon and Delia lay perfectly still, huddled behind a low rock beside the path. Scarcely breathing, they watched the hound wander off in the dimness. The smaller one circled the bottle and shook its coat, holding its head high, testing the wind. It hesitated a moment longer and then turned in the opposite direction from the other.

With a slow, deliberate step, one paw at a time, it walked down the trail, eyes scanning and ears cocked for any suspicious sound. Delia's hand tightened on Jemi-

52

don's padded forearm as the dog drew closer. He touched her hand in reassurance and then quickly began to wind the strip of cloth around the clump of metal. The hound drew abreast of the rock, just as Jemidon finished and ceased all his motion. He gripped the small wad tightly in his fist and tensed the muscles in his legs. He would have one chance; if he missed, there would not be another.

The hound stopped and growled. It was a low and guttural sound, extending into the subsonic, seeming to vibrate even the boulder behind which they crouched. Cautiously, Jemidon rocked himself forward and raised his head. With a barely perceptible motion, his eyes cleared the horizon of the granite and he peered out onto the path.

The hound was looking the other way in a sweeping scan of the darkness, its ears still tensely erect. Gradually it turned back full circle to stare in Jemidon's direction.

For a long moment, nothing happened. Jemidon and the dog stood frozen, separated by the obscuring rain. Then, in a sudden blur, the mastiff leaped forward. With a roaring growl, it vaulted the rock, jaws wide and front legs extended. Jemidon stood up to meet the onslaught. He took aim through the opaqueness and at the last possible moment hurled the cloth-wrapped weight into the gaping mouth. The mastiff plunged onward, grabbing Jemidon about the shoulder and tumbling them both to the ground.

Jemidon felt a stab of pain as the teeth cut through his wet tunic and into his arm. He rolled to one side. With his protected forearm, he tried to pound on the dog's nose. The first two blows skittered harmlessly aside, but the third landed on target. Instinctively, the mastiff snorted to clean the passage and then inhaled to test the result.

Immediately, it released its grip and coughed, trying to dislodge the puzzle sucked into its throat. Jemidon whirled free of the flailing paws and stumbled back on Delia beside the rock. The hound steadied itself to charge, but only a muffled bark escaped from its jaws. Its eyes began to bulge. With great heaves of its chest, it sucked the wad of cloth deeper into its windpipe.

Deliberately, it marched to where Jemidon had fallen, but each step was slower than the last. The mastiff faltered on one foreleg and then collapsed in a heap. With eyes staring in pain, it pawed the ground, struggling for air.

Jemidon rose to his knees, just as another growl warned him to look behind. He whirled and flung up his left arm as the larger mastiff bounded over the rock. The hound bit into the cape-wrapped sleeve and surged forward, landing on top of Jemidon with a rib-jolting crash. Jemidon reached up with his free hand, but his shoulder was already starting to stiffen. His blow stopped short in a stab of pain.

He locked his legs around the dog's barrel chest and tried to tip the mastiff to the side. In response, it spread its front legs in a wide vee and settled its rear to form a stable tripod. Even through the protection of his cape, Jemidon felt the pressure of the teeth and the spasm of the jaw muscles as they gritted down harder on the cloth. The hound jerked Jemidon's arm from side to side, with each tug pushing it backward and up over his head.

For a second, Jemidon ignored the tactic. He concentrated on twisting his arm as much as he could in order to pry it from the viselike jaws. But the hound's grip was too firm; in a moment, Jemidon's arm was well extended above his brow. The dog then suddenly let go and dove for Jemidon's exposed throat. Jemidon reacted instinctively and brought his arm flying back down across his face. In the last split second, he managed to interpose it as a barrier to the gnashing teeth.

Again the mastiff began to work Jemidon's arm aside. This time Jemidon clenched his muscles tight and tried to keep his arm between the foam-flecked mouth and the arteries pulsing in his neck. The beast growled at the resistance. It stopped the jerking back and forth and clamped its grip tighter. The sinews in its neck and shoulders knotted. Then, with a mighty heave, it flung Jemidon's arm aside like a discarded bone.

Jemidon pulled his arm back, but a massive paw stomped on his elbow, pinning it to the ground. Jemidon twisted to the opposite side, but he could not break free.

He tugged and pulled, but he was held fast. The hound saw the end of resistance and howled with success. In desperation, Jemidon flung his other hand palm upward across his throat. The mastiff stared down at Jemidon, clicking its teeth in anticipation. Jemidon closed his eyes for what would happen next.

Suddenly the hound barked with pain. It lurched backward and turned its head to snap at what had dropped onto its back. Jemidon opened his eyes to see Delia astride the huge beast, clutching a small, bloody dagger. The hound's motion threw her to the side; but as she fell, she slashed again between the ribs. The thrust plunged true. In a burst of gore, the mastiff staggered and fell to the ground next to its strangled comrade.

Jemidon rose to his feet. He looked at Delia and pointed at the blade dangling at her side.

"It was to be my last resort, if Drandor had his way," she said vacantly, still not comprehending what she had done.

Jemidon nodded. He looked back to the dead hounds at his feet. Impulsively, he opened the jaws of the one closer. "Fifty-six teeth," he said slowly after a moment. "No wonder they looked so savage." He dropped the head and frowned in thought. "A latticework can be from any smith's shop and an imp from across the sea, if from nowhere else. But there is no breed from which could come such as these."

Jemidon stared back into the blackness. "Drandor," he said. "We still must flee. He cannot be far behind."

"And the lattice and the bottle," Delia answered.

Jemidon grunted and gathered his remaining energy. He ran to fetch the array of wires and beads. "Wrap the imp in what remains of my cape," he called back. "The trader probably knows these trails less well than I."

"Where do we go?"

Jemidon began a shrug and then stopped with the reminder of pain. The cuts in his shoulder were not deep, but they would have to be attended to. And the fight with the hounds had been exhausting. He had no more ideas. "To the hut of Farnel, the master sorcerer," he said as he started to jog down the path, one arm dangling at his side. "We can hope he is already back from the feast." He stopped for a moment while she caught up with him. "I guess I will have to ask for additional favors sooner than I thought," he said.

CHAPTER FOUR

Sorcerer's Gamble

JEMIDON pounded wearily on the rough-hewn door. The rain had stopped. Dawn was breaking over the high hills to the east. Now, with the light, they needed a shelter in which to hide. Because of Jemidon's injury, they had had to move slowly, and Drandor had remained fairly close behind.

"Away with the summons," Jemidon heard Farnel growl from behind the door. Indeed, the master had already returned. "The presentation is not until noon. And I need not rush. The loose tongues of the other masters made clear how their votes would be cast. I have seen enough tokens bestowed on Gerilac. One more time will hardly matter."

"It is your tyro!" Jemidon shouted. "And I have a problem—something that your experience with the ways of the island may be able to resolve!"

The door creaked open. A bleary-eyed Farnel in a rumpled nightshirt squinted out into the growing brightness. He grunted recognition and motioned Jemidon inside. With a second wave, he indicated the fruit on a side table and lumbered back toward the bed.

"Jemidon offered me aid when I was most needy," Delia said without moving. "I hope the kindness of a master will be even greater."

Farnel turned back, rubbed his eyes, and looked closer

56

at Delia. He shook himself suddenly awake. "Speak again," he said slowly.

"I ask for your help," Delia replied.

"And more, something that gives difficulty to the tongue." A hint of excitement crept into Farnel's voice. In an instant, he was transformed from a groggy-headed old man into a straight-backed master of sorcery, dancing eyes hinting at the dart of thought suddenly alive within.

Delia paused, then spoke again, puzzled. "Do you mean things like fresh cheese or six sick sheep?"

"The voice is a pure one." Farnel looked at Jemidon, rubbing his hands in satisfaction. "Perhaps you have been of some value after all."

"Her delights do not matter," Jemidon said. "That is not why I have brought her here." He was still exhausted from the struggle. The pain in his arm was now a constant throb.

"Nor are they my interest," Farnel snapped. "Can you not hear how she speaks? Are you so intertwined with theories that practicalities of the art totally escape you? That voice! No one on the island, tyro or master, has one that comes close to its purity. Wrapped around a charm, it would be perfection. My peers would offer much of their learning in order to cast a cantrip or glamour with such clarity." He stopped and thought. "Yes, we must try it. It is worth the effort. Far better than debating the virtues of Gerilac's style or struggling with meaningless competitions. If the others hear the value of faultless words, then convincing them of the purity of my art will follow easily. How could anyone resist the truth of what I always have maintained, if it is so perfectly spoken?"

Farnel glanced around his hut and scowled in annoyance at the disarray. "Come in. Come in and make yourself comfortable, lass. I am most curious as to how you will repeat what I will tell you."

"But that is not why we are here," Delia said as she and Jemidon passed through the doorway. She looked around the rough furnishings and eventually sat in the only uncluttered chair. "Drandor may have been close enough to see us enter. I do not care to confront unprepared anything else he might fetch from his tent."

"To aid in some petty squabble is not why I have asked you in." Farnel waved away the words. "We will select the charm before anything else."

"Then make it a Wall of Impedance." Jemidon grimaced as he lowered the lattice to the floor. Farnel's flying off on some diversion of the art was not something he wished even to contemplate. And he was annoyed with himself for not recognizing the potential of Delia's voice as had the master. "A Wall of Impedance, some sort of chant to block the hurt."

Farnel noted Jemidon's pained expression, and then his eyebrows rose in question marks as he saw the blood-stained sleeve. "Erid?" he asked.

"Later." Jemidon shook his head. "After I have some rest."

Farnel frowned and looked about the hut. "I have some sweetbalm here," he said. "Payment by an alchemist who wanted a private glamour two seasons back. It is old and stale and, as a side effect, it sometimes produces a great desire to sleep. But it might aid until a charm is cast."

Farnel rummaged through a box at the foot of his bed and then tossed Jemidon a small tube of salve. Jemidon grunted thanks, removed his tunic, and applied the balm to the cuts in his shoulder. Almost instantly, the throb diminished and the swelling began to subside.

Farnel watched the red begin to fade from the wounds and turned his attention back to Delia. "Each of the other arts has its place, I suppose," he said. He smiled at Delia as he approached. "Now the Wall of Impedance. Yes, just the thing to teach the lass. Simple enough that it is one of the first instructed to the tyro, but with enough potency that the enunciation must be exact."

The sorcerer took the imp bottle from Delia and set it on a table. "Pay attention to the beginning," he commanded. "The last few syllables are not quite the same, and that makes all the difference."

"The help I seek is not one of instruction." Delia shook her head slightly and looked out a small window facing the trail. "But if I can remain hidden long enough, perhaps the trader will give up the search and sail on to Pluton, as he had planned before I fled."

"Pluton," Farnel said. "A trader will find little to barter there. Fortunes are measured by sums and abstractions on paper, not by trinkets from faraway lands. Why, even the common gossip of the day must be bought, rather than freely received."

Delia ignored the comment. "Will you provide the shelter and more active aid, if that is what I need?"

"Will you attempt the charm?"

Delia looked once more out the window. She touched the iron around her wrist, and her shoulders sagged. "Oh, if you must, tell me the beginning," she said. "It is far less than what I would otherwise have to pay."

Farnel rubbed his hands together like a small boy anticipating a new toy. Jemidon settled down onto the floor beside the lattice and tried to make himself comfortable. He was still aware of the wound in his shoulder, although the pain was much reduced. And now, without its distraction, Farnel's interest in Delia began to grate as an irritant. Perhaps it was the fatigue and tomorrow he would think more clearly; but, by the laws, he was the master's tyro, not someone of only a few moments' acquaintance. If there was to be instruction, he was the one who should receive it. And with no previous exposure, it would take Delia considerable time to grasp all the subtle shades of intonation.

For the Wall of Impedance, he had required more than two hours, practicing each syllable over and over until it was spoken correctly. The effort had been such a drudgery that he had not even bothered to string them together and try the complete charm when he was done. None of them had he practiced. Once one was explained to the end, his interest had waned. Far more intriguing was how the next cantrip or glamour was begun.

As Farnel droned on and Delia echoed, Jemidon idly fingered the coin about his neck and tried to recapture his feelings when Drandor had projected his images on the beach. He looked at the lattice and frowned as he struggled to understand its structure. Near his arm, the basic pattern was highly symmetrical. Nodes spaced themselves evenly in a cubic array. Connecting vertical struts were red; the horizontal ones were blue in one direction and yellow in the other. Most of the vertices connected only to their regularly spaced neighbors; but along one row, additional green wires stuck out at an odd angle, extending to nodes isolated from all the others.

In other regions of the lattice, orange wires branched in yet another direction; elsewhere there were lines of purple and black. Jemidon followed the progression of wires and saw regions in which green, purple, and orange formed the regular cubic array and the red and yellow connected the outliers. In the dense center, all seven colors competed to catch the eye in some unifying pattern that one could not fathom in a single glance.

Near the edges, the lattice was thin and sparse. Long tendrils of a single color rayed away from the center, like a mine following a vein of ore. At the regularly spaced intervals, stubs of unit length branched off like exploratory shafts, occasionally sprouting little sublattices that ran on other courses for two or three units more.

"Why seven directions, each with its own color?" Jemidon mused aloud as he reached for a bead that clung to one of the nodes.

"The Postulate of Invariance." The imp in the bottle sprang to life. "The Postulate of Invariance. Seven exactly. There can be no more. It is Melizar's, and you must not touch."

"Quiet," Farnel snapped. "I am in the midst of instruction."

"Seven exactly." The imp's eyes gyrated in uncoordinated circles. "Nor can one force there to be any less."

"Cease the provocation so it will be silent." Farnel scowled at Jemidon. "At the very least, you understand how important it is that I not be misheard."

"As you said, the sweetbalm is old," Jemidon answered. "The pain is not totally gone. And an idle wait for several hours to learn a spell I already know is not something I would freely choose."

"An example recital of the completed charm would speed the process, I admit," Farnel said, "but the ale from last night makes me slow enough that I dare not try it myself." He watched Jemidon cautiously test the mobility of his arm. "But perhaps necessity will be a better motivator than a master," he said, rubbing his chin in thought. "Show us what you have learned. Speak the charm for yourself."

Surprisingly, Jemidon felt a spark of excitement through his fatigue. The sense of dread which had accompanied all the other opportunities somehow was totally gone. He felt no confusion, no doubt that he might fail. Instead, it was an opportunity to redeem himself in Farnel's eyes. He glanced at Delia, who was looking at him expectantly. He searched through his memory to see if he still could recall the beginning and found that the first words were there, sharp and firm. Quickly he rose and walked to the mirror.

Jemidon licked his lips and rattled through the first few syllables in a rush. He paused briefly, expecting the nauseating backlash of a miscast charm, but he felt none. He saw Farnel's reflection nodding approval. Encouraged, he concentrated on the next grouping.

Again the words sprang from his lips with crispness. He caught the cadence of the chant and, with rising confidence, completed the first recital. Jemidon smiled as he began the repetition. Each charm had to be spoken three times to be enacted, and the difficulty increased with each enunciation. But his words remained clean and firm, projecting forth without effort, as if he had cast them a thousand times before.

He raced into the final recital like a boulder crashing downhill. The words tripped from his tongue unfailingly. His voice rose from a whisper to a booming shout. Hands on hips like a great orator, he mouthed the last phrases at his reflection. With a flashy bow, he concluded the charm and turned to receive Farnel's reaction.

"Perhaps it is to be sorcery, after all." Jemidon smiled. "It all came easy, both the recall and the casting."

"A bit too dramatic, but well spoken nonetheless,"

61

Farnel said. "It is a pity that you could not have done as well for the other masters."

"But at least it is a better promise of what is to come from your instruction." Jemidon started to wave the thought of his previous failure aside, but winced at a sharpness in his shoulder. "How soon until the pain is totally blocked? It feels no better than before."

"You should be numbed upon completion of the last syllable," Farnel said. "There is no delay in sorcery."

"But my arm—"

Farnel frowned. He studied Jemidon's puzzled expression and shook his head. "Then it is another miscasting," the sorcerer said. "Somehow, with your dramatic flourishes, you garbled the charm."

"I feel no other ill effect," Jemidon said, "and you heard it all the way through without pointing out any error."

"Probably it occurred in the leading phrase of the first recital," Farnel said, "just as the charm was beginning. An error there would render the rest a mumble of nonsense without power or meaning. Yes, that must be the reason. It was indeed too much to expect for you to get through it all so easily."

Jemidon opened his mouth to frame some sort of a reply; but before he could, a heavy pounding shook the door. With a crash, it flew open and banged against the wall. Canthor and four men-at-arms entered the hut. One pointed to Delia and the bottle beside her. Canthor nodded and looked back to Farnel, shaking his head.

"To the keep, old friend," he commanded. "The trader Drandor has charged that you have possession of three of his properties and demands their restitution."

"This is not a matter of harmless bickering, to be forgotten after a night in the keep." Canthor tried to scowl at Farnel, who sat at the other end of the table. "Morgana must show to everyone that its justice applies to master and bondsman alike."

Jemidon and Delia stood between two men-at-arms behind Farnel's chair. Up and down the length of the table sat the other sorcerers of the island, all puffy-eyed and slack-jawed from the night before. When a charge was brought against one, then they all had to be present to hear the evidence and decide what must be done. Drandor paced behind Canthor's high chair, and his footfalls echoed off the round walls. A faded banner hung behind the trader, splotches of mildew mingling with tattered threads. Spiders nervously scampered across the fitted stone and into niches in the crumbling mortar. Recently broken webs hung in the doorway. The council room of the keep was seldom used in Canthor's administration of the island. From two small slit windows, the morning light stabbed into the shadows.

Even though it was a bracingly cool morning, Jemidon felt increasingly tired and disheartened. He had been up all night and dosed with sweetbalm besides. Again he had miscast a spell in front of Farnel, and now there were additional complications, additional obstacles between him and the robe of the master. He gripped the back of the chair tightly to stand erect and grimly forced his sluggish thoughts to follow what was happening.

"Justice I expect," Drandor said. "Of the evidence there can be no denial. The imp bottle, the lattice, the girl, all belong to me and my partner Melizar. I have the bills of possession here for you to examine."

"But it is so unlike a master to bother with material objects," the tall sorcerer on Canthor's right said. "Our work is what we can shape with the mind. And to summon the full council for what surely must be a private matter is most unwarranted. Did you not deal directly with master Farnel? Despite his antiquated techniques, he is most honest and reasonable."

"I did try my own negotiations." Drandor shot Jemidon a glance. "But they met with mishap at the base of the granite cliff. Prudence directed that I appeal to a higher authority, rather than attempt more on my own."

"Trader, justice you shall have." Gerilac rubbed his forehead irritably. "And the quicker you are quiet, the quicker it will be meted." He looked around the table through bloodshot eyes. "After last night, I am sure we all wish to move quickly to settle this matter. And since we are all here, we can also cast the final vote and present the supreme accolade. Let us be done with everything so that we can return to much needed rest."

"You need not show such haste," Farnel growled. "We all filled our cups as many times as you. And the tokens from previous years are keeping you in a pampered style. The five hundred from this season probably will add little difference."

"Five hundred tokens?" Drandor asked. "This sculpting of phantoms brings so much to the one who performs it best?"

"That concerns only the masters," Canthor replied. "We are here at your behest, trader. And when the complaint has been settled, you will be dismissed before we proceed to the other."

"But five hundred!" Drandor persisted. "It is indeed a very large sum."

"Much more than the objects you are making such a clamor about," Canthor said. "You have disturbed my sleep and that of a good many others. Is it not sufficient to return them to you and let the matter drop?"

"The lattice and bottle are the trader's," Jemidon blurted. "Take them and begone." He stepped around Farnel's chair and looked at the assembled masters through heavy eyes. "But surely someone here can meet the price for the girl. Pay what is required so that Delia need not accompany the trader as well."

Jemidon frowned and slowly puzzled out how he felt. He was as much surprised at his outburst as the rest. Delia was an appealing beauty and in need of help. He should have done no less than he did. And yet she was the one responsible for Farnel's present predicament, as well as the cause of the additional complications that could only delay his quest for the robe. In the hut, he had chafed when the master instructed her in sorcery. Certainly he did not want competition. How could she be more than a passing distraction?

"Five hundred tokens." Drandor ignored Jemidon's interruption. "And I infer that the selection of the winner has not yet been made." His eyes narrowed, and he showed his teeth in a crooked smile. "I, too, deal in trinkets for the mind. And if I may be so bold, I wager that what I can create has greater merit than the best you have to offer."

"You are no sorcerer," Gerilac said. "You can do no more than the imitations of the bazaar."

"That is not so." Drandor's smile broadened. "My charms are far more powerful than any you can muster."

"Tradesmen's banter." Gerilac massaged his furrowed brow and slumped his elbow to the table. "Anyone truly trained in the arts can tell the difference."

"Then put it to the test," Drandor said. "I am willing to make a wager. Perform your best sorcery before the masters as judges, and I will invoke mine. Let the better win not only the accolade but five hundred tokens more that I will secure from my partner Melizar."

"Why this sudden interest in our art?" Canthor asked. "You have camped in the harbor bazaar for many days, but never ventured forth before."

"Before, I did not know this recognition carried with it such tangible worth," Drandor said. "A large cache of tokens I must assemble. Melizar wishes it so." He turned and smiled at Canthor. "Besides, I cannot pass an opportunity that is now such a sure proposition."

"All of this is irrelevant." Gerilac deepened his frown. "We are not here to ponder the empty words of someone who is not even a member of our council. Let us be done with his business and proceed with our traditions."

"Our tradition is one of openness to all forms of expression and judgment on merit alone." Farnel rose suddenly to his feet. "Something we masters seem to have a hard time remembering. Yes, that is it. This offer presents an opportunity." He pointed across the table to Gerilac. "Is that the mold in which we shape the thoughts of our tyros who will someday follow? Are they to emulate a sorcerer who fears the challenge of one who is not even a master?"

"I do not fear this tradesman," Gerilac snapped. "His spinning mirrors or whatever would bore us all in a moment. It is an idle exercise not worthy of any of our time."

"Not even worth an additional five hundred tokens?" Farnel asked. He looked around the council room. "It is true that my reaction is one of principle. But additional tokens brought to the island from the outside are eventually of benefit to us all, no matter who is the first recipient."

Jemidon saw a few of the masters nod and then the one nearest Canthor turn his palm upward in agreement with the trader's offer. "Five hundred tokens more," he said. "As if the high prince visited not once this year but twice instead."

Like a rippling wave, the others around the table agreed, one after another, until only Gerilac remained. All eyes turned to the master, and for a moment there was silence. Gerilac looked quickly around the chamber and finally stared at Farnel.

"You do this just for spite," he spat. "But very well. It appears we choose to defend the accolade against this preposterous challenge. Let it be tomorrow morning in the hall. There is no need to wait any longer."

Jemidon struggled to think through his weariness. Dimly he recognized another presentation in the hall, and open to an outsider at that, as a chance to bind Farnel to his bargain. Impulsively he spoke again, not waiting to reason the consequences all the way through. "If there is to be another competition, then it need not be limited to two," he said. "The other masters should have their chance as well."

"What is the point?" Gerilac asked. "The competition among the masters has already been held. Only the best need perform again."

"You have not seen the work of master Farnel," Jemidon said. "This gives him the chance to compete when he is not ill-disposed."

"Enough!" Farnel rose and pushed Jemidon back, his eyes wide at what his tyro had said. "One day is insufficient time. My cause cannot be aided by another hasty preparation."

Gerilac watched Farnel's reaction for a moment, and then the deep furrows in his forehead relaxed. "Insuffi-

66

cient preparation, did I hear you say, Farnel? How could that be if your theories are correct?" He shrugged slightly and beamed a broad smile, his discomfort of a moment before totally gone. "I am a fair man, even though you perpetrate these petty spites. If you wish to present an example of what you define as art with only a day of thought, then let it be so. It is not my intent to bar any glamour so vigorously extolled by its creator. And it is not secret that my production will be the other one the masters will be seeing. Perhaps the contrast will be amusing."

"I do not wish to present." Farnel slammed his fist on the table. "For no such permission did I ask."

"Permission!" Gerilac shot back. "Permission! I do not think this any longer is a matter of pampering your idle whims. You have forced me to recite again. Very well, if I am to dance to your manipulations, then so should you to mine. Present your art in the hall tomorrow. Present it so the rest can compare and then judge the relative merit for themselves. Perhaps when it is all over, you will be silent at last."

Gerilac did not wait for Farnel's reply, but turned to the other masters for their agreement. Farnel started to say more, then clamped shut his mouth as the first few indicated assent. The master watched silently as, one by one, they nodded. With a deep scowl, he slumped back in his chair.

"Wait, there is no need for any other," Drandor said. "We already have agreed on the elements of the wager."

Gerilac frowned at the trader. He looked again at Jemidon and his eyes narrowed. For a moment, he studied the imp bottle and lattice and then shook his head. Finally he ran his eyes over Delia's gown. "Make her part of the prize," he said finally. "As long as you inconvenience the masters of Morgana, you must offer more as your share. And as to what Farnel has to submit, it can only be this outspoken tyro. But then he will be enough. Erid and the others have the need for an experimental subject, and this one already has some practice."

"It is not a contest of equal risks," Drandor blurted;

67

he paused and snapped shut his mouth. For a moment he was silent and then he smiled. "But neither is it one of equal chance. Very well, the girl is part of the final award." He looked at Jemidon. "Melizar will replace my pets with others. They, too, will need amusements."

Jemidon ignored the threat and slumped back against the wall. Now that Farnel was back in the competition, he had somehow to figure a way for them to win. Indeed, his very freedom now depended upon it. But the events of the last day were taking their toll. Jemidon's thoughts were fuzzy and dissolving in a muddle. Fatigue pressed down on him like a great stone. He needed sleep before he could be of much use to anyone.

"Then it is settled." Canthor slapped the table for attention. "These two properties to the trader at once, for which he agrees to mention the incident no further. And all the rest to be decided after a meal or two to repair yesterday's excesses." He waited a moment and looked at each master, but no one protested. With a nod to his men, he left; one by one, the others silently followed. In a moment, only Farnel, Jemidon, and Delia remained in the chamber.

"And what is the rest of your plan, quick-witted one?" Farnel growled. "We have done nothing on the battle scene since we abandoned it. There is hardly time to pull it together now."

Jemidon opened his mouth to speak, but no words came. It was probably best if he said no more. In a groggy haze, he followed Farnel and Delia back to the hut.

Jemidon blinked open his eyes. It was evening. He had struggled to keep alert and be of some help when they reached the sorcerer's lair, but finally had succumbed to a deep sleep that had lasted for hours.

He stretched tentatively and then with greater force. He still felt somewhat groggy, but better than before. Slowly he rose to sitting and readjusted the tatters of his tunic over his shoulder. He centered the brandel on his chest and pushed aside his torn cape, which had been balled into a pillow in the corner of the littered floor. Delia saw him stir and stepped between the helmets and maces to his side. She touched his shoulder, radiating concern.

"The swelling is much less," she called out to Farnel, who sat atop a stool on the other side of the hut. "The sweetbalm, despite its age, has done well."

Jemidon reached for Delia's softness, but she gently pushed him away. "There is little time. Even if master Farnel instructs me through the night, we may not be ready." She smiled and slid away. "But he says that I am an attentive pupil, and I think even his spirits rise as we progress."

"Attentiveness is only a part of it," Farnel said. "She has a natural aptitude—an ability for recall as well as enunciation. I have heard of other instances, but never met such a talent before."

"I am the tyro." Jemidon struggled to his feet and tried to shake the last bit of fuzziness out of his head. "Just a few moments more and I will be able to assist."

"No, it is to be Delia." Farnel's voice was firm. "With her, we just might have a chance after all. Oh, to be ten years younger, lass, with a tyro such as you." He beamed as Delia positioned herself back in the middle of the room. "Gerilac and his followers never would have a chance. Now quickly; the next phrase is but a copy of the previous one with the middle syllables borrowed from the very beginning. Can you feel how it goes?"

Jemidon frowned and tried to figure out what had happened during his sleep. While he pondered, Delia began to rattle off a long string of melody, her voice crisp and pure, like the notes of a harp. Jemidon listened only half attentively at first; then, as she continued, he sagged back to the ground, surprised by what he heard. Most of the charm fragment was familiar, but other parts were new, totally new, phrases that he had never learned in all the months he had studied. Wide-eyed, he looked with respect at the slender form in the center of the room.

"Perfect, perfect," Farnel said. "You know all of the parts. Now we can begin the practice of the complete glamour. Start with Dark Clouds and then slide into Clinton's Granite Spires." He turned and looked at Jemidon.

69

"She even handles the transition without a flaw. It is a rare talent indeed."

A hint of envy crept into Jemidon's amazement. Farnel had given him no such praise, even after the best of his training sessions. "Why spend time now in instruction?" Jemidon asked. "Should not the master be the one to rehearse for the final performance?"

"My head and stomach are not yet clear," Farnel said. "But it does not matter. With Delia's talent, I am sure she will be able to conduct a winning presentation. And enough of interruptions. Tend to your mending and we will pay attention to the sorcery. After all, I doubt you care to become chattel to either Gerilac or this trader Drandor. It is in your best interest as well that we succeed."

Jemidon started to reply; but before he could, Delia began the charm. Almost involuntarily, he closed his eyes and concentrated on her voice, following the flow, hearing the firm command she gave to the words and phrases. His own chanting, the little vocalizing of fragments he had done, was technically correct, but it was the drone of a scribe compared with the beauty of her song. Even though his eyes were shut, Jemidon felt himself being drawn into the enticing web that she wove with her words. Farnel was right; she was the one who had the talent to achieve their goal. Even if he could perform all that he knew with confidence, his glamours would be pale shadows next to the richness that sprang from Delia's lips.

"How is the effect?" Delia asked when she finished. "I felt none of the increasing resistance that you warned me of. It was no different the third time than it was the first."

"You must have made some small error, as Jemidon did this morning." Farnel frowned. "I detected no fault, but I see no clouds and mountains." He stopped and rubbed his chin. "Perhaps we have proceeded a bit too rapidly. Let me cast the beginning. I think that the churning in my stomach can take on something as simple as that. Listen for a difference, and when I am done, you can continue with the rest."

70

Farnel climbed down from the stool, Delia replaced him, and the glamour was begun again. Jemidon heard the same words rumble from Farnel's throat, heavy with the assurance of a master. But the sorcerer took twice as long to complete the charm, slowing the tempo near the end rather than finishing with a burst of speed. As he said the concluding syllable, a look of puzzlement started to grow on the master's face.

"Strange, I would have expected more resistance," he muttered, "especially with the way I feel." He waved his arm at the far wall. "But at any rate, that is the way the scene opens, and you have heard how it is done. Now, with the setting in place, you can begin to bring in the characters and their emotions."

"I am supposed to see a background on the wall?" Delia asked. "It is the same clutter as before."

"What? Impossible!" Farnel exclaimed. "I have not miscast since I was a tyro. One does not become a master with sloppy technique."

"I see nothing," Delia repeated. "If I squint, then some of Jemidon's scrawls resemble a small ship, but that is all."

"It is the joining." Farnel turned to Jemidon. "Your little theory of patching together the charmlets has a flaw. We must go back to Alaraic's Foreboding and Magneton's Walls of Closure, as I first suggested."

"There is no flaw," Jemidon said. "My analogy with the curves was only a means to see which charmlets to couple together. Once that is determined, the transition proceeds in a standard fashion."

"Then the casting, after all," Farnel said. "The ale has addled my senses more than I thought. I have misremembered some syllable and taught it incorrectly to Delia as well."

"But the charm I tried in the morning was a different one," Jemidon said slowly. "Yet it did not complete either." He frowned and rose to standing, clutching at the coin around his neck and reaching for tendrils of thought that danced just beyond his grasp. There was a puzzle here. He could sense it. And as with Delia's trinket in

Drandor's tent, he felt a tantalizing tug, a lure to explore all the facts, to turn them this way and that, and to find the common thread that explained them all.

"No, something else is wrong," he said after a moment. "I can feel it. Somehow, someway, something more basic is at fault. The failures, all of them, are deeply connected. It is not just from lack of precision alone."

He closed his eyes and strained, trying to piece things together, but only incomplete images would form. Miscast spells, whispered commands on a rainy beach, competitions for a thousand tokens, an imp in a bottle, and lattices with shiny beads.

"There is not time for another abstract theory," Farnel said after Jemidon did not speak again. "I must recompose the beginning of the presentation and then teach the lass yet another glamour to replace the one that failed."

"No, wait," Jemidon said as a bizarre thought popped into his head. He licked his lips and moved to the center of the room, not quite believing where his logic was leading him. "There is something important here, and it is easy enough to test its limits. Try the first charmlet without the connection. See if it works by itself."

Farnel scowled, then shrugged his shoulders. He turned to face Delia and quickly ran through Dark Clouds. "Well," he said when he was done. "Surely there was no mistake in such a short glamour. Even a beginning tyro can do it."

"Nothing still," Delia said.

"Then the error is in the first," Farnel declared. "Clinton's Granite Spires is the one I remember correctly."

"Cast it as well," Jemidon said. He felt no surprise at the failure. Instead, a cement of conviction began to connect the framework of his ideas.

Farnel twisted his frown even tighter, but carefully recited the glamour. He paused at the finish, as Delia slowly shook her head.

"By the laws, two misremembered!" Farnel pounded his fist against the wall. "Somehow it is Gerilac's doing. He has contrived the whole competition just to get another chance to display his craft against mine."

"Gerilac did not know of Delia and Drandor until this morning." Jemidon shook his head. "No, the explanation lies somewhere else."

"In any case, I must recompose the beginning with some substitutions," Farnel growled. "Do not waste what time remains with irrelevant suggestions."

"And what of the rest?" Jemidon asked with slow deliberateness, emphasizing every word, his doubts tossed aside. "What of the rest? If the first two have failed, what can you say of the chances of the others?"

"Would you that we fail again? Another prize for Gerilac and more whispers that I can no longer cast a charm?" Farnel snarled in frustration and scooped a dagger from the floor. With a savage fling, he hurled it above Jemidon's head and sent it crashing into the wall. "The hour grows late," he growled, "and it is your glib tongue that has placed us here. By the laws, it is your burden as well to avert the result that surely encloses us in its snares. Stop throwing barriers in the way. If not by charms, then by whatever else shall we enchant the masters?"

"We have a compact," Jemidon said. "I stand by my part of the agreement still. I will help to win the competition, and you will instruct me in sorcery in return." He matched Farnel's angry stare, looking him deeply in the eye. For a long moment, no one moved. Finally the sorcerer turned his glance away, flinging out his arms in disgust.

"And we will accomplish nothing by blind thrashing," Jemidon said. "If we cannot depend upon our charms working, then we must conceive a production that does not use them. We have no choice but to work with what we have."

"A production with no glamours? Impossible!" Farnel snorted.

Jemidon did not reply. His spirits had lifted. He was back in the center of things, part of the solution rather than a hapless bystander, watching others try to unravel problems he had created. If they were to win the competition and save themselves from Drandor or Gerilac, if Farnel were to gain his measure of respect at last, it would be because Jemidon found the key to the puzzle, the means to the end, the plan for their salvation. He was in his element, working with what he enjoyed the best.

Already he had had one flash of insight. Surely another would come soon as well. Slowly he scanned the room, looking for some clue to the way out of their plight. He saw the pikes and long swords stacked in the corner, Delia sitting on the stool in the middle of the room, and, behind her, the walls covered with the outline of their original design. "You said my writing reminded you of a ship," he said to break the tension.

"Over there." Delia pointed. "The one on the left."

"So it does," Jemidon agreed. "But it is quite out of place with the effect we are trying to achieve."

"And an accidental sketch is hardly of sufficient quality for a presentation designed for a high prince," Farnel muttered.

"Although this time it will be for the masters only," Jemidon said. "And they also will know by heart the words that will be—" He stopped suddenly and studied the rough pen strokes that hinted at a galleon on the high seas. Then he smiled. The way to proceed was floating gently in his mind.

"Seascapes, castles, interiors of a palace." He whirled toward Farnel. "Other settings. Can we quickly assemble such properties as well?"

"I have a few stored at the hall from previous years." Farnel shrugged. "And so do my peers. We trade them back and forth as we have need."

"Then let us go and select the best." Jemidon waved at the outline on the walls. "We have until morning to find a substitute for them all."

"But there is no time for me to learn a whole new set of charms," Delia protested. "And they might fail just as surely as the few that I know."

"Practice only what Farnel has taught you," Jemidon said. "You need worry about no more. Your performance tomorrow still must be flawless. Indeed, it remains our hope for winning the prize and keeping our freedom."

CHAPTER FIVE

The Purging Flame

JEMIDON flung open the door to Farnel's hut. Even though he had not stopped to rest since he had instructed Delia to get some sleep, everything was still not quite ready. He looked anxiously at the brightening sky and hurried through the debris that littered the floor between him and the sorcerer's bed. Gently he shook Delia awake.

"It took longer than we thought," he said. "Some of the other sorcerers did not take kindly to Farnel's requests in the middle of the night. He is at the hall trying to put into order what we have already collected."

Delia rose to sitting and stretched. "The list I made for master Farnel before you left," she said after a long yawn. "Did you use it to ensure that a scene was found for each charmlet?"

"Farnel worried about the details." Jemidon shrugged. "For my part, the basic concept was enough."

"Without a plan and attention as things progress, the most brilliant insight produces nothing." Delia shook her head. "My fear of Drandor was overwhelming, yet I did not attempt to flee until I had decided exactly what I would take and knew when he would be preoccupied."

"But despite that, if I had not been on the cliff, you would not have the chance you do now," Jemidon said.

"If not you, then I would have found some other."

Jemidon frowned. Delia laughed as his face clouded over. She stood and smiled. "Indeed you were the one. And please do not think that I am ungrateful."

With a fluid motion, she suddenly clasped her arms around his neck and pulled his lips to hers. Jemidon blinked in surprise, but then felt his pulse quicken. He stepped

75

forward and drew her close. For a long moment they embraced. Jemidon's thoughts of sorcery faded away. Bodies pressed together, he pushed her toward the bed.

Delia teetered for half a step and then suddenly stiffened. "No," she whispered, "that is not what I meant."

Jemidon stroked his hand down her back, pressing her tighter. He thrust his legs against hers, forcing her another step backward.

"No!" She wrenched her face away and pushed down on his entwining arm. "I have given you all I meant to offer."

Jemidon stopped. He backed away as she smoothed the front of her gown. He looked at the hard lines that had replaced her smile and shook his head. "With the bracelet of iron, surely there have been many," he said. "And after your invitation, what was I to think?"

Delia opened her mouth to speak and then snapped it shut. Jemidon saw the anger that flared out of her eyes and twitched the muscles in her cheeks.

"Gambling in the token markets was a choice I made freely," Delia sputtered at last. "And I admit that I knew what the consequences could be." She waved her arm with the bracelet in Jemidon's face. "But despite this, I am still more than a toy to be pawed by an owner and then passed to another when he grows tired. That is my past, not what I will be."

"I have no legal claim over you," Jemidon cut in quickly.

"Nor am I some doxy from the sagas who swoons to do every bidding of her rescuer in boundless gratitude," Delia rushed on. "I am free-willed as much as you. I asked for your help. You gave it without qualification. And I have thanked you. My obligation goes no further."

"A weakness of the moment," Jemidon said thickly, turning away his eyes. He felt foolish that he had misjudged her intent and relied too strongly on some ill-defined feeling that now he could not quite describe. And what would she think of him? Probably as a bumbling tyro from the wheatlands, who thought with his loins rather than his head, or an apprentice puffed with vanity, so sure of his attractiveness that he did not bother to ask.

Jemidon frowned at the direction of his thoughts. And if she did, why was it so important? If Farnel's production won the competition, she would be free to go her own way. After that, could it any longer matter?

For a long moment, there was a heavy silence. "Perhaps if I did not indeed wear the bracelet," Delia said at last, "then the feelings that mold me might be different. But the ring of iron is the reality; I cannot deny all the rest that has happened because of it. I feel a bonding to you, Jemidon, but not like that." Her cheeks colored slightly. "At least not now, not yet."

"We still have business together." Jemidon looked back after a moment, trying to speak as if nothing had happened. "For now, our fates are intertwined. And we must rush. Gerilac has already started. Drandor is ready to be second. And the other masters have made it quite clear: if we are not prepared in time, our chance will be forfeited."

"Then let us be off," Delia said. "A meal can come later."

Jemidon started to say more, but hesitated. The moment had passed. There was too much yet to be done. Without speaking, he turned for the door. In a short while, they were on the path of crushed white stones, walking swiftly to the presentation hall.

Rose-tinted clouds hung low over the hilltops in the center of the island, while the sky above the harbor was just beginning to show its blue. Canthor's banners hung limply from his keep, and beyond it, the details of the hall were muted in shadow. The faint groan of rigging in the harbor mixed with the crunch of their rapid footsteps on the rock, but otherwise the air hung heavy with the morning silence.

"They expect Drandor to be finished when the sun tops that ridge." Jemidon nodded to the east. "There barely will be enough time to get you in the well. But with my sliding about the scenery, I could come for you no sooner."

"I still do not quite understand," Delia said as they hurried along. "The scenery is supposed to be an aid to help the sorcerer cast his spell. An aid to put the watcher in the proper frame of mind. We were working with helmets and pikes, swords and battle-axes, to suggest battle scenes. Now you have replaced them with wavecaps and fogs, totally unrelated to what I will chant."

"Precisely the point," Jemidon said. "The more divergence, the better our chances will be. You see—"

He stopped suddenly and pointed ahead to the hall. "Look, waiting at the stage doorway are some robes of brown. Hurry, we can ill afford delay when dealing with Gerilac's tyros."

Jemidon grabbed Delia's hand, as he had done on the granite cliff, and sprang into a run. Together, they covered the remaining distance in a rush. As they approached the stage entrance, Jemidon recognized Erid and the others, standing with studied nonchalance in the frame of the door.

"Faster, faster," Erid shouted as they drew close. "I want to see your expressions when your entry is barred."

In response, Jemidon put on a burst of speed, tugging on Delia's arm. But she gasped and stumbled; reluctantly, he slowed his pace.

For a moment more, Erid watched without moving. Then, when they were about fifty paces away, he and the other tyros sprang back into the hall and slammed the doors. Jemidon heard the bar drop with a heavy thud.

"The patrons' entrance," Jemidon said. "Before they can secure it as well. Somehow we will work our way back to the stage."

Delia nodded, and they quickly circled the hall. Seen from the front, wings of unlike design jogged away from the central structure, one sprouting twin towers at its far end, the other a staggered tier of small boxes. Four doors cut the entrance facade, each one grander than the one adjacent, the last filling an archway twice the height of a man. Together, Jemidon and Delia bounded from the rock path and through the largest entryway into the hall.

Immediately they plunged into dimness. Two candles in a wall sconce illuminated three identical doors and a single staircase leading off to the right. Delia ran forward to try one of the latches, but Jemidon pulled her back.

"No, let's try upstairs," he said. "These probably all lead into the Maze of Partitions on the first floor. It would take who knows how long to work our way through to the stage. Perhaps in a balcony we can find a faster way around."

They raced upstairs and found a long corridor snaking off to the left. The wall nearest the stage was lined with doorways and elaborate portals that opened onto boxes beyond. Jemidon poked his head in one and saw that it was completely empty, the far wall hung with shutters that had been pulled firmly closed. In the next were lavish furnishings, couches with gilded frameworks, and deep floor cushions of shiny silk.

"Come along," Jemidon shouted as he withdrew. "These probably all open onto a balcony above the Maze. Let's follow the corridor to the end. There should be another stairway there."

Running faster on the smooth floors than they had been able to do outside, Jemidon and Delia traversed the straight runs of the passageway and followed the bends that wound about the outer wall of the hall. Finally they reached a barrier of brick and stone that blocked them from going further. In growing desperation, they looked for another exit, either up or down, but found none.

"By the laws, it is too late to retrace our steps back to the entrance and try again," Jemidon said. He grabbed savagely at the closed door on the last box in line and tried to wrench it open. The thin wood creaked, bowing from the jamb, but bolts at the top and bottom set from the inside held it in place. Tendrils of cold air whiffed from the crack as the door sprang back.

"Someone is in there!" Jemidon exclaimed. "Who could it be? All of the masters will be in the first row, and these presentations are for no others."

"Does it matter?" Delia asked. "I thought our goal was to get me to the well."

Jemidon grunted and tried the door on the next box adjacent to the one that was sealed. It flew open. With no better plan in mind, he motioned Delia to follow him in.

The interior was decorated more luxuriously than most, with patterned draperies hanging on three sides and even a painting on the closed shutters facing the stage. Lighted cressets brimmed with scented oil, and additional bottles stood amidst sand buckets underneath.

Jemidon climbed over a down-filled bed in the middle of the room and flicked at the latches on the shutters, pushing them open to look out onto the lower floor of the hall. His eyes swept the stage, and he suddenly stopped in mid-glance.

"It is like what I saw the night of the storm," he said. "But this time Drandor has made it much more real."

The trader had tilted a mirror over the chanting well. The light that arched upward did not project throughout the hall, but reflected horizontally onto a curtain that hung from the stage. On its surface, Jemidon saw a scene that moved and changed as he watched. From some impossibly high vantage point, he viewed the offshore islands of Arcadia, sparkling in the sea like pearls on a string. Then, in a breathtaking dive, the islands grew and moved from the center of focus to vanish off the edges of the screen. Morgana remained in view, swelling larger with each instant. The hills, the harbor, and the individual buildings resolved into recognition. The detail was not that of a sorcerer's illusion or even of a good painting, Jemidon knew; but somehow the production was compelling, drawing him in so that he could not turn aside. He felt like a hawk swooping on its prey, expecting any minute to see a small rodent scamper among individual tufts of grass.

With a stomach-screeching "turn," Jemidon felt himself stop the plummet and reverse direction above the highest tower of the presentation hall. He raced over the peak with only inches to spare. He banked to the side and glided for a pass over the harbor. With a final turn away from a setting sun, he sailed from the island in a growing twilight.

The first row of the lower level which contained the masters burst into an incoherent babble. Jemidon blinked his thoughts back to attention and saw Drandor emerge from the well with his smile at its widest.

"Most interesting." The sorcerer on the right rose to greet him. He stepped past the small table with the open scroll and bulging bag of coins. "These glamours do not have the detail, but if I had to decide between yours and what I saw of Gerilac's today, my choice would be clear."

"Intriguing, I agree," the next in line said, "but should not master Gerilac be given the benefit of the doubt? We all have seen his Women of the Slave Quarter before. The high prince himself whispered that he enjoyed it well."

"You are to judge only what you see now." Drandor's smile melted away. "Past performances were not to be a factor."

"But it is so little time from our celebration," the second sorcerer continued. "Like us all, master Gerilac was not fully rested. It is no wonder he was unable to weave again the splendid glamour that we enjoyed so well when the prince was here."

"You have seen two performances," Drandor insisted. "It is no concern of mine that the other did not match its expectations." The trader looked about the hall. "And if the last does not start immediately, then we should waste no more time and proceed to your vote."

"A moment more," Farnel called out from backstage. "My tyros will arrive shortly."

"The vote," Drandor repeated, and several masters nodded their heads in agreement.

Jemidon tore his eyes away from the stage and finally looked down to the floor. "There," he exclaimed. "From our vantage point, we can see a path below the long tapestry on the left, a narrow walkway that winds to the front of the hall."

He turned back into the box and grabbed the nearest draperies from their hangings. While the masters argued, he tied several together and threw one end of a makeshift rope over the shutter rail. Delia nodded understanding. With Jemidon bracing against her weight, she shimmied down its length to land on the floor below. She paused and looked up expectantly, but he waved her on, holding

81

up the free end of the drapery still in his hands. As she sped onto the walkway, he glanced back into the box, looking for a means to anchor his own way down.

While he tested the weight of the bed and tried to maneuver it into a position so that it would not slide, the agitation of the masters increased as more joined in the debate.

"But we agreed to three," one shouted above the rest.

"It does not matter," another answered. "Farnel has not yet started and has forfeited his chance. Let us vote and then be done."

Other voices blurred the argument into indistinction, but then suddenly Delia's clear tones cut through them all. Her words pulsed with energy, crystal sharp and demanding attention, filling the expanse of the hall. Not strained or forced, they carried rich harmonics of mystery and allure.

For a moment, the babble rumbled onward. Then, one by one, the masters stopped to listen, their own voices quickly hushed when they became aware of what they heard. Like enraptured children, they settled back into their seats, concentrating on the charm.

Delia ran through the first glamour with the same skill she had exhibited in Farnel's hut. The spell for Dark Clouds blended smoothly into that for Clinton's Granite Spires. As she reached the last syllables, the stage curtains parted in darkness. Then, with the final word, the scene behind sprang to life. Jemidon dropped the drapery and returned to the open shutters to watch what the reaction would be.

On the stage, a two-masted sloop, its sails billowing from offstage fans, frothed in a shallow sea. Bellow-driven sprays dashed against canvas boulders. The largest rock was topped by a light that swept in slow circles and caught the dust that churned in the main vault of the hall.

Then, as quickly as the scene had appeared, the stage returned to blackness and Delia started the next portion of the charm. An excited murmur started to swell along the masters' row. Jemidon smiled. It was working as he had thought. The sorcerers could not have doubted that

82

Delia's words would produce images of the mountains surrounded by high clouds. Her voice was too pure. And to see scenes of the ocean instead had to be an intriguing surprise.

"But that is no sorcery," Jemidon heard Drandor shout. "I have made sure that there is none. I am the one who must win. By logic's laws, there can be no other way!"

Louder hisses for silence drowned out the trader. Except for Delia's voice, the hall quieted like a wizard's tomb. The masters sat attentively now, anxious to see what the next images would be. Drandor stomped his foot in frustration and looked up in Jemidon's direction to the box on his left.

For a moment, nothing happened in response. Only Delia's voice filled the expanses of the hall. Then, as the curtains began to part for a second time, the shutters on the next box banged open loudly and a bottle of oil sailed out to crash onto the walkway immediately below. A lighted torch followed and, in a flash, the long wall tapestry burst into flame.

Two more bottles hurled from the opening and shattered like the first. A brace of torches scattered over a wide arc. In two heartbeats, the first level was ablaze with half a dozen fires.

Jemidon looked back at the doorway and then to Delia, still chanting in the well. He threw the drapery aside and impulsively climbed up onto the ledge. Without pausing to take aim, he vaulted from his perch.

The momentum of his kick carried him past the walkway directly below. He crashed through a thin panel canopy, hit a pillowed divan, and tumbled to the floor. He staggered to his feet and looked about to catch his bearings. The sorcerers were aflutter. They had seen the fire, and Delia's voice no longer held them in thrall. Like huge black birds, they ran in all directions, tripping over buckets and shouting commands.

But the frenzy of the fires was already greater. Licks of flame touched oiled paneling, bursting the wood into glowing splinters that started dozens of additional blazes where they landed. A storeroom of paints and canvas

83

suddenly exploded, sending globs of incandescence throughout the interior. Far faster than one could believe possible, the entire hall was embraced in the beginnings of a fiery death.

Jemidon saw the mirror that projected images from the well; reflected within was Delia's frown of apprehension as she debated what to do. She might remain, struggling to continue until it was too late. He had to get to the well and help her escape. But the walkway she had taken was now engulfed in flame. He glanced to the side and then quickly dove through a low doorway as the expanding fire caught another tapestry that billowed in yellow and orange.

Jemidon raced along the snaky corridor, trying to move in the direction of the stage, ducking at intervals into the boxes to see if they had another exit to shorten his path.

He heard a rush of air like that from an anthanor and climbed a small ladder to peer over a wall. A wave of fire raced down both sides of the hall, exploding the tapestries along the way in globs of blazing anger. The stage curtain caught. To the rear, Jemidon heard the groan of a massive beam sagging as its supports began to burn.

Jemidon saw Drandor appear from an aisle to the side, the imp buzzing free around his head. The trader swiped at the small table near the front of the stage and scooped up the bag of tokens as he ran.

"It is all rightfully mine!" the small man shouted. He looked around once quickly before plunging down the stairs that led to the well. Jemidon heard Delia scream and then only the roar of the fire.

Blistering air rolled past Jemidon's face, forcing him below. He looked back the way he had come and saw it blocked. He touched the wall at his side, and it was hot to the touch. Acrid smoke billowed overhead, stinging his eyes and forcing him to his knees.

Reaching the stage was no longer possible. He would have to get out as best he could. He closed his eyes to block the sting and began to grope along the floor. He felt the cold metal of a water pail and quickly doused it over his head. Pushing along the baseboard, he grasped

84

the hinge of a door. But the metal was hot, burning his hand, and he crawled further down the aisle.

He detected an opening to the left and scrambled into it, only to crack his head against a panel a few feet beyond. He flung his hand about and felt a wall on one side and open space on the other. The smoky air pushed lower. He choked as he gasped for breath. Flinging himself to the side, he proceeded another few feet before again bouncing off a wall directly ahead.

Jemidon opened his eyes. The haze of gray and black was worse than before, but he saw high wooden panels of slick veneers. Like the first storey of a house of cards, the wooden walls zigged and zagged off into an unfathomable distance.

"The Maze of Partitions," Jemidon said aloud as he recognized where he was. He pondered for a moment on how to proceed and then grimly made up his mind. "It eventually leads to another entrance at the front of the hall. If the passages are simply connected, then I may have a chance."

He squinted his eyes shut and placed the palm of his left hand firmly on the panel. Moving slower than he had done before, he crawled on his knees along the boundary and into the Maze. The panel ran for a good distance before it finally ended, abutting another wall at a square angle, barring the way. Jemidon turned to the right with his hand still in front, guiding his movements, and continued on in the new direction.

The air grew hotter. It hurt to take a deep breath. He heard the crackle of the fire funneled down the narrow passageway. With a burst of effort, he tried to crawl faster through the Maze.

Time dissolved into a meaningless agony. Onward he crawled mindlessly, moving to the right when he ran into a barrier directly ahead, in the other direction when he felt his fingertips curve around a corner to a panel going to the left. He snaked into a spiral, back out again, and then along a narrow straightaway. He blindly climbed one set of stairs and descended another. He scrambled through a long traverse and then a set of convoluted aisles.

For what seemed like the thousandth time, Jemidon reached the end of a panel. He slid his hand across rougher wood in front of him and then felt smoothness projecting back along the other side.

"Another dead end," he mumbled as he turned around and continued back in the direction he had come. He winced at the intensity of the heat and coughed with the choking smoke that now filled every breath. Faltering, he pushed himself another step onward.

Jemidon opened his mouth to lick his lips and then quickly snapped it shut again. He steeled himself to slide another half step into the heat, but he could not find the strength. He had to follow the left-hand wall all around the Maze. It was like solving a complex puzzle on paper, horribly inefficient but the only way that was sure. Only then could he be certain of finding the doorway that led back out to the front of the hall.

Doorway, his thoughts dimly lumbered as he laid his head down on the ground. Doorway to the outside. Visions of the Maze, the presentation hall, and the swirling smoke tumbled in his head. He remembered Delia's puzzle, familiar and yet somehow a little strange.

Jemidon felt a blistering pulse of heat course across his hand and he pulled it back. The fire now danced on his clothes. He sprang to his feet and whirled in desperation in the other direction. He clawed frantically at the wall until he felt the wood of the door. With a last effort, he pulled it open and saw daylight ten paces away. He tumbled forward into the brightness, trying to snuff out the flames as he rolled.

Jemidon stretched himself awake and took a deep breath. Vaguely he remembered the helping hands that smothered the fire and then the application of the sleep-inducing salve. Its caressing aroma still lingered. With surprising ease, he managed to sit up on the hard flagstones and look at what remained of the presentation hall.

Only a few charred timbers still stood. The rest smoldered under the collapsed roof and piles of charcoal debris. The onshore breeze had not yet blown away all the smoke and haze. A few of the masters directed their tyros to douse the remaining spots of fire. Others wandered aimlessly around the perimeter, eyes clouded in a daze. A shadow blocked out the sun, now low in the western sky. Jemidon looked up to see Farnel kneel down and touch his arm.

"I can get more," the sorcerer said. "Canthor puts great store in the salve, but if a second application is required, it does not matter."

Jemidon struggled to his feet and shook his head. "It heals burns as well." He waved his arm at the others still sprawled on the entryway.

"I have provided for them all," Farnel said. "Even if there are no tokens to go with the honor, I will not be regarded the same as tight-fisted Gerilac after he has won an accolade."

"Then the spell worked!" Jemidon exclaimed.

"Better than the others." Another master approached and solemnly gripped Farnel's arm. "Better than the others. With what we saw, there was no other choice. Gerilac failed totally. Not one image came to my mind when he was done. And the trader's technique was amusing, but nothing compared with the shock that you produced, Farnel. The effect caught me totally by surprise. I expected mountaintops and clouds; with the words I heard, there could be no other. And then to view the sea—a masterstroke. The image was not strong; it remained entirely on the stage, rather than surrounding my senses as any good illusion should.

"But such difficulty you must have had to make the charm sound so like the other! A little weakness in execution can easily be overlooked. Something only a master could appreciate, it is true. But within our craft, it is a spell that will become a classic. A pity that we were interrupted before you proceeded further."

The sorcerer looked over his shoulder at the ruins and then shook his head. "No, not a new technique from which to build next year's productions to the high prince. But with the work of a dozen generations burned away in a morning, it is unclear that that is very important."

"We must proceed." Farnel straightened to ramrod stiffness. "For the next year, we must make the start of a new hall and a new direction in our craft as well— charms that challenge the mind, rather than cater to its weakest desires."

"Yes, to plunge onward is best." The sorcerer managed a weak smile. "That is why we went ahead with the vote, to salvage as much as we could of our tradition. By eleven to ten, Farnel, you are the winner of the supreme accolade. And perhaps there is even something of value in what you have wrought. You must teach me the technique when I feel I am able."

"Instructing you might prove to be a disappointment." Farnel coughed. "It is perhaps best to wait until the excitement of this day is mostly forgotten. And besides, I have my part of a bargain to honor first. A just payment for favors rendered." He looked at Jemidon and smiled. "No small part of my success today is due to my tyro here. He has helped me to the prize, and in return I must give him the knowledge it takes to become a master."

Jemidon smiled back. His plan had worked exactly as he had hoped. There had been no sorcery involved at all. Delia had failed, just as she had the night before. But her words were so perfectly uttered that the masters could not bring themselves to believe that a charm was not cast. And so, guided by the stage props Jemidon had designed, they saw a sea scene, somehow formed with the words that should dictate mountains and clouds. Of course it had been weak. But, they would have reasoned, what more could one expect with a charm so inappropriate for what was produced?

And from here on, there could be no more stumbles. Despite how it was accomplished, Farnel had achieved what he wanted. Now the others would listen to the sorcerer with more respect. And this time, Jemidon thought, he would study diligently and master each charm along the way before he proceeded to the next. This time he would learn the Power of Suggestion so that it would never be forgotten. This time— His thoughts suddenly faltered and then stopped. He knew the Power of Suggestion. Effortlessly, he could recall the simple glamour and many more. That was not the problem. He ticked off his own failures, Delia's, Farnel's, and now even Gerilac's. He remembered his deduction in Farnel's hut, his conviction on how to proceed to win the prize. Sadly he shook his head. As preposterous as it seemed, there could be no other answer.

"Has any one of you tried to cast a charm since your celebration after the high prince left?" Jemidon asked.

"We were all too indisposed from the revelry," the master answered, "although several did attempt something simple to steady themselves after the fire."

"And the result?"

"Miscast, every one." The sorcerer shrugged. "It is still too soon, and the events of this morning could only make one more upset. And whatever the disturbance is, it will wear off soon enough. We often rest for months after a season to recuperate our powers. When it comes time to prepare for the next, we will all be ready."

"But if the charms continue not to work, what then?" Jemidon persisted.

The sorcerer cast a worried look at the remains of the hall and ran a hand across the nape of his neck. "Then we will be forced to act like all the others. Deep enchantments, cantrips of far seeing, curses, and ensorcellments. All life-draining and making us feared by everyone."

"And if they, too, have lost their power? If the basic law of sorcery, 'thrice spoken, once fulfilled,' is now no more than a rhyme of nonsense?"

"A law no more? Impossible," Farnel scoffed. "A charm is sometimes misremembered or forgotten; that has happened. Or even a master discovers that he can cast no more. But the law applies to all charms and all men, on Procolon as well as Morgana, on the seas, under the ground, and on the stars at the very limits of the sky. Stopping the law from working is the same as suddenly preventing every tossed rock from returning to earth. What mechanism could possibly cause such to happen? How could you even conceive of such a thing?"

"I do not know," Jemidon said, "but for me, the evidence is compelling. Since the night of the presentation to the high prince, there is no charm that has been completed successfully. The simple and the complex, joined or unrelated, they all do not work. What else can it mean but that the law no longer functions?"

"But there was Farnel's charm this morning," the sorcerer protested. "And even, in a peculiar way, the moving illusions on the trader's screen."

"Drandor!" Jemidon cried. "After his ritual on the night of the celebration, there were no more working charms. Yes, somehow the trader is connected!" He wrinkled his brow, trying to piece the events together: the presentation on the screen in the hall; before that, the more primitive enactment at the bazaar; and at the first, the tent with the objects from far away.

"Delia!" Jemidon suddenly blurted aloud. His struggle to reach the chanting well jarred into memory. "What happened to her? Was everyone rescued from the hall?"

"I was backstage directing the change of scene when I heard her falter," Farnel said. But the curtain was in flames before I was able to come to her aid. And I have talked to other masters who were closer. They babble about the imp shielding the trader from the heat as he dragged her away and of something else that met them at the rear door, dark and shadowy—a presence black and cold that directed both Drandor and the imp. But then their burns were bad, and the sweetbalm had not yet begun to work."

"Where are they now?" Jemidon asked.

"A harbor pilot says that Drandor sailed on the tide for Pluton even before the blaze was fully controlled." Farnel shrugged. "Like the tokens, of the trader and the slave girl there is no sign."

"And the one who hurled torches and oil from the second-level box, starting the fire?"

"No trace, either," Farnel said. "Perhaps whoever it was worked with Drandor as well, creating a distraction when it appeared that the trader might lose the competition. But that is all speculation. We cannot be sure.

"In any event, Jemidon, forget all this irrelevant thinking. The important thing is the rebuilding of our craft. If there is some sort of blockage in our abilities, it will pass with time. We will be back at full strength well before the next season." He stopped and looked at the ruins. "We must. There is no other way."

Jemidon nodded slowly, digesting Farnel's words. Perhaps the master was right. How the charms stopped working probably did not matter. They could regain their potency again just as abruptly. And he would be ready with a full arsenal of glamours—enough to hold his own with Erid and advance quickly to the robe of the master. It was why he had come to Morgana. His plan would be successful at last, despite the twists along the way. He would become a master, with no fumbling failures like his first time in the well.

He thought of his first time in the well. He recalled the growing panic as the words slithered away from his grasp, the choking throat that would not respond, and the looks of the masters when he trudged back up the stairs. Jemidon shuddered at the memory and then felt an icy wave of doubt wash over his body.

That was before the night of the storm, he realized, before the final presentations to the prince, before the law stopped working, and before his tongue became so glib. Suppose the law were restored? What then would his abilities be? Would the practice be enough, would the phrases remain firm? Could he spout the Wall of Impedance as quickly as he had in Farnel's hut?

And would the powers really return unbidden? If Drandor's rituals were involved, was there not forethought behind what had happened—forethought coupled with some mechanism that shifted the very fabric of existence, as Farnel had said, throughout the world and encompassing the stars beyond? What a puzzle it was! Yes, a puzzle far grander than any he had worked before. Jemidon licked his lips as he stretched his mind, savoring how he would proceed to find out more, to reach for the insight that hinted at the first exciting clue.

But how could he devote any thought at all to such a mystery while he studied in drudgery under Farnel, perhaps to no avail? Indeed, what was the surest way to the robe of the master? Instinctively Jemidon grasped the coin around his neck to steady his racing thoughts.

"And if the laws do not ever come back of their own volition?" Jemidon broke out of his reverie. "Suppose it takes a positive action to restore things as they were before?"

"What you speak of cannot come to pass," Farnel said. "It is only a matter of time."

"If our livelihood is taken away, by whatever means, and then someone through his own efforts restores it," the sorcerer beside Farnel replied, "then at the very least he would receive the master's robe without question— regardless of his station or his ability to cast a single charm."

The sorcerer looked back at the smoldering embers. "Yes, if by the slightest chance what you say were so, no honor would be too great."

Jemidon's eyebrows lifted. Another path to the robe! And one far more to his liking. It would not depend on innate resonance with sorcery that he might or might not have, but just the solution to a puzzle, a complex one perhaps, but in principle no different from the ones he had solved so many times before.

"And Delia as well," he said aloud in a rush. "The goals are intertwined." His thoughts were still in a tumble, but deep inside, he knew what he must do—track Drandor to unravel his mysteries. At the same time he could also free Delia from the trader's grip. Yes, somehow, he knew he could. And the second time, her gratitude might be worth more than a kiss. Or better yet, he could turn his back and walk away when it was done so that she would know he was made of finer clay. He paused as he remembered their last time together. How did he really feel about her anyhow? But then he brushed the thought aside. That could be decided later, after he had accomplished his new plan.

"Yes, I must go to the harbor," he said excitedly. "I must book passage and sail for Pluton with the next tide."

"But wait," Farnel said. "Do you not understand? I

offer you instruction, freely given so that you may become a master."

Jemidon bolted into a run and headed down the path of crushed stone. He gripped the brandel tightly to prevent it from swinging and called back over his shoulder, "My destiny lies elsewhere. I can feel it. When I return, it will be with sorcery restored."

"But how?" Farnel yelled.

"I must find Drandor on Pluton and learn what he knows. Examine the contents of his tent. Listen to the imp when he babbles about the lattice and his master, Melizar. Yes, the lattice, Melizar, and the Postulate of Invariance."

PART TWO

The Postulate of Invariance

CHAPTER SIX

The Whispers of Memory

JEMIDON paused before he entered the courtyard gate and looked back to Pluton's harbor. The passage from Morgana had been uneventful and the contrast between the two islands more or less what he had expected. The population of Morgana was small, barely enough for a viable community to support two dozen masters and cater to the lords when they came once a year. Pluton, on the other hand, was an active trading and financial center, a stopping point for the traffic between mainland Arcadia and Procolon across the sea, and the nexus for the interisland traders that flitted up and down the archipelago.

The harbor was crowded; several ships lay at anchor in mid-bay, awaiting their turn for a berth. The piers jutted into the dirty water with regular-spaced precision from two arms of land that gently curved into an enclosing circle. A small opening led to the unprotected sea outside the bay. Through the gap, one could follow the shipping lanes to the heartland of Arcadia, which lay beyond the horizon.

A narrow road that ringed the shoreline was a tumult of wagons, dust, and shouting drivers. Small boats pulled by oars and even a few biremes slid over the glassy water, dashing between the waiting ships, moving people and messages too important to delay onto the crowded shore.

Two smaller islands poked above the bay's surface, one covered with trees except where it had been cleared for an elegant estate, and the other rocky and bare, pockmarked with the dark entrances to deep caves that came to the water's edge.

All around the ring of shore, the land sloped abruptly

97

upward to a circle of hills. Jemidon's eyes followed the landscape as it rose. Rough-planked shacks stood adjacent to the wagon road. In the tier behind, single-storey mud-brick boxes painted white crowded together. Above them, the larger structures of brick and iron marked the exchanges and countinghouses that distinguished Pluton from all the other islands in the chain. On the topmost slopes leading to the hillcrests were the manor houses of the wealthy—polished stone, fine-grained woods, and patches of cultivated greens towering over all the rest.

But his search would not take him to the hilltops, at least not initially, Jemidon thought. The advice of all the other passengers was to seek out a divulgent when he first came ashore. Information was a commodity on Pluton like everything else, and he could find out whatever he wanted if he could afford the price.

Jemidon patted his now much lighter purse and frowned. If not, he would have to hope that he could find an old acquaintance who would be disposed to offer him aid.

Augusta! How would she have remembered him? One of the merchants on shipboard had mentioned the name in connection with something called the vault in the grotto. Could she be the same? Unbidden, the whispers of memories flooded back ...

"But I can wait no longer, Jemidon. Please try to understand," he heard the voice from the past say.

"We have forsworn all others, Augusta." Jemidon remembered his reply. His heart had been pounding and his palms sweaty, but he had tried to show an outward calm. "You do not care for this Rosimar's rough manner. I can see it in your eyes."

"But he is already an acolyte, Jemidon. The guild on Pluton has offered to teach him the mastery of magic there. And he has asked me to go with him. Pluton, Jemidon, Pluton! Center of the islands and focus for trade. Why, in a single day there will be more excitement than this outland has in a year."

"And is that so important?" Jemidon asked softly. "When I am with you, the rest does not matter."

"Ah, Jemidon." Augusta smiled, placing her hand lightly

98

on his. "Your sweet words are always a delight. But one must be practical as well. You are only a neophyte; the training of an initiate takes three years more before you can pass to acolyte, let alone a master. I know that within a year I would be longing for the silks, cold fruits, and prestige that the woman of a master magician could command. Rosimar gives me that promise; from you, I can see nothing for a long time to come..."

Enough, Jemidon growled at himself. He covered the old hurt and pushed it away. It would do no good to dwell on opportunities already lost. He was now seeking the robe of a sorcerer, tracking down a trader and a slave girl. He would find out if the Augusta of the vault in the grotto was the one he knew only if he must.

He wrenched his attention back to the courtyard in front of him and scanned its interior. It was large and noisy, crammed with stalls and partitions around the periphery. The scene reminded him of the bazaar that had flourished on Morgana a fortnight ago; but here the structures were more permanent, made of stone and wood rather than canvas and paper. Each was decorated in gaudy colors. Hawkers at the entrances called out what could be exchanged inside. With long ceremonial daggers, they pointed to hastily chalked lists on panels that swung out over the milling throng. From time to time, scurrying messengers flitted through the crowd to erase an entry or change a price.

"For the name of lady Magma's lover," one called, "I have been offered twelve tokens. Does anyone on Pluton desire to know it more?"

"Gold from the west in exchange for grain," another shouted. "Two brandels per bushel. Trade now while my purse is still full."

"A barge for the southern kingdoms will sail on the tide," a third said. "How much for a one-hundredth share?"

At the far end of the court, on a board flanked by pages in silken hose, were listed the trading rates for metals and staples around the world. Gold, silver, wheat, stone, spices, and slaves all had entries scripted in bold black numerals. Below the board sat the changers, huddled between their huge scales and weights. Next to them were the assayers, with rows of reagent bottles and shelves crammed with specimens. Jemidon saw a richly dressed merchant exit from the freshly painted cubicle directly ahead and perfumed ladies duck to enter an equally elaborate facade to the left. He looked down the row and walked toward an entrance smaller than the rest. It had no hawkers outside, but the faded panel of fare was crammed with entries in a small, nervous script. "Tomorrow's departures," the first read. "The true age of the high prince," the second said. "The size of Procolon's fleet," the third proclaimed.

Jemidon ducked through the low opening and saw a room crammed with furnishings. Stools short and tall were pushed against shelves sagging from the weight of leather-bound books. Scrolls of parchment lay unwound on the floor, weaving a coarse tapestry between small chests and smooth boxes bolted shut with massive locks. Two oil lamps on the far wall shone above a high table with chairs on either side. Hunched over a ledger like a mantis watching its prey, a thin and gangly figure mumbled as he scanned entries and made small notes with a quill.

"Tomorrow Gandis will pay twenty tokens for the name of Trocolar's latest partner. And since I bought it from Brason for sixteen, that is a profit of four. Sixty-seven tokens for the week. Two thousand eight hundred and twelve in all. Ah, if only the election were another month away. Cumbrist would not have a chance. Three thousand at the most; he could not be worth a brandel more."

"I seek information," Jemidon said when the other did not look up. "And I think I will not be able to afford the surroundings that the other divulgents seem to offer."

The man behind the table jerked to attention. His elbow bumped the bowl of ink onto the sawdust floor. "Calm yourself, Benedict, calm yourself, or it will be Cumbrist for sure." He breathed deeply as he watched the ink sink into the ground. Then, focusing on Jemidon, he motioned to the empty chair. "I am Benedict, pansophical divulgent," he said. "Ask me anything and I will know. Gossips of the guilds are a specialty. Futures of the exchanges with generous guarantees. For a copper, the use of the seat is yours."

Jemidon halted just as he was lowering himself into the chair. He pushed it aside in irritation. "An unthinking way to treat a potential customer," he growled. "It makes one want to try somewhere else."

"You will find none charge less than a copper," Benedict said. "Everything on Pluton has a price. And besides, you need look no further. Anything you wish to know, I will tell."

"Then what of a trader called Drandor?" Jemidon asked. "How much for where he is now?"

"For two coppers I will speak my fee." Benedict centered the ledger on the table. "How soon do you wish to know?"

"You have heard of Drandor?" Jemidon exclaimed. "What luck on my first try! Then what of Delia, the slave girl with the golden curls? Is she still safe? Who is the partner Melizar? Has he interceded on her behalf?"

"One at a time," Benedict said. "For someone who begrudges the copper for a chair, you talk as if your purse were full. Show me your assay so that I will know you are worth my time."

"Assay?" Jemidon shook his head. "I have come to this exchange directly from the harbor." He furled his brow. "And even that cost two coppers for the directions."

"What, no writ certifying your worth?" Benedict asked. "Not a single token in any of the vaults? Then why are you here? It cannot mean you seriously intend to trade."

Benedict stopped and his eyes widened. He quickly snatched the ledger from the table and raced to the wall. Jemidon saw the divulgent stuff the book into a large box on the floor and slam shut the lid. A flash of painful blue light sparked from the container as it closed. The air crackled and hissed. Jemidon caught the pungent smell that came with a storm.

"Forever protected, save by my command." Benedict shot back a triumphant look. "No hammer can dent the walls, nor can the box be moved from where it sits on the floor. And unless I am calm, even my words will have no effect. A knife at my throat will not force entry if I do not wish it so. A small strongbox as those of magic go, but effective nonetheless. You will have to try your thievery on one who is not so fortunately secured."

"I will take nothing here that you do not freely give," Jemidon growled. "And if I must have some piece of paper before we can talk, then tell me how one is obtained and I will be back."

Benedict paused, eyeing Jemidon critically, but a roll of drums outside in the court stopped him from speaking. He hurried back to the high table and grabbed a belt from a shelf. It was plain leather and buckled on the side. In the very front, it looped through a row of small columns that butted together and protruded with thumb levers. Buckling the belt around his narrow hips, the divulgent dashed past Jemidon and through the opening. "No more time to weigh your merits," he called. "The court is full, and many will want to wager on the outcome with less than a full token."

Jemidon turned to follow, his annoyance growing with each step. He flung aside the curtain, but then stopped as he sensed the sudden change of mood in the courtyard. Except for the drumbeat, the throng was quiet. The jostle of bodies had ceased, and all eyes were on the center of the court. A pathway had cleared itself back to the rate-board. From behind the changers marched a small troop of men-at-arms. The first two pushed the crowd farther back on either side. Behind them came two lines of three, supporting a huge gleaming box on their shoulders.

The coffer was a perfect cube of glistening metal, polished to such a smoothness that Jemidon saw the surrounding scene reflected better than if by the finest mirror. Along the top edge, just below a row of hinges, he recognized the arcane script that magicians had chiseled into the side as part of the ritual of formation. Near one bottom corner, a small pipe protruded from the interior. Except for these, nothing else marred the clean and rigidly flat surfaces.

A whisper of anticipation started through the crowd as

102

the next in the procession came into view. Jemidon stood on tiptoe to look over a shoulder and saw a man with eyes wide with fear, his hands secured behind his back and his neck circled with iron. From the heavy black ring, a chain ran to a second prisoner, similarly bound, and then to a third. The last was a woman, clad only in a thin chemise, stumbling barefooted after the others.

As the procession stopped in the center of the court, the men-at-arms set the cube on the ground and flung open the top face with a crash. Two more guards struggled forward underneath the weight of a pair of huge sandglasses. The last brought up a ladder, placing it against the side of the box. The top rung came to rest near the rim, well above the height of Jemidon's head.

"The men are worth nothing, but for the woman, ten tokens," someone shouted.

"Twelve," another countered, "and one of my own in trade."

"A brandel that the bidding will not go above fifteen," a third called out.

"Ten coppers that she will plead before it is finished."

"A token and three that the first glass will be done before the contraction," a woman in an embroidered gown next to Jemidon said to her companion. "A token and three coppers against your token plain."

The man accompanying her nodded and pulled a gleaming coin from a pouch. The woman produced hers and then frowned as she searched through her purse for the rest.

"Perhaps I can be of assistance to my lady." Benedict suddenly appeared and patted the mechanism strapped to his waist. "Brandels for tokens, coppers for silver galleons, dranbots from the south, regals of the inland. I can change them all. Only one extra for a fee, and whatever you have can be transformed into another."

The woman nodded and reached a final time into her purse. "All copper and silver," she said as she dumped a pile of brass and tin into Benedict's palm. "I expect to wager more before it is done."

With a speed that Jemidon could hardly follow, Benedict inserted the coins into the slits in the top of the device at his waist. As the metal clattered downward, he tripped the levers near the bottom and his palm filled with another collection, different from the first.

"May your wagers be perfection," Benedict said as he handed the money back to the woman. With a slight bow, he darted away into the crowd.

"Eighteen has been bid, but the debt is thirty-five."

Jemidon turned his attention back to the center of the court. A man-at-arms with a red surcoat over his mail paced around the cube, shouting to the crowd.

"Expert trader Trocolar's due is thirty-five, and he will accept no less. Speak now, else the justice of Pluton will run its course."

The crowd again fell silent as the guard made a final circuit of the box. He jerked his thumb upward and the prisoners were goaded onto the ladder at spear point. The first reached the top and hesitated, but one of the guards prodded him over the side. Jemidon heard a muffled thud as he hit the bottom and saw the chain pull tight on the one who followed. When the woman reached the top, she turned and looked out over the throng.

"Trocolar," she shouted hoarsely, "Trocolar. I cannot pay him, it is true, but my spirit will not rest until he suffers the same. If ever he becomes short even by one token only, then I charge your judgment to be no less than what you have prescribed for me."

With her chin thrust out defiantly, she turned and leaped in after the others. Two of the men-at-arms grabbed the lid of the chest and arched it up over the hinges to clang shut. A blue flash like the one from Benedict's strongbox cut through the air overhead. Low-hanging banners about the court seared and smoldered, turning black along a thin horizontal line at precisely the height of the top of the coffer. One of the glasses was tipped over. As the sand began to fall, the crowd broke into another round of spirited betting.

Jemidon looked about, puzzled. No shouts could be heard coming from the box, nor any pounding on the walls. In perfect silence, it stood gleaming in the high morning sun. He watched the sand drain from the glass and, just as the last grains emptied, the starting of the other.

"There are three this time, rather than the usual pair," Jemidon heard someone say. "That is the reason. Without her, it would have long since been over."

"But the pressure does not relent," another replied. "Three coppers that we will not see the turning of another glass."

A sudden shimmer caught Jemidon's eye, and he glanced back at the cube. He saw the walls vibrate as if struck by a hammer and then a sudden jerking movement as they simultaneously contracted. Jemidon blinked at what he had seen. The cube was still perfectly formed as before, but, with no excess material or visible seams, it had shrunk to half its former size.

With a sickening feeling, Jemidon realized what was going to happen. Before he could turn away, the cube jerked a second time and then again. With each movement, it halved its dimensions, confining its contents closer together in smaller and smaller volumes. The vibrations of the walls intensified, so that a low-pitched hum filled the air of the courtyard. Drops of reddish pulp appeared at the end of the pipe at the bottom. With the next constriction, it gushed in a steady flow. Bits of cloth and shattered bone swirled out onto the courtyard. A thick, stringy liquid added its stain to the sun-bleached blotch that was already there.

Jemidon turned away and staggered back through the entrance to Benedict's cubicle. On Pluton for less than an hour, and already he wanted to be away. He thought of the tangle of three bodies as they were cramped together and the woman's face that he had seen just moments before. He sagged into a chair, shook his head to clear the images away, and tried to focus on why he had come.

After a moment, he heard the slide of the curtain and looked up, thankful for the distraction as Benedict entered.

"Still here?" the divulgent asked. "If you stay, the chair rent remains one copper."

Jemidon started to rise, but then slowly settled back into the chair. Disgustedly he threw a coin on the table and placed his arms around his stomach. It would be worth the cost for a few more minutes to allow his insides to settle.

Benedict circled to the other side of the table and scooped up the copper. With a laugh, he slid it into the changer at his waist and patted it affectionately.

"Faster than any of the rest, and they know I am accurate as well," he said. "It garnishes only little profit, even when the courtyard is full, but each token I am able to accumulate brings me closer to Cumbrist's total." With a practiced motion, he levered a half-dozen coins into his palm and then recycled them through the top.

"A curious device," Jemidon said, reaching for any distraction to blur the memories of outside. "It seems to be a collection of distinct columns fused together. The type of coins which come out the bottom of a particular shaft are all the same, even though a mixture is inserted in the single slit at the top. Somehow, internally they are permuted about."

"A minor magic." Benedict shrugged. "Necessary to make the thing invulnerable. More of a puzzle than anything else."

"Do it again, but more slowly so that I can watch."

"Another copper," Benedict said. "I am no practiced performer, but it would be folly to give away my skill when fetching a price would be better."

Jemidon scowled and waved the thought aside. "Never mind, then. Let us return to why I am here. Where do I get this assay? Or must I pay for that information as well?"

Benedict pursed his lips. "Everyone on Pluton would know. The value of the knowledge is worth far less than the smallest coin we could exchange."

"Then answer more questions until I have received full value," Jemidon said, bouncing a second coin on the table.

"Well enough." Benedict nodded in agreement as he grabbed the copper. "As for the first, any vault will perform the service for a small fee—even certify what is deposited in accounts other than their own."

"Another small fee," Jemidon said, "given to a vault which also will probably charge for me to sit while I explain what I want." He paused as another idea popped into his head. For a moment he turned it over, then shrugged, making up his mind.

"And the vault in the grotto," he said at last. "Will that serve as well as any other?"

Benedict ran his fingers over the small, weathered disk. "I owe you still and so I will answer fairly. Of all the vaults on the island, that is the last with which I would entrust my wealth. The others have protection that is true magic, strongholds like mine, only large enough to hold the fortunes of many. But the one in the grotto—" He shook his head. "It depends on the tide to protect it. I would not take the risk. No matter that it means the fees are smaller. Cumbrist does not choose such folly, and neither shall I."

"I have no fortune to be so concerned," Jemidon said, "and on the sloop from Morgana, I heard that an Augusta earns her livelihood there. Perhaps she is none other than an old friend and will be less eager to demand a fee at every turn. Give me the directions to where she is, and then we will be done."

"In the end, you will receive what you pay for." Benedict shrugged. "The difference is the degree of risk. And as for the consequences, think again of the exhibition in the court."

"The ledger does not indicate that you are expected." The clerk on the left looked up suspiciously from the paper-strewn desk. "Surely one of us can handle your needs just as well."

Jemidon glanced around the small room. Neither of the two women could be Augusta, despite the number of years since he had seen her last. And the drab decor was not what he had expected. Simple curtains of cloth hung from the walls to hide the rough wood planking underneath. Candles from a single chandelier overhead added their feeble glow to the filtered sunlight from the windows facing the street on the east. Missing were the fancy divans and tables heaped with fruits and drink. Unlike the other vaults he had passed, there were no laughing women in low-cut gowns to entertain the traders while they waited.

"Tally the account as of the moment." A door to the rear swung open, and a woman with an armful of scrolls bustled through. "Trocolar will be here within the hour, and I do not want him to find some petty excuse to move his funds."

"Augusta?" Jemidon blinked in recognition. She was full-figured, perhaps a trifle heavier than he remembered her. Her face was broad and her eyes wide-set. None would call her a beauty, but few men would ignore her smile. Her hair was clipped short, combed straight back and held in place by tiny combs. She was a year older than Jemidon at most, but already the hint of wrinkles had appeared in the smooth glow of youth.

Augusta frowned at Jemidon and then broke into a smile. "My somber neophyte!" she exclaimed. "A happy event on an otherwise miserable day!" She dropped the pile of paper onto the nearest desk and circled around the side. "Within the hour." She waved back at the scrolls as they fell.

With a fluid motion, she slid her arm around Jemidon's back and pushed her cheek forward for a kiss. "You always were the dreamy one. To seek me out after all these years! It is good to think that at least one man is interested in something other than the number of tokens I hoard in the vault."

Jemidon started to speak, then thought better of it. He followed Augusta back through the doorway into a room scarcely larger than that occupied by the clerks. Slowly he sat on the bench she had cleared with a swipe of her hand.

"Now tell me everything that has happened since we went our separate ways," Augusta said. "Do not hold back any detail. I want to hear it all." She stopped and looked at a water clock dripping on a shelf. "I want to hear it all, that is, until Trocolar comes blustering forth with his accusations and threats."

Augusta breathed deeply. She settled in a chair opposite Jemidon and rubbed the frown in her forehead. After a moment, she looked back at him with a weak smile. Jemidon rose and circled behind her. More sleeping memories awoke as he placed his hands on the taut tendons of her neck.

"You are overwrought," he said as he began to massage the tightness.

Augusta let out a long sigh and patted Jemidon's hand on her shoulder. "It has been too long," she whispered. "Rosimar was the practical one, but his back rubs could never compare with yours."

"Rosimar!" Jemidon stopped. "Are the two of you still—"

"A child's entanglement, no more enduring than our own." Augusta laughed. She wiggled her shoulders for him to continue.

As simple as that, Jemidon thought as he resumed kneading. Rosimar was dismissed with a few words. And he and Augusta were chatting and sharing pleasures together as if they had never been apart—as if there had been no deep hurt, no searing wound that left him so disillusioned. He pushed his thumbs along her spine and arched her shoulders back, digging for the feelings of what had been.

The frustration, the despair, the helplessness had brought him to tears; he remembered them, yes, but now only as abstractions, mere labels for an event which marked his passage into manhood. The fire, the intensity, the overwhelming flood of emotion that had consumed his thoughts—those were hollow voices that spoke no more. And beneath them, the delicate whispers of his first love and the unfolding of his innermost self to share with another were trampled and torn gossamers hidden away in a box as strong as Benedict's. Could he dare to open it again, to hear the broken murmurs and try to make them whole? Jemidon flexed Augusta's shoulders in larger oscillations, watching her gown fall slack and then pull tight

109

across her breasts. And yes, the passion—could that again be as sweet?

"You were going to tell me of your adventures." Augusta cut through Jemidon's reverie. "What made you decide to seek me out at last?"

Jemidon hesitated. He was on Pluton for a different reason entirely. Seeing Augusta was only a means to an end.

He wrenched his mind back to why he had come. "I need an assay, an assay so that I can barter with a divulgent. I had hoped that you might help me for less than others would charge."

Augusta stiffened. She abruptly stood and turned to face Jemidon. "So practical," she said. "Now, so practical and blunt. You have changed, my dreaming one, you have changed indeed." She looked at him intently. "No matter, do not apologize." She laughed. "My vanity has withstood stronger affronts. Besides, there is no reason to rush. I am in such a position now that I do not need to seize the first opportunity that presents itself."

"About your position," Jemidon said. "The vault in the grotto—what role do you play?"

"I *am* the vault," Augusta said. "Those who held it previously were foolish where I was wise. Or perhaps it was the luck in speculating in the exchanges. It does not matter. In the end, their choice was to surrender title to me or accompany the mercenaries and their contracting cube. It is not a bad result for one who once thought trailing the robe hem of a master magician would be enough."

"I saw the cube in the courtyard today," Jemidon said quietly. "For what sort of crime would something such as that be used?"

"For debt," Augusta replied. "For inability to pay. On Pluton, tokens and life are the same. Without one you cannot have the other."

"But why the obsession?" Jemidon asked. "On none of the other islands is there so much focus on one's wealth."

"Because here it truly can be measured. There are no

110

ambiguities or changes other than those of your own making."

Jemidon frowned in puzzlement. Augusta smiled and reached for a small bag piled with many others on a cluttered desk. "It is because of the token," she said, flinging him the sack. "You were a neophyte in magic. You know the properties of something created by the craft."

Jemidon nodded as he reached into the pouch and extracted one of the gleaming disks. He held it in his palm and felt the strong tingling that coursed up his arm. Mirror-flat and unblemished by a single scratch, it vibrated with the magical forces that gave it life. The coin was a geometric perfection that would last forever, long after all around it had returned to dust.

"Yes, 'perfection is eternal.'" Augusta watched his eyes as he fondled the cold smoothness. "A token illustrates so well the Maxim of Persistence upon which all magic is based. At first the small guild on the island made them as curiosities, a training ritual for the initiates and nothing more. They were sold as souvenirs to the traders who stopped on their journeys across the sea.

"But the tingle is addictive. Gradually, as more and more people coveted them, the token's true value came to be realized. They are small, lightweight, indestructible, and impossible to counterfeit. The flutter in your palm is unmistakable. Once you have handled a token, nothing else can ever be mistaken for one. And since Pluton saw goods and moneys from many lands, tokens became the standard by which all else was measured. Even more reliable than gold, they are the medium of exchange. With them are balanced the transactions between Arcadia, Procolon, and the other kingdoms."

Jemidon replaced the coin in the sack and tossed it back on the desk. "Brandels or brass," he said, "it is all the same. The cutpurse or the marauder can take away in a trice what a lifetime has carefully built."

"And so it was on Pluton," Augusta agreed, "until the guilds again exercised their arts, building strongholds both large and small, impregnable havens for the coveted tokens that only a true owner could unlock. With a standard that was unimpeachable and a mechanism that made the possession of wealth secure, Pluton blossomed as a trading center. There is none like it anywhere on all the shores of the great sea."

"And the obsession?" Jemidon asked.

"As in any land, wealth is a measure of power." Augusta shrugged. "But, unlike elsewhere, on Pluton there is nothing else. The stacks of coins hidden away in the vaults are true treasures and forever secure. There is no force that can take that basis of power away. The measure of a man is the size of his assay, not the circumference of his bicep."

"And hence the price on everything?"

"And hence the price. We have no hereditary rulers in any of our guilds. All is decided by election, with each one's vote proportional to the tokens he has on account, even for the ruling council. In a few days we will determine who is to lead us for the next three years. And hence everyone strives to increase his assay by whatever means he can. Why, even information brings a fee; the divulgents scramble to accumulate wealth the same as anyone else. And for those already owning treasures, there are the gambles of the exchange by which they trade back and forth their riches."

"I need to find a trader who has come to Pluton," Jemidon said. "How much will it cost?"

"If you must know immediately, prepare to pay a full token," Augusta said. "All divulgents will profess already to know, but they must spend large sums to ferret out the facts."

"A full token," Jemidon repeated. "Why, I know that even a slave girl can be purchased for fifteen. My purse is not flat, but after I paid for my passage from Morgana, neither does it bulge. It would take me quite a while writing scholarly scrolls to amass the value equivalent to a full token."

"That is the rate, nonetheless," Augusta said. "They are skilled in their trade and will learn far quicker than you would yourself. But without a purse that gleams, then from the divulgents you will gain little."

112

"A full token," Jemidon repeated once more. "And that fee might be the first of many. Perhaps it would be quicker to take a chance with the exchanges."

Augusta paused in thought. She looked at Jemidon and slowly ran her tongue over her lips. Tilting her head to one side, she smiled and casually motioned him to sit again.

"No, Jemidon, not the exchanges or the slow drudgery of the scholar," she said softly. "I can better help you with your needs. The vault will offer you a token in exchange for—for a week's indenture to my service."

Jemidon frowned at the sudden change in her tone. "What tasks would I be called on to perform?"

"You would be an aide, a messenger, whatever I decide needs to be done," Augusta said. "For example, I wish an offer taken to Rosimar's guild. I know that he is close to perfecting a new ritual but does not have the resources to investigate the final steps. He will give a generous share to an investor who provides the wherewithal to see it finished."

"But why a token for a week's labor?" Jemidon asked. "The rate seems far too sweet."

"It is better than you will find anywhere else," Augusta agreed. "And as to why—" She shrugged and laughed again. "I spoke earlier of opportunity. It is an opportunity for us both. I now can afford to indulge in dreamers."

"I do not like the idea of the indenture. I have seen enough already of what the consequences could be."

"In one week you will have the means to locate this trader, and I will have ample chance to convince you perhaps to stay for another. If what you seek is so important, you must risk what you have, in any event. Do you not think it better with me than with some other?"

Jemidon scowled at the rush of ideas. His instincts told him to proceed slowly. His quest was to find Drandor, rescue Delia, and restore sorcery to what it was before. The robe of the master was what he sought—the riches and the power. But as he looked at Augusta's smile, he felt the confusion of his old longings. Her offer was attractive. On his own, could he proceed as quickly? And

113

was not his striving because of her as well? Was it not to see the respect in her eyes, finally to be regarded as more than a comfortable dreamer with nimble fingers, and to savor her words when she apologized for the hurt? Jemidon puffed his cheeks and let out a sigh.

"Prepare the papers," he said at last. "And instruct me to the guild which is to receive this offer of your assets."

CHAPTER SEVEN

The Vault in the Grotto

JEMIDON returned to the drab building at the foot of the Street of Vaults. He was satisfied with what he had done. Augusta's offer had been readily accepted by the magician's guild, just as she had said. He was even invited back in four days to monitor the next steps in the experimental ritual. If eventually the whole sequence worked, then tokens could be produced at a fifth the traditional effort. Augusta's investment would be returned twofold. She could expect an additional ten tokens every month thereafter.

"On this evening's tide. Another day I will not wait," a heavy voice boomed from the back room. "And if you do not comply, I will tell the others that you cannot because they are gone."

"I only point out that the hour is already late and the level is rising," Augusta shouted back. "You speak of risk, but choose to ignore true threat for the insignificant."

Jemidon passed through the doorway and saw Augusta scowling at the heavy-set man slumped in the chair. His sagging jowls gave him a bulldog look that the fine tailoring of his cape and collars could not hide. With watery, pale eyes he returned Augusta's stare.

"Tonight," he repeated. "You can have an oarsman

114

light the way. After all, I would have no such trouble with any other vault along the street."

"Any other along the street would charge three times the fee to hold your tokens secure," Augusta said. "Their precious magic boxes do not come cheap." She stopped and looked in Jemidon's direction. "My newly indentured servant," she said. "And this is Trocolar, elected leader of the tradesmen."

"After the next polling, leader of the council as well," Trocolar said. He ran his eyes up and down Jemidon's frame. "Stocky enough, but I doubt he would last more than a day at the oars. No, tokens are my concern, Augusta, not flesh of questionable value. My tokens are what I want, and I want them now."

Jemidon bristled at Trocolar's rude manner, but he said nothing. Instead, he watched Augusta for the key to how he should behave.

Augusta worked her lips for something more to say, but no words came. After a moment, she sighed and slapped her hands to her sides. "Then let us get to the skiff at once. Because of the hour, you will have to pay my rowers double as it is. And you should accompany us, Jemidon. One more will make the loading proceed quicker."

Trocolar stood with majestic slowness, his face drawn in a slight smile. With a perfunctory nod as she passed, he followed Augusta through the front room and out onto the street. Jemidon came last. In a silent single file, they made their way down the hillside to the harbor's edge.

Soon they were gliding across the water in a narrow boat. Oarsmen front and back propelled them toward the smaller of the two islands in the center off the bay, the one of gnarled rock that was seemingly devoid of life.

Jemidon watched the weather-beaten rock loom larger and larger with each stroke. The sun, low in the west, hid most of one side in soft shadow; but even so, he could distinguish the deeper blacks that marked the entrances to the caves. The boat headed unerringly for one opening larger than the rest. Like the mouth of a large serpent, it

115

opened directly on the water, sucking in each lapping wave and expelling it with the next breath.

The oarsmen maneuvered the boat into the entrance and paddled into the dark tunnel. The oars were secured. In an eerie quietness, the skiff coasted forward on the still water.

A long moment passed, and then they halted with a gentle bump. Jemidon heard a fumbling in the bow, the scrape of flint on steel, and finally a gentle whoosh as an oil cresset chiseled into the rock sprang to life. He saw their way barred by a heavy iron grating that protruded from the ceiling above and disappeared into the dark water. Augusta placed her palm on a small box next to the burning light; after it opened, she extracted a large brass key.

"You see, there is magic protecting the vault that resides in the grotto," she said as she worked the lock on the grating. "But only what is necessary to complete the security. For the large containers, we never had to pay."

"Holgon, my magician, would not be impressed by such items," Trocolar said. "And guarding a single entrance does not guarantee that others do not exist."

"Yet you have seen fit to leave a considerable treasure here," Augusta said. She motioned to the oarsmen. The one in front grabbed the protruding handle of a bolt and pulled it free. The other tugged at a circular chain draped nearby. With a rusty creaking, the grating slowly began to rise.

"A considerable treasure," she continued. "And none of your reasons for withdrawal carry much persuasion."

Trocolar grunted, but did not answer. Instead, he pointed to the red horizontal line painted on the wall.

"Yes." Augusta nodded. "In less than an hour, the tide will be too high. I warned you before we came. All your tokens will not save us if we are caught in the passage between the two pools."

The grating clanged against its upper stops. The two oarsmen rushed to get the skiff back into motion, while Augusta lighted a torch from the cresset. In its flickering light, Jemidon and the others glided deeper into the cave.

Immediately behind the grating, the ceiling and walls

receded from view. As if traveling on calm seas under a starless night sky, the small boat slid through the water. Jemidon breathed still and fungal air, the only clue to his true surroundings. He tried to pierce the gloom, but saw nothing to aid in orientation. The rhythmic splash of the paddles wove complicated patterns with the rustle of Augusta's smoking flame. No one spoke. The feeling was oppressive.

After several minutes, the pace of the paddling quickened. Jemidon sensed the tenseness in the oarsman behind. He looked around and saw the walls again coming into view. Like a crumpled funnel, they converged on the skiff, defining a narrow passage where there had been none before.

Jemidon watched the undulating surfaces resolve into distinguishable textures, dry swaths with large crystals of pegmatite, glistening walls of fine-grained granite, areas of gas-smoothed slickness, and jagged fissures that trickled with rainwater seeping from above. Closer and closer converged the walls. Jemidon felt himself breathe deeply to stave off the instinctive fear of confinement. A boat length away and then barely two arm lengths apart, the rock pushed in from either side.

Augusta lowered her torch. Jemidon looked ahead to see the ceiling crushing inward like the walls. The oarsman in front ducked to the side to avoid a low-hanging projection, and it whizzed past Jemidon's ear. Augusta set the base of the torch on the keelboard and experimented with huddling low at its side.

"We probably will have to extinguish our light on the way back," she said. "There will be just enough clearance for the skiff itself to squeeze by."

"How high does the tide rise?" Jemidon asked.

"Above the ceiling at the narrowest point," Augusta answered. "The vault is shaped like a carnival man's barbell, with this passage the only connection between two large chambers on either end. And for most of the day, the inner chamber is completely sealed off. There is no way to get through. Only at lowest tides, when the water

117

level is under the red line, can one attempt a passage. And even then, the margin of safety is none too great."

Jemidon copied the others, hunching over and then squirming even lower when a sharp outcrop skittered across the top of his head. He heard the rower behind give up trying to paddle the water. Instead, the oar was pushed against the side of the passage to propel them along. The skiff scraped and splintered against one wall and then bounced off to rub along the other. Jemidon felt the unyielding rock press him still lower and then heard a sickening grating as both sides of the boat caught at once. For a second they stopped, jammed against the walls, but the oarsmen rocked back and forth, and the inflowing tide pushed them free.

Jemidon tensed, waiting for the next constriction, but he felt instead the pressure on his back gradually lessen and then abruptly fall away. He watched Augusta stretch and extend the torch as she had done before. Once again, the walls receded to provide an easy passage.

"We are in the inner chamber," Augusta said. "And now to the vault itself. It is a small, separate cavity that took some fifteen years to suck dry, even with pumps of magic. The ledge above it does not provide enough space for the treasures."

As she pointed out the direction, the skiff sailed across the bowl of water. When they reached the wall, one oarsman secured the boat to some iron rings. The second rower sprang onto a rope ladder suspended from above.

Jemidon and the others followed. In a moment, they climbed onto a wide ledge twice the height of a man above the level of the water. Augusta's torch lighted several cressets, and Jemidon blinked at the sudden increase in light.

The shelf cut back into the overhanging rock for a sizable distance, creating a pocket far larger than the size of Augusta's rooms back on shore. Sand and planking made the irregular floor more or less level. A single table supported heavy ledgers, and a collection of scrolls was crammed into the cracks and crevices in the walls. Blooms of mold followed the trickle of water down the sloping

118

surfaces, and Jemidon saw splotches of growth peppering the more exposed parchments. Billowed soot covered one portion of the low-hanging roof where a fire evidently had been tried long ago. Charred stumps mingled with small bones and discarded refuse on the floor. Two spots of blackness led off further into the interior. A heavy cauldron lid covered a jagged hole in the rear from which dank smells rose to taint the air.

"The two side tunnels lead back to smaller caverns," Augusta explained to Jemidon. "And the lid covers a shaft that leads down to the vault itself. All of it is natural; the magic pumps and the lock on the entrance grating are the only indebtedness to the guilds."

An oarsman pushed the lid aside and threw another ladder down the tube. Looking over the edge before he placed his foot in the opening, Jemidon saw a narrow vertical tunnel, knobby and twisted, about five times the height of a man. The shuffle of hands and feet echoed along the shaft, making conversation impossible as Jemidon descended; but as he went lower, he heard the drips and gurgles of running water and then the suck and push of throbbing pumps.

Jemidon's foot hit bottom, splashing in a small, stagnant pool. A glow of imp light caught his attention on the right. From bottles fastened to a semicircular wall, the dim, blue glow bathed lumbering complexes of wheels and levers that pushed water up a tube and out of sight. Behind them was an array of chests, neatly ordered in precise rows and columns into a great square. Splashes of soft greens and yellows covered the tops and side plankings. Long tendrils of oozing growth stretched to the wet and rocky floor. The far walls could barely be seen.

The volume was larger than the hold of Arcadia's biggest grainship. Jemidon calculated how much he had climbed and descended as he made room for the others following. Yes, bigger than a galleon's hold and three man heights beneath the level of the sea.

"What miserable storage," Trocolar sneered as he followed Augusta back to the chests. "Look at this dampness, the cracks in the walls. Even a gentle shift in the earth, and the trickle would become a flood. It is worth the fee to have my tokens reside in a dry, clean vault, rather than in this slimy mess."

"The cloth and oak may rot," Augusta said, "but for tokens, it does not matter. Never will they alter."

"Nonetheless, mine will be gone," Trocolar said.

Jemidon saw the trader's eyes glisten as a chest lid was flung back and the subtle glow of the tokens added to the imp light. Trocolar turned to Augusta and pulled his jowls into a slight smile.

"And do not profess that it is of no concern," he said. "The loss of my fees just before the election will give you a smaller vote. I plan to persuade other traders to withdraw their holdings as well. Altogether, it will make a considerable difference."

"The issue is in doubt." Augusta shrugged. "Neither your faction nor mine has sufficient wealth to win on the first round."

"But there will be the subsequent ones," Trocolar said. "And, in a contest between the vaultholders and the traders, what do you think the outcome will be?"

"The vaultholders have governed Pluton fair and well for two decades," Augusta replied. "Indeed, your trading has never prospered better."

"But not as well as it might," Trocolar snapped as he waved his arm over the chests. "I have not forgotten the innocent-faced girl who charmed a debtholding from me all those years ago."

"I paid you a premium for the writ," Augusta said. "You received more than you were due and a year early besides. You have no cause for complaint."

"No, no cause for complaint," Trocolar spat out. "No cause for complaint. I am reminded of it each time the others ask me again to tell the tale. No cause for complaint, because I did not ask why you wanted the writ. This vault should have been mine, Augusta, not the prize of some barefoot mainland girl who chanced upon it first!"

"You were greedy enough for immediate gain," Augusta shot back. "I took the gamble that months later the vaultholders would not be able to pay. And we have been over the same story many times before. You keep your treasures here for the same reasons as the others. Despite how you feel about who earns the fees, you are eager enough to take advantage of the fact that they are less."

"This time there is a difference," Trocolar said. "This time I am close enough that my faction may win." The trader stopped and grabbed Augusta by the shoulders. "I have paid the divulgents, and they have told me what I needed to know, Augusta. I have learned from what you taught me as well. Your only indebtedness is for the pumps that keep this pit from washing away. Periodic payments to the guild that made them will continue for many years. But you are aggressive, Augusta, always hungry for more, speculating to the limit and holding back barely enough to transfer the sums when they are due."

Trocolar sucked in his breath and raced on. "Know that I am your new debtholder, Augusta. I paid a premium for the writ, just as you had done with me. And if I win control of the council, their first act will be to change the laws governing magical items procured by the vaults. Those are too precious to be so capriciously obtained from the guilds. A proper vault should have title to its items of security free and clear. Someone who places his treasures for safekeeping should expect no less. Yes, there will be a change to the laws so that such liens immediately will be due and payable.

"Think of it, Augusta—in a few days it might all be over. In less than a week, you may be a true debtor, unable to pay. Everything you have, including your life, could be mine to do with as I will."

Trocolar tilted back his head and laughed, his voice bouncing off the walls in booming echoes. Then, with a swirl of his cape, he turned and headed back for the ladder. "I will count them in the skiff after they are loaded," he called back. "Holgon, my magician, has found a potential partner who thinks a few hundred is an impressive sum. Wait until he sees me with some eight thousand more."

In the gloom, Jemidon saw Augusta's shoulders sag and he ran to her side. "How serious is his threat?" he

121

asked. "Can you not pay him from one of the other chests that are here?"

"The total number of tokens on Pluton is known." Augusta shook her head. "And for every credit to an account, there must be a debit elsewhere. These chests are not mine to do with as I please. They belong to many others. And Trocolar's knowledge is accurate. The total of what I owe on the pumps exceeds all that I personally have on account."

"Then a new partner. A share in future profits for someone to pay what will be due."

"If Trocolar controls the council, none would dare thwart his intent." Augusta shook her head again. "No, now my hope will have to be that Rosimar succeeds sooner than expected. When we return to shore, you must go to him immediately and tell him the increased importance of his endeavors."

Augusta started to smile bravely at Jemidon, but then stopped abruptly. For a moment she looked away. Finally she turned back and lightly placed her hand on his arm. "I am sorry," she said softly. "You should not be involved. For a single token, it is too much to risk."

"I will help you if I can," Jemidon said, "although my knowledge probably will be of little value."

"It is more than your knowledge that is bound in my plight," Augusta said. "Your writ of indenture was recorded with the rest of the transactions of the day. And such bindings cannot be revoked, regardless of the sum. For the next week, you are one of my assets, Jemidon, part of what I must surrender to a creditor if I cannot pay." She stroked his arm and finally completed her smile. "You see, I will have company if Trocolar manages to send me to the cube. It is to your benefit as well as mine to speed Rosimar along the way."

Jemidon's late evening message to the guild had first been met with resistance. Rosimar had wanted to proceed at his own cautious and methodical pace. But the threat to Augusta had eventually won him over. The preparations for the next phase of the ritual were ready in three days, rather than four.

When Jemidon returned on the third day to monitor the progress, he did so with more than passing interest. Before the trip to the grotto, Augusta's investment in Rosimar's guild had been an idle curiosity—something to stir up old memories of when he was a neophyte, far removed from his pursuit of the sorcerer's robe. But now his focus had been diverted. He could not pursue one art without success in the other. If the remaining errors in the new ritual could be corrected soon enough, Augusta's fortunes would receive a much needed boost. A hundred tokens returned with another hundred as well would more than compensate for Trocolar's missing fees. Her faction might even win the election after all, and then he would have earned his own token and be free to track down Drandor and Delia.

Jemidon looked up and down the length of the huge rectangular hall called the ceremonium that dominated the grounds of the guild. Scattered everywhere was a clutter of apparatus large and small, giant presses, arrays of pulleys and cogs, cascades of vats and piping, cages of exotic beasts, clockworks, balances, and beams. The roof of the structure arched to a giddy height. Through carefully fitted isinglass panels, the morning sunlight flooded the parqueted floor.

Directly in front of where he stood, Jemidon saw the neophytes straining against the huge lever of a ballista and heard the ratchet click another notch. The twisted leather rope grated from the effort. At the far end of the ceremonium was the target, a row of whirling saw blades with teeth sparkling from the diamond dust freshly applied. Behind them were the grindstones, each the width of a barrel and twice the height of a man.

"Much more impressive than delicate tongs and tinkling finger cymbals, is it not?" The lean man next to Jemidon waved at the equipment while the final adjustments were being made. His nose was pinched between close-set eyes. Bony forearms dangled from a robe two sizes too small. Although his face was smooth, his shoulders slumped forward with the posture of an older man. "The larger guilds boast of innovation, but none of them have dared to take the chance," he said.

"And if the plate of steel can be split into strips by hurling it against the blades, what then, Rosimar?" Jemidon asked. "How soon until Augusta receives her return?"

"The mistress of the grotto." Rosimar's eyes narrowed. "I am surprised that you would bother again to curry her favor. She uses men like honeypods, discarding the husk after she has sucked them dry."

"My fate is intertwined with hers," Jemidon tried to say casually. "The more that her wealth increases, then the greater is the chance that she will be able to pay me my wage when it is due."

"One does not have to be a divulgent to know what is at stake," Rosimar said. "And she needs the aid of a master magician, not one who failed to garner even an initiate's robe. Many saw Trocolar march off under guard to another vault yesterday evening. The trader's factors align; he has her positioned where she has never been before."

Rosimar paused and stared at Jemidon. "And understand that that is the only reason. Understand it well. If Augusta asks for help, I will give my consent. Even if it means a trip through that tiny hellhole to the vault itself. *If* it is for our future business together, to influence the tally when the leading factions gather for the vote, not to recapture what has gone before." Rosimar hesitated a second time. "Besides, she can have no more than a passing interest in you, in any event."

Jemidon blinked at the sudden tension hiding behind the precisely enunciated words. Evidently Rosimar's feelings for Augusta were still strong. The magician might yet prove to be competition, if he were to succeed with his ritual. Jemidon grimaced as he tried to sort out his thoughts. Augusta and Rosimar. Did that really matter? What of Delia, who still had to be freed? He felt guilty that the image of her golden curls, the sound of her voice, the sense of her brave spirit, all were fading next to the sharpness of Augusta's presence. In the end, which did he want? It was a tangle he could not resolve. Better for now, he decided, to keep the conversation on safer ground.

"Augusta has mentioned that this time the polling will be in the grotto," Jemidon said. "On the ledge above the vault. Why not have it instead in some neutral place?"

"No place is neutral on Pluton," Rosimar said. "Each is owned by someone who charges for its use. By tradition, the site is rotated among the leading factions, those strong enough to ensure there is no interruption while the counting is going on."

The magician looked off into the distance for a moment and then shook his head rapidly from side to side. Exhaling deeply, he turned to direct two initiates entering the ceremonium, tugging at the end of a large, woven hose. "Attach it to the flute at the left," he said. "The rest are already connected to the bellows in the outer chamber."

Jemidon watched the initiates screw tight the flange that bound the hose to the large, hollowed log running by his feet. The whole end of the room was crowded with giant caricatures of musical instruments, triangles thrice the height of a man, harps with strings like hawsers, and double reeds as thick as tabletops. From each device that was powered by air snaked a hose through a doorway to the rear.

"It is a matter of scale." Rosimar followed Jemidon's gaze. "The casual travelers think that the magic guilds must be the focus of Pluton's power, because from them come the tokens upon which all else is based. But they do not know the number of steps it takes to make even a single perfect disk, an intricate ritual requiring months and consuming exotic ingredients besides. And with the competition from all who know the secret, and the many mouths to feed between the steps, the profit is small, barely enough to make the whole effort worthwhile. When considered from the standpoint of outlay and return, the boxes and vaults are far more efficient in producing wealth. It is better to receive tokens already made than to struggle to form more with the painstaking steps of our art."

"And yet you experiment with the giant apparatus here," Jemidon said, "and have taken Augusta's writ to buy all these hoses, saws, and weapons of war."

"It is a matter of scale, as I have said," Rosimar repeated. "Why labor to produce a single disk when hundreds can be made with the same steps? Why gong a petite triangle to fill a small volume with sound when the entire hall can resonate from one hundreds of times as large? Instead of cutting each sheet of steel into strips a careful stroke at a time, we will attempt to cleave many at once by firing the plate at the whirling saws and playing the music at a tempo to keep in step.

"The grinding will be done by the big wheels rather than by hand-held files. And all the rest has been proved. If today the cleaving can be made to proceed in concert with what the ritual demands for perfection, then the entire process will work, without a doubt."

Jemidon looked down at the whirling row of saw blades and back at the ballista, as the neophytes lined up the sheet of gleaming steel in the carriage that would hurl it forward. "And yet the scale and weights are normal-sized."

"They control the timing," Rosimar explained. "Now the scale is perfectly balanced with seven weights on either side. When one is removed from the left, the right pan swings to the ground and signals the ritual to start. After the triangle sounds, two are removed from the right, and the scale will move in the opposite direction to pace the next step. Alternately, the balance pans will be unloaded. The rigor of the ritual demands it to be so. And when the last is removed and the scale returns to level, the ballista will be fired. The plate will be ripped into nine strips, each one ready to be stamped with the outline of a row of disks."

Rosimar looked around the ceremonium and smiled. "In fact, all is in readiness, and we will soon know the result. You there, Grogan, I want you to remove the weights while I and the other masters attend to the bellows in the antechamber."

The neophyte sprang to his feet and clutched his hands together. "Not me, master," he said. "The whirling blades and creaking wheels give me a fright. My ears ached last night when the flutes were sounded in the seventh step."

"Your hand is steady," Rosimar said. "It is an opportunity to show what you have learned while all the masters are watching."

The neophyte extended his hands palms upward. Rosimar scowled at the blur they made with their shaking. "Crandel, then," he said. "You probably can do it as well."

The second neophyte did not respond. Together, the two of them raced from the hall without looking back.

"A moment." Rosimar's scowl deepened. "They are young and the task is unexpected. I will have to go to the head master and get permission to use one of the initiates. And if it is not granted, then we will have to wait until tomorrow."

"But if the process is proven, can we have new tokens today?" Jemidon asked.

"Within the hour," Rosimar said. "We could use the very strips produced by the test."

"I was a neophyte at the inland guild," Jemidon said. "You remember that. I would rather not delay. Tell me what I should do."

Rosimar looked out through the isinglass to the bay. "I remember your skill, Jemidon," he remarked. "I remember it all too well."

"I was much younger many years ago," Jemidon said. "And here I have no stake in trying to impress a master."

Rosimar looked at the still swinging doors through which the neophytes had run. "Oh, very well," he said. "The task is simple enough. Just remove the weights in the sequence I have indicated. Make each step clean and sure. Watch for my signal. When all else is ready, I will indicate when to begin."

Without saying more, Rosimar hurried out the doorway. Jemidon watched his departure for a moment and then turned to study the scale more intently. Besides the two pans, each carrying the ornate metal cylinders, he could see an array of springs and switches clustered around the balance arm. From them, ropes, pipes, and pulleys led to other apparatus in the ceremonium. He looked back at Rosimar and saw the magician wave his arm to begin.

A hush fell onto the big hall. All of the other activity had ceased, except for the whirl of the saws. Jemidon was alone to set the ritual into motion. He took a step toward the scale, extending his arm to grab a weight from the top of the stack.

But as he did, without warning, he tripped and stumbled, falling to the ground. Surprised, Jemidon shook his head and looked around for what had gotten in his way, but he saw only smooth planking all about his feet.

Jemidon rose to standing and took a deep breath. Old memories began to stir in their hiding places.

"Away, away!" Rosimar stormed back through the door. "It is just as I remembered. You never had a talent for magic, Jemidon, even for the simplest of neophyte tasks. It is no wonder that Augusta forsook you for my attentions instead."

Jemidon looked back at the master. The contempt in Rosimar's face was sharp and clear. "A moment's spasm," he shot back. "And it has passed. I will do as I have said. You need not summon back one of the neophytes too afraid to be less than perfect."

"I will perform the ritual myself," Rosimar declared. "One side, and observe how it is done."

Jemidon's chest constricted in anger. He whirled from where he stood to face the scale. With a swipe of his hand, he reached for the topmost weight to flick it aside. But as he did, he felt his arm streak off in an uncontrolled arc. His hand crashed into the scale. With a clatter, the weights bounced off onto the floor.

Jemidon lunged for the falling weights, but he managed only to trip over the scale and spin around. His feet tangled in the ropes and levers; with snaps and twangs, they jerked free of their moorings. He heard the giant triangle gong three times and then a sharp crack as the ballista released its charge. The sheet of metal arced across the room, tumbling while it sped, and struck the row of saws broadside rather than on end.

With an ear-piercing shriek, the plate exploded into

128

shrapnel that flew back across the room. One piece bounded beside Jemidon's leg and another grazed his ear, knocking him again to the ground. The bellows started pumping, and the flutes and horns blasted monotones in a giant dissonance.

"A resonance!" Jemidon heard Rosimar's shout mingle with the noise. "There is a flaw in the ritual—a resonance that feeds on itself. Stop the bellows and saws. Shut it all down!"

But the shrieking grew louder. Isinglass buckled from the ceiling and crashed to the floor. The bounding shrapnel continued to carom off the walls and apparatus. A large chunk hit the nearest flute in midsection, smashing a hole in its side. The hot air blasting forth caught Jemidon in the chest and flung him down just as he started to rise. He struggled to stand, but the pressure forced him backward toward the spinning blades. Disoriented, he turned to the side to move crosswind, but then suddenly froze in place. In the confusion, he heard one of the giant grindstones, freed from its mooring, lumber by to crash into the opposite wall.

Instinctively he fell prone to the dusty floor and held his breath. As the crash of breaking wood and the whiz of hurling projectiles continued unabated, he dug his fingers into the flooring and waited for the tumult to pass.

After a long while—how long he could not tell—the instruments, the hurling debris, the runaway equipment all came to rest. Cautiously, he opened his eyes and rose to his feet. He dusted himself off, blinking at what had happened.

The hall was in complete disarray. Two grindstones were tumbled among the wreckage of the musical instruments. One had crashed through to the chamber beyond. The complicated array of ropes and linkages was a tangle of broken beams and knotted loops. It looked like a huge version of Drandor's lattice dashed against a rock. The saws had stopped spinning; one end of the shaft was out of its bushing and leaning against the floor.

"You can tell your mistress that you have performed your mission well." Rosimar glared at Jemidon from across the room. "It will not be from this guild that she will get the tokens to save her fair skin."

Jemidon was stunned. What had caused him to lash out so inaccurately with his arm? And how could such a small error cause all the damage that he saw around him?

"I don't know what spoiled my coordination." Jemidon shook his head. "It should have been simple enough to move weights about the scale. And in any event, a resonance, as you say, is highly unlikely."

Rosimar's face contorted even further. "Out!" he commanded. "Out! There is no time left for excuses!"

Jemidon started to say more; but before he could, one of the oarsmen from the day before raced into the room. "Master Rosimar," he cried, "master Rosimar, come quickly to my mistress' bidding! She will pay you ample fee!"

"What has happened?" Jemidon asked, trying to block out his thoughts about what he had caused to occur. The feeling was all too familiar, and he did not want to wallow in it again.

"Most unexpected," the oarsman replied, "and yet most welcome news indeed. Trocolar the trader has changed his mind. He will redeposit his holdings into the grotto and with even more tokens besides. Augusta will earn her fee and a larger one than before."

"She asks for me?" Rosimar shook himself away from surveying the wreckage. "Augusta asked specifically for me?"

"Trocolar brings with him his magician, Holgon, to ensure that all is secure. The mistress wants to be represented properly as well."

Rosimar straightened and pushed out his chest. He glared at Jemidon a final time. "An opportunity," he said. "An opportunity despite the hellhole. An opportunity for her to realize who is her better choice."

"My original treasure plus hundreds more," Trocolar said. "You may deduct the storage fee from what is there."

"Why the sudden reversal?" Augusta asked.

Even in the dim imp light, Jemidon could see the suspicion in her eyes. They were all huddled together around the chests in the vault, their voices echoing from the walls above the beat of the pumps and the drip of seeping water. Trocolar had already been there when he and Rosimar had arrived. There had been no time to tell her what had happened at the guild—not that he could explain the events in a manner that would keep Rosimar's look of contempt from spreading to Augusta's face.

"Why the reversal?" Trocolar shrugged. "It is because of my new partner, the one whom Holgon found. He has presented to me a plan that is greatly to my benefit. For my part of the bargain, all I have to do is carry out a few simple steps, like redepositing my tokens here, along with his more modest amount. He was furious when he learned that I had made a withdrawal. So many tokens in one spot, he said. Far more than he could quickly assemble himself, each the result of an independent act of ritual, none of them shielded by a magic vault. And the more there are, the easier is Holgon's task."

"What has Holgon to do with this?" Augusta asked.

"He arrives shortly," Trocolar said. "As long as he can perform his ritual of safekeeping here, then these treasures are again yours to guard."

"Other than the pumps and the tokens themselves, there is no magic needed here," Augusta said. "It is the tide alone that keeps the vault in the grotto secure. You know that as well as I."

"Nevertheless, my partner insists," Trocolar replied. "He has prescribed the ritual himself. And you can use your Rosimar here to ensure that nothing goes amiss."

"I am no bondsman to Augusta," Rosimar said weakly. He pushed himself from where he sagged against the slimy wall and tried to fill his lungs. Jemidon saw the color return to his cheeks.

"I serve her for a fee," Rosimar continued, "and be-cause—because that is what I choose."

"Dear Rosimar." Augusta stroked the magician's arm. "Your fear of small places has not gotten any better. I would have asked another master, but you are the one I trust the most in such affairs as these."

131

"No matter." Rosimar swallowed. "My strength is already returning. And I am as curious as the rest about what this ritual of safekeeping might be. At Cantor Guild we have heard of nothing like it."

"Nor has any other on the island," a voice rang out from the shaft leading to the landing above. A magician, robed in black like Rosimar, splashed down onto the vault floor. Heavy-framed and balding, his eyes were deep-set and burned with some hidden hunger. "It is an example of a new departure. Like none you have seen before."

"So say they all, Holgon, so say they all," Rosimar replied. "But somehow, on close examination, the new rituals turn out to be mere variations on what has worked before."

Holgon ignored the remark and turned to direct a neophyte struggling down the shaft with the magician's gear. "Your partner arrived with me, expert Trocolar," he called over his shoulder, "and he says that we may begin. He would join you down here in the vault, except that the air circulates too little for his needs. The landing above is as close as he chooses to come."

"But it was to be this very place," Trocolar protested. "He explained that no other would do."

"He assures that all is well," Holgon said. "Once the tokens are securely hidden in their chests and the pumps are stopped, then I can proceed."

"Stop the pumps?" Augusta exclaimed. "But then the vault will begin to fill!"

"Only for the duration of my ritual, so that there is no distraction," Holgon said. "It will be short enough so that little additional seepage will occur."

Jemidon saw Augusta look at Rosimar and the magician shrug indifference. She signaled an attendant by the pumps, and soon the deep, rhythmic throbbing stopped.

Holgon bowed slightly to Augusta and moved to where his neophyte had erected two tripods in front of an uncluttered stretch of wall. On each was a small box, colored in bright blue with a red sash running around the edges and yellow, five-pointed stars in the middle of each face.

Holgon pushed the tripods closer together and then

132

lifted one of the boxes from its stand. With exaggerated flourishes, he unhinged each side of the box from the top. Holding it in his hand, he slowly scanned it in front of the group. The magician replaced it on its stand and repeated the procedure with the other.

"Street conjuring," Rosimar snorted. "No ritual of true magic has such gaudy display."

Holgon did not seem to notice the comment. With his face frozen in a blank smile, he produced a small dove from the sleeve of his robe and pointed at a jeweled collar around its neck. "A bracelet of teleportation," he said. "Completed except for the final step."

Then he placed the dove in the box on the left and snapped shut the sides and lid. He showed the one on the right a second time and closed it up as well.

"And now we wait a moment until the conditions are right," Holgon said. With a flourish, he drew his arms inside opposite sleeves and stood staring straight ahead.

For a moment, everyone was silent, and nothing happened. Then Jemidon felt a sudden jerk from somewhere deep inside. His feeling on Morgana—the one on the top of the cliff, watching Drandor's projections—swelled up within him, only this time more intense. Again he felt cast loose, as if a tug of the tide had parted a mooring rope and set him adrift. He pressed his hands to his sides and squared his feet on the slippery ground. Inwardly, he drifted, gathering speed, joining an invisible current that was sweeping him away.

"The journey begins." A muffled voice snaked down the shaft. "Set the example so that it can be properly completed."

Holgon grunted and resumed his ritual. He produced a small wand from his sleeve and sent it through a rapid series of gyrations.

Jemidon no longer had any interest in following the ritual. He looked at the others, but none showed any sign of discomfort. All were watching what the magician was doing.

Holgon tapped the box on the left, and the sides unlatched and fell open. It was empty, and the dove was gone. Then he put the wand away and carefully cradled the box on the right to his chest. Opening the top, he reached inside and produced the bird wearing the collar. The magician waved the dove back and forth; with a small bow, he hid it back in the container.

Without waiting for comment, Holgon rapidly repeated the steps he had just performed. When he was done, he showed the right-hand box to be empty and the dove to occupy the left. A murmur of impatience ran through the watching assemblage, but Holgon paid no attention. Again he enacted the ritual and yet again.

"And thus it is finished," Holgon shouted out finally after the ninth performance. "The fortunes and futures of expert Trocolar are now well secured."

Jemidon suddenly felt the drifting feeling stop and things anchor as firmly as they were before. In an instant, there was not even a glimmer remaining of what he had felt. As quickly as it had come, the sensation faded away. He shook his head in annoyance, then released the tension in his arms and legs. He could move about as he always had done. There was no feeling of danger that he might leave the ground and float away.

"That is no ritual of magic," Rosimar said. "And the wand patterns were as ill-formed as those of a neophyte. No circles closed, and the cadence was off by at least half a beat. It takes perfection to perform magic, Holgon. I am surprised that your technique shows such a lack of grace. Is that what becomes of one who indentures himself to a trader instead of working in the security of a guild? Does he become a performer of street tricks that mimic magic and waste the watcher's time?"

"And I am still puzzled as well," Augusta said. "You speak of fortunes and futures, but Trocolar's desires are not enhanced if you give me a greater fee rather than none at all."

"Yes, it would seem to be a conundrum for you, Augusta," Trocolar agreed, "a conundrum to be explained in its own due time. But as for me, it is quite simple. If my partner speaks false, then his tokens are forfeited to

134

me. If his words are truth, ah, then, my scheming one, you will indeed have to worry about the cube."

Augusta's eyes widened, but Trocolar did not explain further. He motioned for Holgon to follow and pushed through the others to the ladder leading upward.

"Send this one following after." Rosimar pointed at Jemidon immediately after the trader's party had climbed to the top of the shaft. "He deliberately sabotaged what has taken us months to assemble. Your investment is jeopardized and also my guild's."

Augusta's face contorted in deep furrows. She rubbed her forehead while squinting her eyes closed. "No, Rosimar, no more for today. Trocolar's threats are enough. For the moment, I wish only to think of the fact that his tokens are back and his fees as well. Perhaps this whole exercise is some elaborate charade just for my discomfort. Possibly his chance in the election is nothing but bluster, and he can do no more than torment me with his words."

"You need a steady hand and experience to guide you through the next few days," Rosimar said, "not an incompetent who cannot perform the simplest magics."

"You stated yourself that the ritual had a flaw," Jemidon said. "And your neophytes were none too eager to perform in my place."

Jemidon drew a deep breath to say more, but Augusta placed her fingers across his lips. "Hush, my dreamer. Do not bother to add your words to Rosimar's din. For now, let me be away so that I can rest. If you truly want to help, then try to understand what lies behind Trocolar's words. Does Holgon's pretty display have any real meaning, or is it merely a fantasy of the mind?"

She looked back at Rosimar. "And with Trocolar's fee, we are better positioned than before. There will be time enough to plan for additional funding for your guild— time enough after the elections are over and we have won."

Without saying more, Augusta glided past all who remained and began to climb the ladder.

Rosimar looked at Jemidon, grunted, and made his way

135

to the tripods. "If it provides her with reassurance, then it will be worth the effort," he said.

Jemidon sighed with relief. His latest failure need not matter. He again could focus on tracking Drandor and Delia. He tried pushing the events of the morning out of his consciousness, back to the deep pit of memory where he hid the rest of the similar occurrences. With a shake of his head to clear his thoughts, he joined the magician in taking apart the tripods.

For over two hours, Jemidon and the magician examined the two boxes and their stands, looking for some trace of true magic, but finding only hidden latches and sliding panels.

"You were right," Jemidon said at last. "It is no more than a conjuring trick from the mainland."

Rosimar started to reply, but the pump attendant approached and pulled at his sleeve. "Master, I need assistance. I have tried all the variations that I know. The pumps! I cannot get them to restart!"

CHAPTER EIGHT

The Essence of Value

JEMIDON waited impatiently while Rosimar struggled up the rope ladder. The magician shook his head, perplexed.

"I thought I knew all the major rituals of perpetual motion," he said, "but apparently the inner mechanism of the pumps is one that I do not understand. And the casings were very strange to the touch, like ordinary metal with no aura of magic about them."

Jemidon frowned. He was bothered about all the events of the day. First, he could not completely forget his inability to perform the simplest of steps in a ritual. Then there was the sensation of pulling anchor and temporarily

136

floating free. And now the pumps were unable to restart after Holgon had performed what he claimed was a magic ritual.

"A token," he said suddenly to the oarsman who had ferried them into the grotto. "Fetch me one from the chests."

"They cannot be removed, once the ledgers are marked. Only on Augusta's orders are the transfers made."

"A single coin and for a moment," Jemidon insisted. "Your mistress is in peril."

The oarsman hesitated, but finally turned from Jemidon's determined stare. He descended the passageway and in a moment returned with a small bag of jingling metal. "From Trocolar's deposit, the most recent change."

Jemidon nodded and plunged his hand into the sack. He plucked out one of the smooth disks and his frown deepened. "Cold," he muttered, "stone-cold. No doubt it will be the same with the rest."

"Put away the distraction," Rosimar said. "The riddle is the failure of the pumps."

"The problem is far more basic." Jemidon shook his head. "Look at what has happened to your craft."

Before Rosimar could reply, Jemidon placed the disk against the wall and pushed it across the wet surface. He looked at the result, grunted, and tossed the coin to Rosimar.

The magician grabbed the token and examined it in his hand. His eyes widened and his mouth dropped open in surprise. "Scratched!" he exclaimed. "Somehow Trocolar managed to slip in a counterfeit among the rest."

"Check the others if you want," Jemidon said, "but, like the pumps, they pulse with magic no more."

"I do not know what you mean," Rosimar said. "Magic items last for eternity. They are perfect. There can be no other way."

"Augusta!" Jemidon ignored the puzzled tone. "Don't you see? She must be warned. Quickly, Rosimar, let us speed to her aid."

"But the pumps! And the rest of the tokens! Yes, we

137

should carefully examine them all and see how many are bad."

"There will be no time," Jemidon insisted. "To the skiff. I will explain as we go."

Jemidon watched Rosimar disappear in the other direction through the waterfront crowd. He sensed that there was no time for further persuasion. Already shouts about worthless counterfeits rang from a stall down the way. The magician would be convinced soon enough, after he had tried some simple rituals with his guild. First sorcery and now magic had been struck down. Somehow the quest was more tightly entangled with Trocolar and Augusta than he had imagined.

Jemidon raced across the shoreline road and up onto the higher streets. He threaded his way though the adobes and past the iron and brick court where he had met Benedict. He breathed deeply as the slope steepened, pushing harder to maintain his pace.

A flash of motion to the left caught his eye. A spicy odor filled his lungs. He looked to the side and saw a sheet of white linen stretched taut over a frame in front of a trader's stall. Painted on the cloth in lush reds and browns was a richly decorated leather sack. Small, translucent stones spilled out to sparkle in outstretched palms. No, it was not a painting, Jemidon decided as he stopped to look closer. The scene flickered. The hands seemed to move and clutch the pebbles in a sequence that repeated over and over.

Jemidon breathed the spicy aroma and felt a rush of pleasure fill his lungs. What did the sign say? Only two coppers for a small stone, three for a larger one. He blinked in surprise at the direction of his thoughts and turned back to the street. He had no time for such distraction. Too much of importance was at stake.

He ran some fifty paces and then saw another flickering sign on the right. It was a huge arrow in a cool blue, pointing in the opposite direction. As Jemidon watched, it grew even larger, from a short stub to an elongated shaft vibrating with energy and somehow promising excitement back down the path.

Jemidon sucked in his breath, reaching to savor the hint of spice that still remained in the air. He took a reluctant step back toward the stall. Two others rushed past to join a line rapidly forming down the way. He shrugged and sprinted to jostle shoulders for a place.

Crammed stomach to back in a single file, Jemidon waited his turn, his mouth watering. With a hand damp with anticipation, he fumbled in his pouch to see what coins were there. Up in front, the flickering scene took on more and more animation. He saw the stones pour in a rushing stream from the sack. The hands clutched backward against a woman's thinly veiled chest. Pale eyes under silky, raven-black hair seemed to look directly at him. Pouting lips beckoned with promises of more delights to come.

When he reached the counter, Jemidon emptied his pouch. "As many as this will buy," he said. "I have no tokens, else I would take even more."

"Your metal is good," the man behind the partition said as he scooped the coins into a large sack. "Or even items in trade. Collecting tokens is not my master's desire. And you are fortunate. These are the first scentstones to go on sale."

Jemidon waved aside the words as a half-dozen small, smooth stones were placed in his outstretched hand. He spun around and shouldered his way back toward the street, carefully clasping his purchase. With a glimmer of recognition, he saw that the divulgent, Benedict, was in the queue, eagerly pressing forward with the rest. But Jemidon had no time for such irrelevancies now. He ran out onto the street and then into the first connecting passage on the right. Hands clutched together, he traced a zigzag path through the alleys and lanes of Pluton, making it impossible for any would-be thief to follow, searching for the perfect hiding place in which to examine his treasure.

Finally, almost an hour later, his energy spent, he ducked into a dim alleyway and pulled to a halt. He brought his fist to his face and cautiously cracked open his grip to savor again the encompassing euphoria. With the first whiff, his fingers relaxed. Slipping into a daze, he contemplated the pebbles in his palm.

"I must withdraw my vaultholdings!" a voice shouted behind his back. "The rumors grow more persistent, and I must make sure!"

Vaultholdings, Jemidon thought dimly as he inhaled. Augusta and the grotto. There is something that I should tell her, something about the—

Suddenly two merchants bumped past, knocking Jemidon to the wall and scattering the scentstones to the ground. A flash of anger burned away his inattention and he swung instinctively at a flowing robe as it raced by. He took one step after, but then halted and dropped to his knees. With a frantic pawing, he ran his hands over the rock-strewn path, searching for his treasure. A hint of purple translucence caught his eye and then a small sparkle of orange.

Hastily, he scooped up two stones and ran back onto the wider street. In the full glare of the sun, he opened his fist to verify that he had recovered what had been dropped. But as he looked in disbelief, he saw that he held only smoky quartz weakly tinted with color. A hint of cinnamon drifted upward. The exotic aroma was no more.

Jemidon scrambled back to the alleyway to search the ground more methodically, but after several minutes he found no pebbles more precious than the ones he held in his hand. He examined them again, but the compulsion was totally gone.

He shook his head at what he had done. He held common rock, inexpertly sprayed with a cheap scent. If they were more clear, the stones might pass for semiprecious citrine and amethyst, rare enough in the islands. But as they were, they should have been no more than an idle curiosity, not worth his time. What gave them such an allure? How could such commonplace trinkets evoke such a desire?

Another mystery! Jemidon grimaced in annoyance.

140

Enough! Developments were piling up too fast. Sorcery, magic, casting adrift, and now plain pebbles with an almost irresistible attraction that had vanished after an hour! There was no time to think of it further. First he must help Augusta and secure his own freedom before investigating additional puzzles. He had spent all his money and had to depend upon her now. With determination, he thrust the stones away. Locking his eyes straight down the path, he ran the rest of the way to the street of the vaultholders.

When he arrived, he saw that the hint of something amiss had already begun to spread. Every office was busy with at least two or three customers. A long queue snaked out of one doorway and down the street. Ignoring the angry glances, he pushed his way through the gathering crowd and into Augusta's anteroom.

"I am not making a formal withdrawal." One of two heavy-set men pressing against the partition waved his arms at the clerk. "I still intend to pay full fee. I merely wish to examine my cache of tokens to ensure that all is well. They will be returned within the hour."

"We keep only a small quantity here to handle the usual transactions," the clerk said. "Your deposit is too large, and we must wait for the next tide to bring back more from the grotto."

"The agreement is for full surrender on demand for any sum less than forty tokens," the second customer said. "Any other vault on the street would not try to delay."

"Our service is as good as any other." Augusta pushed open the door from the back. "It is just that you are the fifth in a row to ask for a large withdrawal with only one depositing in between." She handed a writ to the clerk and then forced a smile back to the customer. "And with a moment's patience, your treasure will be secure. My girl will find a vault that temporarily overflows. I will arrange a loan for the rest of the day and then repay it when the fluctuations balance out."

The clerk ducked under the table and headed for the street, squeezing between three more customers who had entered and crowded behind the two in front.

"Any more withdrawals?" Augusta asked. "Step forward. Sums less than—less than three tokens can be honored immediately. Larger treasures will take a few minutes more. And, of course, deposits of all sizes are readily accepted. There is still time to get them recorded so that your vote in the election will be more."

Before anyone could reply, agitated voices suddenly erupted in the street. Five or six more men surged into the anteroom, jamming the doorway. Through the window, Jemidon saw a large crowd gathering.

"Ah, trader Andor," Augusta said over the noise. "You were here but minutes ago with your withdrawal of twenty-five. No doubt all is well, and you wish to return your deposit to the vault's safekeeping."

"I want my wealth!" the short, balding man in front of the new arrivals shouted back. "This time, tokens of magic, not simple disks of cold steel!"

The crowd strained forward in a chorus of apprehension, pushing Jemidon to the wall and completely filling the small room. Augusta looked about worriedly and ran her tongue over her lips.

"But they are true tokens," she said. "Yesterday evening I counted them into the very sack you hold in your hand. Twenty-five exactly, there is no doubt."

"Twenty-five indeed," Andor snarled. "Twenty-five pieces of worthless metal!" He flipped the sack open and hurled a handful of coins to spatter against the wall at Augusta's back.

"They are no different from the ones securely held in the grotto," Augusta persisted. "One magic token is the same as another."

"Then the ones in the vault are worthless as well!" someone else shouted. "We have been swindled. Our fortunes are gone!"

"Gold or silver," another said. "If she cannot pay in tokens, let it be their equivalent, and we can exchange them elsewhere."

"If you desire another metal," Augusta said hurriedly, "I will do what I can. But, like the tokens, my holdings

142

here are small. The first in line and perhaps one or two more."

"The vault has no more tokens! Only gold for some in the back room. Get what you can! The rest she cannot pay."

With a sudden push, the men in front slammed aside the table and poured through the opening. They knocked Augusta to the floor and pounded into the other room. With raised fists and incoherent shouts, the rest of the crowd cascaded after.

Jemidon pushed forward with the others. He reached Augusta where she had crumpled and elbowed one of the depositors away. A fist slammed into Jemidon's back, staggering him to his knees. He twisted to the side and winced in pain as heavy boots trampled the backs of his legs. Scooping his arms around Augusta, he rolled to the left under the table, which had been banged against the outer wall. He reached out between the impatient feet that were stomping and kicking to get ahead and pulled in her legs. Together, they huddled in a tight ball.

The press of the crowd funnelling through the doorway strained against their shelter. Someone fell next to the table and then another went down. Like building blocks toppled by a single swat of the hand, a whole row staggered to its knees. The ones behind pushed these closer to the floor and scrambled over their backs. The doorway jammed in a squirming mass of entangled arms and legs. Cries of pain and panic began to mingle with the shouts of anger.

The table planking groaned from the pressure, and then suddenly one pair of legs collapsed, confining Jemidon and Augusta to a small triangle. Jemidon looked quickly about. The table would not long withstand the load. They had to get out before they were trampled. He examined the wall planking—long vertical boards, each secured to a crossbeam at his feet. He decided what he must try.

Slowly he maneuvered his back to block the growing press of bodies threatening to squeeze into their shelter from the side. Then, still coiled in a ball, he raised his feet from the floor and centered them on one of the planks.

With a deep grunt, he strained to straighten himself against the unyielding constraints on both sides.

The board shook. Then, with a high-pitched grating, it moved a fraction of an inch. Still firmly secured near the ceiling, it curved in a gentle bow. Jemidon relaxed, breathed deeply, and renewed his efforts. With each thrust, the force required was greater as the plank curved more and more from a plane.

After half a dozen attempts, his leg muscles began to tremble. Beads of sweat broke out on his forehead, and blood vessels throbbed in his neck. Another body crashed against his back; flailing arms boxed his neck and ears. Across the room, an ear-piercing scream rose to a crescendo, then abruptly stopped. With a final gasp, Jemidon ignored the pain of protesting tendons and thrust with his last reserve of strength.

The plank vibrated with resistance, then abruptly swung free, creaking about the nails which still held it to the upper crossbeam. "Out," Jemidon said without pausing for another breath. "Squeeze through the hole while there is still time."

Augusta disengaged from Jemidon and snaked through the narrow opening, ripping her gown in a dozen places where it caught on the rough, splintery wood. Jemidon ducked to follow; but as he did, the mass of bodies behind him suddenly heaved and buckled. Two tumbled into the small shelter over the backs of the ones struggling below. Jemidon was dashed to the floor and pinned under the writhing mass.

He reached for the opening with both hands and tried to squirm loose, but found he could barely move. He heard the table creak and then a sharp crack as the other legs gave way. Desperately, Jemidon pulled against the wall, thrusting his head out into the afternoon light. Gripping the walls as an anchor, he brought one leg slowly up along his side. The weight above pressed relentlessly, and his hip ached from the strain. When he could push his knee no higher, he muscled his foot outward in a slow arc until it butted against something soft yet unyielding.

Jemidon tensed the muscles in his back and arms for

one final shove. He filled his lungs as best he could. With a shout, he kicked savagely and grated across the floor. Gathering momentum, he crashed through the opening and skidded across the rough ground outside.

Jemidon scrambled to his feet, not bothering to notice the scrapes and splinters on his face and arms. "Safe," he exclaimed. "I did not reach you any too soon. A run on the vaults was the logical consequence, once it was learned that tokens no longer hold special value."

He looked at Augusta, expecting her to reply, but found her staring at the street and the vault offices across the way. Everywhere the scene was the same. Crazed crowds carried out what small stores of wealth they could find. In frenzied fighting, they squabbled over what little there was.

"Safe," she echoed vacantly. "Safe. What has happened, Jemidon? I do not understand."

"It is the same for all the vaults, Augusta. All across the island, Arcadia, and Procolon. Magic is no more."

"All the vaults?" Augusta asked, shaking herself out of a daze. "Then none of the holders will have a basis for any votes. Those who have deposited will all demand their due. We are debtors one and all."

She looked at Jemidon, her eyes growing wide. "Yes, we are safe—safe until the election. Until Trocolar has his way."

"His fortune is based the same as yours," Jemidon said. "And so is that of everyone else. It is unclear who will be judged the richest, if tokens no longer matter."

"Not all his wealth is in the vaults," Augusta said. "He owns ships, men, and warehouses full of goods. Bolts of silk, barrel staves, links of heavy chain, seedcorn, and flour. A thousand items that he can barter for advantage. He is well prepared to make profit on whatever strikes the speculator's fancy. Why, on the way back from the grotto, he bragged that he even had acquired a boatload of citrine and amethyst to add to his holdings."

"But at least his threat cannot be the shrinking cube," Jemidon said. "That device now functions no better than the rest."

145

"Then chains and hot needles." Augusta shrugged. "He will think of something else to—"

"Citrine and amethyst," Jemidon interrupted. "You say that Trocolar is the one with the gems?"

"They cannot matter," Augusta said. "Trocolar showed me some samples. At most, they can be made into inexpensive baubles for the wide-eyed visitors from the mainland. He would need a powerful glamour to entice one with any knowledge to pay more than a copper for a barrelful."

"But, like magic, sorcery is no more. No one can mouth a working cantrip. The words have no resistance." Jemidon paused while his thoughts raced. "And yet, if not an enchantment, what compelled me on the way here? Yes, now that I think on it, the displays on the street were like the projections in the storm and the presentation hall—moving images on a screen that somehow shaped one's thoughts. Drandor! His strange animations. The smiling trader and Trocolar. There is a connection. It is too great a puzzle, and the solution can wait no longer. I must find out, Augusta, regardless of the fee."

"Wait, where are you going?" Augusta called out as Jemidon bolted for the street.

"Come. I will take you to Rosimar's guild for safety," he called back as thoughts of Delia formed with a renewed intensity in his mind. "Then I will see Benedict, the divulgent, to ask him how he fared with his purchase of the stones. And this time I will not leave until I have negotiated the exchange of information."

"My blade is small, but I warn you, it bites deep, nonetheless."

"As before, I am here to trade." Jemidon looked at Benedict, who was huddled in the far corner of his cubicle, clutching his strongbox with both arms to his chest. Jemidon's sense of urgency had been growing ever since Augusta had been left at the guild. The cries in the street made it clear that little time remained before a complete collapse of order. But the divulgent could prove to be of value. Jemidon willed himself into the appearance of non-

146

chalant calm and slowly motioned Rosimar to enter behind him as he sat on one of the stools.

"A copper," Benedict said. "And two more for a guest."

"What I have for you is worth far more than three coppers," Jemidon replied. "Even more than the tokens you would charge for the contents of that now-worthless box."

"'Perfection is eternal' indeed!" Benedict spat. "A stronghold impervious to the dent of the mightiest hammer, so I was told. Look at it now. No more than a tray with a well-hinged lid. And no hasp for an ordinary lock, at that. Even a child could flip it open and seize the contents if I did not stand on guard. It is as worthless as the tokens that you offer to pay."

"Let us be gone," Rosimar said behind Jemidon's back. "This is an affair of magic, not gossip of the harbor. If Augusta had not wished that I come along, I would be elsewhere, employing my skills as a master."

"There is no time to learn everything that we must know," Jemidon said. "The knowledge of a divulgent may save us many a step."

"His brain is clearly addled." Rosimar moved to Jemidon's side and waved across the high table. "He can only impede what I must do."

"I plan to convince him that our goal is the same," Jemidon said. "That we can work to the benefit of us all."

"No, not of us all!" Rosimar suddenly thundered. "By no means will we all achieve what we seek." His face flushed; with a deep glower, he raised his fist in the air. "This time I will not be haunted by your memory, Jemidon. This time there can be no doubt about the value of what I provide. This time there will be gratitude without reservation. This time Augusta will not whine and complain about the love she left behind, about how slowly I advanced in the hierarchy of the guild, and about how few were the gowns of silk that I could afford. When I snatch her away from Trocolar's certain torture, there will be no excuse to cast me aside and strike out on her own."

Rosimar's knuckles whitened. His hand shook as he

147

continued. "And this time I will make sure that the credit is properly placed. In the end, it will all be mine, not shared with a would-be neophyte who cannot work the simplest ritual—one who curries favor by resurrecting the past, rather than with solid works expertly done."

Jemidon blinked at the sudden rush of passion. He returned Rosimar's stare, looking for a spark of reason behind the emotion. In addition to everything else, he did not need petty bickering. He pushed the confused tangle that defined his own feelings toward Augusta away and focused on why he was in the divulgent's cubicle. "There is no time for that now, Rosimar," he said. "Three working together will serve Augusta better than each laboring apart."

"If I will not share with one, then neither will I with two," Rosimar rushed on. "And certainly I see no advantage in a timid divulgent who does not know even the value of pebbles I can fetch from an ore dump."

"Did you not see the exchange board as you passed?" Benedict asked. "It is empty, wiped clean in the past hour. No longer is value measured in tokens. Each commodity is individually bartered, and no standards prevail. And I know what will happen as a consequence. There is information from the past and other places that foreshadows the events here. Already I have learned of the effects on the shoreline. Ships have missed the tide because the fee for the crew's provisions could not be settled. Goods will remain to rot in storage because no one is sure of their true worth. Commerce will halt. Many stomachs will be empty before a new order is established."

The divulgent's eyes took on a faraway look as he stroked the lid of the box in his lap. "But scentstones are different. They possess a spicy essence that men will fight for; they produce a thirst that cannot be slacked. And more importantly, there are not enough to satisfy the demand. Already a large one has been traded for a barrel of the purest oil. There is a rumor that my rival Cumbrist will offer the use of his cubicle for the next year for three handfuls.

"I desire them as the rest do, but I can see also a second

purpose they serve as well. The price has doubled in the last hour. In the next, it probably will double again. With only two more days to the election, who knows what one's fortune might turn out to be?"

"I saw you in line to buy some of the first," Jemidon said. "Worthless pebbles with allure for minutes at most."

Benedict's eyes glazed over, and he did not acknowledge Jemidon's words. Looking past Rosimar's shoulder, he stared vacantly at the curtain behind.

Jemidon stamped his foot and then clapped his hands, but Benedict did not move. With little spasms, the divulgent's fingers twitched on the lid of his strongbox.

"The scentstones," Jemidon said. "Benedict, pay attention. Do you have them here?"

"My dagger." Benedict shook out of his reverie and fumbled with a blade at his belt. "It will be my answer if you press too close."

"Yet before today, did you care at all about such pebbles?" Jemidon continued. "Does it not strike you as odd? Yes, think of something else besides the stones. Break the connection as I did on the street. What of the threat to what you have in your arms in addition to the chips of rock? Jerk your attention away."

Benedict huddled in the corner and raised his dagger threateningly. Slowly Jemidon slid from the stool and advanced. "All of your information," he said. "Is it worth sacrificing that to save what rattles between the scrolls?"

Benedict's face froze in a mask of tension. He tentatively jabbed the blade forward as he watched Jemidon approach. He started to speak again, but then paused, squinting his eyes.

"Now the stones themselves," Jemidon said, coming another step closer. "What allure can they really have? Look at them quickly. Make sure that they are worth the risk."

Benedict shook his head in denial. But as Jemidon moved forward again, the divulgent quickly thrust his hand inside his box to withdraw one of the stones. He looked at the rock hurriedly and cast it aside. Throwing back the lid, he reached to the bottom and extracted a handful of pebbles, the smaller ones slipping between his fingers to bounce on the floor.

"Cinnamon," the divulgent said, puzzled. "Only cinnamon! By the looks, the magician is right as well. Murky stones with inclusions and flaws."

Benedict looked back at Jemidon. "But how can that be? It is as I have said. Some purchased after mine have traded hands many times, and each exchange has fetched a more princely sum."

"I know who is responsible for the mysteries," Jemidon said, returning to his stool. "And I hope that you know how to gain entry into his keep by some stealth. If we exchange what we know, then perhaps in addition to who and where, we will be able to learn how."

Benedict looked at the pile of rocks as they dribbled out of his hand. Slowly he inverted his palm to let the last few drop away. "Penniless," he mumbled. "Everything I traded for worthless rock. And more I borrowed from others, besides."

Finally he looked up at Jemidon. "You may have information of some value," he said. "And as things stand, I have few options, other than to hear what you have to say. Perhaps the fee for the chairs can be waved."

Jemidon smiled and motioned Rosimar to the other stool. But before the magician moved, one of the pages thrust his head through the curtain leading to the court.

"The men-at-arms," the boy said. "They are searching each cubicle, one by one. It is to impound the assets. All property belonging to the vaultholders is to be seized against payment of their debts."

"Another exit," Jemidon said. "We cannot exchange information if I am bound."

"The debts of the vaultholders are no concern of mine." Benedict retreated back to the far wall. "From the mercenaries I have nothing to hide."

"And neither will you learn about the stones," Jemidon said, "nor of what has happened to the tokens and sorcery. Without information, how can you hope to repay your newly acquired debts?"

Benedict bit his lip. His eyes darted around the small

room. He looked from Jemidon to Rosimar and then at the pebbles at his feet. "Why did I care?" He shook his head. "The allure was so real. And no doubt Cumbrist pursues them still. The divulgent who first understands it all will have knowledge of great value, to be sure."

He paused and looked at Jemidon a final time. "Quickly." He motioned to a hinged panel in the rear wall. "We will strike the bargain, once we are away from the exchange."

Benedict ducked through the opening. Jemidon rounded the high table to follow. He turned to look at Rosimar, who was slowly descending from his stool. "The two of us will proceed without you if we must," he called back, "but a master's knowledge of magic may be useful as well."

Rosimar hesitated a moment and then frowned as he heard the clink of mail. "Until you are to be cast aside." He shrugged. "Until then, I will permit myself to follow."

CHAPTER NINE

The Shadow in the Keep

IN the moonlight filtering through the trees, Jemidon shifted position to get a better view. He looked down to the shoreline where their small skiff could be seen bobbing on the gentle waves. Farther back across the water were the lights of Pluton, some mere pinpoints, but others the flickering brightness of fires out of control.

Jemidon looked back at the rising slope of the island. The trees blanketed the hillside toward the crest, except on the right, where they had been cleared away for the garishly decorated structure of stone and iron. Behind the crest and out of sight was the other island in the bay, the one that contained Augusta's vault. Jemidon had not

151

guessed that the larger of the two islands in the bay was owned by Trocolar. The leader of the tradesmen had indicated nothing when Augusta ferried him to her vault three days before.

But Benedict had been insistent. The island and the estate were indeed Trocolar's. The divulgent had said that, if there was more to be learned, it would most likely be there. And so, under the cover of nightfall, he, Jemidon, and Rosimar had rowed across the bay and landed unobserved where the green canopy came nearly to the shore.

"I will have the correct amounts in a moment," Benedict whispered above the soft jingle of coins. "My sorting device barely functions; the output from a single column is more often a scramble than not."

"Why not carry a pouch the way everyone else does and dip into it, once the price has been settled?" Rosimar growled in irritation. "The guards on the wall or some patrol will soon find us if you continue to fumble."

"A full purse is no way to bargain for several favors," Benedict said. "You will empty it for the first and get no other. I acknowledge your mastery of your craft, Rosimar; respect my skill in mine. A divulgent prepares his cape with many pockets, each with but one coin or two."

Benedict moved slightly, and Jemidon saw the glint of the coinchanger at the divulgent's waist. He watched as Benedict fingered the levers and scowled at the results in his palm. The divulgent selected a single coin from the pile to put in a pocket and returned the rest to the top of the device.

"I am ready at last," Benedict said as the jingle stopped. "The guard at the postern gate has told me much before, but never have I convinced him to let me enter. What we learn in Trocolar's private estate had better be of supreme value to justify our risk."

"Then perhaps I should proceed alone," Rosimar said. "I would have expected something more from this skill of yours than a simple bribe."

"A secret passage, perhaps," Benedict snapped back. "Or maybe a ring that levitates the bearer over walls. You

152

are the magician. What do you bring to our agreement in addition to your razor-edged tongue?"

"Enough!" Jemidon waved his arms for silence. The muscles in his neck were knotted from anticipation. Keeping the other two from bickering was an added irritant that he could well do without. "Enough. Just get us inside. The rest does not matter."

"You are the least qualified to speak," Rosimar said. "Except in stealth, you cannot move about on Pluton at all. The mercenaries will make sure all frozen assets are properly impounded; their annual fee depends on how well they perform."

"Our goal is to learn how the laws of magic and sorcery have been turned off," Jemidon said. "And, if the random factors align, how to reactivate them as well. With the tokens in Augusta's vault once more a well-regarded tender, she will be no debtor, and I can act as I choose."

"But if not within two days, the election will be over and Trocolar will prevail," Rosimar said. "After that, it will not matter for you whether the craft is again operative or not."

"If you see all outcomes so bleak, then why continue?" Jemidon asked. "Return to your guild and wait out the storm. From the safety of your surrounding walls, try to convince Augusta of your aid in her behalf."

Rosimar glared at Jemidon, then at Benedict. Finally he shrugged and folded his arms inside his robe. Benedict hesitated a moment, but no one said more. The divulgent nibbled on his lip and started to move farther into the shadows.

They traveled the rest of the way to the estate in silence, filtering among the trees. While Jemidon and Rosimar waited on the edge of the clearing, Benedict darted across to confer with the guard.

The moon was bright in a cloudless sky. Strong shadows of the roofline traced a jagged pattern across the naked landscape surrounding the keep. The structure was not large—two storeys with perhaps a half-dozen rooms in each—but the facework resembled that of a large castle from the mainland of Arcadia or even Procolon across

153

the sea. Miniature bartizans budded from crenellated walls. Tiny loopholes dotted shallow bastions. Each row of square-cut stone was slightly smaller than the one upon which it rested, giving the illusion of greater height as one scanned upward.

While Jemidon watched, Benedict appeared out of the gloom of the small gatehouse, beckoning him and Rosimar to come forward. In a moment all three were inside, examining the dim walls and a grim-faced guard still clutching a fist full of coins.

"He says that they all are at their evening meal," Benedict whispered. "Including Trocolar's new partner, who spends most of his time in the dampness below."

"Then to the dungeon," Jemidon said softly. "We may learn everything we need before they have finished their wine."

"The stair is on the south wall." Benedict motioned with his head. "But the guard will not escort us down. And the entry is barred and locked, besides."

"A simple lock will not stop us." Jemidon felt his excitemment begin to rise. "Come along. I will show you how it is done."

Without waiting to see if the others would follow, Jemidon turned and ran down the steps. It felt good to move quickly after all the cautious stealth. The passage was narrow, dirty, and hung with cobwebs. Just enough light to guide his feet flickered down from torches set high in the wall.

On the landing below, Jemidon paused a moment for his eyes to adjust to the gloom. He saw a single short passage leading to heavy wooden doors barred by a single beam chained in place. From his cape, he pulled a finger-length shaft of metal with a narrow flange on one end and inserted it in the lock. After a few experimental probes, he rotated it a quarter turn to the left, and the hasp snapped open. Just as Rosimar and Benedict came up behind, he carefully pushed the bar aside and motioned them to enter.

The doors opened onto one vast room, the view interrupted only by stout posts that supported the beams and planking of the ceiling above. In each corner, small

154

alcoves projected off at odd angles, their entrances barred by grates of iron. Each was filled to overflowing with sacks, barrels, and wooden boxes. Stuffed in crannies were heaps of chain, shafts of steel, shields, pikes, and bowls of polished copper. More goods cluttered the main floor—piles of linen, bins of grain, huge leather volumes bound in groups of six, and rough tarpaulins covering stacked crates and lumpy mounds. In the very center, barely separate from the piles which pushed in from all sides, was a small anthanor with its coals still smoldering. Next to it was an array of large sacks, one tipped to the side, spilling hundreds of small, translucent stones on the floor. The smell of cinnamon mingled with the musty and humid air. Pokers and tongs lay scattered about, and pushed to one side was a large lattice of wires and beads.

"Drandor!" Jemidon exclaimed, forgetting the hushed tones he had used before. "I knew I would track him down. And this time we will examine his wares with far more care to learn what secrets they possess."

Jemidon eagerly moved across the room toward the lattice. He looked up at one of the supporting beams and saw the familiar form of the guarding imp asleep in its bottle. Staying far enough away not to excite the sprite, he slowly began to examine the structure, looking for any differences since he had seen it last.

"Why is it so important?" he muttered aloud. "So important to Drandor that Delia took it rather than anything else when she fled? If only she—"

Jemidon stopped and looked around the room. Except for Benedict peering curiously into one of the alcoves and Rosimar standing in the entrance, there was no one else there.

Jemidon grimaced in disappointment. Although he had never expressed it consciously, he had evidently envisioned Delia to be with the rest—a daring confrontation and a final rescue. But what if he could find the secret of how the trader suspended the laws of sorcery and magic and be away before anyone returned? He would have all that he needed to obtain the robe of the master. Why then track down Drandor to ask what he had done with a slave

155

girl? Jemidon's scowl deepened with his hesitancy. He tried to force himself to examine the lattice, to focus on what was most important before being distracted by anything else.

Tentatively, he took another step closer to the structure, but stopped in midstep as a chorus of footfalls echoed down the passageway leading above. Benedict dropped the book he was examining, flung open the grating in front of him, and squirmed into the alcove behind. Jemidon looked back at Rosimar and saw the master standing rigidly erect, making no attempt to hide himself.

Jemidon ran back across the room. "Quickly," he said. "Into one of the side rooms. Apparently the iron gates are unlocked."

"Too small," Rosimar moaned feebly. "Too small. The gloom, the musty walls. I cannot. The room, it confines. I must be away."

Jemidon looked into the sweating face and dazed eyes. He had seen the same expression when Rosimar had ventured into the grotto. The noises outside became louder. Jemidon stepped to the doors and pulled them shut. He turned back to Rosimar and grabbed him about the shoulders. "This way," he commanded. "Control your feelings. We must hide without delay."

Rosimar opened his mouth to protest as Jemidon herded him toward one of the alcoves, but Jemidon clamped his free hand over the magician's mouth. He hooked the grating with his foot, swung it open, and pushed Rosimar inside. With a final swirl, he looped his foot behind the iron bars and pulled them shut. Just as the wooden doors to the room creaked open, he shoved Rosimar behind a crate and tumbled on top of him.

"Strange, I was sure we secured the entrance as Trocolar had directed when we left." Jemidon heard a voice he recognized as that of Holgon the magician. "But it is no wonder. Nine passes with the dove were boring enough. Today's tedium dulls even the brightest mind."

"Continue as you have been told, and you will be rewarded well," another voice answered. "The Maxim of Perseverance, 'repetition unto success,' may not be as precise as the one before, but the results are nearly the same."

Jemidon strained to hear the second speaker and frowned. The voice was not unfamiliar, but he could not place it for certain. He looked down at Rosimar and saw the magician's knuckles pressed to his teeth. Cautiously, Jemidon released his grip and waited for a reaction. Rosimar remained still, rigidly stiff and unmoving. Jemidon paused a moment more and then, indicating silence, slowly rose to peer through a crack between the stacked crates.

He looked out to see Holgon, tightly bundled in a heavy cloak and wearing woolen gloves. The magician huddled over the furnace and was talking to someone just outside Jemidon's view. Two guardsmen with bored expressions lounged against supporting posts, ignoring the conversation. From the metallic rustle of mail, Jemidon could tell that there were more men-at-arms in the room as well.

"It will take nearly a hundred times," the soft voice continued. There was a hint of some accent about it and a breathless quality, as if each word would be the last before a massive gulp of air. "But with each repetition of the ritual, the effect becomes more likely to happen. You rushed the first stones to the marketplace, Holgon, with barely a dozen complete enactments. Some of the purchasers were able to shake the illusion that compelled them to buy and saw what the pebbles truly were. Only when you increased the repetition for the next batch did the images hold firm beyond the first hour. And without the subsequent trades, an increase in value would never have happened."

Jemidon nodded in his hiding place. That explained why there had been no outcry about worthless stones as there was for the tokens. Except for himself, Benedict, and a few others, the illusion had held. After the glamour that compelled him had faded, something else convinced the owner that they were still very special. With growing excitement about what he was learning, Jemidon strained forward to catch more.

He saw Holgon sigh and then dip into the sack for one of the small stones. The magician gripped it with tongs,

157

inserted it into the furnace, and began to stomp his feet. The guard on the left unbuckled his sword and lowered it to the ground. He then joined Holgon's beat, clapping his hands to the rhythm while simultaneously banging together two cymbals strapped to the insides of his forearms. The other guard scooped some pieces of rope from the floor and tied them together in a series of intricate knots, while puffing his cheeks with air and then swallowing in noisy gulps.

"The Rhythm of Refraction," Jemidon muttered to himself. "Except for the use of cymbals instead of drums, it is the magic ritual for making a lens that focuses all of the colors the same."

"Enough," the soft voice commanded abruptly. "It is the number of repetitions that count, not the perfection of each step as it is performed."

Holgon grunted and extracted the stone from the furnace. With his free hand, he flicked open a small vent above the coals. A brilliant yellow shaft of light shot out into the room. Holgon held the stone to intercept the beam, and one of the guards scurried to hold a scrap of cloth on the other side.

"Nothing," Holgon said after a moment. "It is no different from all the times before."

"Patience," the soft voice commanded. "I suffer without comment the small air volume of this room. Repeat the ritual as you have been told."

Holgon shrugged and began to move the stone slowly back and forth across the beam, momentarily blotting it out and creating bursts of light that hit the cloth. Another guard extracted a poker from the coals; with each pulse of light, he gently dabbed the cloth with the tip.

"And again enough," the voice said. "After a dozen passes, the burning point grows too cold. Start from the beginning and proceed as before."

Everyone returned to his former position, and the sequence was reinitiated. Holgon heated the rock in the furnace and stamped the dust, while the others executed their parts of the ritual in step with the cadence.

"Eventually there will be transparency," the voice con-

158

tinued. "Never as fine as the most exacting lens, but with each heating, each bathing in the flow of the flame, each burning of the cloth, the barrier to the light weakens. Eventually it will suddenly shine through."

"But why not have the glamour carry it all?" Holgon asked. "If the owner believes, it does not matter whether the scentstone truly is flawed or not."

"As I have already explained, the glamour can do no more. It is the Rule of the Threshold, or 'fleeting in sight, fixed in mind.' The subtle messages that flash on the screen with the animations cannot be too short, or they never would be noticed. But if they are presented too long, the mind becomes aware that they are there, and their power is lost. The glamours in the marketplace strain to the limit. They can convince no more than they do now."

"It still sounds better than this excuse for magic." Holgon extracted the tongs for a second time. "Perhaps I should become like the archmage and learn more than one art."

"Your archmage!" The voice tinkled in what Jemidon took to be a laugh. "Soon his skills will be no more. The imps twitter that he has heard of the strange failures of sorcery all around this globe and that he finds no explanation at home and plans even to strike across the seas in search for the cause. But by the time he gets to Arcadia, Trocolar's payment to me of Pluton's mercenary constabulary will have long since passed. And then for the rest, it will be too late."

Jemidon strained against the crates which defined his hiding place, trying to ferret out the true meaning of all the words. He shifted his position slightly and then felt a sudden kick from Rosimar's legs. He looked back to the ground just in time to see the magician explode in a frenzy of motion, his eyes twitching in a wild panic.

"Air, clear air! I can withstand no more!" the magician screamed. He bolted upright and shouldered against the crates in front, sending them in a crash to the floor and knocking open the grating to the larger room. Instinctively, Jemidon pulled at Rosimar's robe, but grasped only

159

emptiness. Together, they clattered out onto the dusty stonework for all to see.

"Seize them," the voice commanded as the men-at-arms sprang to life. "This is not according to my plan."

Jemidon turned for the doorway, but managed only half a step through the clutter before he was hit from the side and hurled to the ground. He rose to one knee, but two more guards joined the first, pushing him to the stones. He looked quickly about to see another slap the flat side of his sword against Rosimar's head, crumpling the magician in a heap. Benedict bolted from his hiding place and tried to rush past Holgon, but the master thrust his glowing poker between the divulgent's legs as he dashed by, crashing him to the ground, where he lay gasping in pain.

"Trocolar advised me well to keep his dungeon secured," the voice said with the same soft cadence that had come before. "When these are fettered, search the other alcoves. There may be more."

Jemidon struggled to look in the direction of the anthanor and, for the first time, saw Holgon's companion. The figure was thin and tall, easily a head taller than even Canthor, the bailiff on Morgana. He was totally covered from head to toe with a dark brown greatcloak and deep hood that shielded his face entirely in shadow. The cloth hung heavy and limp, water glistening among the coarse threads. A small pool had formed from what dripped from the low hem to the floor. A belt of gold braid cinched in a narrow waist, and a multicolored cube hung from the clasp. Jemidon saw a tiny circle of imp light dancing around the hood and heard the hiss of gently moving air behind the soft tones of the accented voice.

The guards dragged Jemidon to his feet and, with his arms held tightly behind, pushed him toward the stranger. As he drew closer, Jemidon caught his breath. Cold air rolled around his knees and swirled up to his chest. As if stepping out onto an arctic meadow from a well insulated hut, he found himself shuddering and tried to turn away.

But as he did, he suddenly remembered the suggestion of coldness in Drandor's tent and the wisp of icy air behind the latched door in the presentation hall. They had been only hints before; but now, in the almost overpowering numbness, he was sure they were the same.

"Delia," he blurted. "What has become of her? Your presence is tied closely with that of the smiling trader; I can sense it. You must know where they are. Where is Drandor and how did he cause the changes to come to pass?"

"Drandor?" the voice asked. "Drandor, the cause of the changes?" The soft burble of laughter continued for more than a minute. "He has served his purpose well and now he sleeps with my manipulants."

A long, thin finger with smooth, unwrinkled skin poked out from one of the draping sleeves and touched Jemidon's chest with an icy coldness. "Know Drandor for what he is. A minion. A minion like Holgon here and no more. A minion who has traded his talents for what he might have when I am done."

The finger retracted and touched the center of the greatcloak. "It is I, Melizar, who is the master. Melizar, the first among the pilots."

Jemidon peered into the inky blackness of the hood, but only a hint of the dark features could be discerned. He tested the grip of the guard behind; the man was well trained and held him firm. "But what of Delia?" he insisted. Somehow he felt he wanted to know that the most of all. "What has been done with her?"

"Drandor does not always show good judgment in the treatment of his property," Melizar said. "Especially when it is jointly owned. I have done what is necessary in her regard."

Jemidon's thoughts raced to frame another question; but before he could speak again, more footfalls sounded on the stone passageway outside the room. All turned to look. In a moment, three more of Trocolar's men raced through the doors.

"The stones, the scentstones! The trader needs another chestful of them now."

"They are not ready," Melizar said. "We barely will have a gross of them finsihed by the eve of the election.

161

As they are endowed now, too many purchasers can break out of their spell."

"The spell does not matter," the first of the newcomers said. "It is enough that they can be distinguished from the opaque pebbles on the beach. The demand exceeds the supply. Already a woman is the price for the smallest. Not even a fine team of horses will serve for one bigger than a pecan. Who cares about scents that eventually decay away? With the collapse of the token, it is the new fever of the hour. No one bothers to trade in anything else. Everyone scrambles to recover in a day the fortunes that have vanished.

"And the prescription is so simple. Buy in the morning and sell at noon for a return that nets you tenfold. One cannot fail. Why, Trocolar is the richest man on the island. He has been offered an estate on the crestline for a chestful. Make haste with the whole sack. We are all to come as guards, the entire household. The mercenaries cannot keep order everywhere at once. He has promised us each a handful if we are prompt."

"It proceeds too quickly," Melizar said. "It is not according to my plan. The crowds may prove fickle without the full use of the arts."

"Our orders are to transport them now. Stand aside. Our own fortunes are at stake with the rest."

"It does not follow the dictates of my plan," Melizar repeated. "The stones are not properly prepared."

"All of us here serve Trocolar the trader first." The speaker's voice grew threatening. "The wishes of his partners, no matter how well reasoned, must come later."

"Wait!" Melizar suddenly waved his cloaked arm over his head. "Wait until I have calculated the consequences. Do not show such haste."

Jemidon heard the gentle hiss about Melizar's head abruptly increase to a roar. The imp light intensified into painful stabs of light. Frost began to form over Melizar's cloak as he drew his arms to his chest and slumped into a ball. The cold air billowed down his sides, and a wet fog rolled across the floor. Trocolar's men hesitated, stepping back from the dense air as it encircled their boots.

162

They looked from one to another, trying to see who would take the lead on what to do next.

For several minutes, no one moved. The air in the room grew chillingly cold. Jemidon could tell which held their breath by the absence of cloudlets about their faces. Then, as quickly as they had started, the noise and lights began to fade. Melizar stood erect and unfolded his arms. Small shards of ice tinkled to the floor.

"Enough." Melizar waved his arms again. "Enough. I have thought through the pattern of events." The imp light dimmed to almost nothing. The whistling sound receded to the distant murmur it had been before. "I will do as the trader suggests and let you transport the stones now. It is as Holgon says. If the beholder perceives value, then intrinsic worth does not matter. But I must go along to ensure that Trocolar does not act too precipitously or even forget all the conditions of our bargain."

The deep shadow turned back to face Jemidon. "And as for these, place them in one of the side rooms. They perhaps are the minions of a disgruntled vaultholder. Or maybe even his assets. Yes, it will save Trocolar the trouble of searching. For their capture, I will ask an additional fee."

Jemidon watched sullenly as he and the other two were thrust into one of the alcoves and the lock snapped shut. He saw Holgon remove a crucible of molten metal from the anthanor and pour it into the keyhole as the rest of Trocolar's men prepared to leave.

"A more difficult challenge than the outer lock," the magician said. "I am sure that Trocolar would want you here when we return."

Melizar exited with the last, pausing as he left to examine the lattice beside the furnace. Slowly he ran his slender hands along the wires and fondled the beads with his fingertips.

"So close and yet so different," he said, touching one of the vertices and tapping it gently. "So unlike where we almost succeeded before."

He ran his finger down one of the wires to an adjacent vertex and then at right angles up to a third. "And yet, two steps already taken. The basis is set for one more. And three should be enough. Three changes to the unfamiliar, and none here will be able to cope. The remaining four shifts will come with ease. And then I can traverse at will, move back and forth between what I know and the unexplored, and add new vertices with no threat of dissent."

Melizar sighted down one of the slender tendrils that arched from the dense central maze. "I shall discover what lurks beyond the last node in the thaumaturgy line. Yes, the satisfaction will be great indeed."

He turned back to look a final time into the cell that confined Jemidon. "Drandor the causes of changes, indeed! Not in this place and time."

As the last footfalls of Melizar's departure faded, Jemidon shook the bars in frustration. He had learned much, but was no closer to his goal than before. He had to escape soon, before the trail once again grew as cold as Melizar's cloak. He looked at the broken sword blades on the floor. Trying to pry back the bolt had served only to snap the finely wrought steel. The rest of the crates contained nothing of value to aid in their escape.

Benedict huddled on a small keg in the corner, wringing his hands and moaning softly about the burns on his legs. "I should not have been swayed by the value," the divulgent muttered. "The risk, the risk, it was too great."

A loud groan cut off Benedict's whispering as Rosimar flailed his arms through the air and pulled himself to sitting. The trickle of blood from his scalp had clotted in a stringy cake that ran over one eye and down his cheek. "Air," the magician croaked hoarsely. "I must get out to the fresh air."

Jemidon looked from one to the other and sighed. He moved to allow Rosimar to stumble forward and rattle the grating.

"Air!" Rosimar shrieked again. "I cannot withstand it. Give me air."

"The magician awakes." Benedict rose to his feet. "It is his magic that is our hope." He climbed over the intervening boxes and grabbed the front of Rosimar's robe, twisting him around. "You boasted of your worth. Now is the time to prove your mettle. You must get us out before that cold one returns."

"Magic." Rosimar shook his head vacantly. "Magic, magic swords and rings of power. Magic to give me air. If I had but one such object, I could barter my way to freedom." He turned and stared at Jemidon, squinting through the clotted blood. "But this one says that magic is no more. All my craft is gone, vanished like a demon's wind." He sagged to the floor. "And in truth, none of my rituals work as they should. Empty forms that might as well be abstract dances for entertaining a prince! My magic is gone and I cannot get my air."

Rosimar started to say more, but stopped and turned to the grating. He gripped the bars and tried to thrust his face between them, gasping for breath.

Benedict watched for a moment and then placed his hand tentatively on Rosimar's shoulder. The magician did not respond, but continued to stare out into the storeroom, eyes bulging and forehead glistening with sweat. The divulgent nibbled at his lip and darted his eyes about the alcove. With a long sigh, he slumped his shoulders and resumed wringing his hands.

"They left the equipment here untouched." Jemidon grabbed at Benedict as the divulgent started back for the corner. "Look about, man. Maybe there is something we still can learn by keen observation or something that Melizar said that can yet key a discovery."

"So close and yet so different," Benedict replied absently. "So unlike where we almost succeeded before."

"Yes, that is the idea," Jemidon said. "Melizar's words when he touched the lattice. You remember them well."

"Those are his exact words. A divulgent must retain what he is told with no repetition, else he will find he has paid for nothing."

"You remember all the conversation?" Jemidon asked. "Everything?"

"Strange, I was sure we secured the entrance—" Ben-

165

edict nodded and began again, but Jemidon excitedly waved him to stop.

"Never mind about Holgon. Concentrate on Melizar. What did he say when they were heating the stones?"

"Eventually they will be sufficiently transparent. Never as fine—"

"No, after that."

"The Rule of the Threshold, or 'fleeting in sight, fixed in mind.'"

"And the Maxim of Perseverance," Jemidon added. He began to pace within the small confines of their cell, nervously fingering the old coin around his neck. He squeezed between two open crates and flexed his palm around the grip of one of the unbroken swords.

"'Repetition unto success.' Melizar spoke of laws. As if they guided his efforts like those that apply to the crafts—"

Jemidon paused as his thoughts suddenly exploded. "The glamours of the marketplace," he said after a moment. "And a ritual almost the same as the Rhythm of Refraction. Sorcery is governed by the Rule of Three, and Melizar spoke of a Rule of the Threshold. Magic obeys the Maxim of Persistence, and he talked of perseverance instead."

Jemidon's eyes widened and he slapped his thigh. "That's it, Benedict, don't you see? Sorcery and magic are not merely inoperative. There are still seven laws, just as there were before. The laws have not simply vanished. They have been replaced, substituted by ones similar but not quite the same. Seven laws. Seven before and still seven after the transformation."

Jemidon stopped a second time and looked out into the storeroom. The leap of intuition was based on nothing substantial, but somehow he knew he was right. He grabbed a piece of debris and threw it through the bars to strike the imp bottle attached to the overhead beam.

"The Postulate of Invariance." The imp fluttered to life. "Seven exactly; there can be no more. The lattice, it is my master's master's. You cannot touch."

"Yes, the Postulate of Invariance!" Jemidon yelled,

166

grabbing Benedict by the shoulders and shaking him back and forth. "Invariance. A constant. Seven laws. There can be no more or no less. Whenever one is turned off, another must take its place.

"It is a new law of the arts, Benedict! We have found another law! No, wait, not a law but a metalaw. A law about the laws. A statement that there are many, but that only seven can be in effect at any one time. Different arts, many principles that guide them.

"And no one even suspected. Not even the archmage. It has been the same throughout history, from the very first sagas. The seven that we know so well were painstakingly discovered, and then no more were found. For at least a thousand years and, who knows, maybe back to the beginning of time, there have been seven constant laws and no reason to suspect that there could be more."

"You gibber too fast for even a divulgent," Benedict said. "Laws or metalaws, such abstractions make little difference. There is more to be gleaned from the tangible. What of this lattice of which the imp speaks?"

"The lattice is the proof," Jemidon said. "It is the— the road map by which one navigates through the realm of the laws. The first vertex Melizar touched represented the seven laws as we know them. Move one node to the right and the Rule of Three was replaced by the Rule of the Threshold. Continuing in that direction would change sorcery to something more exotic still. Instead, the next change was in a different direction, changing the Maxim of Persistence to the Maxim of Perseverance. The lattice has seven distinct axes—seven directions, one for each of the laws and the many possibilities along each one."

"I see no sevenfold mapping throughout that structure." Benedict squinted at the framework. "Only in small sections and there for a few nodes at most."

"It represents only what Melizar has explored," Jemidon said. "It is how he keeps track of where he has been. Yes, that is it. Melizar cannot turn off a law; he cannot create one. He can only replace it by the next in line. At the edges, if he moves in a direction for which there is

167

no node, a new law is invoked that must be found through experimentation, one that he does not know."

"Your thoughts gallop too fast for me to judge their significance," Benedict protested. "And they seem to infer too much from the small hints we have heard tonight. How can you construct such fanciful structures from so meager a basis?"

"I—I do not know." Jemidon slowed his patter. "It—it just came to me in a rush. I have always been good at seeing the whole from the parts. Perhaps it is because I have had other hints along the way."

Jemidon stepped back from the grating and took a deep breath. His present danger, his link to Augusta's fate, even if he could escape, and his longing for the robe of a master all faded away in the seductive rush of a new discovery. He felt the exhilaration of finally solving a complex puzzle after many abortive attempts—a last turn that removed a ring from a string or the final piece that made a picture complete.

"In any event, the knowledge is of little value." Benedict jarred Jemidon's thoughts back to their plight. "Knowing all the secrets of the universe is of no help if we still must remain here to receive Trocolar's displeasure. If he is indeed elected head of the council, he can make the penalty for trespassing what he will." The divulgent lowered his eyes. "Although I doubt it will be as severe as what he would do with an impounded asset."

"But there are still sorcery and magic," Jemidon said, "or at least something very close to them. We can use them to find our way out. As for this new sorcery, or whatever it is called, it involves animations on screens and messages flashed in the blink of an eye. There is nothing here that will aid us to construct a glamour.

"But the new magic gives us the Maxim of Perseverance," Jemidon continued, picking up the sword from the crate in front of him. "Perhaps we can use it to enhance this blade and make it strong enough to pick out the mortar between the bricks."

"A magic sword," Benedict scoffed. "You have read too many of the sagas. If indeed there could be such a thing, the guild that could make it would charge two king-doms' ransom. Producing such an object would require many lifetimes and the labor of hundreds."

"The Maxim of Persistence is no more," Jemidon said. "I am not talking about a blade that forever retains its sharpness. We are dealing now with perseverance instead." He looked down to the magician at his feet. "Rosimar, my thoughts still churn too quickly and I cannot remember. What is the ritual for the hardening of the steel that was used in the manufacture of the tokens?"

"The Aura of Adamance," Rosimar mumbled without looking up. "It is one that must be mastered before the robe of the inititate is received."

"And the equipment?" Jemidon asked. "What is needed to act out the steps?"

"Bells and candles," Rosimar said, "magic hexagons drawn on the floor, chalk and pearl dust, and a bottle of ten-year-old wine."

"We will improvise the best we can." Jemidon began looking into the storage crates with a fresh perspective. "Explain the details so that we can begin."

"No, I am the master," Rosimar said weakly. "All credit for magic will be mine."

"You are indisposed. Rest. Benedict and I can do as you direct."

"No!" Rosimar struggled to his feet. "Magic may no longer work, but all rituals will be mine. You stand aside while I perform. I will get the credit. There will be no mistake about who performs with skill."

Jemidon looked at Rosimar's glistening forehead, the whitened knuckles that gripped the bars, and the eyes that twitched in erratic patterns. "It is not that important, Rosimar," he said. "You perform the ritual if you wish, and I will watch. But be warned, it will not be a single time that we must see it through."

Rosimar stared at Jemidon for a moment; then, with a snarl, he staggered to look into the crates stacked against the wall. "Tin cups," he muttered, "and metal spoons. They will have to serve for the pealing of the bells."

All three turned to rummaging through the stored goods

and shortly had assembled the required equipment as best they could. Rosimar directed Benedict in the striking of the bells and the drawing of the hexagon on the alcove floor. He selected the longest sword of the lot and placed it within the pattern. With trembling hands, the magician decanted vinegar over a sack of flour while stomping a complicated rhythm with his feet.

When he was done, Rosimar picked up the sword and pressed it against the wall. With a grating sound, it skittered along the stone, leaving a faint trail where it had scratched the rock.

"And so much for this nonsense." The magician slumped back to the ground. "Magic is no more. We will not free ourselves by such misplaced cunning, regardless of your theories of lattices and hopping between vertices in some realm that cannot be seen."

"Again," Jemidon said, pulling Rosimar back to his feet. "The Maxim of Perseverance works on repetition. We must try the ritual again."

"And if I do not?" Rosimar asked.

"Then I will continue with Benedict as I had originally planned."

Rosimar grumbled and reached for the bottle of vinegar. "It distracts my mind from the closeness of the walls, at the least," he said. "One more time probably will do no harm."

Jemidon clutched his hand to his stomach to stop the growling. He ran his tongue over the dry walls of his mouth and eyed what was left of the vinegar. Benedict slumped against the far wall, the makeshift string of bells dangling at his side, mouth open and eyes drooping with fatigue. Rosimar sat on one of the remaining unopened kegs, head bowed and shoulders slumped.

"Enough of a rest," Jemidon said. "We must keep trying until there is a change in the sword."

"Enough, indeed," Rosimar growled. "It is an insanity. We are like children repeating a mindless game. There is no magic. It is gone. How can a few words by a stranger make you so sure?" The magician rose and lumbered to the wall. With the remains of the chalk, he added another stroke to the ones already there. "Five hundred and seventy-two times," he said. "Over five hundred Auras of Adamance. More than what is performed in a guild in a year."

"Once more," Jemidon insisted. "Once more and then we will reconsider what we must do."

"You said that the last time," Benedict whined. "For over two days, we have stomped and chanted to no avail. In a few hours at most, the election will be over and Trocolar will return in triumph. We will not escape. To continue wasting his wares will only increase his displeasure."

"Once more," Jemidon repeated. "What other plan do you have to offer in its stead?"

Rosimar grumbled and kicked at the sword that lay in the center of the hexagon on the floor. Both edges of the blade were dull. Dozens of knicks and gouges marred the sides. He stooped to thrust it out of the way and then stopped, his eyes opening wide through his fatigue.

"It feels different," he said softly. "Not the tingle of magic, but somehow different all the same." Holding his breath, he clasped the hilt tighter and experimentally touched the blade tip to the wall. He started to scratch the dull point across in a great arc to match the other scars which crisscrossed the stone.

"There is resistance," he muttered. "It seems to take a great deal of strength to move it to the side." Tentatively, he increased the pressure on the guard and then staggered forward, mouth agape. The blade had quietly slid a finger's length into the stone.

"A guild's endowing fortune," Rosimar said in wonder as Jemidon and Benedict sprang forward. "A stone-cutting sword as true as any in the sagas."

"Let us be gone." Benedict tugged at Rosimar's sleeve. "Save the marveling for when we are free. Try the iron bars and see if it performs there as well."

Rosimar grunted and slowly extracted the blade from the wall. He slashed across the grating with two swift strokes. Instantly, the central portion of the bars fell away.

171

Rosimar blinked in disbelief at what he had so effortlessly done. Jemidon gently touched the freshly cleaved surfaces and felt a polish as smooth as if they had been ground. While Rosimar stood staring at the sword in his hand, Benedict pushed him aside and scrambled for the opening. He ran across the storeroom and cautiously tried the heavy wooden door. It swung open easily. There was no sound from above. Apparently the keep was deserted. Everyone had gone to the harbor with the scentstones.

"I will not wait at the skiff," Benedict called back as he ran for the stairs. "I have gathered enough information to last me a goodly while."

"But the lattice," Jemidon said. "It will do no good unless we learn how to restore things to the way they were."

"I doubt that you can add to your theories without more hints from this Melizar." Rosimar climbed through the hole and headed after Benedict. "And he no doubt will be with Trocolar in the grotto. It is there that I am headed, to help Augusta before it is too late."

Jemidon hesitated for a moment and then scrambled after. As he ran past, he cast a last reluctant glance at the lattice.

A few minutes later, they were in the forest and running for the small boat that had brought them to the island.

"If this Melizar is in the grotto, we should head for the city instead," Benedict shouted as they reached the shore. "With what I know now, I see it is folly for the three of us to proceed unaided."

"The mercenaries will be in the grotto to preserve order for the final vote," Rosimar said, scrambling on board the skiff. "I will speak to them there. But with this blade, I will need little else. Benedict, you can row," he commanded as the divulgent sat down in the bow. "No wavering when it is time to press advantage. Direct to the grotto. The voting should soon begin, but I judge by the tide that there is still some time.

"And as for you," the magician continued, turning his attention to Jemidon, "not another step. You can stay here until Trocolar's men find you upon their return."

"Put away the sword," Jemidon said in annoyance, stepping forward. "We are all in this together, and I have contributed my share. Without my insistence, the blade would not have been made."

"Your proper share is not of importance," Rosimar snarled. "I have what I need, and that is enough. Back from the skiff, or we will see how well I can cut through soft flesh."

Jemidon hesitated and then lunged to the left. But Rosimar rapidly swung the sword in a flat arc to cut off the advance.

"Be off, I say," the magician ordered Benedict, and the divulgent pushed against the beach with the oars. The skiff bounded away on a receding wave, while Jemidon stood helplessly watching the retreat.

"I may change nothing," Rosimar called back, "but at least Augusta will know who tried at the last."

CHAPTER TEN

Fleeting Treasure

JEMIDON watched the boat bob away and pounded his fist into his palm. It just wasn't fair. If Rosimar succeeded, he would garner all the accolades, and none would be left. Rosimar would be the one who restored the vanished crafts. The power, respect, and riches would all fall to him. Jemidon's own quest would be over; there would be nothing left with which to claim a robe.

Besides, how would Rosimar proceed, once he gained access to the inner chamber of the grotto and climbed onto the ledge above the vault? Probably by whirling the sword over his head like some hero from the sagas and challenging any man to take Augusta from his side. There would be no careful confrontation with Melizar, no appeal to the confused voters to turn away from the stones. The magician was likely as not to fail. And if he did, the arts would remain lost. Trocolar would win the election, and all of Augusta's assets, including Jemidon, would default to him.

Jemidon kicked at some driftwood washed up on the beach. Somehow he must also get to the grotto and be part of the final confrontation, no matter which way it went. Success for Rosimar or a failure—neither augered well, but Jemidon could not wait on the periphery for the result. Even without a clever scheme, he had to pursue his destiny.

He stopped his gestures of frustration and made up his mind. He ran back to the deserted structure and down into the dungeon. Hastily, he grabbed one of the tarpaulins, the rope on the floor, and a halberd and sword. He staggered up the stairs and back outside with the load, dropping it onto the beach. With only the halberd, he sprinted into the forest and began to fell the smallest trees he could find.

Two hours later, he shoved a makeshift raft into the waves and hoisted the tarpaulin on a mast barely as high as his head. Strapped precariously on board were three of the remaining sacks of raw scentstones. Perhaps, if everyone could see what they truly were, the spell could be broken. Paddling with a stubby log, he cleared the island and set a course for the grotto.

Low tide had already been reached, and the water level was on the way up when Jemidon maneuvered into the opening from the sea. He struck his sail and released the guy ropes that held the mast in place, letting the log topple over the side. The portcullis was drawn up and the wall cresset danced with flame.

He cut a square from the tarpaulin, wrapped it around a small branch, and dipped it into the burning oil. Resuming his paddling, he headed for the narrow opening that separated the two large chambers.

His raft was narrow, and he navigated the tunnel with ease. Emerging from the other side, he saw the ledge on the far wall ablaze with light. Dozens of torches cut through the blackness from the opening in the rock. Others bobbed from the flotilla of small boats anchored below, many with oarsmen waiting in them. As Jemidon drew closer, he could see the cut in the cliff jammed with people to the very edge, shirts of mail, embroidered robes, and flowing capes crowding together shoulder to shoulder. The slurred mixture of many excited voices radiated out into the vastness of the cavern and echoed faintly from the other walls.

"Take me above," he ordered one of the oarsmen when his raft finally bumped against the cliff. "There is much that I wish to relate." Cautiously he reached for his sword and swung it upward.

"Watch out, it may be a blade like the other." An oarsman stepping from one skiff to the next suddenly stopped.

Jemidon smiled at the rower's words. In his haste, he had not thought about how to get everyone's attention. But perhaps Rosimar's interruption would give him the means. "Fetch these sacks of stone," he replied quickly before any of the others could think. "And watch your backsides. Like that of Rosimar's above, this broadsword slices through mail as if it were gossamer."

The oarsman closest to him jumped to the side, and Jemidon boldly stepped forward, waving his sword. "The sacks to the landing," he said. "Make haste before my patience is tried. You will be easy targets if you flee."

The oarsmen nodded and cautiously came forward to pick up the bags Jemidon indicated. With repeated glances over their shoulders, they preceded him up the rope ladder to the landing.

"Make room, make room," the rower in front directed as they reached the top. "Another of the devil shafts. Move aside so that he can pass."

A space opened up along one wall, and Jemidon crowded by. In the rear of the cavern, next to the hole that led down to the vault, he saw Rosimar standing with his back to the downward-sloping rock and waving the magic sword in jerky arcs. Benedict huddled to one side, his arms intertwined around his chest and his teeth working furiously on his lower lip. On the other side of the

175

magician was Augusta. Her eyes darted back and forth over the group that surrounded them in a wide semicircle. Some stood with swords drawn, and others waved at the men-at-arms, encouraging them forward. Behind the front row stood Trocolar and other influential voters. Melizar and Holgon conferred in soft tones near one of the other openings that led further into the interior. At Rosimar's feet, two bodies were piled, one missing a hand and the second the side of his face.

"You are no swordsman, magician, and eventually you must tire," the red-surcoated man Jemidon had seen in the exchange with the shrinking cube called out. The constable's eyes flicked over to Jemidon and then back to the magician. "And even with three of you, you cannot manage to descend the rope to the boats and guard at the same time. Drop the broadsword, Rosimar, and save us all unnecessary grief."

"I am no part of this," Benedict whimpered. "He forced me to row into the grotto against my will. I am a captive, no more free than the rest of you."

"Silence, divulgent." Rosimar gasped for air and waved the sword threateningly to the side. His face glistened with wetness and his eyes had a wild and panicked look. "As for you and your men, constable Nimrod, if I do tire, which of you will rush forward first to engage the cutting edge?"

"Nimrod, do your duty," Trocolar said. "That I will be the winner when this interruption is over there can be little doubt. And the bonuses that I would be inclined to bestow for the previous year's service will be greatly influenced by your actions here and now."

"You have not yet won, Trocolar," someone shouted from the crowd. "The final tally is still to be summed."

"I know very well the number of scentstones that have been sold from my stock these last few days," Trocolar turned and called back. "I have had my clerks keep careful count. Even if every one of you decided on someone else, the total would be less than what I have held for my own. You see the sum that shows for me already on the slate. Now it is just a formality, and we are done."

"But it is unfair," the voice persisted, and several others joined in the chorus. "Forget about the madman. The important thing is how we consider the stones. Of them I have none. My ship docked after the price had become too dear. I possess only a cargo of leather leggings from the mainland and some curious flexible pipes from the southern kingdoms across the sea. I have brought samples of each for assay. The entire lot would have fetched fifty tokens. Surely they still have value against something else."

The hubbub of dissent rose in volume, but Trocolar waved his arms for silence. "We have insufficient time, Luthor. Insufficient time to bicker the proper balance for each commodity. We would be here from one election to the next, trying to redetermine the relative merit of each. But nearly everyone has some stones. I have released enough to make sure of that. In point of fact, they are the new foundation by which all else is judged." The trader paused and looked toward Augusta. "If you have none to assay, then the logic admits of no alternative, Luthor. Your vote is null. Just thank the random factors that you are not a debtor as well."

"Rosimar, the stones," Jemidon interrupted. "Did you explain how they came to be?"

Rosimar turned in Jemidon's direction and his eyes widened. "An impostor," he wheezed, wiping his forehead with his free hand. "I have the sword of power. I have the only one. Take him away. HIs fate is no concern of mine."

"Stand back," Jemidon replied quickly. "You have no need to put it to the test. Just listen for a moment. What I have to say concerns you all."

"Attack, Nimrod. Do your duty," Trocolar said. "Secure these malcontents before there are any more."

"Do not listen," Rosimar shouted as he moved out from the wall and flailed his weapon through the air. "I am the one who is rescuing the lady. It is me to whom she will belong. I am the master who has forged the sword. He had not enough time. The one he holds can be only common steel and no more."

The men-at-arms at Jemidon's side looked at Rosimar, then to the scowling face of his constable, and finally back to Jemidon. He hesitated a moment, but then drew his own blade partway from its scabbard.

"Back, I say!" Jemidon moved to the wall and held his sword menacingly outward. "I have no quarrel with you. I want only the freedom to have my say."

"Impostor, impostor!" Rosimar shrieked. "If it possesses true magic, have him show what it can do." With a sudden rush, he whirled to the wall and sliced off a knob of rock as if he were cutting cheese. The outcrop crashed to the ground, and the magician attacked it with a two-handed grip, thrashing the stone to jagged slivers and crumbling slices.

"And yours," Nimrod called out quickly. "Indeed we have not seen you cut nearly so deep."

"I did not come for petty display—" Jemidon began, but his hesitation was enough. The man on his left completed his draw and pushed to attack. Jemidon danced to the side to avoid the downthrust, looking quickly about for something he could use as a shield. He jabbed to his right and the guard there gave ground, not yet sure of the potency of what he faced.

Jemidon slid along the wall, kicked a stool out of the way, and vaulted a small table at its side. A low slash nicked his calf as he flew past. When he landed, his leg buckled in pain. Down on one knee, he looked frantically about and saw that the men-at-arms still gave Rosimar a wide berth. With one leg dragging on the ground, he scrambled toward the magician. If there was an opportunity to grab the magic sword, he would have the means to make them listen.

As Jemidon slowly approached, Rosimar turned and raised the blade up over his head. But when they closed, Benedict bolted from behind Rosimar's back and tumbled over a stack of scrolls to Nimrod's side. "It is the amount of space!" the divulgent shrieked. "The magician can barely cope as it is. Confine him! Restrict him! It is the only weakness, as long as he wields the weapon!"

Nimrod frowned in puzzlement, but Benedict did not

wait. "It is information," he said while he ripped off his robe and thrust it into the constable's hands. "Use it. There will be no fee."

Nimrod nodded. While Rosimar tensed for Jemidon to come another foot closer, Nimrod circled behind the magician and flung the robe over the magician's head. Where the material touched the blade, it immediately parted; but enough fell on Rosimar's face to prevent him from seeing. Dropping the sword, he grabbed for the robe with both hands. "Air!" he shouted suddenly. "Air! Give me room. Let me out. I must have more air so that I can breathe."

The sword spun to the ground point first. Silently it slid into the stone halfway to the hilt. Jemidon shuffled forward as Nimrod wrapped his arms around Rosimar and hurled the magician to the ground. The constable quickly disengaged and prepared to lunge for the weapon, but Jemidon waved him away with the tip of his own blade. Then, grasping the guard awkwardly with his left hand, he strained to pull the magic sword from the ground.

The grip was hot; stabs of pain coursed through his palm. Jemidon flinched in surprise but determinedly tightened his fingers, ignoring the biting teeth that seemed to gnaw through his flesh.

He tugged gently and then with greater force, but the sword did not budge. He saw a flick of motion out of the corner of his eye and moved aside, just in time to avoid a thrust from two men-at-arms who converged from the right. Positioning his back toward the wall, he swung his blade in a wide arc to keep all hands away from the sword in the stone. As he saw the guardsmen pause, he decided what he must try. With a blurring motion, he dropped his own blade and placed both hands around the broadsword's grip. Rising from his knees and using all the strength in his back, he strained to pull it free.

But again the sword did not move. Except for a slight quiver of the hilt in response to Jemidon's tugs, it remained frozen in the rock. In desperation, Jemidon jerked to both sides and tried to twist the shaft. For a moment, the men-at-arms stood motionless while he struggled, but at last they saw he would remain unarmed and converged from all sides.

"No!" Jemidon heard Augusta shout from his rear. He turned just in time to see the stool she held descend toward his head. In an explosion of light, he fell forward, his grip on the magic broadsword sliding away.

The scene blurred as if it were viewed through cloudy water. A ringing persisted in Jemidon's ears. His calf throbbed with a dull pain, and his arms were bound tightly behind his back. He was propped against a wall, and Augusta huddled at his side. Near her feet, Rosimar twitched in his bonds and stared vacantly into space.

Nimrod now sat at the small table in the rear of the chamber. Solemnly, he examined the outstretched palm offered by the first in a queue which ran along the wall to the right. Behind his chair stood the cloaked form of Melizar, and next to him, holding the magic sword gingerly at arm's length, was another man-at-arms. In the center of the first row of the encircling throng, Trocolar stroked the bulge of his stomach with a jeweled hand.

"Eight small stones and one twice the size," Nimrod boomed over the buzzing all around. "An equivalent of ten altogether. Very well, Cumbrist, how do you vote?"

"For the head of the council, it cannot matter." Cumbrist looked up at the chalked totals on the slates erected behind the table. "But for the record, let is show that I add my support to the expert trader."

"Trocolar is right," another voice rang out. "There are barely a dozen of us left. And the common street hawkers have less than anyone here. We waste our time for the sake of tradition. Let us declare the trader the leader by acclamation and be done. It is in all our best interests to return to the shoreline quickly to protect what remains from the looters."

Jemidon saw Trocolar smile and bow slightly to the speaker. "I am pleased that others also see the practicalities of the moment. If now no one objects, I am ready to assume the responsibility of restoring order and issue my first edicts."

The murmuring stopped. Everyone present looked to his neighbor to see what he would say. For a full minute, no one spoke, and then Trocolar strode deliberately to the rear of the cavern where Rosimar had made his stand.

"Constable Nimrod, you are now mine to command," the trader said. "No one voices dissent. And my first instruction is for you to seize the vaultholder Augusta and transfer her writ of personal ownership to me. Her and her remaining assets. She is a debtor, and as senior lien holder, I have first rights to do with her what I will."

"It is the rule for the surrender of the body to come after transfer of the other assets has been duly recorded," Nimrod said. "Three days' grace is given to settle one's personal affairs. That has been the custom for many years."

"My first instruction," Trocolar repeated. "Carry it out quickly, or a reprimand will be the second."

"Our charter is to enforce an equitable peace." Nimrod's tone hardened. "Not to serve as the instrument for some private intrigue." He waved at Jemidon and Rosimar. "It is for the likes of these that we administer swift justice. The fate of the vaultholder should follow the due course of law."

"The intruders concern me less," Trocolar said. "They strove to disrupt the orderly transition of power. Every faction here supports the retribution that is its due. All would help to heat the shears and turn the cranks. But Augusta's crime might go unpunished, were I not to exercise my responsibility as leader."

"Some inner desire warps your reason." Nimrod scowled. "The danger of the day is from the two who are bound. Indeed, it is well that the younger was somehow unable to remove the sword from the rocky floor before he was felled. He was no stiff-armed magician. With the blade in his hand, it is uncertain what the outcome would have been."

Jemidon frowned and tried to reason through the implications of what was being said, but his thoughts were slowed. He had been unable to budge the sword, even though he had strained with all his might. Yet now the constable held it free and clear of surrounding rock. Had

181

it lost its magic while he was unaware, or had something else prevented him from wielding it?

"As you say, they are bound." Trocolar paid no attention to Jemidon's puzzlement. "But as yet the vaultholder is not. Seize—"

"Your petty vendettas can be no more than second priority, Trocolar," Melizar suddenly interrupted. "Foremost, you must honor the terms of our agreement that made your victory possible. You now lead the council. My skills put you there. In payment, you are to provide me a year's service of your constabulary to follow my instructions and not your own."

Trocolar scowled. He turned to face Melizar's shadowy hood. "There are riots in the streets," he said. "Warehouses are being plundered. Already two passing ships have refused to anchor. When we made our bargain, you did not hint at the turmoil that would result. As elected leader, I also have the responsibility to see that order is restored."

"Assemble and train a new cadre of warriors," Melizar said. "My need now is greater. The unrest in the wheat fields may not last beyond the season."

"I did not think that your scheme had any merit." Trocolar shook his head. "It appeared a risk-free means of securing five hundred tokens with which to augment my vote. I had no intention of surrendering such a central element of power after I had won."

"Nevertheless, I provided the skills without which you could not have been guaranteed victory," Melizar replied. "We have an agreement. I have honored my part. You must do the same."

"And I had the clerks, the distribution, and the strategic locations for the glamours," Trocolar snapped back. "I exploited the use of your wares as I would any other's. The triumph is of my own making. No other credit is due."

Trocolar paused for breath and then smiled. "You speak of agreements to honor, but what have you truly offered in good faith? Worthless disks of metal, five hundred circles of dull steel. And the stones—they have value of their own creation. Intrinsic worth because demand exceeds the supply, independent of the rituals in the confines of my estate. You have given me nothing, Melizar, and expect a largesse in return." Trocolar licked his lips as if he were savoring the taste of his words. "Nimrod, escort him away," he said. "I hold no writ of indebtedness, but this cold one would be well advised to make Pluton no longer a port of call."

"Another lackey's task," Nimrod mumbled. "Will sweeping the dungeon floor be next?"

"It is the fee that binds you to the island, is it not?" Melizar pushed a slender hand palm outward from his cloak as Nimrod hesitated. The dance of imps above Melizar's head quickened. Their glow of light throbbed from dull red to energetic yellow. "Do you hold the concept of honor the same as your new master?"

"My troop has fulfilled its contract faithfully for over four decades," Nimrod said, "through the tenure of more than a dozen councils. And we expect ample bonuses with our recompense for the year just past, as we have been rewarded many times before."

"For the year past." Jemidon heard Melizar's voice quicken slightly. "Fees rendered after the service is done, rather than before! What perverse logic you use to conduct your affairs! Had I but known, I would not have even bothered with this Trocolar. Name your price for the year to come, warrior, and it shall be yours."

"There is the matter of custom and tradition," Nimrod said. "We have been treated well." He paused to turn a scowl at Trocolar. "Heretofore the leader of the council has been able to judge between private interest and public need."

"Nimrod, to your duty," Trocolar commanded. "Use the sword you pulled from the rock, if you must. It is the cold one's own folly if he does not move aside when you thrust."

"Then is it the sword that gives you such presumption, trader?" Melizar asked. "Without it, how would you regard the bargain then?"

"Indeed, with the sword and the scentstones, I need

little more." Trocolar laughed. "I have enough to handle easily a simple peddler with a few tricks such as yours."

"Swords and scentstones." Melizar's own voice lowered until Jemidon could barely hear. "You compare them with the resources of a pilot?" He whirled and motioned to Holgon, who was still standing near the cavern wall. "Forward, magician. Perform the ritual as you have been instructed."

"But that was before the sword was captured and Trocolar's election completed. He is my master, and now I do not see the need."

"The ritual," Melizar repeated. "Think. Where should your allegiances truly be? With a petty island trader without honor or with one who can show you secrets that none of your kind has ever dreamed?"

Holgon looked at Trocolar and then to Melizar. He stepped backward until he touched the rough wall. He glanced at the wooden box at his feet and shrugged. Stooping down, he dragged the crate to the middle of the floor.

"I will allow no more of your strange games," Trocolar said. "And as for you, Holgon, remember that you are still in my debt."

"If you have so much power, then why do you fear the simplest of your children's toys?" Melizar asked. "Show him, Holgon. The scentstones are one and the sword is the second. From the container, you must bring three."

Holgon grunted and produced a smaller box from the first. With a flourish he removed the lid.

"Dominoes!" Nimrod snorted. "A game with which my men sometimes wager their rations."

"Here the use is even simpler," Melizar said. "A quaint practice of no utility, but somehow of amusement to your smaller minds. The next is a simple rat trap—and after that, the bladder of a pig."

While Melizar spoke, Holgon quickly stood the dominoes in a row, one after the next. He cocked the trap so it was triggered when the last domino fell, then bound a pin to the metal loop that was flipped shut by the spring.

"Finally the bladder," Melizar directed. "Inflate it quickly and place it so that it will intercept the sharp point as it flies upward."

"Enough, enough!" Trocolar said. "Scoop up this refuse and be away."

"In a moment, it will be done," Melizar said in his soft voice. It projected no strain and only a hint of the need for speed. He drew into a tight ball and huddled to the floor. "The nexus can be no stronger," he said, "and the contradiction is easy enough to make."

Jemidon struggled erect to see better what was happening, but his vision suddenly swam when he moved his head. A wave of disorientation swept over him as he collapsed weakly back to the floor. He closed his eyes to steady himself, but the feeling cut deep, down to his core. It was more than a loss of physical balance; his whole being was adrift. The sensation was like what he had felt when Holgon performed his ritual with the dove, but with much greater intensity. Trivial facts, flashes of memory, subtle concepts, intuitive insights, and all his thoughts mixed in a jumble. There was no framework to sort one from the next. Childhood delights blended with logical deductions. Intense passions blurred slender shafts of subtle reason. Simple hunger engulfed algorithms that solved complex puzzles. In a swirling sea of abstractions, he floated away from a sharp focus.

"Rest, Jemidon. Do not give them cause." A gentle touch ran across his forehead.

Looking up through glazed eyes, Jemidon saw Augusta kneeling beside him.

"I am sorry for the blow," she said, "but I did not know what else to do. Surely if you resisted further, you would have been slain."

"But the election," Jemidon managed to say. "Without an explanation, it is all over. Trocolar has won. Our fate has only been postponed while his attention is elsewhere."

"I said I am sorry," Augusta repeated. "But forgive me the one last weakness in wanting to have someone at my side when the trader finally forces his way."

"And thus it is done." Melizar's voice cut through the

ringing in Jemidon's ears. "The domino, Holgon. With the softest touch you can manage."

Through the haze, Jemidon saw Melizar return to standing. He watched the magician strike the first wooden block in line. One after another, the rest tumbled in order across the rough floor. The last hit the trigger on the trap, flipping it into the air and hurling the pin into the inflated bladder, which exploded with a loud pop.

"And now you will be gone," Trocolar said when the action had stopped.

"Two more simple demonstrations," Melizar insisted, waving off the man-at-arms who moved forward to grab his shoulder. He huddled a second time for a brief moment and then rose again with majestic slowness. "Two more and then I will depart."

Jemidon breathed deeply. He had to regain control. With determination, he held himself perfectly still and concentrated on Holgon's apparatus. Item by item, he willed that he should see. For a long moment, nothing happened; but then, gradually, the swirl started to subside. Dominoes became distinct in the blur, then the sprung trap. Finally the entire cavern returned to focus. The pain in his calf sorted itself from the rest as the disorientation ebbed away. His thoughts resumed their order and wispy phantoms disappeared.

"Holgon, clap your hands in the rhythm of the Adagio for Perpetual Lights, but as softly as you can muster." Melizar's voice cut through Jemidon's concentration.

Holgon's face registered confusion, but the magician began to push his palms together, so that Jemidon could just barely recognize the familiar cadence of a neophyte's training. On the final stroke, the ground rumbled. A spout of water coursed up the hole that led to the vault. A great spray of cold and slimy wetness struck the low ceiling and showered down on those nearby. The ground trembled slightly, and Jemidon thought he heard the grinding of great masses of rock.

"The vault! It's flooded! The weak walls have given way!" one of the men-at-arms shouted as he peered down the hole to see what had happened.

186

"And now the Stomp of the Forging Presses." Melizar did not pause. "And then a taste of other forms of power."

Holgon complied. Beginning with his third step, the ground shook, this time not in slight trembles, but in great jerks that tumbled Trocolar and those around him to the floor. The basin of water below the landing began to slosh. With creaks and groans, the moored boats crashed into one another.

"Stop them, Nimrod!" the trader shouted. "Stop them before they collapse this cavern as well!"

"The Maxim of Perturbations." Melizar's voice competed with the shriek of tearing rock. "With it my minions can shake the earth or skim carpets across the ground. And beyond that, there are other maxims as well. Those of perspective, of penetration, persuasion, and pomp. You speak of power, insignificant mite, but know not one hundredth of all it entails."

"The sword," Trocolar demanded. "Nimrod, use the sword."

The constable snapped shut his gaping mouth and sprang into action. He ripped the blade from the man who held it and slashed at Holgon's legs. The magician's support buckled, and he tumbled to the ground. With eyes wide in fear, he threw his hands across his face, awaiting the next blow.

But the rumbling instantly stopped, and Nimrod hesitated before continuing the attack. He grunted as he saw a crimson stain begin to glisten in the hem of Holgon's robe and turned his attention back to Melizar.

"Yes, the sword." Melizar stepped forward to meet his assailant. "The sword that once sliced through rock. Until a moment ago, it held great power. But now, did it really feel all that different from any other when you tried it on the magician's flesh?"

Nimrod paused in mid-strike and turned the blade aside. It plunged toward the ground at Melizar's feet. With a shriek, it skittered across the rough stone and suddenly snapped near the hilt.

"And the scentstones." Melizar glided to the three bags that Jemidon had brought to the grotto. "Holgon's stomp-

187

ings have done more than rearrange the structures of the caverns. See also what they have done to crystal impurities."

With a surprising grace, he dumped the sacks to the floor, one after another.

"Cloudy!" someone exclaimed as the stones poured over his feet. "Not even citrine or amethyst. Milky quartz and no more!"

"Look closely, Nimrod," Melizar continued over the din that arose as everyone present began to examine his own collection of stones. "It is with this simple rock that you will be paid for your labor and the past year. Who knows what it will be for the next? Come with me to the wheat fields of the mainland, and there will be plunder enough for all."

The wave of white pebbles spilling onto the floor acted like a catalyst. The voices competing with Melizar's rose in volume. First had come the shock of the ruined tokens and now of their glittering, worthless replacements—financial ruin twice within a week. Traders and vaultholders began to push between the men-at-arms to side with trusted comrades. Swords rattled with anger in their scabbards.

"The stones are nothing!" one of the men-at-arms shouted. "And I am in debt! I depended on my fee to settle free and clear."

"Then to the mainland with the cold one," the guard next to him said. "Enough of dull sentries and shrinking cubes."

"Trocolar is the one at fault," a trader cried. "Without his tampering, this election would have proceeded as all those before."

"To your positions," Nimrod ordered. "We have an obligation still to discharge."

"For what?" one of his men shouted back. "For ballast, good enough only to weight a ship's keel?"

"Divulgents, to your guildsmen. Protect one another until we are safely away."

"Trocolar is not a winner. His clouded gems can be

worth no more than mine. Now is the opportunity, vault-holders! Seize the records. Once again, the island can be ours."

"Those for the mainland, to my side," Melizar said. "Do not let them dishonor you more."

"Death to the schemer!" Luthor pushed his way through the crowd and headed for Trocolar, waving a small dagger over his head.

Another trader crumpled as he was hit from behind. A torch went sailing overhead to crash into the throng. Someone screamed, and then one guardsman tried to prevent another from reaching Nimrod's side. In a moment, the scene swirled into a chaos of motion, flashing blades, and flowing blood. The shouts and cries of pain mingled with the echoes reverberating from the walls. Torches were ripped from their sconces. In growing dimness, fists, daggers, and swords flailed at whatever was closest at hand.

A richly robed merchant dropped at Jemidon's feet, clutching his stomach, with spurts of gore pulsing between his fingertips.

"His dagger!" Jemidon shouted. "Quickly, Augusta, cut my bonds so we can be away."

Augusta grabbed the blade just before another body fell. She severed Jemidon's bonds with quick slashes. In an instant, he was on his feet and testing his leg. "Into the passage." He pointed at one of the tunnels leading from the cavern. "On the way, you can tell me where it leads."

Limping as rapidly as he could, he pulled her into the opening and away from the fighting.

"It dead-ends after a twist a hundred paces farther along," Augusta said as Jemidon hobbled after. "There is no other way out, except back the way we came."

"A place of defense, then." Jemidon grimaced. "And time to tell me of what you saw happening through clearer eyes." He stopped a second and thought back over what he had seen. "From what Melizar had said, the sword

189

still held power when I tried to withdraw it from the rock. And then, almost without effort, the laws have changed again. Another node in the lattice—and Melizar selected exactly which one it would be."

CHAPTER ELEVEN

The Final Tally

JEMIDON flexed his back and peered around the corner. He saw only pitch blackness. Except for the soft splash of distant oars, there was no sound. No one had pursued them. For over four hours, they had waited for the chaos at the other end of the tunnel to die away and the last survivor to leave.

"Let's hope that in the confusion at least one boat was left," Jemidon said as he straightened to full height. "Come, I think it is safe enough now that I can get you out."

"But what has happened?" Augusta asked in the darkness. "Does one faction now rule the island?"

Jemidon frowned. He was a good deal less confident than he was trying to appear. Twice he had rescued her from an immediate danger. But he had done little to free her from her ultimate fate. Now it was more than Trocolar's minions they had to fear. No faction on the island would aid the ones who disrupted the election with the magic sword. Likely as not, they could become the common focus for the frustration and anger, an outside enemy that everyone could hate, a catalyst for uniting into a new order out of the destruction of the old. And what could he accomplish now that he could not before? With an invisible shrug, Jemidon ignored Augusta's question and started down the passageway.

Cautiously he fingered the cold and damp walls and stepped over the rough variations in the rocky floor. Still limping, he guided Augusta back to the landing above the vault. In the entranceway, he stumbled over a lifeless body. He moved to the side, but ran into another. He felt Augusta tense to scream and put his arm around her shoulder.

"It is to our good fortune," he said. "Surely one of those who remain has a flint and steel."

Positioning Augusta near the wall, he gave her a reassuring pat and then, on all fours, began to explore the floor of the cavern. After several minutes of distasteful groping, he found the necessary tools on one of the victims. Soon a single torch illuminated the arching ceiling with its flickering glow.

"Half the wealthholders of the island are gone," Augusta gasped. "Look, there is Cumbrist and next to him Benedict, his principal rival. Beyond them, I think I see even Trocolar among the rest."

Tears welled up in her eyes as she looked at the form barely an arm's length away. "Poor Rosimar," she said softly. "He came for my sake and now he will play the hero no more." She sank her head on Jemidon's shoulder and shook with a spasm. "And he was bound, with not even the slightest defense. When I freed you, I should have thought of him as well."

"You have seen enough." Jemidon tugged her away. "Let us go to the cliff edge to see what remains."

The torchlight cut through the darkness down to the water. Only two skiffs were left. Even Jemidon's raft was gone. Sprawled over the side of one, with hands dangling in the water, was a trader with a dagger in his back.

"Luthor." Augusta squinted through the gloom. "He wears the embroidered leggings from his last trade. And look at the tide. I have never been here when it was so high. Quickly, Jemidon, we must leave."

Jemidon nodded and started to move along the edge of the cliff toward the rope ladder. He looked back at the carnage and saw the sparkles of light that reflected from links of mail and broken blades. Would any of Melizar's equipment still be there? Or perhaps even the body of the stranger?

Jemidon stopped and frowned. He and Augusta must flee. Clearly that was the best course of action. Any other was folly. But other currents also swirled in his mind. Slowly he placed one foot on the ladder and then hesitated again. Flee into what new uncertainty? His thoughts tumbled. How had anything he had done led him any closer to what he truly wanted? The Postulate of Invariance was only a beginning. With more information, who knew what he might be able to deduce? The urge to explore, if only for a little longer, began to well up inside. He could not put the feeling away.

"The secret may yet be here," Jemidon said half aloud. "Outside is more peril and, if we are lucky, another flight." He returned to Augusta and drew her close. "I cannot abandon the quest. You saw how Melizar so easily changed the laws. It seems he has discovered a greater magic than the five we know. Call it a sixth magic, something governed by a metalaw different from all the rest. And perhaps among the bodies there is some clue that will explain more. It does no good to understand what was done unless I also know how."

"But the tide," Augusta protested. "We have waited long enough." She looked about the landing at the bodies and shuddered. "I cannot remain here while the passageway submerges."

"Then you go ahead," Jemidon said gently. "You have traversed the tunnel many times, and I am sure you can manage alone. Wait just behind the portcullis that opens onto the bay. At most, I will be a few minutes behind."

Augusta started to say more, but Jemidon drew his face into a mask of rigid determination. "Every minute we delay, the water rises higher," he said. "You help me best by making haste."

Augusta nuzzled closer for a moment and then sighed. "I am not so much the dreamer that I would offer also to stay," she said. "But take care, Jemidon. The events spin too fast. I seem to need your comfort more and more."

She disengaged and descended the ladder. With the precision of an oarsman, she maneuvered the empty skiff away from the cliff and toward the narrow opening in the

192

far wall. As she disappeared from view, Jemidon saw her wave a final kiss.

Jemidon cleared his head. Now he must hurry to find out what he could before the tide rose any higher. He would first explore the other passageways, then whatever remained among the wreckage on the landing floor, and finally the vault itself.

Quickly he crossed back over the bodies and debris to begin. He entered a side tunnel and examined the ceiling and walls for any trace that Melizar might have left behind. Falling into the pattern of the scholar, he investigated to the end of the passage and then started to explore the next, losing track of the time.

An hour later, Jemidon emerged from the last, as empty-handed as when he had begun. He turned his attention to the floor of the cavern and located Holgon's body sprawled across Melizar's toys. In the torchlight, he examined each one—the broken bladder, the sprung trap, and the painted blocks of wood. They felt quite ordinary, and no arcane symbols were anywhere to be found. Nearby was the broken sword of magic; when Jemidon grasped it, only the sense of cold steel greeted his fingertips. The shocks of electric pain were gone.

In frustration, he rubbed the worn coin about his neck. There was nothing here that told him anything more than he already knew. Somehow, with greater ease than the simplest glamour, Melizar had changed the laws, replacing the substitute magic with yet another.

Jemidon gripped the broken sword tighter, twisting its strange, unbalanced feeling back and forth with his wrist. Perhaps later, in the light of day, there might be something else that he could not see now. Yes, that was it—take an example of each form of magic and study the connection at a better time. He placed the sword hilt where he could easily find it again and then scooped up a handful of dominoes that lay next to the guard. He looked around for some example of traditional magic and saw Benedict's coinchanger reflecting the torchlight from a few feet away.

Jemidon stooped and pried loose the divulgent's stiffening fingers from the device, which was still strapped to his waist. He cut it free and experimentally tripped one of the levers. A pile of worthless tokens fell into his palm and bounded onto the cavern floor.

Jemidon continued his search, but found nothing more. Finally he knelt by the side of the shaft leading down to the flooded vault and peered into the inky blackness. Impulsively he gathered the tokens he had spilled and dropped one of the coins into the opening. Almost immediately, he heard an answering splash.

The water level was halfway up the shaft, he decided. There was no way to see what had happened below. Exploration was impossible. If any secrets were in the vault, they would forever remain there. One by one, he dropped the rest of the tokens into the dark water, trying to visualize the imagery of their grave.

As the last one left his fingers, he bolted upright with a sudden thought. The tokens in the vault were totally submerged and inaccessible. It might work at that. It offered no bearing on the riddle of the changing laws but was useful, nonetheless. Why hadn't he thought of it before racing after Rosimar with no idea of a detailed plan?

With a rush of excitement that blotted out the pain in his leg, Jemidon decided what he must do. He had learned all he could. There was no reason to remain. Now the feeling of urgency returned. He must get out ahead of the rising tide, out to safety so he could tell Augusta what they could do.

Quickly he scurried around the landing, gathering up his loot. Balancing the load precariously, he descended the rope ladder to Luthor's skiff. With no hesitation, he pushed the trader the rest of the way over the side of the boat and kicked the wares to the bow. "Forgive my disrespect," he muttered, "but if the grotto is ever used again, you will be given the proper rest."

In a few minutes, Jemidon was at the tunnel opening that connected to the outer chamber. The water level was far higher than he had seen it the week before. On his first passage, only the narrowest part near the center had been confining. Now, even at the entrance, he had to duck his head. Cautiously he paddled forward and peered

194

into the receding darkness. The tide was still rushing in, and each stroke of the oar was an effort. The ceiling hung oppressively close.

As he stroked, Jemidon concentrated on the small knobs and folds protruding from the tunnel wall ahead, measuring his progress as these landmarks slowly passed by. He ducked to the side to miss a low monolith and then paddled furiously to avoid an outcrop that narrowed the passageway from the left.

For a moment, he stopped rowing and let the stream blunt his forward momentum. Perhaps it would be better to return to the landing and wait half a day for the next tide. But who knew what would transpire outside in twelve hours? He had sent Augusta ahead to wait in the outer cavern. He must increase his effort in order to pass through the neck of the tunnel before it was too late.

Jemidon resumed his rowing. He sucked in lungfuls of air and concentrated on delivering powerful strokes to either side. For a few minutes his pace increased noticeably, but then another low dip in the ceiling forced him to duck and wait for the obstruction to pass. When he continued, his burst of energy was spent. He felt fatigued and winded. His wound and the confinement in Trocolar's dungeon were taking their toll. It seemed he could just barely make progress against the force of the water.

The ceiling sank lower and the walls closed with unrelenting menace. The skiff jammed into a narrow restriction, and Jemidon had to use his good leg against the wall to break free. He ducked beneath a projection and found that he could no longer sit erect. With each passing moment, he hunched lower and lower, barely avoiding blows against the top of his head.

Eventually rowing became impossible. Jemidon switched to pushing his oar along the wall, as he had seen the oarsmen do before. He adjusted himself to be as comfortable as possible, lying chest down on the keel, propped on one elbow while he pressed the oar against the wall. His progress slowed, as more and more frequently the skiff became jammed between the confining rocks. And with each foot forward, the ceiling sloped lower; with each passing second, the water rose to meet it.

The gap between the side rail and the ceiling diminished to less than a foot. His forehead beaded with sweat as the truth of his situation began to sink in. He was not moving swiftly enough. There would be too little room. Before he reached the narrowest constriction, the boat would jam against the ceiling, and he would be trapped.

Jemidon groped around the bottom of the skiff, trying to trigger a fresh idea. He saw the pile of Luthor's leggings and, behind them, a coil of the flexible tubing, animal intestines wrapped in cloth and stitched together into great lengths. He frowned and looked at the ceiling. He visualized the skiff pressed firmly against the rock and cold sheets of water spilling over the rails on both sides. With a shudder, he convinced himself of what he must try.

He pulled one pair of trousers from the pile and looped shut the waist and one leg with some of the twine that held the bundles together. He inhaled deeply and blew into the open leg, as Holgon had done with the pig bladder. Again and again he emptied his lungs, until the leggings bulged like a misshapened balloon. Then he collapsed the hem in his fist and forced the end of the tubing through the constriction. With the last of the twine, he bound the end of the pipe into the opening, sealing it shut. It did not hold much air, but that was all that he could muster. Finally, he grabbed the other end of the coil in his right hand and pushed one of his feet into the gap above the railing.

Struggling awkwardly, he worked his calf through the opening and then his thigh. The splintering wood dragged against one side of his leg and the rough rock ceiling against the other. With each wiggle, he felt the resistance increase.

Using both arms for leverage, he forced his other leg out and then, with a burst of strength, shoved himself clear to his waist. He inhaled deeply, preparing for one more thrust to push him free. He looked around the skiff a final time and blinked in surprise about what he had almost forgotten. Scattered on the keelboard were the

196

sword hilt, dominoes, and Benedict's changer. If he escaped without them, then it would have all been in vain. He might as well never have come into the grotto. But there was not time to pack them away, and he could not carry them all when swimming.

Then one, just one, part of his mind demanded. If he could take one, from it there still might be some clue with which to continue. But which had the best chance of assisting him toward his goal? he argued with himself. The water continued to buoy the skiff upward. The railing pressed harder and harder against his chest. Each breath became a painful effort that could not be ignored. Jemidon waved his arms in indecision and then impulsively grabbed the changer. Now both hands were encumbered, but he had made his choice. He pushed his knuckles against the keelboard, trembling from the effort, and somehow squeezed the rest of the way over the side.

There was barely a handbreadth clearance between the water level and the rock, but Jemidon began kicking away from the skiff.

He glided into the dark water, turning his head to the side for gulps of air and then floating forward, propelled by his kick. With each gasp, he saw the ceiling press closer and then finally felt it drag along the top of his head. He tipped his neck lower until his chin bore down on his chest; then he felt the ribs of rock scrape along his back. He could proceed no farther without resorting to swimming underwater. He took one last gasp of air and then thrust the end of the tubing into his mouth. Holding it in position with his hand, he angled downward and continued his glide.

In what seemed like too short a time, Jemidon was out of breath and he sucked on the tube. The pressure from the leggings was not great. He gasped for air. He felt his lungs expand, but sensed no great satisfaction from the musty smell that filled his mouth. He pulled himself through the water, not quite believing that he had received any nourishment at all, but somehow managing to complete another two dozen gliding strokes.

Again he gasped for breath and received the tainted

air from the tube. He banged against one of the tunnel walls in the darkness and angled slightly to the side. He reached upward and felt the ceiling scrape across his knuckles, in contact with the water and just inches from his head.

Onward he stroked, trying not to think of what would happen if the leggings finally collapsed or the hose was too short. In a mindless daze, he paddled through the darkness. Time lost all meaning. Despite his efforts to concentrate only on his swimming, the sense of panic slowly grew until he could contain it no longer. After countless gulps of air, he missed a stroke and floundered, slipping deeper into the water and rolling on his side. And as he tumbled, the tube jerked from his mouth. Quickly he reinserted it, but coughed as he inhaled water. He tried pinching off the opening with his hand while he prepared to draw again and then felt a sickening release of tension as he jerked the hose about. It had extended to its full length, and he had pulled it from the leggings at the other end. The air he had in his lungs would be his last.

Jemidon somehow maneuvered back into a horizontal position and touched the side of the tunnel for orientation. With a spasmodic kick, he floundered a few feet more down the passageway. He tried to resume a smooth stroke for one final try, but his bubbling thoughts swept all co-ordination away. Like a child splashing in a bath, he jerked forward in uneven spurts. His lungs emptied past the point where he previously had gulped more air. He gnashed his teeth together to resist the desire to exhale. It seemed he could feel each thrusting limb pumping air from his lungs like a piston and replacing it with a foul odor he must expel.

Jemidon began to feel dizzy. Strange dots of light appeared before his eyes. His diaphragm began to twitch against his will to hold it firm. In a last desperate test, he thrust his hand toward the ceiling and felt the same cold wetness. He was still submerged, and there was no more air.

Reason snapped, but surprisingly, Jemidon suddenly calmed. The dark spots of light grew into fuzzy images—

his sister, the golden coin, Delia, the robe of the master. They all began to shimmer and wave in his dimming consciousness. Almost without knowing what he was doing, Jemidon rolled over on his back. He placed his palm upward in front of his face and walked his fingers along the rock as his kicks became mere twitches, moving him barely inches at a time. Finally he stopped moving altogether, letting his fingertips splash in meaningless patterns on the water's surface. With an inward sigh, he released the tension in his body and prepared to sink into oblivion.

Water's surface! He choked suddenly. With a gasp, he instinctively thrust his head upward and inhaled the sweet air. There was a sliver of open space between the water line and the upsloping rock. He had passed the narrowest constriction. Now each length forward would give him more room to breathe, not less. The tide was still rising, and he must not tarry, but at least he had a chance. He would not drown. He would keep the rendezvous with Augusta after all. Lying on his back and inhaling deeply, he slowly floated through the rest of the tunnel into the outer cavern. As his senses returned, he noted almost with amazement that in his left hand he still tightly clutched Benedict's changer.

For a few moments, Jemidon continued to float, savoring his close escape. Then he rolled onto his stomach and saw Augusta maneuvering the skiff in his direction, a single torch bound erect in the stern, lighting her way.

He waited, exhausted, for her to draw alongside and provided only feeble assistance to her tugs to get him on board.

"There is a large sloop nearby in the harbor," she said as she resumed rowing. "I saw it through the portcullis. We may as well head directly for it, rather than hide in the hope that it goes away."

Jemidon did not protest. He lay in a limp huddle in the bottom of the skiff, trying to recover his strength, while Augusta propelled them through the opening to the grotto and out into the bay. In a few minutes, they rendezvoused with the sloop, and eager hands pulled them aboard. Over the far rail, Jemidon saw two more ships with the same rigging and, beyond them, a flotilla of many more. On the shoreline, flames still danced among some of the smoldering ruins, although not as many as before. The sky was smeared with dirty browns and grays. A rain of ash covered the rail and deck with a fine powder of grime.

A row of grim-faced traders whispered among themselves near the main mast. The eldest noticed Jemidon and Augusta coming aboard and broke off from the rest to see what his men had found.

"It was a good thought indeed to wait outside after we departed the grotto," the trader said after he had scrutinized Jemidon for a while. "Even though the one called Melizar was able to sail for mainland Arcadia with the constabulary on the tide, not everyone responsible for what has happened has managed to escape. I recognize this one as one of the sword wielders, and the woman is a fugitive as well," the trader continued. "No matter who wins, there will be a reward for their dispatch. Save their heads so that we can collect a bounty, if one is offered later."

Jemidon tried to shake himself to full awareness. He remembered in a rush what he had concluded in the cavern. "Wait," he croaked weakly. "You need not bother with such insignificant tasks. I greet you with the news that you can again be a wealthy man."

"Tokens and scentstones," the trader said. "I have gambled and lost with both. A bounty will be enough. Even if it fetches only a bowl of gruel, your demise will be well worth the effort."

"But if you have holdings in Augusta's vault, you can have means once again," Jemidon rattled quickly as he struggled to his knees. "The tokens in her vault—what if their magic has returned, as if nothing had happened, the way they were before?"

"An easy enough tale to weave," the trader spat out. "No one could prove you wrong."

"Exactly so," Jemidon said. "And why indeed should anyone of wit choose to disagree? Is it not in your best interest that the value of the token be restored?"

The trader squinted at Jemidon with beady eyes. Slowly he ran a hand across his chest. "The tokens have not been restored to magic," he said. "There are probably some here on deck, and their tingle is gone. The masters of the guilds moan the loudest, because their craft is no more."

"Only tokens, and only those in the grotto."

"The token was the medium of exchange. How can it be that, buried under the slime?"

"As it was before," Jemidon replied. "Only rarely were they moved about as you conducted your trades. Far more often, it was pieces of paper that you exchanged—writs that certified the shifts in ownership and the new balances that corresponded to them. It is the ledgers all carefully kept that told the story of your wealth, not the pieces of metal hidden away."

"But I had no deposits in Augusta's vault." A second trader came forward. "There is no gain for me to consider as truth what you claim."

"Dump your tokens down the shaft to join the rest," Jemidon said. "When they hit bottom, consider their magic restored as well. Again the ledger books will reflect your true wealth. Things will revert to exactly as they were before."

"It is too illogical to believe," the second trader objected. "Magic restored to the tokens in an inaccessible vault—there and nowhere else!"

"The consequence of not accepting the possibility is to continue the way things are now," Jemidon said. "The riots, the barter, perhaps the end of Pluton as a port of trade. But if everyone agrees to accept the tokens in the vault as they were before, then what difference does it make what truly happens with steel disks buried under the water?

"Indeed, if you agree in addition to pool the tokens from all of those who died in the grotto and then divide them up among those of you who survived, you will in fact come out all the richer from what has happened."

The eyes of the first trader widened at the mention of additional wealth. "The rates with the other commodities would be fixed as before," he said slowly. "I could buy

201

from Tobruk and pay my debt to Demson with the usual exchange of writs."

"And I could take the cargo from the ship that lies just outside the harbor," the second mused. "And credit the captain's account with some of my tokens so that he could buy from others for a return voyage across the sea."

Jemidon quickly scanned the faces of the other traders. On some, the hints of smiles indicated their acceptance of his scheme to recover their fortunes. Others were blank with confusion, and a few were drawn in stiff lines of rebuttal. He sighed. It would take longer than he had first thought. But even arguing for hours was better than how the traders had suggested they pass the time.

Jemidon slumped down on the deck. Seventeen traders in all had needed convincing, and the last had been the most stubborn. But finally they all had agreed on the merit of his idea. They could find no better alternative.

"Call the rest of the faction together," the first trader instructed the rest when the last had decided. "We must send signals to the others so that they, too, can quickly agree. With that soft-voiced Melizar sailing with most of the mercenaries, almost everyone will have the sense to see that this is the only way to restore order to the isle."

"What about Trocolar's assets?" Augusta asked. "I am in his debt for the pumps in my vault. And he threatened to make the sum due immediately rather than over a period of years, as is the custom."

"Trocolar!" the trader snapped. "He was the one responsible more than any other. His wealth will be pooled and divided just like the rest. And I doubt that anyone will be interested in carrying out his plans. The prudent will disassociate their inclinations from his faction as much as possible. I was a member of that faction, but my votes will be cast in another direction. There is little chance that one of his followers will garner anywhere near enough to win a position on the council."

"Then, Jemidon, you have saved me indeed!" Augusta exclaimed and hugged him close. "With Trocolar dead and none to follow in his steps, I can continue to run the vault as I did before."

"And with considerably more influence." The second trader eyed Augusta critically. "The other vaultholders may still hoard gold and other metals that we will need for minor exchanges, but only you will receive the holding fees for all the tokens on the island. Congratulations, mistress of the grotto; your future prosperity seems assured."

Augusta tightened her grip on Jemidon. "The week is over, and your indenture is fully expired," she whispered. "It will appear unseemly for one partner in the vault to be the property of another."

Jemidon looked at the group of traders. On every face was an expression of self-importance. Once they had all agreed, they were no longer paupers, but holders of great wealth and power. Augusta was no more the fugitive, but again the prestigious vaultholder. The fires on the shoreline, the dead in the grotto, and the realities of the outside world melted away. As long as there were tokens, the rest did not matter.

"But Melizar," Jemidon said after a moment. "The power that is at his command cannot be ignored. It is not for a peaceful intent that he leads men-at-arms into the rebelling wheatlands."

"The mainland can be far away, if we choose to ignore it, Jemidon," Augusta replied. "Concentrate instead on what I have just offered—a partnership in what will become the wealthiest vault on the island. It is not something to be dismissed lightly, even by a dreamer."

Jemidon felt Augusta press against him. Even through his fatigue, his pulse quickened. Perhaps this was to be the end of his quest. He had vindicated his worth with his first love. Now she was his for the taking.

After all, why had he pursued the robe of the master? Were not the arts the means to the end, the paths most likely to lead to success, despite his failures along the way? Now he could have them all—the gold, the nods of peers, the bows of servants, and adoration in a woman's eyes. A mantle of black was no longer necessary.

There was no need to restore the art of sorcery, no reason to rescue a slave girl to prove that it could be done.

Or was there? Jemidon looked down at Benedict's changer. He pressed a lever, and a shower of brass and silver spilled into his hand. A single gold brandel gleamed on top of the pile. He picked it up and compared the sharp contours of the embossing with the dull indistinctness of the coin about his neck.

Jemidon stiffened. He ignored Augusta's suddenly questioning eyes. Did anything that she offered wipe away the guilt of his sister's death, the humiliation of failing the initiates' examinations time and time again, the frustration over the formulas that would not work, and the slight shake of Farnel's head when the glamour did not complete?

"No, they are not enough." Jemidon surprised himself with the intensity which the words blasted forth. "The prestige, the power, the wealth—I want them, yes. But if I could trade them all for my own self-respect, then gladly would I deal. I have the knowledge, the intuitive skills, and the deep understanding of the arts that few will ever possess. Dullards ten times my inferior have succeeded. By the laws, then, why can't I?"

Clumsily, Jemidon pushed Augusta away. With a booming thud, he crashed his fist down upon the rail. The taste of victory soured in his mouth. What did it matter that he had escaped the cube if he still must carry his burden?

"Gently, my sweet." Augusta wrapped her arms around his waist from behind. "The poisons of your exertions have not yet run their course. Be calm and fight inner demons some other day."

"But I am not a master," Jemidon exclaimed. "I found the reason for the vanishing of sorcery and then I let it slip away."

"No man can be a master solely from desire," Augusta said. "Each must have inherent aptitudes, as I am sure you have amply learned. But put the thought from your mind. You have shown me skills that I have found in no other."

204

Jemidon gently pulled Augusta's arms from around his waist and turned to face her. He attempted a smile; but despite her words, he was not comforted. For a long moment, he pondered all that he had experienced.

"I have learned much, Augusta," he said at last, "and solved more than a single riddle—the vanishing of sorcery and magic, and their replacement by new arts heretofore unexpected." He held out his hand and began to coil his fingers into his fist, one by one. "But there is more still unanswered. First, why have I had the feeling of drifting? From where does it come? Second, it may indeed be that my tongue is ill-suited for sorcery, but what forced me to trip and stumble when attempting the simplest of rituals in Rosimar's guild? Third, the skill of Melizar—how does the stranger change the very fabric of existence to move from one law to the next? Somehow, with certainty, he can direct where reality is to go."

Jemidon started speaking faster as he realized where his thoughts were leading him. "And lastly, the Postulate of Invariance. If there is one metalaw, can there not be others as well?

"Yes, yes, Augusta. There is a way for me to be a master yet. I need to learn just a little more of how to guide the laws to ones that fit. My quest goes on. It is of Melizar I must learn more. From him, I will extract what I need to know."

Jemidon looked into Augusta's eyes and stopped. He sighed and then spoke softly, almost not believing the words as they came forth. "The cold one travels to the wheatlands; the high prince must be warned. And, and— there is a slave girl who must be freed. The reasons are too great, Augusta. I must be gone."

"You speak nonsense," Augusta said. "How can such a course compare with what I can give you here?"

"It is nonsense," Jemidon agreed, shaking his head. "I do not fully understand the feeling, but I know it cannot be denied." He touched the cold, unresponsive metal of the changer and felt a longing swell. "I must follow the nodes of the lattice until I find one that is meant for me. I must return, Augusta, return home to the wheatlands, to discover what Melizar means when he speaks of contradictions."

Augusta looked intently at Jemidon, searching for some hint of doubt, but he stood unmoving, his decision firmly made. Finally she drew him close, turning her head away.

"Indeed, there has been change in you, my gentle one," she said at last. She looked back at him and smiled weakly, batting away a tear. "But no matter; I am still mistress of the grotto and will have a wide selection from which to choose."

Her cheeks trembled as she struggled to broaden her smile. "You will need the means for your passage, shelter, and food. Let me refill your purse for services rendered."

"There is no great need," Jemidon said. "As a scholar, I can—"

"Hush." Augusta put her finger to his lips. "One of the traders here, Martin, I think, has said that in three days' time he sails for the Arcadian mainland. No other leaves before him. And I am sure he will be happy to take you along, provided you have the means to pay your way."

"Augusta, if it were not for the master's robe, I—"

"You stomp and shout about riddles and robes," Augusta said, "but I wonder. How much of your quest is for them and how much for this slave girl whom you mention the last of all?"

PART THREE

The Axiom of Least Contradiction

Chapter Twelve

Spring Harvest

Jemidon walked down the deeply rutted path, guided only by the moonlight. Little was different in his native village, despite seven years' absence. As he walked, he pondered the logic that had brought him home.

Two months had passed since he had left Pluton. The lingering winter rains had slowed his journey; the accompanying chill had made travel a definite displeasure. And Melizar's path was as cold as the weather. Nowhere could he find anyone who remembered the passage of a cloaked stranger in the company of a small band of men-at-arms.

And so, when he had learned that the high prince also journeyed to the wheatlands, he made the royal party his quarry instead. Along with everything else, the regent should be warned of what Melizar had done and of the stranger's interest in unrest and plunder. Perhaps, with the minions of the prince looking as well, Melizar would be found all the sooner.

But then the random factors must have aligned for him to catch up with the prince when he visited the barony of lord Kenton. Now there was no reason for Jemidon not to visit his father's hut as well. Indeed, it probably was no less than his duty. But what would he say? Could any words match the expectations and finally obtain forgiveness for what had happened so long ago? He would have to be assertive and somehow cast an image that emphasized accomplishment, rather than additional failures along the way.

Jemidon wrenched his thoughts away to something less distasteful. Having the conversation with his father once would be enough. For perhaps the hundredth time, he turned back to another puzzle, one that he had played with ever since he left Pluton, Augusta and Delia. Where did his true feelings really lie? If it were not for the quest for the robe, which, then, would he choose? Augusta had made very clear her feelings for him. In her eyes, he was already what he wanted himself to be. And she was intelligent and perceptive—perceptive enough to suspect that Delia was more than a casual interest.

But why should Delia be more? He had known the slave girl for a few days only. True, she showed courage and independence. She probably had the makings of a great sorceress as well. But a deep-felt relation built on so little acquaintance was substance only for the sagas. In life, it would have to take much more.

Jemidon suddenly recognized a familiar structure and broke out of his reverie. His father's hut stood to the side of the path. It seemed unchanged from the image painted by the wash of memories. As before, the tattered curtain which served as a door fluttered against its lashings in the quickening wind. The feeble wisps of smoke from the tin stack indicated that the fire inside was little more than smoldering coals. The light of a single candle winked through a high window stuffed with rags.

Jemidon hesitated. Then he gathered his cloak tightly around his chest and decided that it was foolish to stand in the unseasonal cold any longer. He sighed and approached the cloth-covered opening.

"Jemilor, freetoiler Jemilor, are you there?" Jemidon called out. "The air chills deep, and I ask to share your fire."

A moment passed, and then a hand that was beginning to show the blotches of age fumbled with the thongs holding the curtain closed on one side. The drapery fell open and Jemidon looked into watery, blue eyes. The cast of the chin was like his own, but the face was deeply lined with rows of coarse furrows that remained, regardless of the expression.

"Father," Jemidon said, as the other squinted and did not speak. "It is your son. At last I have returned home."

Jemilor's face moved almost imperceptibly in recognition and then hardened. He reached out a hand and ran his fingers over Jemidon's new cloak. "Freshly woven, but without the logo of a master," he said. "Your status is little different from what it was when you left."

"Father," Jemidon said, "it has been almost seven years. There is much that I have learned. Much that I want to hear from you as well. A scribbled note reached me on the shores of the inland sea. Mother was failing. No more have I heard."

"She is with your sister, almost two years past." Jemilor motioned toward a small patch of rocky ground to the left of the hut. "Daughter, wife, son—they all have passed beyond the need for me to care."

He turned without saying more and shuffled back toward the dimly flickering fire. Jemidon watched the hunched shoulders retreating and followed into the hut. "But I am here," he said. "And with a far better future than when I left. Isn't seven years enough to mellow the keenest disappointment?"

Jemilor slowly settled onto the small stool before the fire, lowering himself as if the slightest miscalculation would result in a broken bone. "Your sister gave her life so that you might have a chance, Jemidon. A chance to find the means for the rest of us to break free from lord Kenton's bonds. Each year he has grown more oppressive. Each year his masters come forth with more abuse of the craft. Before you left, there was only the ripening. Now there are even harvest cages and sadistic amusements in the keep.

"But if not by thaumaturgy, then with one of the others, you said. Not immediately, but perhaps next season or the one after that. For seven years I have waited. When you return again a failure, then I am entitled to keep my judgments."

Jemidon looked about the interior of the hut. The painful memories bubbled forth. The little cot was no longer against the wall, but the image of his sister was bright and firm. He clutched the brandel about his neck and for a moment swayed from the rush of emotion. He thought of his decision in Pluton and tried to hold firm to why he

211

was going on. "I return with the means to see you away to something better," he said evenly. "A vaultholder from Pluton gave me a full purse before I journeyed here."

Jemilor looked critically at Jemidon's dress. "A merchant, then," he said softly after a long while. "A partner in some trade with the islands. Perhaps it would not be so bad. As long as you managed well, you probably would fare better than your cousin Anton. He runs a mill now, but is forever in debt, trying to maintain lordly airs." Jemilor rubbed his hand along his chin. "Yes, it might be possible. These purses you receive—how often does one come and how many coppers does it contain? Do you have a chance of increasing your share if your work is good?"

Jemidon turned his head aside. "I refused the offer," he answered slowly. "The one purse was a gift. There will be no more."

"A single purse." Jemilor's tone regained its harsh edge. "A single purse for fine capes and expensive leggings. And, no doubt, for fancy meals and down-filled beds as well. After it is gone, do you plan to labor seven more years to get another?"

"No," Jemidon said. "I plan for my next reward to come much sooner. I have tracked the high prince here to warn him of great peril. If I can unravel its true cause as well, then the robe of the master may yet be mine."

"The high prince!" Jemilor snorted. "It is true enough that he is here. He shares the bounty of the village's labor with lord Kenton in his castle on the rise."

"For nearly two months, I have been following his party," Jemidon said, "up the river from Searoyal harbor and through the midland baronies to the central plains. I just missed him at lord Burdon's as it is."

"Burdon has accompanied the prince to Kenton's keep," Jemilor said. "But the movements of the nobility do not matter. You are as likely to audience with the prince there as he is to grace my hearth here in the village."

"He will lead the incantation for the spring harvest in the square tomorrow. The winter wheat is to be reaped despite the lingering cold. I hope to have a chance to speak to him then."

"And he feasts with Kenton in the keep come nightfall, as well. But in either case, what will you say to the thaumaturges who will block your path?"

"I will talk to them with these." Jemidon growled. The desire for forgiveness suddenly no longer mattered. If his father could be so unyielding at every turn, then so could he. He reached under his cloak and withdrew his purse. Reaching inside, he scooped out two gold brandels and threw them at his father's feet. "Use them for firewood," he said as he turned to leave. "Perhaps they will warm more than the air in the room."

Jemidon grimaced as the butt end of the spear jabbed into his back. All morning he had simmered over his father's treatment the day before. And now he had wanted to wait until the incantation was finished before approaching the high prince. But the men-at-arms made it clear that it would do no good to protest. Everyone was to watch. Packed shoulder to shoulder with the others, he shuffled forward against the line in front.

Jemidon had been herded into the south end of the square, well away from the high prince and the double row of thaumaturges who flanked him on both sides. He looked around the familiar sights of his childhood and saw the same rough-hewn boards showing through blistered paint, the tattered awnings flapping limply over empty storefronts, and the drab signs that signaled little commerce and even less life. Only the thaumaturges carried an air of freshness. The morning sun filtered through tiny clouds to cast pale shadows of their crisply pressed robes on the cobbles of the square. A hint of wind from the west shook their hems as they moved toward the central fountain in stately cadence.

The high prince wore the robe of a master, although Jemidon knew that it was only a courtesy for the sake of tradition. The thaumaturges would speak the incantations and invoke the words of power. The prince was an actor, miming the motions for gullible subjects, and no more.

He was not the one who brought the crop to ripening at the desired time. It would mature as the thaumaturges directed, whether he gave his benediction or not.

Jemidon stood on tiptoe to see over the shoulder of the villager in front. He saw the procession stop its march next to a huge, banded candle. The tallow column was an alternation of white and gray disks that towered well above the tallest head. On the prince's signal, a journeyman climbed a ladder to light the wick. With the first spark, it burst into flame. Faster than one would have expected, the topmost layer burned away.

"Less than a minute for a full day," the swarthy man on Jemidon's left grunted to his comrade. "They will have to move quickly to ensure that each field is serviced at the proper time."

As the candle began to consume the second layer, the master thaumaturges broke from their precise line and scattered around the courtyard. Each ran to position himself in front of an earthen pot from which sprouted a single long stalk of golden wheat. They began chanting a nonsense harmony, a complicated sequence of phrases and syllables that meant nothing to the untrained ear and disguised the words of power when they were spoken.

While the candle burned through the second layer, the journeyman scampered to the thaumaturge the farthest distance away. He carried a giant lens, and the master grabbed it from his hands when he approached. Carefully judging the distance and angles, the thaumaturge focused the sun's rays onto the ripening plant. Jemidon heard him grunt with satisfaction as a small billow of steam almost instantly snaked upward from the drying grain. The master handed the lens back to the journeyman and extracted the kernels, one by one, from the tassel of the tall grass.

As the candlewick began to expose the next level, the journeyman darted back across the square to another waiting master on the other side. The same steps were repeated with the second, while the first thaumaturge recited a solo incantation and then sat on the ground, his task done.

One by one, the masters tended to their singular crops,

each one acting within the time span specified by the melting of a single band of wax. When the last was completed, nothing remained of the rapidly burning taper. All the masters focused their attention on the high prince.

"The rocky ground to the east." The man on Jemidon's left spoke again. "They ripen those fields last because Ocanar and Pelinad are so near. If any fields are to be sacrificed, they will be those."

"Pelinad and Ocanar will be far away when the harvest starts tomorrow," another said in reply. "A large troop presses upriver from Searoyal at the high prince's command. Lord Kenton has convinced him that the threat is more than a brigand's idle boast."

"Yes, that it will be," the first growled, rubbing his stomach. "Kenton again has increased his rents, and the late warming will mean the yield is poor. They call us freetoilers, but the margin between that and bondsmen has grown exceedingly thin. Pelinad might find many more in his camp."

"Pelinad!" The other snorted. "It would be a shame if any of stout heart hearkened to his banner. It is to Ocanar that the support must come. Of the two, only he has the wits to give the high prince any cause for alarm."

"Yes, wits and craft enough to barter his own daughter for advantage, if he saw the need," the first said. "And if he were to win, then for us it would be no better. Kenton or Ocanar, to tithe to one lord is as good as to another."

"You mention a troop from Searoyal," Jemidon interrupted. "Do you know the names of any who make the trip? Is there a Melizar as well as men-at-arms?"

The two men abruptly stopped speaking and looked at Jemidon critically. "The cape is not the fashion here," the first one muttered. "Not one of our own." The second nodded. "He should ask our good lord himself at the feast tonight. The one to which no freetoiler is invited."

Jemidon frowned. Perhaps a bribe would help. He reached for his purse, but stopped as the words of the high prince echoed across the square.

"Freetoilers of Arcadia," the booming voice said, "again the nobility has granted you a boon. Again you will harvest fine crops from the plots scattered around your fair plain. And again the wheat will mature and ripen in the proper sequence so that none is spoiled while waiting the thrasher's flails. Rejoice in your good fortune. Exult in the high yields. Thank the graciousness of your lord Kenton that you have the means to be, not slaves, but free."

At the mention of Kenton's name, a low murmur started in the crowd, and the men-at-arms straightened from their slouches to a state of alert.

"Yes, thank your lord for the way that he has analyzed all elements of the cycle." The high prince raised his voice above the buzz. "The seed selection, the fertilization, the water channels, the grain barges, and the pushing back of the harvest of winter wheat to early spring, so that there are two crops a year instead of one. Without his guidance, you all still would be scratching out barely enough to feed yourselves. Instead, you nourish all of Arcadia and, indeed, even baronies across the sea. Tonight in his feasting hall, the millers, the barge captains, the traders, and the grainkeepers all come to pay homage to your lord's great use of craft."

"And had he not been so clever," someone shouted, down the line from where Jemidon stood, "then at least we could have starved with some leisure. As it is now, we toil from sun to sun, and our stomachs growl all the same."

"You need not avail yourselves of your lord's machinery and arts," the high prince replied. "Farm your rented land as you see fit. But if you rely only on the natural climate and soil, your neighbor who gives his labor in exchange for the benefits of the art will have a production that exceeds yours manyfold."

"And so only the ones who march in step in the cages will be able to pay the increased rents that rise every year," the man next to Jemidon muttered.

"And once you miss payment, you are trapped as a bondsman and forced to labor just the same as the rest," a second replied. "Free or fettered, it makes little difference. We will all be Kenton's in the end."

"But if you owe nothing at the close of the season,

unlike the others, you can leave," a third said. "Only if you are in debt are you legally bound."

"Walk away to what?" The first one spat. "The plain over the mountains to the east is ruled by a lord, just as is the one here. The walled cities will not admit one who does not have a craft." He paused and shook his fist. "A pox on whoever first applied thaumaturgy to the fields. It has tied us to the land far tighter than any edict ever could."

The hubbub intensified. The high prince stamped his boot for silence, but no one heeded. A few of the men-at-arms pushed the shafts of their spears menacingly into the crowd. The agitation grew. The prince tried to speak once again, but he was drowned out. He paused for a second, then whirled about in disgust and waved his arms for the thaumaturges to follow. Rigidly erect, he marched through the small archway that led from the square and disappeared. The thaumaturges hastily shouldered their way after. In an instant, the square was deserted by the masters.

The men-at-arms became more aggressive in their pokes and jabs. Without any focus for their hostility, the feeling of the crowd ebbed away. The ranks to the rear started to turn. In twos and threes, they stepped back into the alleyways and disappeared. Those in front shouted one last defiance as they retreated into the empty space at their backs. Far more rapidly than it had filled, the square was emptied of everyone except the men-at-arms.

Jemidon frowned. His father had been right. He was no closer to the high prince than he had been at the start. The incantation for the spring harvest had presented no opportunity at all. He could only hope that, if somehow he got into Kenton's keep, his chances would be better. But for that he needed to accompany a grain trader or a miller.

A grain trader or a miller. Anton. Anton was a miller and forever in debt. Yes, that was it. Jemidon touched his full purse. Perhaps his cousin would be receptive to a little transaction to the benefit of both.

* * *

217

The afternoon passed swiftly before Jemidon found his cousin. Anton was as his father described, long on appearances but short of coin. And once the agreement was struck, the rest had been surprisingly easy. As darkness fell, Jemidon found himself in the feasting hall of lord Kenton and mere yards away from the high prince.

But barely an hour had gone by when Anton drained the last of his fifth goblet and waved it over his head to be refilled. With a lurch, he sagged against Jemidon's shoulder.

"You cannot empty the kegs alone, no matter how hard you try," Jemidon whispered beneath the din. "Pace yourself, Anton. The bargain was a seat at the table against the gold for a feathered cape. I did not offer to carry you home to your mill."

"Nor did I agree to hear pious judgments from a free-toiler's son," Anton slurred. His face was puffy, like rising dough. Beads of sweat trickled down ruddy temples, even though the huge room was cold. "Had I not the need to dress to catch lord Kenton's eye, a sweet doxy would have been my choice for companion, not a cousin suddenly visiting from afar."

Jemidon started to reply, but a page arrived with a flagon, and he contented himself with pushing Anton erect. He had far more important things to attend to. For the dozenth time, he looked around the large, rectangular room. All four walls were hung with tapestries from floor to ceiling, with cutouts for high doorways that led to the kitchens beyond. In each corner was a treadmill, a belt of wooden planks tied together with rope and looped around two axles in a tight band. An ambulator sat on each, muscular legs dangling over the sides. Long tables defined the perimeter of a central square. Around the outside edge sat over fifty revelers, eating Kenton's fowl and drinking his wine. The table to the south was slightly higher than the rest, and its center was the focus of Jemidon's attention.

Lord Kenton's loud and commanding presence dwarfed even that of the high prince, who sat on his right. The two men were most unalike. Prince Wilmad's face was thin, like a hatchetfish, and his eyes were set high above a nose that seemed razor-sharp. His head was always tilted slightly back. From under half-closed eyelids, he slowly scanned the room, daring anyone to relieve a majestic boredom. Kenton's face was round, with full cheeks that pushed his eyes into tiny dots. His chin bristled with a two-day growth of beard. After perfunctory wipes of a gravy-laden hand on a soiled surcoat, he was as likely as not to run his fingers through a tangle of jet-black hair. At his left was what looked like doll furniture, an array of tables and chairs, laid out in a scaled-down replica of the feasting hall.

With a booming command, Kenton slammed down his flagon and beckoned the wine steward for more. Pushing aside Wilmad's hand with a laugh, he grabbed the skin from the steward and filled the prince's cup until it overflowed. With what appeared like an afterthought, he splashed a few swallows into his own.

"Do not be so cautious, my liege." Jemidon strained to catch Kenton's words. "You are among friends, as safe as in the highest keep in Searoyal. Everyone here is a man of at least some means. Master thaumaturges, barge captains, millers, and sackmakers. The last harvest incantation is done. It is an excuse to enjoy yourself. Even a prince must sometimes indulge in simple pleasure."

"Our interests in a successful harvest are mutual," Wilmad said. "The mood throughout the kingdom would grow more ugly if it fails, I do not deny that. But the whole does not necessarily follow from one of the parts. The crude humor of a misplaced melon peel does not compare with the experiences one can feel on Morgana."

"Yet what will you do next season, my prince?" Kenton smiled. "The rumors have it that sorcery is no more. Perhaps it is time now to cultivate new tastes."

With a wave of his hand, he signaled to the far corner of the room. Jemidon turned to see the ambulator stand up and begin to pace on the treadmill. With a fluid kick, the man picked up speed, pushing the planks under his feet faster and faster. The creak of the boards as they rounded the axles added to the noise drowning out the prince's reply. Jemidon tensed. He knew the ambulators were one of the ways for providing the energy to an incantation. Kenton would not have started one running unless he intended to exercise the art.

"And now let me see," the lord boomed. "Who is in most need of stretching his legs to relieve the tedium of the feast?"

A sudden blur of motion streaked by Jemidon's side. He turned just in time to see Anton fall to the floor, his chair tumbling back to the wall.

"Ah, you always were the alert one." Kenton laughed as the miller struggled to regain his feet. The buzz of conversation transformed into a chorus of laughter as Anton stomped on his new cape and fell again to the ground. Jemidon glanced back at the ambulator and confirmed his suspicion. The man now panted heavily, trying to rebuild the treadmill's speed. And where was the simulation? Jemidon scanned the hall for something that would be related to the chair. When he saw the small model held in Kenton's fingertips, he stopped and nodded. A trivial case of thaumaturgy, but an exercise of the art nonetheless.

"In the wheatlands, it is polite to help one's cousin." Kenton caught Jemidon's eyes. With a deft motion, the lord flicked another model chair with his thumb. Jemidon felt his own seat scoot away. He grabbed for the tablecloth as he fell and crashed to the floor in a pile of plates, flagons, and spilled food. The laughter increased, and even the tapestries could not muffle the roar.

"Two chairs. They account for two of the treadmills," Kenton continued. "But with four ambulators in the hall, there must be additional bindings."

As Jemidon struggled upward, he saw a wine cup across the way suddenly jump from the table, splashing its contents down the front of a woman's dress. A turkey thigh rose from a platter and plunged into the beard of a grainkeeper on her right. For several minutes, the laughter continued as Kenton manipulated the objects, dashing the chairs into anyone who lost track of where they were, bouncing the cup off heads and elbows, and thrusting the

220

turkey leg into mouths not discreetly shut when it passed by.

"Enough," the lord said finally. Jemidon saw the ambulators collapse to sitting, their chests heaving from their effort and their treadmills still. The laughter died away.

"Release the bindings," Kenton ordered, and the thaumaturges started to sing as they had done earlier in the day. The lord turned to the prince. "This is just a sample of what the other arts can do to amuse one nobly born."

"It is little different from last year's," Wilmad said. "And a few minutes' entertainment at that. You presume too much, Kenton. Guide your masters in the production of wheat. In that, you have shown much skill. But leave true art to those who have the sense to judge the subtle from the mundane."

"But the goblet," Kenton protested. "Have you no idea the difficulty involved in fashioning a replica on such a small scale?"

"The craft of your masters is well regarded, even in Searoyal," Wilmad said. "The candles that they carefully build, taking a full day for each layer, are used throughout the plains."

"You waste time in debating the merit of foolish games when you should be attending to the responsibilities of being lords," Jemidon suddenly interrupted. The snickers and the hot gravy soaking down his legs as he tried to blot the wine from his tunic had proved to be too much. He had come to tell the high prince of an impending danger, not to be the butt of a baron's jokes.

Jemidon's outburst brought the hall to silence. He immediately realized what he had done, but there was no way to turn aside the look that began to etch itself on Kenton's face. A growing sense of apprehension began to mingle with his flash of anger. Boldly, he plunged on before the lord could speak.

"First sorcery, then magic. Can you not see that even thaumaturgy might be next? How will you harvest all of these ripening fields if the art gives you no aid?"

"The last incantation of ripening has been performed," Kenton said in a surprisingly quiet voice. "The thauma-

221

turges stood in the village square in exactly the same geometric pattern as that of the fields upon the plain. The crops will mature, each field one day after the next in lock step, just as the representative stalks did in the square." The lord glowered at Jemidon. "All that remains is to ensure that the labor for the reaping is properly applied to the task."

"Not the cages again," another voice on Kenton's left interrupted. The man stood and faced the prince with his palms spread wide. He looked like the senior master of a guild instructing a first class of neophytes; a ring of white hair circled a completely bald crown. Burst veins of blue netted his cheeks, and flesh hung limply from slender arms. "The freetoilers work to their limit as it is. Another fetter will drive them directly into the brigands' hands. Instead of eleven bushels where you used to have ten, you will have none at all."

"I have eleven where you have only six, Burdon. Eleven to your six because I know better what effort the free-toilers are capable of exerting. If it is the cages that will increase this year's yield to the desires of the high prince, then cages I shall use." Kenton waved his hand in Jem-idon's direction. "And for every one that I can fill with legal cause, it is one less that the freetoilers must elect to enter by choice."

"I do not care to interfere with your methods," Wilmad interjected. "As long as the grain is produced in sufficient quantity and my house gets its rightful share, the means are not my concern." The high prince paused for a second, eyeing Kenton down the length of his nose. "They are not my concern, as long as Arcadia remains at peace with itself and I do not have to explain to my doddering father why the royal garrison must be pulled from the coast to the inland plains. One company from Searoyal is quite enough, Kenton. Do not overstep the bounds, so that next year I again must shout apologies about a vassal's conduct to the rabble in the village square."

"The chance of rebellion is not to be lightly dismissed, my liege," Burdon said. "Each day the brigands add one

222

or two more to their cause—one or two more cursing Kenton's abuses of the art."

"Abuses!" Kenton snorted. "A weak excuse for those unwilling to toil as they should. Why, of the five arts, thaumaturgy is the least sinister; it has the smallest potential for true harm. There is no opening of a channel to the frightening power of the demons with which the wizards toy. Nor the possibility of lifelong enchantment that can come from a sorcerer's gaze. No awesome weapons, like those from a magician's guild. No salves or philters of evil intent from an alchemist's anthanor. No, just two simple principles to aid in the production of our crops."

Kenton paused for breath, but then raced on before Burdon or the prince could speak again. "Even I understand their intent, if not the incantations that invoke their uses. The Principle of Sympathy, or 'like produces like.' Because of it, when I move the model chair, the one in the room responds in kind. A whole field ripens as does a single stalk.

"And the Principle of Contagion, or 'once together, always together.' Both the full-size chair and its model were made from the same log. The wheat maturing in the square is coupled to the field from which it came and no other. These two concepts, plus the binding of a bit of energy to make it all come about, span the full scope of the art. It is so simple that, as I have said, no great harm can result.

"And look at what we have accomplished by dutifully applying the craft to our fields year after year: seeds placed in straight rows to equal depth merely by inserting one; germination in unison of all that is sown; accelerated growth, as if each plant were nurtured in the finest of fertilized soils; and an entire field ripening at once, while its neighbor is delayed for a day, so our limited tools can be used for each at the optimal time."

"The harvest incantations occur in my villages, as well as in yours," Burdon said. "We all understand that each layer of candle wax was made a single day before the one underneath, and hence lives one more sunset from birth to death, and that each field's ripening is bound to a layer, so that it matures in the same sequence. All of that is not the point. You see no abuse, yet it is all around you, Kenton. What of those misshapen ambulators? Their thighs are as big as their waists, and they are of no use other than to provide the energies that your incantations demand. If by some chance the art were to go away, to what other craft could they be employed?

"No, the issue is not the principles of thaumaturgy," Burdon continued, "but the degree to which magic robs our people of their will. Now the freetoiler has little choice. He must volunteer to man the cages in step with the bondsman so that his own field yields as much as yours. If you have your way, ultimately he will be little more than a machine, locked in a grotesque dance that stomps the stems and separates the chaff with jerking steps precisely placed."

"My masters have not yet perfected their craft, it is true." Kenton smiled. "But it is a goal well worth striving for, nonetheless. The cage that you show so much concern about is no more than the logical extension of what we have been doing for years. And the freetoilers need not employ it. As long as they can get eleven bushels from each acre, where last year they harvested ten, how they accomplish the task I do not question."

"Yes, eleven bushels." Kenton turned his attention back to Jemidon. "For one of the miller's trade, it will be a grand experiment. It is the form by which you will accept the punishment for your impertinence. Eleven days in the cage. Let us see if you are as skillful as the rest when you are done."

Kenton smiled but said no more. He rang a small bell at his side; from somewhere in the castle, a huge gong sounded. He motioned to his thaumaturges and ambulators. The treading resumed. The words of a binding incantation again filled the air. A squad of men-at-arms marched into the feasting hall, carrying shackles and chains.

Jemidon turned to meet the new arrivals. His apprehension was well founded. In the hallway behind the men, he glimpsed iron bars and a steel plate. He heard the rumble of wooden wheels on stone. What they were he knew he was soon to learn.

CHAPTER THIRTEEN

Fugitive's Choice

JEMIDON gasped when the cold water hit his face, snapping him awake. Squinting into the dawn sun, he saw that he was outside Kenton's castle at the edge of a field of wheat. A steel belt and chains fettered him to the sides of a large metal cage. He was the only occupant, although the volume could have accommodated many more. Straining as far as his bounds would allow, he came nowhere near to touching one of the walls. Bars were spaced a handspan apart on all four sides. A steel plate formed the ceiling, its underneath side bracketed with tools, gears, screens, and other machinery that Jemidon did not immediately recognize. The bottom was open; he stood on the rough ground. And all of the bars were attached only at the top, like the teeth of a giant comb. In each of the four corners, large wooden wheels pressed into the damp earth. Identical cells formed a precise line staggered into the distance, each one placed a cage length behind the one in front and offset half a width to the right.

The man-at-arms who had splashed Jemidon awake continued down the row, waking others who hung slumped in their bonds. A sergeant followed behind, tapping each cage with a baton and barking the order to make ready. He stopped at Jemidon's cell and pointed at the scythe attached just within arm's reach to a bracket on the ceiling.

"You must cut it all," he said. "If any tickles the touch-

225

plate in back, the flagella will whirl. And get rid of the cape. It will merely get in your way."

Jemidon did not reply. Only with great restraint had he not resisted being seized the night before. It had saved him from certain injury. He had been thrust into the cage in such a hurry that he was still dressed for the feast. In silence, he watched the sergeant look at the gently waving stalks and then turn a crank that led into the top of the cage. As the handle spun, a coarse screen lowered from the ceiling to about waist level, directly behind Jemidon. Twisting to look over his shoulder, he saw a cylindrical drum mounted above the screen, with its axis parallel to the back of the cage. Long strips of leather coiled around the drum, and sharp metal brads covered the loose ends that dangled in the air.

The sergeant looked a second time at the grain, made a small adjustment with the crank, and then nodded to himself in satisfaction. He tapped his baton once more on the metal bars and turned his attention to the next in line.

As the sky brightened, Jemidon gazed across the field down the long lines of tall grain. In the distance, he could see more treadmills like those of the feasting hall, but built on a larger scale, with ambulators four abreast.

Jemidon watched the ambulators start the treadmills in motion and expectantly waited for what the thaumaturgical effect would be. Almost immediately, a strange rustling shimmered throughout the grainstalks. Thin tendrils of vapor snaked into the morning air. Triggered by the incantation the day before, the crop had matured and was ready to harvest. His cage lurched and began to rumble forward toward the high-standing grain. Jemidon looked forward and back and saw the rest of the staggered line move in unison. Somewhere, a thaumaturge was guiding a small toy to which all these were bound. He stumbled on a rock and missed a step, but the cage continued forward, pulling him by the fetters tied to his waist.

Jemidon saw the man in the cage directly ahead enter the field and grab his scythe. With a practiced stroke, the prisoner felled the stalks that filtered through the vertical bars in front. His path was such that the left edge of his swath matched the right of the prisoner who preceded him. Jemidon grunted understanding as he saw what was happening. The cages were large enough to give each man room to swing, yet they were grouped in such a way that, once they had all passed over the field, no grain would remain standing.

Jemidon watched the uncut grain dance into his cage as he reached the field. But his anger of the previous night still lingered. Nurturing a spark of defiance, he folded his arms and stomped on the grain as it came underfoot, letting the growth on either side pass by untouched. He looked over his shoulder, to see it spring back to nearly full height, almost as if he had not gone by at all.

He saw the tall stalks poke through the screen that the sergeant had lowered into place. As the first tassel passed through the grid, one of the gear trains on the ceiling began to creak. A lever pulled a pawl from a ratchet, and suddenly the disk at Jemidon's back whirled into motion. The leather thongs uncoiled and whipped from their resting place, striking his back with a barrage of the sharp metal tips. Hot bursts of pain exploded across his shoulders and neck, staggering Jemidon almost to his knees.

The sergeant's words suddenly had meaning. Jemidon grabbed the scythe as quickly as he could. With a slashing abandon, he hacked at the grain that continued to pour through the bars of the cage, toppling all the stalks before they slipped past him to be detected by the screen. The swinging blade tangled in his cape. With a rip of his free hand, he flung the garment to the ground. He looked again at the methodical sweep of the other prisoners' scythes in front and tried to imitate their economy of motion. He felt his own cage pick up speed and fell into a rhythm to keep up with the pace.

The rate of progress increased two more times before Jemidon reached the end of the row. With leaden arms and gasping lungs, he mowed the last few lengths. He was not used to the hard labor. Already he felt his coordination deteriorate from the fatigue. He dropped the scythe to the ground, then thought better of it and barely managed

227

to retrieve the blade as the cage continued to trundle along its predetermined track.

Jemidon was led to a second field adjacent to the first and placed into another staggered line. While the last of the cages were finishing their swaths and being moved into position, a small, hinged door opened from the ceiling and a cup of dirty water descended on the end of a long rod. Jemidon grabbed the offered liquid and drank deeply, thankful for a moment of rest.

On the first field, another row of prisoners had begun to move across the mowed ground. Their cages were different, with deep wooden bins hanging along the interior walls on both sides. Through a complex of linkages and springs, the suspended hoppers were connected to a circular disk, faced with two rotating pointers like the hands of a clock. One seemed to circle of its own volition, revolving at a steady but fairly rapid rate. The other bounced and jerked, moving forward through short arcs only whenever another armful of shorn stalks was dumped into one of the hoppers to increase the weight it contained.

Most of the time, the weight indicator led the other, but occasionally it would be passed and lag behind. And whenever it did, the drum in back of the occupant of the cage whirled into life, lashing out with the barbs of sharp metal. Snatching and scooping in a fury, the harvesters made sure that little of what had been mowed was left on the ground.

Without warning, Jemidon's line began to move again. The cup retreated back into the ceiling. In an instant, his cage lumbered into more uncut grain. Again he was late to stop the screen behind his back from being touched, and again he felt the incentive to leave no stalk uncut. Grimly he swung the scythe and tried to take his mind off anything more than ensuring that his task was perfectly done. Before the sun had reached its zenith, Jemidon had cut six more rows of wheat. By dusk, he had lost track of the number.

With the last rays of the sun, he was allowed to stop at the end of the row he had just worked. His arms, his back, his legs, and every muscle were throbbing in protest to the strenuous labor. His waist bled from a dozen sores where the metal belt had dug into his flesh. He hung like a damp rag in his harness, feet dragging on the ground and arms dangling with no life.

The blankness of his thoughts was interrupted by the sergeant, who placed a bowl beside his cage. The man-at-arms paused a moment, looked hastily over his shoulder, and then scooted a second bowl between the bars. "The first day is the roughest," he said, "but if you do not eat to get strength, then the next will be your last."

Jemidon raised his head and eyed the sergeant dully, too tired even to offer thanks. "I earn no favor with the lord if one of the cages stops working during the day," the guardsman said gruffly as he unknotted one of the chains binding Jemidon to the bars. "Take advantage of your good fortune so that I can ensure mine."

Later, with food in his stomach, Jemidon felt a small degree of reason return. Another ten days of this he could not endure. He slowly stood and looked around the cage. With only one fetter, he could reach the side, but rattling the bars revealed no looseness; they all held tight and firm. Tentatively at first and then with greater vigor, he sawed with the scythe against the linkage that still bound him, but the blade just skittered across the harder metal, refusing to bite and make a notch.

Jemidon grasped the tool in both hands near the neck where the blade joined the wooden handle, trying to imagine how he might separate the two pieces and turn them into something that would be of use in an escape. He ran his hands over the gears and levers of the ceiling, pulling at protrusions and trying to break something free. Each object he could reach he studied in turn, grasping for some idea that would help his plight.

But try as he would, all his thoughts were leaden. Evidently he was too tired from the labor to think anything more than the obvious. With the certainty of failure, he went through the motions, making the escape attempts that every cage occupant probably tried.

Finally he turned his attention to his own possessions. He ran his hands over his newly purchased tunic, now

229

deeply creased and smelling of sweat. As he touched his pockets, he felt the reassuring lumps of their contents; his purse of gold, Benedict's changer, and the various curios of his seven years of wandering were still there. In the haste to have him confined, no one had bothered to take anything away.

One by one, he removed the items, trying to couple them with something else in the cage. When he reached the changer, he idly thumbed piles of coins into his palm and poured them back into the slit in the top.

As the metal disks slid into the opening, Jemidon could hear the soft click of some sorting apparatus that directed them to the various columns. But the output of each was a jumble—gold, silver, copper, and steel, diameters of all sizes, coins with central holes and those without, all mixed when a dispensing lever was depressed.

Almost hypnotically, Jemidon cycled the coins, letting the soft jangle soothe the soreness from his limbs and back. He found himself watching the pattern of types as they emerged and trying to guess what the next might be. Silver, he thought, fingering the lever for the leftmost column. Silver again; he smiled when his choice proved correct. "And again," he muttered half aloud when he was right a second time. "Perhaps, even without magic, the box can still sort, if given enough tries."

Five silver coins in a row fell from the column before a brass dranbot ended the string. "An interesting puzzle," Jemidon mused, putting the device aside as he tried to visualize what the internal mechanism must be. After a moment's thought, he lifted the changer again. With a rapid series of motions, he emptied the entire contents of coins onto the ground. Then he selected one copper and inserted it in the slit. Trying the dispensing levers one by one, he found that the third column had received the coin.

Two coppers in sequence were partitioned into columns three and four. And if they followed a silver, they went instead to two and five. In a rapid series of experiments, Jemidon used longer sequences of coins, trying to deduce the rule by which they were distributed. He inserted runs of all one coin and then two types, interleaved in pairs. Cycles of four, mixed triplets, groups of seven—the various combinations filled his thoughts as he struggled to assemble all the results into a coherent whole.

The sky dimmed into night, and then the first stars twinkled into view. The moon streaked pale shadows of the cage bars onto the ground, but Jemidon continued on unheedingly. He divided the coins into distinct piles that he could locate by feel in the darkness. "Suppose we limit the problem to five of each type," he muttered. "And the challenge is to choose the order so that in the end they all will be sorted. Yes, I will call it Benedict's problem. The path each one takes from the slit depends not only on its type but on what the columns already contain as well. It cannot be done in one pass. When four coppers are in column one, unless a silver is in both two and three, the last will go to five instead. So one must carefully remove some from the bottom and intermix them with those remaining to be added at the top. Only then can there be a chance."

"With the setting of the moon! Pass it along." A whispered voice broke Jemidon's concentration sometime later. He had not noticed that another of the harvest cages had moved to barely ten feet away.

"With the setting of the moon. Do not sleep. Pass it along," the voice repeated. "The message comes from one of the Pelinad's band. Kenton expects him only to touch the fields on the east, if at all. But it will be tonight. Here. They will make the attempt."

Jemidon shook himself alert. He frowned at the scatter of metal disks that lay in front of him. He looked at the sky, now quite different from when he had last noticed it. "What have I been doing?" he gasped aloud. "Frittering away time on a meaningless puzzle, and one of my own making at that. I must be more tired than I thought." Disgustedly he scooped up all the coins and inserted them in the changer. He shook his head, confused about his actions, and thrust the device away. The visions of sliding mechanisms and clinking coins began to fade. He wrin-

231

kled his brow and forced his thoughts back to his immediate plight.

"Wait," he said to the occupant of the other cage. "The setting of the moon. Pelinad's messenger. What do you mean?"

"The reward justifies the risk. With common laborers too tired to lift a sword, there was no reason for taking the chance. But two new ones were added to the cages today—and one is a sorcerer from Morgana."

"I am no sorcerer," Jemidon said. "I was only on a visit to the island to learn the craft."

"Not you, dolt. The big man farther down the line. Now pass it on, before the guardsmen hear your chatter and come to investigate."

Jemidon started to ask more, but the other cage began to move away. Silently, he cursed himself for not noticing sooner that the message was close at hand. Sorcerers and Pelinad's rebels, he thought. They were far more important than the tinkle of a few pieces of metal. Determined, he made up his mind to recover the time he had lost. He checked the ground to ensure that all the coins had been retrieved and then began to push his cage in the direction of the next in line.

And at the next, rather than returning to his own position, he offered to carry the message farther down the row. At each stop, as he whispered the words, he stared into the darkness, trying to recognize a familiar face. The practice of sorcery in Arcadia had been confined to Morgana. A master sorcerer would have to come from there. But it would not be tradition-bound Farnel and certainly not Gerilac. And why would any of the other masters journey to the wheatlands?

A dozen stops produced nothing, and Jemidon felt his fatigued legs begin to tremble from the effort of pushing over the ruts that ran alongside the lines of wheat. But the memory of his mental lapse goaded him on, and he continued to the next. He lost track of how many cages he visited. The end of the line finally came within sight.

As he approached the fourth from the last, a sudden scream jerked him alert. A drum sounded to the left, and the guard fires sprang back to life. Shouts of alarm came from all along the line. Steel clanged against steel three cages away. In a matter of moments, Jemidon saw dark figures running from cell to cell and keying open the doors. He heard the jangle of freedom in the back of his own cage and tugged with an energy he was surprised he still had to free himself of the metal belt.

He bolted so quickly to the outside that he nearly knocked down the man racing from the adjacent cell. Together, they flailed to regain their balance in the dimness. As they spun about, the moon on the horizon caught the other man's features. Jemidon's mouth dropped open in sudden recognition.

"Canthor!" he exclaimed. "Canthor, the bailiff of Morgana Island. Why are you here? You are no more a sorcerer than I!"

Jemidon looked around the campfire in the small bowl framed by the rising hills. He tried to stretch himself into a more comfortable position. His linen tunic was now bunched in thick creases beneath a vest of stiff leather. The equally fine leggings hung in tatters beneath his knees. There had been no pursuit for over two days. And now Pelinad's band was high enough in the foothills so that the lookouts would be able to spot any activity out of Kenton's castle on the plain below. The slopes rapidly merged into the higher mountains in the east, and escape was possible in a dozen ways. Not that flight was the only option. Before the attack, Pelinad's brigands had numbered about sixty. Now they were three times the number. Not a single one of the bondsmen or freetoilers had elected to stay. Even the troop from Searoyal would find the rebels more than a mere nuisance.

In small groups of three and four, they huddled around the sprinkling of morning fires. Some sprawled exhausted, still asleep despite the cold and rocky ground. Others talked with loud animation, slapping the arms of old acquaintances and testing the feel of the newly supplied hide-covered shields. Behind them, the silhouettes of craggy spires were just barely discernible in the brightening sky. Slightly north of where the sun would rise, Jemidon saw the dark crestline dip into the deep notch that was Plowblade Pass.

Jemidon watched Canthor return from a huddled conference with Pelinad and his lieutenants around one of the fires to the left. The bailiff squinted off into the distance, then looked at Jemidon and smiled.

"Farnel's tyro," he said as he approached. "Who would have guessed it? Returned to his homeland, no doubt to seek his fortune the same as an old soldier who knows that where there is turmoil, there is also the opportunity for gain."

"But the message said that there was a sorcerer among the captives," Jemidon whispered. "Did you come with someone else?"

"I am the master." Canthor patted his chest and laughed. "It is for me that Pelinad staged his raid. And he has just told me why. He is to meet this morning with Ocanar, the leader of the other rebel band, and the village whispers say that this rival has acquired the aid of a master of one of the arts. Pelinad feels that he must show equivalent strength if he is to bend Ocanar to his will, rather than the other way around."

"But you do not practice sorcery," Jemidon said. "Pelinad has made a mistake."

"And one that I have chosen not yet to correct."

"But why?"

"Why not? For all intents now, I can weave illusions as well as any master." Canthor grimaced and looked in the direction of the sea. "No need, they said. No need for a bailiff or men-at-arms. With no art, there would be no visitors. What little order they needed they could manage by themselves. Booted out from the keep with wages a month in arrears! A fine thanks for services almost two decades done. And so it was either starve or beguile the weak-witted with impressive-sounding chants that I have heard repeated over and over. A wave of the hand, a penetrating glance, a deep-pitched voice in a dimly lighted room. There are enough begging to imagine some fantasy

234

in the air that the coin was easy enough to come by along the way."

"Pelinad rescued us for no less," Jemidon said. "With sixty men or three times that, he will not directly challenge Kenton's sharp steel and tight mail. The rest are all babbling about their good fortune. They think that finally they have a weapon to use against the catapults and the lord's missiles of war. You had better explain quickly that you are a fighter like them and no more."

"You did not seem so quick to speak when they filled your bowl with a double portion," Canthor remarked. "Even the tyro of a sorcerer rates more than an even share."

"I put forth no such claim," Jemidon protested. "The forced march was enough, after a day in the fields, to keep any man's mouth from wasted chatter."

"Nevertheless, they have accepted my word as to your budding proficiency." Canthor waved down the volume of Jemidon's voice. "And, as I said, Pelinad needs to have a sorcerer in his retinue for the parlay. For the moment, it is better that things proceed as they are. Besides, with two we should be able to carry out the illusion all the better. There will be time enough to reveal the reality. And if no harm is done in the process, then what can it really matter?"

"My purpose for coming to the wheatlands was not to fight in a rebellion," Jemidon said. "Rather, I intended to warn the high prince of the power of a stranger who has mercenaries of his own."

"Indeed." Canthor flicked another branch onto the fire. "Then perhaps you should demand an immediate audience with Pelinad and inform him forthwith where your allegiances lie. I am sure that the others who were released with you would delight in the presence of a representative of the prince."

Jemidon scowled and looked about the campground. What Canthor said was true. None of Pelinad's rebels would care anything about warning the prince. Perhaps he should slip away when there was opportunity. But slip away to what? Certainly not back to the toil of the cages or the oppression of Kenton's barony. Was it for the benefit of the Arcadian nobles that he was to offer his aid? He shook his head in confusion.

But if there was no warning to the prince, then how could Melizar be apprehended? And the secrets of the stranger were the slender threads from which everything else hung. There would be no robe of the master, no calming of the strange longing that made him turn away from all that Augusta had offered.

Jemidon lapsed into a deep contemplation, clutching the coin about his neck and cutting out Canthor's words. He tried to dissect the compulsion that apparently lay behind all the reasons he had thought were driving him on. What was the allure of Melizar's lattice and the soft, cold words that issued from the dark hood? Why did he care about the Postulate of Invariance and the new laws, the new sorceries, and the magics that somehow switched on and off, according to the stranger's commands? Lattices, drums and weights, flitting imps, visions of changers, and stacks of coins danced in his head. Copper and silver slid into the slit, and precise columns of gold issued from the bottom. Benedict's problem—inserting three regals followed by one galleon should produce—

"Alert, to arms," he heard Pelinad say. "Ocanar comes for the parlay, and I do not trust his intent." The tall, angular warrior thumped his fist on his chest. "Stand upright now and show them, each and every one, that you are the equal of any whom he has to command."

Jemidon groaned and willed his body erect. Understanding the puzzle of his own mind would take more than a few minutes in a crowd of men pursuing a desperate cause. Without words, he accepted Canthor's nimble fingers tightening and adjusting his leather vest. He grasped the scythe in one hand, wondering how well he would fare against someone who knew how to use a blade. Pelinad shouted orders, drawing his men into a jagged line that faced the direction from which Ocanar would come.

After a few moments, the trail sounds that had alerted the lookout grew loud enough for everyone to hear. Shortly thereafter, the first of Ocanar's band topped the small rise to the west. Murmurs of surprise arose among Pelinad's own troop as they saw the procession come forward.

"Mail," the rebels whispered. "Some of them are in mail."

"Yes, Ocanar and at least a dozen more."

"And the total number—he comes with unexpected strength."

"Silence," Pelinad snapped, but Jemidon barely noticed the command. He had expected Ocanar's master to be the same as Canthor, another fraudulent sorcerer manipulating the gullibilities about an art that was no more. But instead, what followed the line in front was a shock.

"Melizar!" Jemidon cried. "And the men in mail. They must be Nimrod and the Pluton mercenaries."

Canthor cuffed Jemidon in the arm as a warning. Jemidon looked back, surprised, and then dropped his eyes from Pelinad's disapproving stare. Fidgeting uncomfortably, he waited with the others, watching the troop pour over the hill and form into another straggly rank, a few pike lengths from Pelinad's own. He saw his father march up with the last, in a clump of older villagers, all with faces set in grim lines. But he was already numb from the jolt of Melizar's appearance and gave the second surprise little thought. Both troops spread out to span the depression from lip to lip, each a single row deep, alternating clumps of men and large gaps. Despite the attempts of each leader to make his following appear the larger, Jemidon estimated that the forces numbered about the same.

"Greetings, brother," the red-bearded man in front hailed. He alone wore an embroidered surcoat, and the morning sun glinted off a cap of steel. "The hills speak of an increase in your might. Had I not been augmenting myself, then your size might have begun to rival even my own."

"The lord's burden grows too oppressive." Pelinad moved forward to answer the greeting. "Two nights ago my following tripled. Tomorrow, if I approach the village, it will probably double again."

"A day too late." Ocanar forced a laugh. "I have already made the sweep while you were fussing over the

237

harvest of a single field. Look at my legion." He waved a thick arm to those filling in behind. "At least two hundred, trained freetoilers, and ready to fight. Yes, two hundred. It is clear that the momentum has swung my way. The rebellion is growing, and I am the center. The time for timid confusion is over. I charge you to accept my command, Pelinad. Swear allegiance to me as leader, so that we may strike Kenton's strength rather than poke with petty irritations at his periphery."

"Command is not measured by mere numbers." Pelinad pointed at Jemilor and those around him. "If I wanted to enlist the old men and the lame, I could have done so a year ago. No indeed, my raid was strategic. Because of it, I have garnered an element of great power." He motioned Canthor to come forward. "Henceforth I battle with a craft far removed from simple thaumaturgy. Here is my sorcerer, Ocanar, and from no less than Morgana itself."

Ocanar looked at Canthor as the bailiff walked forward. He frowned and pulled at his beard. "The village whispers that sorcery is no more," he said slowly. "And this man wears no robe with a logo. His walk is that of a fighter, not the shuffle of the masters I have seen."

"Look me in the eye and we will test the truth here and now." Canthor put his hands on his hips. "Let us see to what extent the village talk is true."

Ocanar took a step backward and threw his hand across his face. "Whatever resources we have should be tested in battle," he said quickly. "It is folly to waste them fighting between ourselves."

"Allow me to accept the challenge to your place." Melizar glided forward to stand by Ocanar. "Let the so-called master pit his skills against the powers that are mine."

"Ocanar speaks with good judgment." Pelinad put his hand on his sword hilt. "There is no need for confrontation."

Melizar hesitated. His deep cowl slowly scanned the line of Pelinad's men, all grasping weapons. Like cranked crossbows, they tensely waited the signal that would release their restraint. Ocanar's troop responded in kind.

238

For a long moment, no one moved. All eyes were on the leader to see what would happen next.

"A fight here in the foothills sheds none of Kenton's blood," Melizar said at last. "And it is not according to my plan. Perhaps I do agree, Ocanar. The battlefield is best. There is no need to test this so-called master now. Let him show his merits in the pass, and then all can judge the true prowess of his craft."

Jemidon bit his lip. Melizar knew full well that nothing remained of sorcery. The stranger was maneuvering Canthor and Pelinad into a position from which they were bound to fail. But right now, he could say nothing. His own position was too tenuous. And it was just as well that Melizar did not recognize him as one who had disrupted Trocolar's scheme in the grotto. Later, when he knew more, he could formulate the best course of action.

Ocanar tugged on his beard, looked at Melizar, and then glanced across to where Canthor stood. "Yes, tomorrow can be the judge. Pelinad, do you abide by it? The one of us whose power best decides the battle, then he is to lead us both."

"What battle?" Pelinad asked. "We do not yet have the strength to confront Kenton in his keep, even with both of us acting together. And soon he is to be fortified by a troop of the prince's own from Searoyal."

"It is your good fortune that we have met," Ocanar said. "Your ignorance would otherwise prove quite costly." He turned and forced a laugh that his men picked up in chorus. "This troop from Searoyal. No doubt you have seen some trace?" He turned back to mock Pelinad. "What would happen if they came upon you unaware?"

"In truth, we have seen nothing," Pelinad said. "We have been in these hills, planning for our successful raid."

"You would have seen nothing, even if you had been on the plain!" Ocanar roared. "They do not beat upriver for all to see, so that we can melt away." He waved a fleshy palm to the east. "No, they proceed by stealth in the next valley. Through Plowblade Pass they intend to come—to fall upon us in our lairs and thrash us from behind is their plan."

Ocanar paused, sucking in his breath. "But we are the ones who will stage the ambush. It is into our trap *they* will fall, not us into theirs. And after our victory, the plains will erupt with fire. Not a single man will hold back. Kenton and the others will be swept from the fields. It will be a true rebellion at last." Ocanar gazed off into the distance, savoring his thoughts, then fixed Pelinad with a hard stare. "You dispute my leadership, Pelinad. But by the laws, on what grounds? Certainly not your vision; you show as much imagination as an ambulator upon his mill."

"It was I who found the truth," Melizar said before Pelinad could reply. "Nimrod has many friends in the royal garrisons. Let us keep the importance of my contributions firmly in focus, Ocanar. I have been deceived once by your kind. This time there is to be no misunderstanding."

"Our agreement still stands," Ocanar said. "I see no reason to change it. You come with a dozen men in mail, fully trained fighters whom you offer to be my captains. And they have bullied my rabble into fighting shape, I do not deny it. Aid me in plucking Kenton from his keep, and what you ask shall be yours, even if I do not understand why you want it so."

"You find it strange, do you not, that my lust is not for a manor and rows of humble servants? Those trappings, Ocanar, will all come in the proper time. For now, I desire only a halt of all thaumaturgy. After the unlocking, I will need nothing more. And what better way to achieve what I wish than the chaos of insurrection? Unlike sorcery and magic, the craft is too widespread for the contradiction to be effective any other way."

Melizar paused, and his voice hardened. "And in the end, we shall see whose fiefdom is the greater. A single valley is not enough to interest even the least able pilot, and among them I am the first."

"As I have said, it is agreed." Ocanar waved his arm in irritation. "I have heard enough of your mumbled nonsense before. Just make sure that your rock rumblings and strange images are ready when they are needed."

240

"I begin my preparations for tomorrow now," Melizar said, motioning back to the hill over which he had come. "It is somewhat paradoxical that the power of thaumaturgy, which makes the transition so difficult, also greatly mitigates the unlocking."

"Your cozy tent provides the catalyst for much grumbling among the men," Ocanar said. "You should sleep on the ground like my men."

"Warmth?" Melizar said. "Rest? It is not for those that the Maxim of Perturbations was vitalized in the grotto. Which would you rather? Push a pack train along these trails, or have a single minion effortlessly guide my possessions as they are guided now?"

Ocanar did not respond. Jeminod looked to the crestline and saw a large tent float over the rise. It was Drandor's, the one that had caught his eye in the bazaar on Morgana. Its faded canvas hung in loose folds; coarse stitching bound swaths of different colors together in jagged seams. But, unlike the structure on the island, no guy ropes or stakes were to be seen. The bottom side panels gently rippled over the rock and scrubby plants, like the hem of a woman's dress. All the cloth danced and wavered as the whole structure bobbed along. A single man-at-arms held the end of a rope that ran to a ring attached above an entrance flap. He tugged the structure along without effort into a quickening morning breeze.

"Perturbations," Melizar repeated. "Perhaps not as dramatic as a dance which crashes open fissures in the earth, but guidance of small swirls of air at the right place and time can produce buoyant effects as good as the largest balloon."

With a soft whoosh of the tent, the men-at-arms halted a short distance behind Ocanar's line of men. Melizar glided into the opening and returned shortly with the drums and weights that Jemidon had seen briefly in the interior of the tent when Drandor had shown him around.

Drandor's tent. Drandor. Drandor and Delia. Jemidon's thoughts took another sudden turn. He ran his tongue over his teeth, trying to recapture the taste of his thoughts before Ocanar's band had arrived. The slave girl still felt important, as important as the lattice and the rest. But he was no closer to understanding the other pieces of the puzzle than he was to why she held such an allure.

"These will be used for our common benefit." Melizar waved the drums in Pelinad's direction. "Simple devices that aid me in my craft. Hold your men silent, so that I may receive all that they tell." He looked at Canthor. "If your master has any preparations to make as well, then gladly will Ocanar's legion return the favor."

Pelinad glanced at Canthor and then scowled. He flung his arm to the side in acquiescence and prepared to watch with the rest.

Jemidon tried to concentrate on what Melizar was doing as the cold one set the drums up in a row between the two lines of men and adjusted the tension in the heads, one by one. But the surge of his thoughts increased rather than subsided. He felt wispy tendrils in his mind, tantalizing glimmers of some insight that eluded his grasp. Deep inside, there seemed to be a tiny box whose lid was slowly beginning to open, oozing out marvels that had never been suspected, but which were nonetheless true.

Jemidon stared at Melizar. Even the proximity of the stranger was suddenly unsettling. Before, he had been mysterious. But now his every motion seemed to have an effect on Jemidon's thoughts. Each precise flick of the long, thin fingers crashed the images about in Jemidon's head. He felt the muscles tighten in his back. His mouth grew dry. A hint of queasiness floated up from his stomach. Something unpleasant was about to happen. For whatever the reason, now he wanted nothing to do with this stranger, nothing at all. Cautiously, Jemidon slumped to the ground and tightened his arms about his chest.

"Seven drums," Melizar said to Ocanar. "Seven drums, one for each of the laws."

"I am a fighter, not a practitioner of the arts," Ocanar responded impatiently. "The details of your craft are not my concern."

"Perhaps it is a weakness," Melizar said. "It gives me a perverse pleasure to display my workings for all to see and have none understand the slightest glimmer of what

242

truths they mirror. Well spoken, Ocanar. It is the blind devotion to the narrow perspective of your kind that gives me the greatest assurance that a pilot and his manipulants shall succeed."

Melizar selected a small weight that was not wired to a drumhead and gently placed it in the center of the first tight membrane. The tare barely dimpled the surface. "The new sorcery," Melizar said. "And there are no animations, as the lack of depression shows." He placed another weight on the next drum in line, and it sagged further into the thin, translucent covering. "The tent," he said. "So close to the nexus that it alone has a strong effect."

The next three were tested in quick succession, each one pulling down the drumhead by about the same amount. "Alchemy and wizardry, three laws in all," Melizar continued. "They will be the last, after we are sure of the victory." He looked at the final two drums in the line and simultaneously moved a weight to the center of each one. Instantly, the tares snapped from his fingertips and, with what looked to Jemidon like a force far stronger than the pull of the ground, the weights distorted the planes with deep, cone-shaped depressions.

Melizar rubbed his fingertips together and then looked through a collection of small metal rings mixed with the weights. He selected one from the rest and placed it on the warped drumhead, over the indentation caused by the tare. Instantly, it disappeared from sight into the hole. "Excellent," he said. "The workings of the art are not as nearby as a vault, but they are widespread and strong. The unlocking will proceed better than I first would have thought."

"Well," Ocanar demanded impatiently, "what does your reading portend?"

"That the unlocking should be now, when it is easiest," Melizar replied. "Before, I was too cautious, when there was no need. Now I know that it does not matter. There are none here who can tug in directions other than my own. Yes, I will unlock the nexus now and then be ready when the rebellion has reduced thaumaturgy to a level from which I can proceed."

Melizar bent to the ground and released the tension in the drumheads. He stored the apparatus back in the tent and then indicated silently to Ocanar that he would be but a moment more. In a fashion almost as theatrical as Holgon's, he removed from a chain on his belt a small cubical structure that was painted with a crosshatching of smaller squares.

No, not painted squares, Jemidon thought as he watched Melizar manipulate the solid, twisting faces in a series of rapid rotations that his eye could barely follow. It was a collection of smaller cubes, bound together and yet able to move in several independent directions, creating and destroying intricate patterns as they came together in varying juxtapositions. There were six sides and six different colors on the small cubes. Could the structure be manipulated so that—

Just as the thought formed, Jemidon saw Melizar stop and display the solid for all the onlookers to see. The random patterns of the small, colored squares on the faces of the larger cube were now all homogeneous. In less than the time one could hold his breath, Melizar had solved the unusual puzzle.

Puzzle? Jemidon frowned at why he thought of the cube in that way. It was a puzzle, yes, but certainly of much greater significance than that. And what sort of mechanism inside would allow the small cubes in the corners to rotate about three independent axes—?

Jemidon gasped. The impending uneasiness that had forced him to sit roared suddenly through his being like a wild wind. He was aware of a great snap that released some inner restraint and cast him adrift. Like a swimmer struggling against the current for the shore, he felt himself swept away. Like one diving off a cliff in a dizzying spin, he sensed a tingling thrill radiate out from the pit of his stomach to his fingertips.

Jemidon closed his eyes, but it did not help. Coins, changers, cube puzzles, all danced in his head, streaking by faster and faster, becoming glowing blurs that fused into a distant background with no landmarks. Jemidon clutched his arms around his chest tighter and slowly rocked back and forth. With deliberate effort, he breathed deeply and tried to blot out the dizzying thoughts. The words of Melizar and the others dimmed as he concentrated. He was missing the preparations for the battle, but he did not care.

Onward he seemed to streak, lashing out to grab at the formless glows as they sped by. With numbing impact, they ripped through his hands as he continued on his way. Jemidon strained to strengthen his grip and, after countless failures, held one for a moment, before his fingers let go. His body seemed to whip around, losing some of its momentum and slowing its mad rush. He reached out and held onto the next a little longer, pulling the glow along, his fingers slowly sliding off its rough and bumpy surface. Again and again, in the image in his mind, he flailed his arms to grasp the blobs and, with each successful contact, he decreased the blinding rush. The forms took on detail and shape, as individual coins, changers, and cubes, each with a unique structure differentiated from the shapeless glows farther away. He seemed to slow to a fast run, then to a trot, and finally to a gentle drift that carried him along.

Gradually, after how long a struggle he could not tell, Jemidon opened his eyes. The sense of motion persisted, but with a much lower intensity. He still felt as if he were falling, but the acceleration was not nearly as great as it had been at first. The images of the streaking lights faded into the background of the reality around him. Melizar and the tent were gone, presumably back over the hilltop. Both Ocanar's and Pelinad's bands were in their separate camps. Jemidon looked up at the one man standing patiently before him.

"If you are finished with the dreaming, then I have a suggestion," his father said. "Ask to be that Melizar's apprentice. Perhaps he can teach you a thing or two."

CHAPTER FOURTEEN

The Pendulum Swings

JEMIDON stirred uneasily and flexed his cramped muscles. The advance scouts had moved through the pass at dawn. The main body of the troop from Searoyal should have marched into the ambush over an hour ago. But the road winding down the mountainside was clear. No cloud of dust or creaking wagon wheels disturbed the serenity of the morning.

The pass itself was still in shadow on Jemidon's right. A narrow cleft barely four men wide, it looked like a deep furrow in freshly plowed ground. From where Jemidon was hidden behind the rocks at the side of the trail, he could not see all the way through the notch to the other side. Beyond the crest on the downslope that eventually led to Kenton's barony, Ocanar's band huddled in concealment, waiting for the royal companies to march by. They lay armed and ready, as did Pelinad's men across the wagon ruts from where Jemidon crouched.

Inwardly, Jemidon seethed. Why was he behaving the way he was? The object of his quest had appeared virtually as a gift, and aligned on the same side, at that. For over two months, he had pushed to achieve an encounter and now, with it in his grasp, his thoughts kept dancing aside to other things.

Jemidon looked at Canthor, slumped peacefully beside him, and shook his head. "How can you be so calm?" he asked. "You understand as well as I that Ocanar has manipulated Pelinad into an impossible position. Melizar is on the top of one of the crags which frame the pass. He will be able to shake the earth and deliver the avalanche on schedule, splitting the royal troops in twain. I have

246

seen his prowess before. But you can make no illusion that will terrify those on this side as we fall upon their rear. Pelinad will have no special aid."

"The avalanche will be enough." Canthor stretched and yawned. "That and the attack from behind will make up for our lack of mail and sharp weapons. I will say some meaningless words and then join with the others pouring onto the trail. And when the swords start swinging, no one will remember whether the hesitation of the opponents was due to surprise or a fanciful image."

"But experienced troops from Searoyal!" Jemidon said.

"The toll will not be light," Canthor agreed. "Yet there will be enough booty in the end for those who are quick and skillful."

Jemidon looked at the scythe that was lying nearby and then at the thick-bladed sword in Canthor's lap. "Such a view is perhaps easier for one who has seen battle before," he said. "Easier for one who, at least, has the proper tools of the trade."

"Stay close and guard my rear." Canthor shrugged. "You will fare as well as I. And speak no more of tools. My head is full of your babble about drums and weights."

"I cannot help it," Jemidon said. "My thoughts keep circling what I have seen. Like a rhyme that persists in your head, the images remain fresh and do not fade. You see, the distortion of the drumhead must indicate the degree a craft is being exercised. When Melizar placed a tare on the one that he said represented sorcery, it remained flat. That is reasonable enough, since, except for one of his followers, there are none who know how to practice it. But the drum for thaumaturgy became a deep cone. The art was widespread, he said. It seems clear, once you think of it. What else can it mean?"

"Why speculate when the answers are so near?" Canthor asked. "You had a whole day to ask this Melizar of his craft and yet you did not. He is an ally. We strike for a common cause. At worst, he would refuse the request. Anything else would teach you more than you know now."

"So says my father." Jemidon sighed. "So cry my memories of Kenton's feast hall and the fields of wheat. And

247

Melizar is the very reason I have returned to the land of my birth."

He paused and tried to sort out his feelings. "And yet, now that I have the opportunity, I am indeed quite hesitant. Somehow, I do not trust this strange one; yesterday, just his presence made me uncomfortable. In truth, his skills I long desperately to know. But now, now that I have experienced him more, something tells me that they must be ferreted away, not received as a gift."

Jemidon hesitated a second time and then smiled. "Besides, I have not done so badly on my own." He numbered the facts on his fingertips. "The first change in sorcery took place on Morgana; nowhere else in all of Arcadia was the craft practiced more. Magic has been nullified on Pluton, where the hoards of tokens were greatest. Here in the wheatlands, thaumaturgy dominates the other crafts. We have seen his use of the drums. It is as if Melizar seeks out where the concentration of the arts is strongest; somehow it makes the changes easier to come about."

"You have the heart of a master and not that of a warrior, to be sure." Canthor laughed. "All of your kind place so much importance on your secrets. And yet, what is the value of any of your efforts in the end? Petty entertainments, bookkeeping devices for trade, machines for the harvest. If not with your arts, then by some other means the same results would have been achieved."

Canthor patted the hilt of his sword. "Even in battle, it is still muscle and bone that determine the final result. Illusions of great monsters or slides of rock perturb the outcome this way or that, but in the end, a blade is in your gut or it is not. It is the warriors who sit on the thrones of Arcadia, Procolon across the sea, and the other kingdoms. Warriors are kings, and not the masters. Why, even the archmage commands only a small guard and a modest house of stone.

"Yes, embrace this Melizar. Learn what you can. In the end, he will be an advisor like the others, bowing deeply to some baron and scrambling for the gold that drops to the floor."

"If it is so simple, then why did I feel such uneasiness

248

yesterday when he was near?" Jemidon insisted, but Canthor stopped paying attention. The warrior put a finger to his lips and pointed down the trail.

Jemidon turned and saw a puff of dust billowing lazily skyward. The royal troop was coming at last. He felt the muscles in his face tighten. The feeling of drifting was still in his stomach, but it faded into an uncomfortable dimness. Now there were more immediate concerns than Melizar's manipulations with the drums.

Eventually, the marching column came into view. Triple file across the trail, the men-at-arms snaked into the cleft of the pass. A mounted commander, with pennant bearers stepping smartly at either side, led the procession. In full armor, he prodded his sweating horse up the incline. Behind the leading officers came the first company. On foot and dressed in mail, they breathed heavily from the labor of the climb.

Jemidon tensed as the head of the troop disappeared from view. After the second of the four companies had gone by, the rocks were to tumble. Each of the two outlaw bands would fall upon those on its side of the pass and then come to the aid of the other, if it were able to. The last of the first company entered the notch, and Jemidon waited expectantly for the next to follow.

But suddenly, just as the pennant bearers of the second group approached, the ground shook. A grinding rumble filled the air.

"Avalanche! Look out!" Jemidon heard someone shout. The flag carriers threw down their standards and turned to run. Small rocks and then heavier boulders began to rain down from above. Streaks of blurring gray fell from the cliffs. The groans of breaking stone and then of wounded men sounded over the deep, teeth-shaking rumble. Clouds of white and dirty brown billowed from the crest of the pass.

One pennant bearer was hit in the shoulder by a rock ricocheting in a flat arc, but he managed to stagger back before the larger boulders smashed him to the ground. In momentary confusion, the marching column stopped in the swell of dust and noise.

A horn sounded from the cover on the other side of the trail, and Pelinad's band jumped to the attack. With swords raised high, they thundered into the third company's flank.

"But Melizar was supposed to wait until two companies had passed through!" Jemidon shouted to Canthor. "And you were to stage your glamour among the wagons from behind! Now Pelinad charges on the side, rather than into the rear."

"A misbegotten plan, to be sure," Canthor said, suddenly alert. "Leave it to a practicer of the arts to bungle what chance we had." He grabbed his blade, bounded around the rock, and looked up and down the trail. "Quickly, follow me," he said after a moment. "With three companies rather than two, the line is too long; we are blocked from the others. But despite Pelinad's odds, we will fare better on his side of the trail than here. There is no time for a pretense of sorcery. Our hope will be to circle through the confusion of the avalanche, if we can."

Jemidon scooped up the scythe and ran after the bailiff as Canthor scrambled toward the pass. The attention of the royal troops was focused on the charge of Pelinad's men, and no one noticed them in the swirling dust. With practiced precision, the middle company turned its shields to meet Pelinad's attack, while the ones on either side made ready to engulf the flanks as the ragged line drew closer. Soon the rumble of the rock was replaced by the clang of steel and cries of pain.

Canthor jumped among the boulders with an agility that belied his age. He headed directly for the broken rock that had spilled out of the confines of the pass. The royal troops were giving the area a wide berth. In the confusion, Jemidon and the bailiff managed to reach the edge of the rubble before they were noticed. Without slowing, they climbed onto the fresh talus and began to scramble toward the other side of the trail.

But three-quarters of the way across, they were spotted by a pennant bearer. Before Canthor could reach him, he cried out an alarm. In answer, half a dozen men-at-arms turned from the rearmost line and started to climb the rubble. As they approached, Jemidon flung out the scythe at arm's length and struck the nearest in the temple. Two more closed on Canthor, who slashed with his blade, biting deep into the wrist of the one on the right. Undaunted, the other four pressed forward, one waving an axe, and Canthor stepped back in order not to expose his side. Watching the bailiff out of the corner of his eye, Jemidon retreated as well, taking a few steps up the slope.

One of the men-at-arms tried to circle from the left. Jemidon picked up a jagged rock at his feet and threw it squarely into the attacker's face, breaking his nose with a splash of blood. The remaining attackers continued forward, waving their swords in menacing arcs. Jemidon found himself retreating farther up the jumble of rocks, swinging the long scythe back and forth as best he could.

As he retreated, Jemidon jabbed tentatively point first, using the shaft like a pike. The man he faced reacted swiftly. Before Jemidon realized his mistake, a slashing sword hacked the blade from the head of the pole. Jemidon instinctively jabbed a second time, but saw his adversary continue forward, this time removing two more feet from the shaft. Jemidon threw the useless pole aside and turned to look at Canthor, to see what he should do. But as he watched, the bailiff stumbled on loose rock and fell onto his back, his sword sailing out of his hand.

The man-at-arms on the left ran forward, seeing his advantage, and swung his axe high over his head for a fatal plunge. Canthor threw his hand upward in a desperate attempt to ward off the blow, his eyes wide with the image of death. Then, like a drowning man grasping at leaves on the surface of a lake, he sang one of the sorcerers' chants. The three recitals tripped from his tongue faster than Jemidon had ever heard a glamour spoken before. He recognized it as the illusion for a windstorm. He saw Canthor scoop up a handful of dirt and pebbles and throw them in the axeman's face.

Then, as Canthor threw, Jemidon experienced a great lurching in his stomach. The feeling of drifting that had been submerged by the danger of battle boiled upward from where it had been pushed away. With a breathtaking

251

blur, Jemidon felt himself flung across some measureless space and time. His senses reeled. He was overcome by the same disorientation he had felt in the presence of Melizar and his drums.

As suddenly as it had come, the feeling vanished. Like a speeding arrow wrenched from the air in midflight, he jarred back into focus. His stomach was calm, the sense of falling was gone; everything was sharp and clear. It had all happened in an instant, and Jemidon blinked in surprise. He looked at Canthor's adversary and saw the man clutching his face and staggering backward, the axe flung aside on the rocks.

"The sand, the wind!" the man-at-arms shrieked. "It is worse than the high desert. We will all be buried alive!"

Canthor turned to face the others, who now approached with hesitation, looking at their comrade out of the corners of their eyes. Then they, too, dropped their weapons and staggered back. One threw up his forearm across his face. The other dropped to his knees, burying his head in his hands. Canthor turned questioningly to Jemidon. As their eyes met, Jemidon felt a sudden rush of skin-blistering wind and the bombardment of stinging sand.

"What is happening?" Canthor asked. "I do not know why I spoke as I did. It is strange what a man will say when he thinks the words are his last."

"Louder," Jemidon gasped. "Speak louder so I can locate where you stand." He staggered forward, arms across his face, hunched against what seemed like a buffeting gale. His ears roared with a deafening whir that almost drowned out all other sound.

"What nonsense is this?" Canthor persisted. "Stand straight and grab a weapon. We are not yet through."

"It is your charm," Jemidon shouted, trying to hear his own voice above the windscream that surged through his mind. "Somehow it worked. Somehow, someway, sorcery has been restored."

For a moment Jemidon heard no reply, and then, above the roar, Canthor's voice shouted back.

"Wait here," the bailiff yelled. "Wait here until I am

done. I will release you from the glamour after I have helped the others as best I can."

Jemidon tried to crack open his eyelids, but a feeling of swirling grit and dirt immediately forced them shut. He sighed and curled into a ball, helpless to do more than await the outcome of the battle.

After some measureless time, Jemidon heard the words that ended the illusion of the blasting sands. He stood and stretched, then blinked at what he saw. It was night, and the moon had nearly set. Upslope, barely a hundred feet from where he stood, ran the crestline of the mountains.

"I remember being led like a blind man and stumbling upward for an eternity," he said. His mouth was dry and felt full of old rags. "What happened? Why are we here?"

"My apology for taking so long to release you." Canthor clasped him on the shoulder. "But others had wounds more greivous than your discomfort. Putting as much distance between us and the pursuit was the primary goal. Enchanting away the pain, when we finally were able to stop, was the next. The royal troops have camped for the night. We can rest here until the dawn."

Jemidon looked about a second time with more care. The trail and pass were nowhere in sight. Below him stretched the downslopes of the mountains. Like the crumpled robe of a master, the ridges and folds disappeared into the blackness. The ground underfoot was smooth and nearly devoid of plants; it curved gently in a flat arc to form part of the rocky spine that ran to the horizon. Except for the camp, there were no other lights. Of Pelinad's band, barely forty remained huddled around two small fires of brush.

"I caused enough confusion with the glamours for the prince's men to fall back and regroup," Canthor answered Jemidon's questioning gaze. "It gave us enough time to withdraw. But by then, Pelinad and most of the others were gone." The bailiff shrugged. "The shirts of mail were too many. We did not attack from the rear as was our plan."

"Ocanar—why did he not appear?" Jemidon asked. "If we had to bear the brunt of three companies, then he would have had to face only one. He should have finished up quickly and scrambled over the rubble to come to our aid."

"It was only byrnies from Searoyal that we saw pouring back through the pass," Canthor said. "Not vests of leather, or scythes and flails. Somehow, despite the strange one's craft, I suspect that Ocanar fared no better than we."

Jemidon wearily sagged back onto the hard ground. "But why did we then retreat into the mountains?"

"There was no open path down the trail in either direction," Canthor said, "and by striving for the peaks, we were more likely to link up with what remained of Ocanar, if he was doing the same. Indeed, his thoughts did run in a similar path to mine. The lookouts on the crest have seen a tattered band on the far-side downslopes. In a few moments more, he will be here."

Jemidon grunted and looked at the dark line that marked the skyward limit of the peaks. Almost instantly, he saw Canthor's pronouncement come true. A triangle of black shadow poked above the crestline and then, beneath it, a rectangle with gently undulating sides. With a whoosh of air that Jemidon felt from where he sat, Drandor's tent settled on the crest.

Weary fighters appeared on either side, some dragging scythes and others totally unarmed. In twos and threes, they staggered down the slope into Canthor's camp. Silently, they slumped around the small fires.

One of two shirts of mail mingled with the rest. In a clump of lieutenants, Ocanar stomped down the slope, each step a thump of anger rather than the stumble of fatigue. The leader looked about and saw that only Canthor stood, of all of Pelinad's men. Stroking his beard, he approached and squinted in the dimness.

"Pelinad?" he asked.

"They follow me now," Canthor said.

"But you were only the sorcerer," Ocanar said.

"It was my skill as a man-at-arms more than any craft

254

that saved the few whom you see here." Canthor shrugged. "Glamours do not organize a retreat or pick the course of the march. But that is of no consequence. Because of the odds, how we fared should be no surprise. Why are you running along the crestline, too, rather than polishing shirts of mail and bragging to the villagers about your victory?"

"Ask the cold one who claims to be a master," Jemidon heard Ocanar growl. "We would rout them all without the loss of a single man, he said. And so, after the scouts had ridden by, we stood by the mouth of the pass, not even bothering to group into any sort of formation. It seemed amusing to watch instead the elaborate preparations, lanterns and focusing lenses, and the vast expanses of white linen on which some great glamour was to play. The royal troops were to be petrified, frozen in mid-stride. We were to be able to move among them unchallenged and slit their throats at will."

"The rock slide started prematurely," Canthor said. "Three-quarters of the men-at-arms were left on our side of the pass. What upset the timing of our plan?"

"The timing was perfect," Ocanar spat out. "That part Melizar accomplished as we had—" Ocanar stopped and looked at Canthor through narrowed eyes. He tugged at his beard, waiting for the bailiff to say more, but Canthor remained silent. "Yes, prematurely," Ocanar said slowly at last. "I meant to say the rock slide came too soon. Undoubtedly another miscalculation like the rest. It was all Melizar's fault and none of mine. Now he hides in his canvas contraption and awaits my wrath.

"But none of that matters. One hundred men-at-arms slashed their way through the white linen as if it were not there. My men in leather were unprepared. Nimrod tried to rally them, but they did not stand a chance. Of all who waited this morning, hardly a fifth are left alive."

Jemidon followed the wave of Ocanar's arm, as the last of the men came over the crest. He saw his father trudging down the slope, one leg ringed with a dirty rag. He scrambled to his feet and ran to greet the older man

255

with an embrace, relief mixing with guilt that he had forgotten about the perils that Jemilor must have faced.

"Melizar let me ride in his tent," Jemilor said as they disengaged. "Without his assistance, I doubt I could have kept up the pace. But I had followed his instructions well, just as he taught. There should be no blame for me that the sorceries did not work as planned."

Jemilor sagged to the ground and motioned Jemidon to follow. "Listen, my son," he said, pointing at his leg. "The cut is jagged and is slow to close. I am lucky to have gotten this far. An inch to the left, and tomorrow you would be questing on your own once again."

"Do not speak of such things as this," Jemidon chided. "If you can walk away from the battlefield, you will live to see the next. You know the saying as well as I."

"Melizar's apprentice." Jemilor waved away the words. "I want you to promise me now. He is most eager to take on all who will follow his direction without question. Do as he says and you may yet serve my memory with pride."

"But who is he and where is he from?" Jemidon asked. "I want his secrets, yes, but what is his ultimate intent?"

"He fights to overthrow Kenton and his barony," Jemilor replied. "That is enough recommendation for me. Promise me, Jemidon. Without that, I will not rest in peace."

"You will feel much better in the morning," Jemidon said. "And I do not think that the strange one will accept kindly one who sent magic swords swinging through his plans in the grotto."

"Promise me," Jemilor insisted. "After all that has passed, do not deny me one last kernel of hope."

Jemidon looked again into his father's pale face. He sighed and placed his hand on the older man's shoulder. "It is not that I have not tried, Father. Believe me, I want the robe as much as you."

"We could have served him both together today," Jemilor said. "Setting up the lantern and stretching the sheets you would have found easy enough to do. And your arms are yet strong and your reactions quick. Who could say

256

what the difference might have been as we raced for the protection of the tent?"

"I am a man, full-grown," Jemidon said. "The quest I pursue is now my own."

"Your own?" Jemilor turned his head away. "Was it for that that your sister gave you the coin?"

Jemidon rose and stretched. His father had long since fallen into a fitful sleep. And he had made up his mind. Whatever caution his instincts threw in the way could not stand against the logic of everyone else's counsel. Slowly he climbed the distance to the crestline. Puffs of air skittered around his ankles as he approached the tent. The flicker of candlelight escaped from the hem of the canvas as it danced over the uneven ground.

At the tentflap, Jemidon reviewed what he planned to say. Perhaps stressing what he already knew would be best. He believed in the Postulate of Invariance, even if no one else seemed to give it great weight. Besides, ferreting out the secrets was no longer to be his intent. Despite his reservations, he would ask to be taught. He would find out by direct explanation, rather than by deduction, what he needed to know. He would learn the means to become a master and to cast off at last the burdens that pushed him on.

Nervously, Jemidon fingered the brandel about his neck. He felt the uneasiness in his stomach begin to grow. He could sense how the discomfort would increase as he drew closer to the cold one inside the tent. He did not want to enter, or to offer assistance, when deep inside he felt a distrust that no argument would chip away. Somehow in the end, their objectives could never be the same. But he thought of his father sleeping restlessly down the slope and of Canthor's advice given with no hidden bias. Against their words, he had only vague feelings to argue himself away. Cautiously he pushed aside the flap.

Melizar slowly turned as Jemidon looked inside. "Yes, what more does Ocanar want? I have given him the explanation. It must have been a great attempt at sorcery on the island. Probably far more powerful than this world

257

has ever seen. So great that even here, the intensity was strong enough to force the animation to be the least contradiction. The effect varies as the cube of the distance. It is not my concern if he refuses to understand."

Jemidon tightened his arms around his stomach to quiet the rising discomfort. He saw that the interior of the tent looked much as it had on Morgana. Two small candles provided most of the light. The flap leading to the rear chamber was closed. The now-familiar lattice leaned against one of the supporting poles. Delia's counter was gone. On the bare ground, Melizar had been studying his drums and weights. Except for the buzz of the imps about the cold one's head, there was no other motion.

"You have worked with others before," Jemidon said. "Drandor the trader and Holgon the magician. Do you have available the position for yet another apprentice?"

Melizar glided forward until he stood directly facing Jemidon. A slender hand jutted from the flowing robe and poked Jemidon in the shoulder. A wave of intense cold that numbed his arm sent a shiver down his back. He looked from the darkly painted nails, up the draped arm, to the cowl that hid everything but reflections of the candlelight in deep-set eyes.

"But more important than that," Jemidon blurted, "who are you? From where do you come?"

"Inquisitiveness is not the mark of a good follower," Melizar replied as the cowl moved closer in the dimness. "Obedience is the virtue that will garner the greater reward."

"Even if the reward is knowledge?" Jemidon asked.

"Even if the reward—" Melizar stopped and studied Jemidon's face. "I have seen you before," he said at last. "You were the one who tried to imitate the magician in the grotto."

"That is in the past and does not matter," Jemidon said quickly. "We now work for a common cause. Teach me more of the Postulate of Invariance. I wish to learn."

"The Postulate of Invariance! Who told you of that?" Melizar asked softly. "The demon swore on his eggclutch that it was only me and my manipulants. None of the rest were able to follow."

"I deduced it from what I have seen," Jemidon answered. "Sorcery deactivated and another craft in its place." He paused and wrinkled his forehead. "Only now it seems the pendulum has swung back the other way. The Rule of Three possesses vigor. Even Canthor was able to use it to delude the royal troops. No doubt that was why they were able to march through the animations on your side of the pass. They saw only a clever lantern show with no power to enchant."

"Of course," Melizar said slowly. He grabbed the cube at his waist and fondled it with his fingertips. "The sorcerer with the deceit that his powers were still whole. I had dismissed him entirely. He must have tried a glamour in the battle, just before the animation was to begin. Not many leagues, but only yards away. I was close enough for the shift to take place."

Melizar paused, head bowed for a moment, and then turned his attention back to Jemidon. "But the words would not be enough. Merely mouthing the charm without producing the effect does not give any contradiction."

Jemidon frowned, trying to follow the train of Melizar's thoughts. "It was the Song of the Shifting Sands," he said, "and Canthor threw a handful of dirt into the face of an assailant as he spoke."

"As simple as that." Melizar's voice took on a soft tinkle, like that of a delighted child. "I need not embellish my original plan. There is not some great sorcerer against whom I must pit the excuses for masters that I have. A simple animation will be more than enough to make the charms down the slope the smaller contradiction."

Melizar waved his arms at the drums. "The surface is merely dimpled. Two weak glamours, at most three or four. I will awaken Drandor to perform the animation and another to witness the effect. It will be enough within the confines of the tent."

"My apprenticeship," Jemidon said as Melizar started for the rear chamber. "You have not yet answered to the reason why I have come."

"The Postulate of Invariance is not the concern of any manipulant," Melizar said. "To him, such information is utterly of no use. And the fact that a metalaw holds interest for you harms, rather than abets, your suit. Wait patiently. I will decide your fate when the more important task is done."

Jemidon frowned as Melizar disappeared behind the flap. For a moment, he debated whether or not he should follow. But before he could decide, the strange one returned, stroking the cube at his side.

"They will be fully awakened in a moment," Melizar said. "Time enough for the part that I must perform." He unlatched the cube from his waist and began to twist it as he had done the day before.

Jemidon started to reply, but suddenly he felt the queasiness in his stomach grow and he sagged to the ground. Once again, his thoughts began to take off on their own, running through chains of discordant logic that he could not control. Events and random facts danced in his head. Pieces of the puzzle, all perceived at once, somehow fitted into a coherent whole. Morgana, the center of sorcery, on the night of celebration before the awarding of the prize . . . Pluton and the vault in the grotto—taking away tokens and then adding to them with more . . . Stopping the pumps before Holgon worked his transformation with the dove . . . The rebellion in the wheatlands—Melizar's being delighted that thaumaturgy was so strong, after he had told Ocanar that his goal was for it to stop . . .

The mental brew frothed and bubbled, growing in intensity and carrying Jemidon farther and farther away from where he willed. He imagined a box of secrets with the lid cracking open and the scent of its delights swirling out, to mix with the other experiences he had witnessed along the way.

Through glazed eyes, he watched Melizar finish his ritual with the cube. Dimly and uncertainly, he perceived someone—Drandor, perhaps—manipulating what might have been animated projections. But as before, the scenes blurred in streaks of light and dark. He felt as if he were on some great beast, charging across a featureless plain,

260

or like the shot of a catapult arcing across the sky, a monolith of energy that crushed whatever was in its way. He cried out, trying by sheer will to force the plummet to stop. The last of his senses whirled into incohesion.

Then, after an indefinite time, and with a lurch that shook his body in a giant convulsion, Jemidon darted his eyes open. The feeling that had built so intensely was just as suddenly gone. Everything was clear and in focus. All senses were restored. From outside the tent, he heard a cry of pain and, following that, another louder than the first. Instantly he knew what had happened. "Sorcery again is gone," he mumbled. "Canthor's soothing charms are no more."

He looked quickly around the tent, hoping to see what he wanted. "Delia!" he exclaimed as her slender form caught his eye. He felt his heart race with a surge of pleasure. "You are here, as I suspected. And Drandor—"

Jemidon stopped short as he looked more closely at the trader, now standing beside a small lantern and a scatter of transparent images on the floor. One arm dangled at his side, flat and shapeless, like an empty glove. His face sagged to the side, lips curving down to where the firm line of the jaw should have been; the cheek was only a loose bag of flesh.

Jemidon's eyes darted back to Delia and scanned her body from head to toe, searching for additional disfigurements. But except for the vacant stare produced by the animation, she was apparently whole. She wore the same gown in which he had seen her last. A band of iron still circled her left wrist. He let out his breath and finally looked back at Melizar as the strange one put away his cube.

"What has happened to him?" he asked, pointing at Drandor. "Was he exposed to the fighting as well?"

"My helpers, my manipulants," Melizar responded, accenting the last word. "No, they are too precious to waste in such a manner. But negligence cannot go unpunished." He swept his arm in Delia's direction. "This second one

261

should never have been allowed to get away. Nor did the pets I gave him thrive under his care."

"By all the laws," Drandor slurred, "stop him before he does more. The cave beneath the tent, the sleepers, the sucking! I can feel the dissolving inside. Stop him before there are more."

"Silence," Melizar commanded. "Silence, or the manipulants shall have fresh marrow before it is needed." He turned and faced Jemidon. "You spoke of apprenticeship. There is more than one way that you can serve."

Jemidon rose groggily to his feet. Something significant had just happened. It was another fact to add to the other thoughts that his insides insisted were important. "Your sorcery with the animations," he said. "Now it has the basis of law, and not the other."

"This woman was the first to experience it," Melizar said. "The enactment was simple, but it was sufficient to tip the scales."

Another moan pierced the canvas walls of the tent. Jemidon thought of what it must be like to have pain suddenly return. The first crisis must have been in surprise as much as in anguish. As Melizar said, a simple performance of the animation and then sorcery was no more.

Jemidon sucked in his breath at the thought. First must have come Drandor's performance, and then afterward there was no more sorcery. Just as Canthor had flung the rocks before there was any effect. Animation preceding the Rule of the Threshold. Blinding with pebbles because the words did not yet work. The action and then the law.

Suddenly everything fell into place. The whirling events of the past marshaled in step and left him with no doubt.

"Contradictions," he said. "You speak of contradictions and which ones are the least. When things are drifting, when somehow the laws are cut loose, the seven that will be chosen will be those that best explain what is happening—the seven which leave the least contradictions outside their scope. The node of the lattice will be the one which best fits the happenings around it. Enactments of others become exceptions and wither away.

"And you performed the unlocking with the cube," Jemidon rushed on. He had to articulate it all before the thread faded from his grasp. "Yes, an unlocking, a release of the grip which holds the laws as they are. With the cube, you control when the change has an opportunity to take place. Only when you set the conditions can the various laws compete for dominance.

"The unlocking is easier when you are near the power of the crafts, but once it is done, you want it the other way. Otherwise things will remain exactly as they are. On Morgana, you must have decoupled during the performance for the prince; and then at the celebration afterward, when all the masters were filling themselves with ale, Drandor enacted his animations on the beach. It was what I saw from the cliff top—a single glamour that would have power according to the new law, but far closer to you than any sorceries is Procolon across the sea. It was the least contradiction; the law that explained more then was the Rule of the Threshold, not the Rule of Three.

"And in the grotto, you had Trocolar add the additional tokens to the vault holdings so that the strength of magic would be stronger and the disconnection easier to make. Many magic tokens; that is why you had Drandor seek the sorcerer's prize. But before Holgon walked through his ritual, the pumps were stopped and all the tokens safely secured in chests out of sight, so that no one could see. Again the new magic was the one that held sway.

"Later, when I returned with the sword, you were sure to have three instances of the Maxim of Perturbations to two for that of Perseverance."

"You are not speaking like a manipulant," Melizar said. "You have thought about things too much."

"And these first attempts have no real power at all." Jemidon ignored the interruption. "Drandor's initial screening used some natural property of the eye to simulate motion; Holgon's sleight of hand in the vault moved the dove. They were contrived to be as close to the new laws as possible, even if they were shadows of what would come to pass. They were boosts to shove things from one node in the lattice in the direction you wanted, rather than in a random drift you could not control.

"And even Canthor in the pass! You unlocked the laws when Ocanar and Pelinar met. That was responsible for the drifting feeling I felt—the feeling I experienced each time the laws could be shifted from one node in the lattice to another. Only this time you planned to wait until after the insurrection had spread before nudging the transition on its way—until the practice of thaumaturgy had fallen to a low enough level that the shift could be easily made. But by chance, Canthor's attempted glamour came first. His words and the tossing of the sand were an example of a traditional charm. Without the planned animation, of the Rule of the Threshold there was none. The Rule of Three dominated, and sorcery was restored.

"It fits, it fits, all of it. There is a second metalaw. The, the—the Axiom of Least Contradiction, you probably call it. Yes, the rule follows from the example. That is how you have manipulated all the transformations that have swept sorcery and magic away."

Jemidon paused for breath. His skin tingled with excitement. Coming to Melizar directly had not been such a bad idea after all. The closeness of the cold one and the swing back to the Rule of the Threshold together had catalyzed the synthesis that had been building in his mind all along.

"You asked to be an apprentice," Melizar said in a whisper that Jemidon could barely hear. "Perhaps it is indeed better that you serve." He waved his arm over his head, and imp light twinkled into tiny points of brilliance. The air in the tent grew chillingly cold. "I demand complete obedience. When lithons soar close to one another, there is no margin for less. The three metalaws are for my concern. You must forget the two you have learned."

"Your plan is to change them all, isn't it?" Jemidon asked. "One by one, until only your minions can perform any of the crafts. The thaumaturges, the alchemists, the magicians, the sorcerers, the wizards, even the archmage, all will be powerless against you. Despite what Canthor says, it is not men-at-arms who hold the balance in their

264

hands. One who has exclusive command of unknown crafts would rule the world against the sharpest blades."

"This world, the stars, your whole universe," Melizar said. "Ocanar sulks in defeat; but for me, the battle has accomplished almost as much as I planned. I now know why the animations did not work and have no great sorcerer with whom to contend. Tomorrow, with the help of some simple animations, the villagers will believe in a setback of the royal troops, despite whatever else this Kenton may say. The timing is right; the passions will be inflamed. In a fortnight's time, the plains will vibrate to the stomp of thousands of scythes and flails. More than four companies from Searoyal will have to come. And with the harvest stopped, thaumaturgy will be easy to push aside.

"I will have gone from a single greedy trader, from a dozen men-at-arms, to a whole kingdom at my command. Alchemy will be next and wizardry after that. In the end, everything will be mine."

Melizar paused and jabbed Jemidon on the shoulder. "Yes, be my apprentice. The choice is a wise one. Serve without failure and you will be rewarded well."

Jemidon held his breath. The goal that motivated his coming to the tent had been achieved. Even more, he now understood not one metalaw but two. But the disquiet that had impeded him before was still there.

He looked at Delia, who was still staring blankly into the distance, and fingered the coin around his neck. He thought of his father sleeping on the downslope and what the old man would say. With one decision, he could exorcise all the ghostly burdens and be close to what he wanted for himself as well. Perhaps with time, when Melizar realized his true worth, he could learn more and complete the last pieces of the puzzle. He glanced at the cold one's cube and then looked up to stare at Drandor's slack-jawed face.

But at what price was he willing to pursue his quest? The robe of the master was supposed to bring the respect of peers and followers—a proof that he, too, was a man. Would it be there, if won by treachery and guile? If the

265

order of all things were destroyed in the process? If he were the lackey of one so cold and strange? Jemidon drew his lips into a firm line. He wanted the robe, but not if he lost everything else in exchange.

"No," he said quietly, his voice as soft as Melizar's own. "I have changed my mind. It is too much power. The laws were not meant to be altered."

"Whence I came, the laws were not meant to stay the same." Melizar stepped forward. "But no matter. By one means or another, you will serve. Seize him, Drandor. If he chooses not to offer his mind and muscle to me, then the manipulants will enjoy his marrow."

Jemidon stepped back, wishing that he had a weapon. As he did, he saw the imp light about Melizar's head brighten to a fiery incandescence. Too late, he tried to dodge a handful of dust that Melizar splashed into his face. He felt the beginning of a numbing torpor. Then nothing.

CHAPTER FIFTEEN

Door into Elsewhere

JEMIDON felt a gentle touch on his forehead and forced open his eyelids. A bouncing glow of reddish light and strands of golden hair filled his view.

"Delia!" he said thickly. "It was you whom I came to rescue."

"With about as much forethought as when we raced into the presentation hall." Delia pulled away to give him room. "And your discussion with Melizar seemed to focus on other things. Even though bound by the animation, I recall most of what was said."

Jemidon rose to sitting. He felt stiff and sore. His mouth was dry and the taste rancid, as if he had been awakened

266

from the middle of a drunken sleep. Hovering a few feet from his head was a large, glowing sprite, its bony arms crossed in front of a shallow chest and its legs coiled into a knot. The forehead bulged with bumps and mounds. Tufts of coarse hair protruded from tiny ears. The nose lay smashed across a broad and pockmarked face. Except for the whine of rapidly beating wings, it seemed like the well-preserved remains of a grotesque child.

Jemidon ran his hands over his leather vest, touching the reassuring smoothness of the coin about his neck and the lump of Benedict's changer underneath. He placed his palms down at his sides and felt a tingling from a surface that was glassy-smooth. As his senses returned, he detected the same vibration through his thighs. He looked around in the sprite light and saw rock everywhere. He and Delia were enclosed in a perfect sphere, centered on the small demon and showing no seam or exit. As if from the polished face stone of some great palace, specks of quartz and mica cast back pale reflections of the flickering luminescence.

"A rockbubbler," Delia said. "It can maintain a void several arm spans about itself in all directions, even at the greatest depths. One of the score or so that keep open a pit under Drandor's tent. And apparently I have some degree of control over this one. He responds to my bidding, as long as it does not conflict with his other instructions."

"The Law of Dichotomy," a small, squeaky voice radiated from the gently bobbing devil. "One of the two upon which wizardry is based. 'Dominance or submission.' There is no other choice." One small eye cocked to the side and stared at Delia. "I have a master and I must obey. I fulfill your request because it does not contradict and it is my choice."

"By whatever justification, the end result is the same," Delia said. "I instructed him how to trick two others of his kind with which he had a petty feud. And now he has kept his sphere just tangent to the others so that the manipulants could not find you, Jemidon, before you awoke." Delia stopped and shuddered. "Although with the fighting that will eventually happen above, they will have many from whom to pick."

"What has happened?" Jemidon shook his hands at arm's length to restore the circulation. Any excitement from being with Delia was muted by the remains of a deep lethargy. "Where are we? The last I clearly remember is Melizar casting some powder in my face."

"Torpordust," Delia said. "Something that can be made with the new magic. He uses it to slow prisoners for the manipulants."

"I thought it might have been a freezing."

"The cold does not come from Melizar. It is generated by the imps that circle his head. Without them, he would have to sleep with the rest. I suspect he can barely tolerate moving among us as it is. When he must concentrate deeply, he requires it to be even more frigid."

"Then where is he from?" Jemidon asked. "From what he has said, not across the sea or from another star in the sky."

"No, not another star." Delia shook her head. "Somehow, it is farther than that. I asked him once and he laughed. He said that on all our worlds the laws are the same. It was only through the demon's portals that one could journey whence he came."

"The realm of demons," Jemidon said. "It may well be the lands beyond the flame from which the djinn appear when they are beckoned."

"My master forbade me to speak of it, or I would tell," the sprite said. "But even in sleep, I must honor his will."

"These manipulants?" Jemidon asked. "Are they demons too?"

"No, I think not," Delia said. "Even demons would not behave as they do."

"But if not djinns, how can they exist behind the flame?"

Delia reached out and grabbed Jemidon's hand. "There is little else that I know. Little else except for some of the workings of Drandor's animations. Melizar has been teaching me the craft and has made sure that I remained unharmed. The cold one wants the trader to know he can be replaced if he does not continue to comply. There is

268

nothing with which Drandor can bargain, not even the exercise of the new sorcery."

"And I?" Jemidon looked around the featureless sphere. "What do I have that is any better?"

"At least you are fully awake," Delia said. "For four days you have slumbered, while I kept the rockbubbler apart from the rest. Now you must use your wits to aid me as you have done before. Come," she said. She turned until she was on hands and knees. "Follow the sprite. You will see what else lies in the rock under Drandor's tent."

Jemidon frowned as the small demon turned in Delia's direction and began to drift slowly away. Delia's answer to his question was not what he had hoped to hear. But before he could say more, he felt the sphere rotate beneath him, pushing with increasing firmness behind and then finally toppling him forward to sprawl by Delia's side. He looked up to see what appeared to be a tiny opening form in the curved wall directly ahead.

As Jemidon scrambled into a crawling position, the circle grew, revealing a larger cavern beyond. Sliding his hands along the smooth surface and pushing with his feet on the slope behind, he managed to keep up with the slow rotation of the sphere.

In a moment, the opening had expanded to the maximum extent. The rear of the bubble became a hemispherical bulge on a larger volume. Like a sealed chamber in a dungeon, the void in the rock was heavy with damp air and the smell of decay. The floor looked like the crate for an array of eggs, a lattice of shallow depressions that matched a similar set of indentations in the ceiling above. In between, in a more or less geometrical precision, hovered other rockbubblers, eyes closed and arms and legs crossed.

Like a rag doll flung aside, Drandor lay in the centermost sphere. The trader's eyes were barely open and his chest heaved with deep breaths. Occasionally he lashed out with his good arm, swatting the empty air. Dots of light showed where imps, much smaller than the hovering rockbubblers, flitted above him, dropping a fine mist of sparkling sand.

"More torpordust," Delia said. "It keeps the trader in lethargy until Melizar requires his efforts." Delia paused and swallowed. "And except for those, the manipulants, it would not matter."

Jemidon followed the sweep of her arm. On a large sled with rounded runners that fitted the curves of the floor, he saw six humanoid forms, dressed only with loincloths and all lying prone in apparent slumber. They were tall and slender, more suited for the dance than for wielding blades. Their skin was an almost translucent gray. Beneath the tough elasticity, Jemidon could see the course of the major arteries and veins. Half wore massive ornamentation, nose rings, necklaces, and anklets, their fine black hair coiled in elaborate swirls. Sharp planes of bone defined blocky faces. Filmy lids covered deep-set eyes. Below the bulge of the nose, each had large pinkish lips that looked like the suction cups of an octopus or squid. Cupped in each left hand was a can with holes in the lid. On a chain from the waist dangled small picks like those used in gemstone mines.

"I have seen them before," Jemidon said, "on Morgana, in Drandor's animation the night of the storm, the one that shifted the Rule of Three to the Rule of the Threshold."

"Too close," one of the nearest sprites interrupted Delia's reply. "First you move away, barely maintaining contact. Now you press in on my space, my innermost core. Back whence you came, prickly one. I would rather you not support my flank than push with so much pressure against my chest."

"Poxblisters," the sprite above Jemidon's head shot back. "For you there is no distance that pleases. You would be better off as a solitary. Always bickering, trying to force the swarm to your own natural harmonics. Never just accepting what resonates with the entire clutch."

"You are no better, mintbreath," the other replied. "Your wings must have been unbalanced in the egg. They have vibrated your brains to mush. You have no fre-

270

quency that stands above the noise. You keep flitting like a djinn in heat around the soft and golden one—and not even your master."

"Vibration is what makes the lips quiver and the foolish noises issue forth," Delia said. "It is strange that you would be one speaking of balance."

A high-pitched whine bounced around the room. Jemidon guessed that the other sprites were twittering at what she had said. The demon directly ahead snapped shut his mouth and, except for the hum of wings, the pit plunged into silence.

For a moment, nothing more happened. Then one of the manipulants suddenly stirred and crawled from the sled, sluggishly groping over the dimpled floor. Like a newborn puppy, he seemed to flounder instinctively toward food and comfort. The manipulant bumped against Drandor. With uncoordinated jerks, it closed around the trader's boneless forearm. Drandor's eyes flickered and his face contorted into a mask of strain. With glacial slowness, he struggled to crawl away, but the manipulant was slightly quicker and pinned him where he lay.

In staccato bursts of motion, the left hand with the shaker positioned over the trader's elbow. Jemidon saw a fine powder fall onto the pliant flesh, and then, after several misses, the large lips contacted the glistening surface. A loud slurping noise blended with the demons' hum. Drandor's entire body trembled; he opened his mouth with an ear-piercing scream.

"As Melizar would look without his hood," Delia said. "They suck the marrow through the skin after somehow dissolving the bone. That must be what keeps them alive as they wait. Apparently this place is so warm that they languish like lizards in a desert sun.

"Melizar let me remain awake so that I could avoid the manipulants," Delia continued. "He did not suspect that I would influence one of the sprites as well." Her voice shrank to a whisper. "I could have dragged the trader away, just as I did you. But each time I think of it, I also remember his crude sketches of my disfigurement, his tongs and pinchers, and the fact that it is because of him that I am here."

Jemidon hesitated, wondering what he should do. Drandor had released the beasts after them on Morgana. He had abducted Delia to this oppressive tomb. Jemidon looked again at the trader's mutilations. He felt the line of his own jaw and then the reassuring firmness of his forearm. He saw Delia shudder and instinctively drew her close. She did not resist, but rested her head on his shoulder. The touch of her cheek was cold.

While Jemidon wavered, the manipulant suddenly released its grip with a loud pop, like that of a bursting bubble. Drandor struggled away to collapse in the bottom of an adjacent sphere. His eyelids snapped firmly shut. His chest resumed its slow and steady cadence. The manipulant groped over the cupped floor, bumping into Drandor a second time and then one of the walls. Eventually it found the sled and crawled sluggishly back into its space.

"Their needs are minimal," Delia explained. "It will be another week before that one ventures forth again. Drandor is safe until the next arouses in perhaps the length of a day."

Jemidon let out his breath and patted her reassuringly on the shoulder. "Do not build a pit of guilt in which to trap your thoughts," he said after a moment. "Believe me, they can be a stronger master than any other."

"I am in command of my own spirit. Nothing would be served by succumbing to despair."

Jemidon looked into Delia's eyes and then back around the entombing rock. "That is a spirit I must admire," he said. "There are few who could keep their minds intact when faced with such as this."

Delia rubbed his hand on her shoulder. "And when I was summoned above and saw it was you, I felt the first real hope since I was confined."

Jemidon smiled. "It has been an eventful quest," he said. "Let me tell you what I have learned while we were apart."

Quickly he related all that had happened. To his sur-

272

prise, he found that mentioning Augusta made him feel awkward. With a wave of his hand, he passed on to talk in more depth about meeting Melizar and the discovery of the two metalaws.

Somehow as the words came out, the driving force of his quest seemed to be more for Delia and less because of his hunger for the robe. But she listened quietly and did not contradict. With an intense concentration, she absorbed everything that he said.

"And now that you have rejected Melizar," she whispered when he was done, "how can you hope to achieve what you truly seek?"

Jemidon shook his head to calm the rattle of conflicting thoughts. He had wanted the mastery of a craft above all else. And yet, when faced with the choice, he could not submit to the one with the power to guide him to his goal. A few months ago, such an act would have been unthinkable. The quest for the robe was everything; his entire life had been bound up in it. But now there were other goals, other values that tugged on which way he should go.

Jemidon sighed. He should have followed his original instincts all along. There was no doubt Melizar must be stopped. The cold one admitted that no less than complete control of everything was his plan. The universe, he had called it—this world and all the others in the sky. And if he succeeded, the oppressions of Kenton and the other nobles would be nothing compared with what could transpire. As Jemidon had first decided in Pluton, he must aid the forces opposing the changer of the laws.

"We must escape and convince the masters the world over," Jemidon said at last. "Convince them to exercise the remaining laws to their fullest extent. Melizar has to be prevented from changing any more."

"I agree. Melizar must be thwarted," Delia said, "but that is not the answer to my question."

Jemidon frowned. He clutched the coin about his neck. What was it he truly sought? Saving a world from the domination of one such as Melizar was far more important, to be sure. But still, if not a master, what could he possibly—

Suddenly a flicker of light near the ceiling broke Jemidon out of his reverie. He watched one of the small imps appear through the solid rock and the rockbubbler in the center of the cluster rise to meet it.

"Curse the binding," it grumbled as it rose. "With any normal master, my decisions would be my own while he slumbered. But no, I am to bounce like a ball every time an imp flits into view. Such was his last command before he drifted into slumber."

Jemidon watched a column of rock seem to rise beneath the ascending bubble and a hemispherical void push into the ceiling. At the apex, a tiny iris of black widened into a larger circle. Through it, Jemidon caught glimpses of stacked crates and flickering light beyond.

"Another compartment of the tent," he mumbled as he recognized some of the contents. "The one behind the counter where we first met. This pit was beneath it all along and I did not suspect."

Delia grabbed his arm and pointed at the opening. Jemidon saw two boots drape over the edge to dangle into the void and then the rest of another body crash down into the sphere. The sprite increased the beat of its wings in response to the load. Slowly it reversed its direction, settling back to the same level as the others.

Jemidon shook himself out of what remained of his lethargy. He groped his way from one circular depression to the next, reaching the slumped form and turning him face up. "Burden," he said over his shoulder as Delia followed. "One of the lords at Kenton's castle when I was there. Melizar grows bold indeed if he can snatch away the nobility as well as bondsmen."

Jemidon looked down at the sleeping lord and rubbed his chin. "He may know something of value. If we secure him away as you did me, how long until he can speak?"

"It took you four days," Delia said. "For someone older, who knows how long it would be?"

"We can ill afford to wait." Jemidon frowned. "How deep is the sleep?"

"If you stimulate him enough, he might respond," Delia said, "but only in snatches and they will be incoherent, at that."

Jemidon reached down to roll Burdon over, but felt a numbing twinge in his shoulder. He looked up to see one of the dusting imps hovering overhead and quickly sprang aside.

"Drag him back into my sprite's sphere," Delia said. "We will withdraw from the rest."

Jemidon grunted and pulled at Burdon's bulk.

"Rebellion," the lord mumbled. "The archmage, wizards, and wine."

Jemidon ducked to the side as the imp made another pass and then heaved Burdon from one sphere to the next. In a few minutes, he had crammed the lord into Delia's globe. Awkwardly, he squeezed in beside her and tried to keep his balance as the giant ball of emptiness rolled away from the rest.

"Thirty years," Burdon mumbled. "Who would have thought of treachery by my steward after thrice a decade? They have all lost their senses. Drugs in the wine. Swinging scythes like madmen, not caring whom they struck down."

"Where is the high prince?" Jemidon shook the man's arm. "What did Kenton do after the battle in the pass?"

"Kenton, Kenton." Burdon's eyes flickered open for a moment in a glassy stare. "Of his, I am not surprised. So hard. He pressed them so hard. But my own. My very own, along with the rest. As if ensorcelled, although that can no longer be.

"And now it is full rebellion. There are thousands up on the slopes. No matter how many the high prince and the others muster, they will not easily storm these cliffs against the flails and rakes. They have even taken the cages and dragged them up the mountainside for all the plains to see. They are a symbol, a measure of their defiance, and a taunt for the high prince's men to mount an attack."

"Another battle!" Jemidon exclaimed. "I would think

the high prince would move with caution after what happened at Plowblade Pass."

"The pass. The battle," Burdon wheezed. "This is far graver than the skirmish of a few companies. Far graver, no matter which side you believe was the final victor. Now all the baronies, and all their minions, are drawing together to put down the insurrection. But what if they fail? Yes, what then? Everyone is afraid to uncover what he knows to be true. If the leather vests carry the day, there is nothing standing between them and the palaces in Searoyal.

"And I saw the gravity of the situation, even if no one else did." Burdon waved his arm, suddenly more alert. "I sent for the archmage. It is not only catapult and shield that we are dealing with. The wizards and alchemists and all the rest whom he can muster will be needed as well. I rode with an escort of six to where he had agreed to meet at dusk. A few swallows of wine from the flagon on my saddle horn quenched my thirst. There is something wrong. I feel dizzy. I must sleep."

Burdon's face relaxed. His arm fell to his side. Eyes snapped shut; lips vibrated with the beginnings of a snore.

"The archmage is nearby," Jemidon said. "He would listen for sure. Far better than Kenton or the high prince."

Jemidon looked up and surveyed his surroundings in a new light. "Exactly where are we now? How far to the archmage and in what direction?"

Burdon did not answer. Jemidon shook his arm and then both shoulders with more vigor, but nothing happened. Frowning, he let the lord slip back into the bottom of the sphere.

"Each passing moment is time in Melizar's favor," he said. "We must be away." He looked around the small bubble again, this time more critically, searching for some clues that would lead to an escape. He studied the walls in the hope of seeing a fissure and then stared up at the ceiling, trying to imagine exactly where they might be.

"Delia, your sprite," he said suddenly. "How can it be that you can order him about? Certainly you are no wizard. And I know the basics of the theory. There is no gratitude or courtesies with the likes of an imp or a sprite."

"I do not dominate him as would a wizard," Delia said. "He already has a master." She shrugged. "And despite whatever you say is the theory, he states he has done what he has for favor received."

"You were able to persuade him to pull this sphere away from the rest," Jemidon said.

"It is not truly separate. To tangency was as far as I could persuade him. And for that, even in his misshapen face, I could see the struggle not to comply. He says he can act only insofar as it does not conflict with the instructions of his master."

"But to give him instructions at all, somehow you must—"

Jemidon halted and snapped his mouth shut. He frowned as he felt his thoughts begin to race off to solve a new riddle. There was no time for that now. Their escape was the important matter at hand. Resolutely, he forced his concentration back in the proper direction.

He turned his attention to the walls, judging distances in the featureless surroundings. "The void seems larger in area than the tent that rests upon it," he said. "Did you try sending the imp upward as well as to the left and right?"

"To what purpose?"

"We might not be that far beneath the surface."

"I thought of that myself," Delia said. "Even if the sprite were to break through to free air, there would be no way for me to climb. The curved walls are too smooth."

"Not the walls, but my shoulders," Jemidon said quickly. "I saw the distance Burdon descended. It cannot be far. Yes, that is it, Delia. We must burst through to the surface and then run for the archmage as best we can. Tell your sprite to rejoin the rest and then to ascend above them as the one in the center did."

"A moment." Delia grasped at Jemidon's arm as he squirmed to turn around. "You act no differently from the way you did at the presentation hall. All inspiration, but with no plan to see the idea through. Suppose I were to get to the surface. What then? More likely than not, I would find myself in the middle of some armed camp. And even if I could escape and flee to the opposition, what tale would I tell? How could I do better than you at Kenton's feasting?"

"We have no time for detail," Jemidon said. "I will think of more as we go along."

"As no doubt you did before charging into the vault in the grotto?"

Jemidon opened his mouth to rattle off a rebuttal, but then stopped and frowned. "Those are hard words for one whose intent was to save you from your fate. Despite what I said to Melizar above, the quest was at least in part for you."

"You are like the raw elixir of the alchemist, Jemidon." Delia reached out and stroked his arm. "I mean no disrespect of what you say. The power of your thoughts fumes and sparks. You show a great talent for seeing the solution where for others the goal is unclear. But as for means, you dash forward, grasping the first thought that comes, without a hint of a plan."

"I cannot help how I think." Jemidon pushed her arm away, suddenly irritated. "And it has served you well on more than one occasion already. It was not detailed instructions that slew Drandor's pets. A carefully reasoned treatise did not misdirect Erid's blade in the presentation hall."

"Nor was it your forethought that brought the dagger when the second of the beasts was at your throat. Your inspiration did not list all the props that made Farnel's glamour possible in such a short time."

Jemidon scowled and grabbed at the brandel dangling about his neck. He ran his tongue over his lips, formulating what to say. He looked deeply into Delia's eyes.

She moved her hand forward a second time, but stopped short of placing it on his arm. Palm upward, it rested on the curve of the sphere halfway between where they knelt.

Jemidon looked aside and let out his breath. He rubbed the brandel stiffly between his fingers. The hint that she was a piece of the puzzle ricocheted through his mind.

And she must have some feelings for him. Why did she not express them instead of dwelling on irrelevant faults? Why couldn't she be more like Augusta, warm and friendly, rather than carefully meting out favors only in exchange for some gain?

Jemidon looked back at Delia and saw her patiently waiting, her face a pleasant mask. For a long moment there was silence.

"You are right in that the solution to any puzzle can be improved if it is studied again," he said at last. "The number of steps until the pieces disentangle can be lessened, or the beauty of how one manipulation logically follows another enhanced. It is Burdon we must free from this pit. Burdon, more so than you or I. He was the one who has called the archmage. And failing that, it is he to whom Kenton and the other nobles might listen. We must wait until he awakens—until the right time when he can make good his escape."

"So it would seem to me as well," Delia said softly. "We must stimulate his recovery as best we can and then tell him everything we know. Give him a plan, something he can carry back and put to work against the magics Melizar will employ. We can use the time while we wait to explore all the details of what we will do."

"Then let us begin with formulating the message to the archmage." Jemidon released the coin about his neck. The tension was gone just as suddenly as it had come. He looked down at Delia's outstretched hand. "Anything else?" he asked.

Jemidon watched impatiently as the ceiling dissolved. Under Delia's direction, the sprite rose slowly, creating a void above its head. As the sphere drew farther away, the intersection with the bubble in which he was standing became less. He saw a circle of rock squeeze in from the sides, restricting the view into a smaller and smaller area. When the diameter had shrunk to barely three feet across, a beam of light burst through at the apex, outshining the feeble glow of the imps dancing over the manipulants. An incoherent mixture of excited voices tumbled through the opening and filled the den with sound.

"A little bit more," Jemidon said. "We can still squeeze through the constriction between your sphere and the one below, if you separate them somewhat farther. But we need at least the length of a forearm for the diameter of the one at the surface of the ground."

The sprite halted at Jemidon's words and folded his bony arms across his chest. "You are not the one who took my side against the mushbrains who babble so," he said. "It is to the golden curls that I choose to show my favor."

Jemidon waved his arm in exasperation and motioned Delia to come forward. In a few moments, using words hardly different from his own, she molded the passage to the surface in the proper proportions.

Without saying more, Delia placed her foot on Jemidon's intertwined fingers and boosted herself into the upper sphere. Jemidon wriggled his torso after until he stood erect between the two globes. Delia climbed on his shoulders and cautiously raised her eyes above the level of the ground. She paused a moment to look in all directions and then stretched to full height, scrambling out of the hole.

An instant later, a crude rope made of belts and torn clothing snaked back into the pit. Jemidon pulled himself up and out. Together, they hoisted out Burdon and the still slumbering Drandor.

Jemidon looked quickly about. His pulse began to race. They were on a flat ledge on the slopes of one of the mountains. The folds of Melizar's tent stood immediately to the left, quietly flapping in a midmorning breeze. The excited shouts came from a second ledge immediately below. Much wider, it ran out of sight around the curve of the mountain in both directions. All along, its length was packed with men, some dressed in leather, some with helmets of horn, others in bare-sleeved tunics, waving flails in the air.

With hoarse shouts and cheers, they rained abuse and taunts down on the valley below. Everyone's attention was turned away. No one bothered to watch what was happening in the vicinity of the tent.

Below the lower ledge, the ground fell rapidly away. Like a blanket covered with crumbs, the slope was littered with boulders. Cracked rocks and gaping fissures laced the slanting ground in intricate patterns. Halfway down the slope, Jemidon saw tangled masses of steel bars and dented plates. Next to them, still undamaged cages sprawled to the ground. In twos and threes, they formed a line of demarcation that divided the high slope from the plain.

Sweeping to the horizon were the wheatlands of Arcadia, all scoured black and sending wisps of smoke into the air from still smoldering flames. In the near distance, the humps of thatch and precise lines of stone marked the village of Kenton's barony. Approaching the very foot of the slope was a vast army of armored men. Squares of marchers, their mail gleaming brightly in the sunlight, stood ten rows deep. For every four companies on foot, there was a squad of richly decorated cavalry. Even from the distance, Jemidon could hear the nervous whinnies of the horses as they approached. In the very center flew not one royal standard but two. The rebellion had become far too grave for the high prince to handle without the presence of his father.

Behind the front ranks were arrayed rows of catapults and ballistas. Pressed closely together, they looked like the wall of some huge fortress that kept the mountain from creeping further onto the plain. In contrast to the slow and stately march toward the slope, Jemidon saw robes of black busily flitting among the throwing machines, adjusting their tensions and making ready the arsenals of stone arrayed by each.

The first contingents of the army were already climbing the slope, breaking precise formations and picking their way among the loose jumble of rock that littered the surface. Jemidon looked again at the thaumaturges, who were preparing their weapons, and then back at the rock-strewn slope. "You must convince them to use the engines without any magical aid," he said to Burdon. "Otherwise, it will only make it easier for Melizar to break the coupling."

"But without the aid of thaumaturgy, they project no more than blind missiles, hardly worth the effort to have dragged them across the plain."

"Nevertheless, you must do as I say," Jemidon snapped. The sense of urgency within him began to boil. He had little patience for delay. He looked at the slope and then at the army slowly making its way uphill. "Come along," he decided suddenly. "Throw off your cloak so that they will not know you are a lord. We must reach them before they come any closer."

Without waiting for an answer, Jemidon broke for the edge of the cliff and began to scramble to the one below. "But our plan," Delia shouted as Burdon started to follow. "We were to wait until the first skirmishes had started, so there would be a better chance to pass unnoticed. You will arouse Melizar. What about Drandor?"

"Not now, Delia," Jemidon shouted back as he bumped into the rearmost row of peasants watching the royal advance. "There is not time for debate." He turned the man in front aside and worked his way forward, barely offering apologies to those he pushed away. Burdon followed immediately after. Delia hesitated a moment more, then scrambled to catch up before she was permanently cut off. In a moment, they were in the front line.

Jemidon did not pause. He vaulted the edge and plunged down the mountainside, raising a billow of dust. Delia called out, and he reached back to grab her wrist, pulling her after. Burdon, puffing from the effort to push through the throng, awkwardly clambered over the edge into the cloud that marked Jemidon's path.

Down the slope Jemidon dodged, dislodging small streams of pebbles that cascaded in front and bounced off the larger boulders in the way. Barely in control of his motion, he careened between two rocks and then cut sharply to avoid another directly ahead. Delia stumbled and tripped. For a moment, only Jemidon's grip kept her from tumbling to the ground.

A small stone whizzed past Jemidon's ear, and then a

282

shower somewhat farther away. The throng on the ledge was not sure who the runners on the slope were, but the targets were much closer than the ones at the base of the cliff.

"Why so fast?" Delia managed to pant. "Their aim is not all that good, and none come in pursuit. We can reach the royal army without the haste."

"They are almost all on the slope." Jemidon pointed ahead. "I think that Melizar will not wait much longer. We have to convince them to turn back before the cold one acts."

Almost in answer, Jemidon felt a sudden rumble in the ground. He missed his step and skidded to his knees. A large rock on his right began to pitch back and forth in its shallow depression. The shower of pebbles from Jemidon's feet was joined by additional rivulets across the entire face of the cliff. A stone the size of a child's head skittered down to follow.

Bigger rocks began to move, crashing into those in front and dislodging them from their rest. Two large boulders rumbled from their moorings on the left and plowed smaller debris down the cliff to augment the cascade.

The quaking increased in intensity, so much that Jemidon could barely move forward. Like a drunken man, he stumbled down the mountainside, tripping on the obstacles thrust suddenly in his way. He gritted his teeth to ignore the sharp snaps of pain, as small missiles hurled into his ankles and legs.

"Avalanche," Delia shouted, finally realizing what was going to happen. Her cry was drowned out by the one on the ledge, as truly massive monoliths began to lumber down the slope.

Jemidon looked over his shoulder to see a dense wave of dust mask the shouting rebels. The hillside was alive in a fusillade of hurling death. For a moment, he watched the cloud gather momentum and then turned to judge the distance remaining to the bottom of the slope. Instinctively, he swung to the side with the thought of moving out of the way before the avalanche roared past, but then halted, realizing the length of the line was too great.

He scanned the downslope, desperately looking for some natural feature that would give them a place to hide. But except for the moving boulders, the terrain was smooth.

"To the cages," he said at last. "Farther down the hill. It is the best we can do."

With a snap, he spun Delia after and scampered down the slope toward the wreckage of Kenton's machines. He heard Burdon trip behind him, but now there was no time to turn back. Without thinking about how he would stop, Jemidon vaulted a stone in the way and skated on a wave of pebbles for a good thirty feet. Regaining his balance, he twisted past a boulder bounding by on the left, savagely whipping Delia to the side.

The roar of the falling rock became deafening as they reached the first of the cages. Without dwelling on how close they were falling, Jemidon thrust Delia inside and snapped shut the belt around her waist. "Keep your arms and legs inside the bars," he yelled. "Hope that the chains prevent you from slamming into the sides."

He turned to grab Burdon's tunic as the old man tumbled past, completely out of control from the motion of the dancing mountain. "Into the next," he shouted, jumping out of the way as a large rock sailed past his shoulder and then bounced off the bars of Delia's cage. Without looking to see how the lord fared, Jemidon dove for the last cage in the cluster. Fingers suddenly numb and unresponsive slid on the belt. He curled into a ball as best he could.

Just as he did, the wave of dust engulfed him completely. Small pebbles and rocks sailed through the bars and struck his head and back, producing painful welts. Larger rocks clanged off the bars and continued down the slope. A huge boulder crashed into one end of the cage and spun it around. A second hit broadside, bending the bars with a shriek of protesting metal.

The hail of crashing rock became a torrent. Like a tropical cloudburst, the tap and clang merged into a continuous stream of sound. The larger stones shook the cage with gut-wrenching jolts. Twice more, the metal box jarred from where it was poised and then, under the nudge of a boulder, it joined the stream tumbling end over end, another piece of debris in the sweeping storm.

Jemidon gasped from the tugs of the belt. He shut his eyes to block out the dust and the swirl of rock. All sense of orientation vanished in the dizzying tumble. He was barely aware of the cries of men and shrieks of horses as the avalanche roared through their lines.

Then, as suddenly as it had began, the tumbling stopped. A sudden quiet replaced the roaring cascade. Jemidon opened his eyes and peered through the dust. His cage was upended in a pile of granite, one end crushed within inches of his head and the steel ceiling plate dented with pits a foot across. He reached out and grabbed a bar to steady the whirl in his eyes. After a few moments, he was able to release the grip of the belt and scramble out onto the mound of stones.

He blinked in dust-sprayed sunlight. Where there once had been an army was now an area marked only by a few shards of mail scattered amidst the piles of rubble. To his left, Jemidon saw what remained of the rows of catapults. Half were splintery rubbish; on others, thick-beamed spars dangled like broken limbs. All were immersed in a sea of stone that extended farther back onto the plain.

One or two of the machines had survived unscathed. Jemidon saw the thaumaturges hastily cranking back the great arms to release their flights in retaliation.

"Wait, wait," he heard one yell. "The incantation. Something is wrong. The small sliver is not still bound with the whole. Sympathy and contagion. They no longer seem to work."

Jemidon clutched his arms around his stomach and turned his attention back up the mountainside. After the harvesting had stopped, Kenton's throwing engines were all that remained of thaumaturgy. For Melizar, that had been enough for the uncoupling. Now even they were stilled.

Jemidon looked across the slope through the haze and saw what he thought was Burdon climb out of his cage and limp off into the distance. He searched the rubble for signs of Delia and sucked in his breath when he glimpsed a few twisted bars poking out from beneath a boulder the size of a small hut. He ran to examine the wreckage, not daring to think of what he might find.

As he drew closer to the monolith that must have crushed flat whatever stood in its way, he heard a faint, high-pitched hum and the squeak of a tiny voice.

"The time has already been many seconds. At this distance, I can remain no more. I must return and fulfill the obligations to my master. I am to maintain the void under the tent. Little else do I have leave to do."

Jemidon ran around the rock and blinked at what he saw. Delia was huddled in a small ball inside a shimmering transparent sphere that was centered around the rock-bubbler sprite.

"Nevertheless, you have saved my life," Delia told the demon. "You see where the cage came to rest in the monolith's path. There was barely enough time to get out and call for your aid before it hit."

"Your thoughts were compelling and clear." The sprite unfolded its arms from its chest. "I do not understand truly what made me come. But no matter. In a few heart-beats more, I must—"

The imp stopped, and then a spasm ran through its body. "The packing of the spheres has shifted. The others have told. My true master calls. He has been awakened and commands that I return." The demon closed its eyes and slowly pivoted, pointing a thin arm up to the ledge from which it had come. "See, he walks among you mortals and has summoned another to do his bidding as well."

Jemidon looked up the mountainside. The rebels were quiet, stunned by the awesome power of the avalanche. He saw a small flash of white-hot flame that suddenly cut through the swirling dust and then a blur of motion, fiery oranges and burning reds. As he watched, the patch of color soared up into the air. In a breathtaking glide, it arched down to where he and Delia stood.

"A djinn!" the rockbubbler shrieked. "Master, have pity on one who has honored the letter of your law. I have kept open the void under the tent. I left only when the others were so positioned that I contributed nothing to the total volume."

Jemidon watched as the dance of color formed into a large demon. Unlike the sprite, its limbs were full and bulging with muscle. Thick, overlapping scales covered its entire body, except for the tenuous membranes of bat-like wings and the pockmarked cheeks and forehead. Without effort, it descended from the sky, its long tail dangling far below its cloven hooves, testing the ground for a place to land.

Jemidon followed the trajectory with a mixture of fascination and dread. "Not since the agreement between the archmage and the demon prince has one been summoned," he muttered. "The wizard who conjured him is a fool or a true master indeed."

As it grew closer, Jemidon saw that the djinn carried a bundle in each arm. One was dark-cloaked Melizar, the other a manipulant, now fully alert.

"Have him release me." Melizar coughed as they settled to the ground. "A moment of heat will not destroy you. For months, you have been peacefully resting. It is only fair that you should carry some of the hardships as well."

The manipulant motioned with his arms and then collapsed to the ground as the djinn released its grip. Melizar momentarily staggered, but quickly regained his balance and drew himself to full height. He looked at the cowering sprite that had moved away from Delia and then pointed at Jemidon.

"In the grotto, at the pass, and now even one of my manipulant's sprites you have subverted," he said quietly. "Your persistence begins to mark you as a captive of some quality. Perhaps I judged too quickly in placing you in the pit. Your marrow should touch the lips of no less than the first among the pilots."

Jemidon grabbed Delia and closed his fist defiantly. "Numb us again if you will," he heard himself say. "Somehow, we shall escape as we did before."

"Apparently the torpordust is insufficient for one such as you," Melizar said. "That you have already demonstrated." He waved his cloaked arm through the air. "But now there are only alchemy and wizardry left. I will meet this so-called archmage of yours, and then the victory will be complete. You will be the first I will savor when I have gained control of them all. In the meantime, I will place you where I can be more sure you will stay."

Melizar kicked the manipulant huddled at his side. "Send them away. Back whence we came."

Jemidon tensed as the figure on the ground somehow managed to start a small fire from implements tucked into the waist of his loincloth. He tried to ignore the sense of helplessness that welled up within him. He faced no less than a long-tailed djinn that could slice him in two with the snap of its claws. No mortal who was not its master could stand against one. There was no point in even trying to resist. With round eyes, he watched the demon step forward and spread its blood-red wings. As its arms closed around him and Delia, the smell of burning sulfur made him gag.

"Elsewhere," he heard Melizar's muffled command. "Send them through the flames to elsewhere. Let him see if he can fare in my domain as well as I have in his."

PART FOUR

The Verity of Exclusion

CHAPTER SIXTEEN

Skysoar

JEMIDON could not judge the passage of time. There was a moment of disorientation and then he heard sharp cries of surprise. The wings of the djinn unfurled. As quickly as it had engulfed them, the demon stepped back into the flame and vanished.

A blast of numbing cold air ripped at Jemidon's uncovered hands and eyes. A sense of weightlessness rose from his stomach; his feet slowly left the ground. He looked up and blinked. He was surrounded by a vast expanse of reddish sky, not the robust oranges of sunset reflected in clouds, but a soft color that washed from horizon to horizon, full of a diffuse light for which no source could be seen. In the far distance, spanning completely across the ruddy glow, were dim hints of long, straight lines, a trellis of triangles like the facets of a gem.

Where were they? It was a scene that could not possibly exist in the experience of man. Everything was alien—the colors, the smell of the air, and the sound of the whistling wind. The shock hammered at Jemidon's senses and froze him in place, a mute statue totally without comprehension of what he saw.

A hand grabbed his shoulder from behind. He was thrust into a shallow pit carved from solid rock and saw Delia pushed to his side. Long, slender fingers pointed to small indentations in the walls, and he understood what to do. Gripping tightly with his hands and feet, he prevented himself from floating away.

For the longest time, Jemidon remained huddled in the pit, pressing against Delia to share her warmth and feeling the wind whip over his back. He kept his eyes screwed shut, all muscles tensed to lock him into position, not wanting to move, trying to will away what he had seen as part of a flawed glamour. But the thought of what really must have happened bubbled in his mind, gathering strength and dripping with desolation and helplessness.

Finally Jemidon had to be sure. Cautiously, he opened his eyes and looked about. He saw about a dozen figures, dressed only in loincloths like Melizar's manipulants, huddling in depressions similar to his own. They were arrayed in a circle about a deeper pit that contained the last flickers of the fire, a complex linkage of mirrors, and a flat tablelike stone with strange glyphs marked around the periphery.

Like Melizar's manipulants! His sagging spirits plummeted with the thought. Like Melizar himself! Here the beings appeared to move about in comfort, to be the norm. He and Delia were the exceptions, the outcasts trapped far away from home. The strange one indeed had made good his threat.

"Where are we?" Delia came to life at his side. "Is this the realm of demons, the world behind the flames?"

Jemidon looked to the horizon. They seemed to be on the top of a rocky mound; the terrain fell away in all directions. But the proportions were all wrong. There was nothing in the distance beyond the curve of the hill, no plain stretching away or other mountains, only reddish sky and the distant lines.

"It is totally unlike what the wizards have recorded in the sagas," Jemidon said. "But I fear that, for us, it will make little difference."

Jemidon looked again at the men clustered about them. They talked in a soft chittering and ignored him completely. In the pit with the tablestone, one obviously older than the rest and cloaked in gray spoke in hoarse whispers, gesturing commands. His sleek black hair had turned pale, and deep wrinkles furrowed a caved-in face. Pus ran from one half-closed eye. With a gnarled hand, he idly fingered the bead at one of the vertices of a lattice. It was like Melizar's, although it was far less complex.

Beyond the large pit stood a scaffolding and next to it

a line of crudely built wagons, wheels of solid wood and tongues with handholds rather than yokes. Behind them were several hoists, complicated constructions of levers, pulleys, and slings. Shovels and coarse woven sacks were piled everywhere, battened down under tightly stretched nets.

Farther to the right, at the end of what might be a safety rope, looped through a series of metal eyes, was a large indentation in the rock. When Jemidon craned his neck, he could see steps leading down into an interior and the hint of torchlight casting dull shadows on the roughly hewn granite. Except for these features, all else was bare rock, a gently curving expanse with sharp ridges hammered and polished away, the texture of the sea frozen in sculpture's stone.

The old one gestured dramatically at the horizon. Jemidon turned his head and saw a new line of hills where there had been none before. And as he watched, the crest-line grew taller and extended farther to both sides. The undulations of the peaks were ripples on a more gentle curve that bowed up into the sky. For a moment Jemidon was puzzled by what he was seeing, but in a few seconds more, the rising ground began to fill his view. In a flash he understood where he was. They were riding a boulder, a large one to be sure, over a thousand feet in diameter from what he could see, but no more than a mere hunk of rock, slowly rotating and hurtling toward the ground.

Jemidon realized dimly that he should have some reaction to the impending collision, at least a sudden flash of anxiety from the primitive fear of falling, but he felt instead only the huge weight of his increasing despair. Almost dispassionately, he saw the growing details of ragged peaks and scarred valleys as they closed. Here and there were small craters, and in other places long slashes gouged the surface. He looked back at the men. Calmly they went about their tasks, seemingly oblivious to the danger of a collision. Two sighted the approaching body through a telescope and sextant, while another moved small markers around the edge of the tablestone in response to what they called out. A fourth reached from his pit and placed two pale blue stones onto the tabletop, each the size of a fist. Through his good eye, the old one squinted up at the approaching sphere. He glanced at the markers the others adjusted around the periphery of the stone and nodded. Reaching into his loincloth, he removed a small pyramid, each side covered with variously colored triangles much like Melizar's cube.

The old one twisted the faces of the solid, and Jemidon suddenly felt his stomach contract, almost anticipating what he would feel. The sense of letting go and drifting built in an instant, overwhelming even his sense of defeat. In his mind's eye, the rush of motion increased in intensity and began to whip him along at a hurricane's pace. Fanciful convolutions of shape and color streaked by in a blinding blur. But despite the speed, surprisingly, his disorientation was not great. He felt less need than before to fight the flow, to lash out and grab for any anchor as it sped past. He watched instead the swirl of meaningless flotsam about him and concentrated on the box he visualized in the distance, the box he had imagined before, the box slowly opening its lid and tipping to spill out its secrets.

The old one wiped the pus from his eye. He squinted at the approaching ground. While a manipulant began to push the blue stones apart, he leaned forward, extending his arms to surround them with his flesh. Suddenly there was a ground-wrenching lurch, a groan in the granite that vibrated the entire mass on which they rode. Jemidon felt a deceleration, a resistance in the direction in which they sped. The inner sense of a mad rush was just as suddenly gone, leaving unmasked only the dull weight of his failure to escape from Melizar.

The old one twisted his pyramid a second time, and another of the attendants performed complex motions on the tabletop, this time with sparkling crystals of pale violet. Again Jemdion felt the inner rush and the shudder of the boulder as it responded. Craning his neck backward, he saw their rotation slow and the uprushing ground now directly overhead.

The whispering chatter became more intense. The old

one worked with his pyramid almost continuously. Jemidon felt a series of short rushes and re-anchorings. Like gambling in a complex game of chance, the manipulants alternately placed small colored stones on the table, maneuvered them briefly under the old one's hands, and then shoved them away.

Suddenly the one with the sextant waved his arms and all activity stopped. The old one slumped down beside the tablestone, apparently exhausted. Two of the others cautiously rose out of their pits and headed for the scaffolding. Jemidon looked upward to see the ground rushing closer, not quite as fast as it had before. More importantly, it also began moving to the side.

As he watched, the rate of closing became less and less. The lateral motion increased until the features on the ground streaked by in a rush. Finally they seemed to stop falling altogether and flew over the surface at a blistering pace, skimming along over the ground faster than any bird could fly.

For a long moment, nothing happened; then the sextant holder shouted, pointing to the left and far ahead. Jemidon saw the old one direct one more manipulation, and they resumed their descent to the surface. Smaller features resolved as they grew closer, the wrinkles of mountain slopes, the canopy of individual trees. Jemidon held his breath as they skimmed over a small ridge and then above a marshy plain. He recognized the grazing animals that had appeared in Drandor's initial animation and, stalking them behind the cover of tall grass, the strong-jawed dogs.

Out of the corner of his eye, he saw a net billow from the scaffolding to catch the wind. Working two-handled cranks, the manipulant at the scaffolding let out enough line so that each end of the net skimmed along the ground. With a hoot of panic, the grazing beasts saw it coming and began to stampede out of its path. The race of the boulder was too swift, however; in an instant, two or three were caught and scooped from their feet. Jemidon heard a soft, tinkling laughter and saw the manipulant next to him beat his thigh with his palm in apparent delight. The crank handles spun, slowly drawing the trapped beasts from the surface up onto the rock.

Jemidon noticed that the distance between the boulder and the surface began to widen. They had passed the point of closest approach. Gradually the lateral motion turned into one of recession. As quickly as they had come, they were now speeding away back into the reddish sky.

The tension seemed to dissolve from among the manipulants. They all gestured at one another with a curious contortion of the fingers of the right hand. While two hauled in the catch, three others helped the old one out of the pit and into the opening that led inside the rock. Another manipulated the mirror linkage, and coded bursts of light radiated out in all directions. Finally one returned to where Delia and Jemidon lay still, huddled in their pit. He brandished a short sword of copper and motioned them to follow the others inside. Jemidon looked into the manipulant's face and slowly released his grip. The sword he did not mind. What disturbed him most was the smacking of the thick, pulpy lips. Perhaps it would have been best if their encounter had not been a near miss after all.

Jemidon stared at the pile of coins in his lap. Slowly he put them back into the battered changer, one by one. Playing with Benedict's problem was probably what had kept him sane. Besides Delia, it was his only contact with the realm from which they had been cast.

Marooned in Melizar's universe they were; there was no doubt about it. And time was running out. There was no easy way to measure it here, but it was slipping away nonetheless. Over twoscore times they had slept while nothing else seemed to have changed.

Despite what he had suspected after the encounter with the larger sphere, he and Delia had not felt the sharpness of the copper blade. Instead, they were shown to small caverns carved from the rock. And once cautious tastes of meat from herd animals proved to produce no ill effects, their basic needs were provided for as well. The manipulants were even friendly in an offhanded sort of way. Teaching each other their languages had begun almost immediately. He had learned much after a few sessions of struggling with the basic concepts.

They were not prisoners; they could come and go as they chose. But as Jemidon had soon learned, their freedom meant very little indeed. Melizar had been right. Isolating him on a hunk of granite was a perfect prison. There were no exotic powders with which to summon the stronger demons. He and Delia were trapped, hopelessly trapped, far more removed from freedom than in any pit a few feet beneath the ground. How could they possibly escape before Melizar summoned them back to enjoy his meal?

Jemidon looked at the sky. And even if they could escape, escape to what? One speck of rock apparently was no better than any other. The djinn would find them, no matter which they were on. And even if they were able to make the transition back on their own, would even that be in time, before whatever they returned to was totally lost?

Jemidon pulled the leather vest tighter, but it did not help. He massaged one cold hand with the other. At least their worst fears had yet to be realized. The old one and the others seemed to have enough marrow from the grazing animals to keep them satisfied. There was no need for either hibernation or feasting. Other than a few appraising leers and teasing grasps, he and Delia had been left fairly well alone.

Not that anyone could ever be very far removed from the others. Jemidon was able to visualize almost every feature of the rock in his mind's eye. Honeycombed with caverns, a thousand feet across and almost perfectly round, it would have been an impressive monolith on an Arcadian plain. But here it was a mere speck, smaller than most of the others that floated in the sky.

Jemidon felt a slight twinge in his stomach and absently rubbed his side. He was aware of the drifting all the time now, although they all seemed mild and quite far away. Since the initial demonstration upon their arrival, the old one had made no more displays of his craft.

Jemidon looked down at his changer. He had mused

over the facts so many times that even the critical nature of the situation could no longer stifle the undercurrent of boredom that mingled with the threat of ultimate doom. It was indeed fortunate that he still had the collection of coins to divert his attention when the level of frustration was particularly high. Not that Benedict's problem was proving any easier to unravel. With his latest sequence for loading the changer, the five coppers came out of a single column and the silver did, too. But the brandels were interleaved with the rest. The initial condition still was not set right. And any small change in the order with which he inserted the coins made the confusion worse. Perhaps there was no solution—a bad omen for the other, more important problem he somehow had to solve.

A shadow crossed the doorway. Jemidon looked up to see one of the rock's inhabitants enter and settle cross-legged on the other side of the floor. His face was old and, save for the operator of the pyramid, more leathery than any other in his small band. In large patches, the translucence of his skin had dimmed to milky opaqueness. Deep wrinkles surrounded his eyes, like waves gently lapping on a shore. His black hair was streaked with white on a head that peaked in a slight ridge running from the brow to the base of the skull. He held his token of leadership, a small shovel with a long and deep blade, in stiff fingers that did not completely curl about the shaft.

"The other, the one you name a female," the visitor said softly, "she is tired. Tired of teaching to me your speech."

"Anything tires with repetition, Ponzar," Jemidon said as he puzzled through the accent. Ponzar had shown an amazing aptitude for vocabulary and syntax, but his diction was distorted and hard to understand. "Delia has spent many of our hours with you over twoscore of our days. She probably is no more bored than I."

"Repetition?"

"To do something over and over, again and again," Jemidon explained.

"Ah, then life is repetition," Ponzar said. "Forever we drift in the sky. Swoop to the larger lithons. Trade for

298

water. Fly away from the air that is foul. Harvest the lodestones that have the power. The Skyskirr have done this since—since the great expansion. Until the right hand wills a change, we will do so forever after."

"And yet you show an interest in our tongue," Jemidon said. "Perhaps the time between encounters does not pass so swiftly for you either."

Ponzar twirled the shovel in what Jemidon had learned was the equivalent of a shrug. "It is the talent of a captain. To be such, one must speak with all who soar. And I am counted with the quickest. My memory is almost perfect. I can learn in a few sleeps what takes a common mason hundreds. And there is more. You have traded thoughts with the outcast, Melizar. Many lithosoars fear that he will return. It is worth the effort to talk so that I might learn."

Ponzar closed his eyes in thought. "I no longer trust the others," he said. "I do not believe the silvered words they flash by mirror. The more I can speak of your lithon, the more Valdroz will pay me honor when we meet to trade. Also, it is to your worth to tell me all. You will last longer if others think you have value more than common marrow."

"I seek knowledge as well," Jemidon said. "Tell me of Melizar. What are his powers? What has he done?"

"You are only the bounty of the skies," Ponzar replied softly. "You do not have the honor to question those who harvest what has been provided by the great right hand." He twirled the shovel through several full circles. "And I do not know if your words are true. If you are not another of Melizar's manipulants. Sent back to help his return. A manipulant of one people who resonates with the pilot of another."

"But I may be of help," Jemidon said. "I have deduced two metalaws. Melizar hinted that there is a third. If I know them all, I might be able to thwart his plans."

Ponzar threw back his head, and the small cavern echoed with his tinkly laugh. "You against Melizar. You, who have not been excluded. Against the one who piloted a course with nine changes in the laws. Even old Utothaz, may the right hand make his bones tasty, could not keep the coupling tight. Keep it tight if Melizar chose to break it. Speak, by your own telling, you have faced his power. How well did you fare?"

Jemidon frowned and waved his arm in irritation. "If Melizar is so powerful, how did he become an outcast?"

"He is the greatest of the pilots," Ponzar said. "The first among the first. No one in the 'hedron says it is not so. But he reached too far. He studied his craft above all else. Studied it instead of the greater needs of the Skyskirr, of our people."

Ponzar looked toward the sky. "Each lithon must have its turn. It is the way of the great right hand. Every sphere, no matter how small, has the right to unlock the laws. The right to change which of the minerals have the force of attraction and repulsion. The right to choose which are without power like common rock. Each must be allowed to avoid collision. Each to harvest from the larger, to explore where no other has gone.

"But Melizar had eyes only for the others. Eyes for the strange laws which have nothing to do with the walls of the 'hedron or the stones of power. He would decouple the binding when there was no need, demanding many strange rituals until he discovered what would move the laws to other vertices of the lattice.

"Each uncoupling made him stronger. More able to force a translation, if other pilots wished it or not. And every new vertex, each pebble of knowledge, increased his hunger for more. His thoughts became less and less about the soaring of the Skyskirr. For his own lithon, he planned fewer and fewer courses. To his own captain he would not answer. Except for his manipulants, he cared for none at all.

"Finally, his perturbations conflicted with another's. A conflict, even though there was no real need. Azaber's lithosoar was in trouble. They wished to close with a watery orb and break a long drought. But the lodestone, yellow orphiment, was with power at the time. And both the wet sphere and their own lithon carried the negative type. With strong force, they were being repulsed. Azaber's manipulants saw boulders of rusty cairngorm on the orb. The positive kind, opposite to their own. If their pilot could shift to give the brown stone its power while turning off that of the yellow, then they could converge in time.

"And so the manipulants signaled by mirrors to all the lithons. All others agreed not to work the craft until Azaber's pilot was done. A common enough request. When one is far away from other lithons and moving swiftly, it does not matter which of the laws are in effect."

The Skyskirr twirled his shovel and pounded it on the ground. "All agreed, that is, except Melizar. His sphere was one of the largest, a huge lithofloat, far grander than the one that soon we will see. And he had thoughts only for his own searchings. He held the lock tight against Azaber's pilot. The bond did not break. Slowly the lithon was pushed away with no chance to choose speed or direction. It drifted into a region of poisonous vapors. A region with no lodestone strong enough to alter its path for a return. Only the gentle force between the plates carried it along."

Ponzar shook his head. "Even in sleep, the ones who soared with it were without the means of guidance for too long. In the end, they all gave their marrow to one another. The last reflections said they were drifting out of mirror range toward the realgar wall.

"Azaber's pilot took a great risk when he ran their course so close to a void, it is true. It is one of the risks for the lithons that soar rather than float. But if Melizar had loosened his grip, as was his duty, then the lithon would have spun around its target. Spun around and returned to better air."

"After all the Skyskirr learned of what had happened, the rest of the lithons sailed as one. United, they manipulated the laws to converge on Melizar's orb. Never since the great expansion have so many been in one small portion of the 'hedron. Ten times a hundred swords of precious copper were drawn. A thousand were ready to ride the smaller lodestones down upon the floater. To seek the vile one out, to break his bones and scatter his marrow to the twenty planes."

301

Ponzar drew his wheezing breath. "But Melizar and his manipulants escaped. Through the laws of what you call wizardry, he conjured a lodestone that was not made of rock. A strange being that whisked him and his manipulants away, out of the boundaries of our 'hedron entirely, to some other 'hedron whose nature we can only guess.

"All of the other pilots labored to move the laws away from the vertex that made your strange rules work in the Skyskirr 'hedron. Even Utothaz added his failing powers to the rest. But Melizar had translated the laws far into a strange portion of the lattice. The adjacent vertices were known to none. We could not manipulate what would make a smaller contradiction. The portal stays open. And as long as it does, he may return. That you are here from somewhere else is proof enough."

"The laws that are strange to you," Jemidon said, "I know them well. They are the Law of Dichotomy, 'dominance or submission,' and the Law of Ubiquity, 'flame permeates all.'"

"So well that after thirty-seven sleeps, you are still here." Ponzar laughed softly. "If you can do this wizardry, why not return? Return by commanding the strange being which brought you here."

"I—I was never able to conjure up the simplest imp." Jemidon hesitated for a moment and then rushed on. "Besides, a true djinn will not come in simple flame. He needs the burning of special powders, and you have none of it here on this rock."

Ponzar did not immediately reply. He shut his eyes again and slumped forward in thought. "Most interesting," he said after a moment. "I will add that to what I will tell."

"You speak with some apprehension about this rendezvous," Jemidon said. "Why bother if it gives you any concern?"

"Utothaz calculated the course long ago." Ponzar looked back at Jemidon. "And once we spun past the sphere with the grazing beasts, the path was set. Only when we near the lithofloat will there be another chance to alter our track." Ponzar twirled his shovel and tapped the ground. "Our caverns are overflowing with harvest. The floaters are too big to move as swiftly through the sky as we. They gather instead what they can capture as it floats by. If there is trust, there will be good to both sides from the trade."

"And if there is not?"

"Valdroz is a greedy captain. He is not at peace that his lithon is so big and slow. Were it not for the way of the great right hand, I fear he would plunder all that I have. Plunder all and give nothing in exchange. I also think of the strength of the lodestones. Valdroz's lithon has huge boulders of positive cairngorm. Our own are not small. As long as its law remains inert, it acts no differently from baser rock. But if we shift to a vertex where it has power, we could be hurled to only the great right hand knows where.

"But my heaviest thoughts are about the portion of the sky in which we meet. Behind the floater is a great sea of base stone lithons. Some are larger than the greatest floater, great enough for hot rock to flow and clouds of poisonous vapor to hurl in the air."

"Why should that be your greatest concern?" Jemidon asked. "If lava flows on the surface, you need not swoop close. And the fumes should dissipate on the currents of the air. It sounds not so very different from what I would call a volcano."

"There are few enough winds in the 'hedron except for those made by our flight," Ponzar said. "Only in time is the foul mixed with the pure. The poisons move out slowly from where they were born. And the vapors of which I speak fill a very large volume. Even though a lithosoar can fly for many sleeps on a drifting course if its supply of marrow is high, no Skyskirr can hold shut his lips for as long as it takes to pass through such a cloud."

Ponzar waved his small shovel in front of Jemidon's face. "The great right hand guides. It is the duty for all the Skyskirr to follow. Whatever happens is by his design. And I have a duty, as shown by my token of office. The pilot uses his key for the unlocking. The manipulants chip precious lodestones from baser rocks with their picks. The others, the scribes, the smiths, the skinners, all have their duties and tokens as well. And the captain of a lithosoar must scoop the treasures from the skies and provide for his people so that marrow is for feasting and not for survival in the voids."

For a moment Ponzar sank into silence, oblivious to the fact that Jemidon was even there. Then he rose abruptly, apparently satisfied with the conversation. In the doorway, he shifted his shovel to his left hand. He extended his right index finger pointing at Jemidon, thumb upward and middle finger bent to the side. Jemidon returned the signal as he had been taught.

When the captain had gone, Jemidon turned his attention back to the coin changer and sighed. There was nothing else for him to do but wait. "If I start with three silvers before the galleons," he muttered, "then the first brandel will fall into the third column. That means that a dranbot must be next to deposit into the fifth."

Jemidon felt the slight tremble as their small boulder began to slow in its passage, rather than continuing to hurl past the larger sphere. Compared with the agonizing slowness during over a dozen sleeping periods with which their target had come into view, first as an indistinct speck and then gradually growing into a discernible disk, the motion now seemed rapid indeed. He knew that soon they would reach a perilith, then loop back in a long ellipse. Ponzar had said that the trade delegation would come when they were almost skimming the surface.

Already the other lithon blotted out a good portion of the sky, fissures and crags becoming more distinct with each passing moment. Details were more regular, indicating the effort of intelligent minds. Larger squares of greens and blues checkered a relatively flat plane. Upthrusts of rock were sculptured with spiraling steps. Hundreds of lights blinked in small clusters that covered the orb like a great pox.

Jemidon and Delia stood with the Skyskirr, awaiting the arrival, crammed among sacks of bones, twisted branches of trees, wagonloads of sparkling rock, and other objects that Ponzar's group had scavenged in their trek across the sky.

Jemidon twisted restlessly as the large sphere gradually drew closer. He had been able to deduce some additional facts about his surroundings, but even more time in his own universe had been lost as the lithons converged. With no periodic repetitions in the heavens, he could not be sure how much. But at least Melizar's djinn had not reappeared. Now, with contact with other Skyskirr imminent, perhaps he could find something more than bare rock to bridge the gap to the demon realm and home.

"I still do not understand about the forces between the special stones," Delia said at his side. "How do their attractions affect the direction in which we will go?"

Jemidon smiled at the sweetness in her voice. For most of their journey, she had remained to herself, gladly accepting a separate cavern when it was offered. Now, like a weathervane, her charm was again pointing his way.

"It is the construction of this universe," Jemidon answered. He grabbed a shovel from her hand and with its blade scratched a crude figure in the surface of the rock. "Ponzar is reluctant to say much; but from his small slips and what we have seen, I have figured out much of their laws."

"You know the third metalaw?" Delia's face brightened. "Does it provide the means to see us back?"

"Just laws, not metalaws." Jemidon shook his head. "It all began to make sense when I finally recognized the pattern of the distant lines in the sky." Jemidon looked upward and nodded his head. He had carefully walked all over the surface of the lithosoar and seen them all. There could be no other answer. "We are in a box, Delia—a giant icosahedron, it properly would be called, a regular solid with twenty triangular sides. All that the Skyskirr know to exist lies within the walls of this crystal. From the triangular surfaces they get light and heat. The closure of the 'hedron keeps the air from whirling away to whatever is beyond."

"Like the edges of the world in our own sagas?" Delia

305

asked. "If you sailed too close, you ran the risk of falling over the side."

"Here the risk is not one of falling off," Jemidon said, "but of never being able to return. I suspect that the planes are covered with the lodestones that the scavengers find so dear."

"It is these rocks that pull them through the air?"

"Exactly so," Jemidon said. "Positive cairngorm is attracted by one of the plates and repulsed by another on the other side of the 'hedron. For negative cairngorm, the effect is the reverse. Even when it is near no other sphere, a lithosoar can be accelerated by the forces between the walls.

"There are twenty faces in all and ten opposite pairs. For each pair, there is a corresponding rock: black sphalerite, violet spinel, rusty cairngorm, orphiment, realgar, anatase, chrysocolla, epidote, beryl, and serpentine. I have seen the rocks on the tablestone and as they have spilled from the manipulants' pouches—ten types of lodestones in both positive and negative varieties. And for each type, a rock of one variety is attracted to those which are opposite and repulsed by those which are the same. The force falls off with some power of the distance."

Jemidon paused and contorted his hand in the sign of greeting. "Actually, it is a little more complicated than that. Two additional plates interact with each type of lodestone as well. But only when it is moving and at an angle to the direction of motion. It is the meaning of the right hand. If the thumb points in the direction of the primary tug and the forefinger in the direction the lodestone is moving, then the additional force will be in the direction of the curling fingers. The extended fingers of the hand are a simple mnemonic from a distant past to aid in the calculation of trajectories. If there were only one lodestone and no others to perturb its path, its motion would be a helix that would eventually reach one of the walls."

"But our flights are anything but so simple," Delia said. "Utothaz maneuvered us almost at will."

"There are other bodies in the 'hedron as well, each with its own complement of rocks that attract and repel."

"But what of the control?" Delia asked. "He maneuvered our lithosoar over the other as if we were a docile bird."

"It is the—the metamagic. Yes, that is the word for it," Jemidon said. "The laws of attraction for the stones can be turned on and off at will. To approach a target, you invigorate the law that attracts the two bodies together. To break before collision, you switch instead to one that repels. Far away from any lithon, you rely on the forces between the walls. Indeed, that is the role of the metamagician in this domain. He is the pilot who calculates the courses and steers the scavengers through the sky, guiding them from one stone to the next to collect whatever of value they can. The laws themselves are simple. Attraction or repulsion, falling with distance, and a second force at right angles to the velocity. Once a law is in effect, it permeates the entire universe; but with a few observations, anyone can calculate the trajectories that result. There is little of the arts as we know them here, Delia. No complex rituals or incantations that only a master can control. It is metamagic instead that is supreme."

Jemidon broke off and pointed skyward. A swarm of small figures rose from the surface of the larger lithon and accelerated swiftly to catch their lithon as it hurled past. When the visitors grew closer, Jemidon saw that they looked much like Ponzar and the rest, dressed only in loincloths, despite the stinging cold. Each carried a huge pack on his back, and a copper sword dangled from his side. Arms were extended directly forward. In one hand, each held a fair-sized stone of blue that seemed to pull its owner along; in the other was an inert crystal of black.

Partway on their intercept trajectory, Jemidon experienced the feeling of disconnection. It was stronger than any since Utothaz's sweep of the beasts, but the disorientation was totally under control. It was merely an irritation that he hardly noticed any more.

"They have deactivated the attraction of the blue stone and changed to the repulsion of the black," he said. "When they arrive, their relative speed will be almost zero. Then the law will be shifted to another and the lodestones will have no special powers until they are reactivated for their return."

In a few minutes, Ponzar climbed with a slow, careful step to where the first visitor had landed. He signaled with a finger-bent right hand and ordered the security of a well-anchored rope. The new arrival accepted the hospitality with a quick patter of soft tones.

Immediately, Ponzar pointed in Jemidon's direction, and several members of both parties approached to view him better. He scowled back at the rude stares and put up his hand when one reached forward to rip away the front of Delia's gown.

"Careful, faraway one," Ponzar warned so that Jemidon could understand. "Your value is less if you are no better than the beast."

"Far away, a man is valued by the keenness of his mind," Jemidon answered.

"As it is here," Ponzar said. "And in your case, there is perhaps a little interest. It would help if you would show them how you fail to conjure up a demon."

Jemidon's scowl deepened. "There would be nothing to see, only empty flame," he said. "Let me show another art. I have been trained in them all."

"Very well," Ponzar said. "Make it one that catches the eye. The Skyskirr of Valdroz trade with sleepy faces."

Jemidon did not relax his frown. Aiding in Ponzar's petty exchanges did little to help his own plight. Still, what the captain had said was true enough. As long as he and Delia had some value, they had remained away from the sucking lips. And on a bigger sphere they might have a chance to find some of the powders for which they were looking. But what craft to demonstrate? None save wizardry would work here at all. He needed something that appeared impressive, despite what the outcome would be. Quickly he looked around the various items stacked for trade. He dug his hands into one of the nearest sacks and extracted a fistful of soda, originally from the edge of a great salt lake. He rummaged among the small collection

308

of bottles obtained from some previous trade and sniffed for one that had a vinegary smell.

"Alchemy." Jemidon turned back to face Ponzar as he prepared. "A craft governed by the Doctrine of Signatures, or, simply stated, 'the attributes without mirror the powers within.' And these powers are invoked by writing a formula, a series of arcane symbols in a precise order. I will try to make a Foam of Wellbeing by mixing what I have found. If things proceed successfully, there will only be a small bubbling in the bottle before the reaction is complete. The natural propensity to produce large volumes of gas will be suppressed. On the other hand, if the formula fails, the vapor will evolve with explosive results.

"Now, no alchemical formula is guaranteed to work every time, and here I doubt that any will succeed at all. But explain to them what I am doing. The effect should still be good enough."

Ponzar began to translate while Jemidon opened the stopper in the flask and tossed in a handful of soda. He plunged back the cork and, with a quick motion, hurled the bottle up into the sky. While it sailed away, easily escaping the feeble grip that held it to the lithosoar, he rapidly scribbled the formula for producing the foam on a nearby piece of hide, somewhat surprised at how sharply the symbols came back into his mind. He finished the last and held his breath. If the formula worked, nothing would seem to happen. The ingredients would modify internally. But if the natural reaction were allowed to proceed unchecked—

A sharp pop and the glitter of tiny shards of glass cut short the thought. The gas from the reaction had exploded the bottle into smithereens.

"If properly done, the bottle does not burst," Jemidon explained with a shrug. "There, that is a failure as good as any other."

Ponzar twirled his shovel of office in response, looking at Jemidon for a long while. "I cannot be sure," he said. "You still may be one of Melizar's. But if Valdroz's traders accept, you will be their problem and not mine. Wait with the rest of the harvest. I will see what agreement the great right hand will provide."

Jemidon clenced his fist. Ponzar's attitude was no surprise but it grated nonetheless. Certainly he and Delia should be regarded differently from a bundle of sticks. He would speak out despite Ponzar's instructions.

But before Jemidon could respond, the tablestone pit suddenly erupted in agitation. Valdroz's traders drew their swords and bolted for the scavengings. Ponzar slapped his shovel against the rock in alarm. His own followers snapped to attention and scurried after. More poured out of the cavern entrance, waving their copper blades and yelling in high-pitched shrieks. Jemidon felt an unlocking begin but then snap back firmly shut. He saw Utothaz totter to standing and grasp hold of his pyramid, holding it tight with both hands.

Jemidon grabbed Delia about the waist and pulled her away from the Skyskirr as they raced among the sacks and crates. Before Ponzar's fighters could catch them, they poured crystals of black sphalerite from their packs into the containers they had brought and then sealed them shut. One of the traders cried in shrill pain as a blade cut deeply into his shoulder from behind. Ponzar's Skyskirr ran in among the scattered goods, hacking to the right and left, trading blows with whoever turned to resist.

Jemidon heard Utothaz scream. He saw the pyramid tumble from the pilot's hands, wisps of smoke coming from the smaller vertices as they rapidly whirled. The feeling of unlocking grew and then burst through whatever was holding it back. Valdroz's traders lunged for the sacks and crates they had augmented as they suddenly soared into the air.

Ponzar looked at the stricken metamagician and then at the Skyskirr shooting away. "Hang on, hang on," he warned as he struggled toward a pit. "The lithofloat. The cairngorm. Its activation is the next vertex in line."

Instinctively, Jemidon pushed Delia down into one of the many depressions on the lithosoar's surface. He knelt beside her, and the rock almost tore from his grip. Desperately, he reached again to grab hold as it seemed to

310

slip away. He jammed one hand into the indentation and flung a leg across Delia while she struggled to catch on herself. He felt his body move sluggishly as the boulder gathered speed.

His legs slipped from where they were braced and he hung only by his arms. The wind whistled around his head, and he saw small bits of wood, sacks, and ropes seem to come close and whip out of sight, falling behind. Jemidon gritted his teeth and pulled with all his strength, trembling from the effort, somehow drawing himself closer to the receding rock. Using all the muscles in his back, he gradually drew his legs parallel to the curving surface. With one great lunge, he touched the granite and his foot caught in the proper indentation. Straining from the effort, he slowly pulled Delia in front of him to the safety of the pit. Firmly braced with all four limbs, he dared to chance a look at where he had been.

He gasped in surprise at what he saw. The other globe was rapidly shrinking. Like the shot of a catapult, it was hurling away. Their lithon was soaring into the unknown far faster than he had ever traveled before.

CHAPTER SEVENTEEN

Foul Air

JEMIDON turned his head away in disgust. Utothaz's body, sprawled on the tablestone, could barely be seen beneath the huddled forms of his manipulants bending over him. The smacking of lips competed with the whistle of the air. He looked in the direction of the wind. In the distance, he could just discern a tiny speck against the reddish background and, around it, the shading to brown that indicated the concentration of toxic fumes. They had soared for another dozen sleeping periods, and the careful observations through the telescope had long since confirmed that there were no deviations in their flight. By whatever chance, none of the lodestones they carried had a repulsive counterpart on the poison-spewing rock. And no other lithons were anywhere in sight. Still, it seemed little enough reason for Utothaz and the others to abandon hope so quickly.

Ponzar appeared at Jemidon's side and tapped him on the shoulder. "It is no more repulsive than the way you tear the flesh from the bone with your teeth," he said. "And if he is not a criminal, we leave the skull—leave it so that the features remain when the body is cast off into the sky."

"The air is not yet so foul that it cannot be endured," Jemidon replied. "Utothaz has not breathed his last." He shook his head in amazement that the captain still spent his entire day in language drill. Even the accent showed hints of fading.

"He may just as well." Ponzar twirled the shovel blade. "The struggle to hold the laws bound was too great. He knows that he will decouple and move to another vertex only a few times more. It is better for him to give the rest the sweetness of his marrow while he is still fresh."

"But the manipulants," Jemidon protested. "They bicker on who is to be fed upon next. What have they done to deserve such a fate?"

"It is our way," Ponzar said. "Without the pilot to guide them, their lives are as lost. The bounds will be broken. There will be no resonances. It is for few others that they can manipulate the stones."

"It seems to me that the last thing you would want to do is rid yourself of the only talent that has any hope of reversing your direction."

"We will hold trials for another pilot. Although, even if we find one in those who remain, it will little matter. Our flight is swift. There are no other lithons nearby."

"How can you be so calm?" Jemidon growled. "Your very life is in peril. This may be your last soar across the sky. Why are you not straining to invent a scheme, some plan that will save us all?"

312

"It is the way of the great right hand," Ponzar said softly. "Valdroz wanted us repulsed after he had plundered our harvest. But I do not believe that he would want us to be pushed where the air hangs foul. No, we must have been touched by the great right hand as well. Life is repetition, but Skyskirr do not fly forever. For each comes the time when the tugging lithons are far away and the drift leads without change to the walls. For this small stone, that time is now, and we must accept. Our duty is to give our fellows the pleasure of the feast before it is too late to be enjoyed."

The captain eyed Jemidon speculatively. "And as to your own marrow. We have treated you well. Better than some of the other lithons might. It would be to your honor if you do not wait before offering yourself and the female for the benefit of the rest."

Jemidon instinctively drew his arms back to his chest. "I am not Delia's owner," he said. "Any more than you are of me. She will decide in her own mind how she will face the end, if it is to come."

Ponzar closed his eyes for a moment and then pointed with his shovel at the speck in the distance. "The question is not if, but when," he said. "Make peace with the great right hand in your own 'hedron. We would prefer your gift freely given, but will not wait long for it."

Jemidon scowled and turned his back. The helplessness of their situation tore through him like stinging acid. More time had slipped through his fingers. Now it was possibly too late for his own world. He looked again at the growing cloud of dull brown. And soon it also would no longer matter here. Not only was he to fail once again, but in a strange universe, far from home, unmourned, and his body mutilated by fatalistic ghouls.

He heard Utothaz cry in discomfort and clutched at the brandel around his neck. Ponzar had refused to tell him more of metamagic, even after the treachery of Valdroz's floater. In total isolation from the rest of the Skyskirr, the captain still was taking no chances regarding Melizar and his suspected return.

Jemidon felt the battered coinchanger at his waist and

313

idly fingered a dozen coins into his palm. Looking down at the mixture of metal, he smiled ruefully. Benedict's puzzle of the twenty-five mixed coins was probably the only conundrum he would solve—a meaningless pastime instead of the foundation of the universal laws. He looked back into the sky and shrugged. A child's puzzle or keystone to the universes. In the end, was either more important than the other?

A hacking cough at his side broke Jemidon out of his reverie. He turned to see Delia leaning against the safety rope and clutching her other fist to her chest. Her skin was pale. Her golden hair hung in limp snarls. Deep wrinkles had appeared under her eyes, and her cheekbones cut sharp angles in her face.

"The air affects you more than the rest," Jemidon said softly. "You should remain in one of the caverns. Perhaps we can rig up a seal so that the most foul will not as readily mix."

Delia snapped closed her lips and tried to gain control of her spasms. She settled slowly to the rock surface and motioned Jemidon to follow. "It is so cold," she muttered. "So cold. I wonder which of the perils will get me first."

"Do not talk that way," Jemidon said. "I have not given up, like Ponzar and the rest. Perhaps some other pilot will change the laws in a way that will repulse us from this outgassing lithon. Perhaps we will manage to sail on through to greater possibilities beyond."

He pounded his fist into his palm. "If only I had the wit to master wizardry! Even an imp might give us more resource than we have now."

Delia managed a wan smile. "You have saved me twice," she said. "I have no right to expect more. And if it is to proceed to an end, I could have done far worse than to share it with one such as you."

Jemidon looked into Delia's eyes and drew her close. A few times before, they had huddled together for warmth. But this time she melted into his arms in a way that he knew was different. The passion that he had held in check since the rebuff in Farnel's hut flamed anew.

"You are not without virtue yourself," he said thickly.

"A gambler in the markets of Pluton, the organizer of Farnel's presentation, a survivor of the confines of Drandor's tent, the seducer of a rockbubbler sprite.

"That is another part of the mystery." Jemidon paused for a moment. "I had put it out of my mind. How could you possibly get the demon to do as you commanded? He was bound to one of Melizar's manipulants. A master he already possessed. Perhaps wizards can wrest for control of demons, just as the metamagicians contend for the unlocking here."

"I did not seek you out to push the beads about a puzzle," Delia said. "There is little enough time. Come, let us go into one of the caverns while the Skyskirr are occupied with their feast."

"I thought it was my analytical bent that had finally worn down your resistance." Jemidon laughed.

Delia did not smile. "As I said, there is little enough time and certainly no other choice. Let us make the best of it that we can."

Jemidon frowned at her serious tone. "But what if I were the one with the heavy cough and you the more able-bodied?" he asked. "Would you still seek me out? If somehow we return, what then of your closeness?"

For a long moment, Delia was silent. "I do not know, Jemidon." She sighed. "You are a puzzling mixture. Flashes of brilliant insights, caring, and sentiment, but also a skittering focus and a disregard for discipline. I do not know, Jemidon, and abstract conjectures no longer matter. We are here, and the time is now."

Jemidon pulled Delia tighter, and she kissed him on the cheek. He ran his hand down the length of her arm and felt his pulse quicken. But what she had said also began to gnaw at the back of his mind. Like a piece of sand in the corner of his eye, the words detracted from the anticipated pleasure. He thought of Augusta and the way she had looked when he decided to leave. He remembered the contrast of Delia's coldness when he tested her intent in Farnel's hut.

"It is because you have a need, isn't it?" Jemidon stiffened and pushed Delia away. "On the cliffs of Morgana,

315

beneath Drandor's tent, speaking the charms for Farnel—in each case you gave because of a necessity. An even exchange, one favor for another. And when we soared through sweet air, you were sufficient unto yourself. It is only when you desire a windshield against the cold or the cradle of an arm at the last that you come slithering back. Farnel, Gerilac, Burdon, whoever's comforting presence, it would not matter as long as you get what you want."

"Your pleasure will be as great." Delia's tone hardened. "I do not take that for which I cannot provide adequate compensation."

"Nor do you give without expecting payment in return," Jemidon snapped. "You are a woman with many skills, Delia. I am attracted to you in a way I cannot explain. But my thoughts were not of grateful favors when we raced down the cliffside in Morgana or struggled into the cages above the Arcadian plain." He placed his finger under her chin, raising her eyes to his. "You might try an unfettered gift once. There is more than one way to interact with another."

"That is easy enough for you to say." Delia pushed his hand aside, her eyes suddenly flashing. "You did not have your innocence ripped away by dirty-handed traders only too eager to offer so-called advice in the token exchanges. You were not the slave of foul-breathed ruffians who delighted in making you a gaudy display. I have done my share of giving and learned full well what is the result."

"And have I been like the others?" Jemidon asked. "When we huddled for warmth, were my dirty hands misplaced?"

Delia turned away from his stare. She caught her breath and roughly twisted the iron bracelet around her wrist. Jemidon waited, breathing rapidly despite the tainted air.

"No, they were not," she whispered after a long moment. "From the first you have acted as a hero from the sagas, just as I visualized in the dreams I have long since thrust aside."

She glanced into his eyes and then darted her sight away. "You state that I deliberately stayed apart. Indeed

I did, Jemidon, indeed I did. But not because of what you think. It has been so long, yet I am still afraid. You are soft and tender; I felt the walls I had so carefully erected melt away. But I cannot be so foolish. Even at the end. What if you turned out to be no better than the rest?"

Jemidon's anger melted. Beneath the exterior barrier, there was feeling for him after all. He reached out tentatively, but halted before he touched her arm. "I thought that no one's burden was greater than my own," he said softly. "I have spent my life reaching for an elusive goal. But perhaps it is worse to be running away from a past that can never be changed."

Delia took his outstretched hand and pressed it to her cheek. "Your insight pierces more than the interior of lifeless puzzles," she said with a small smile. "You are right, Jemidon, I have used you as I have many others; and even now I came to use you still."

Delia placed her finger across Jemidon's lips. "No, say no more. There is too little time left to be so ill met. I wish to try again. But first I must think of a gift, a gift freely given without any obligations attached."

After a moment, Delia dropped her hand. The passion ebbed away. Jemidon took a deep breath and then joined her in a chorus of coughs. The air had a distinctively metallic taste, with hints of sulfur, like the breath of the djinn which had transported them here between the universes. He tried to think of something more to say, but the words would not come. In silence, they stood facing each other, with the foul wind whistling between them and tugging at their clothes.

After a few moments more, Jemidon felt a tap on his shoulder. He whirled to see Ponzar and two others standing in a row.

"Yes," Jemidon snapped. "What do you want? If it is our bones, you have come too soon. We are not ready yet to give ourselves up."

"It is the matter of Utothaz's final peace." Ponzar ignored the tone. "It seems that the removal of the ribs gives him some pain. And at the convergence, you had mentioned a Foam of Wellbeing."

317

"The law is not operative here," Jemidon said. "I would produce only a minor explosion as before."

"But if there were an unlocking," Ponzar said, "and you attempted the formula within the confines of Uto-thaz's palms."

Jemidon frowned for a moment and then nodded in understanding. "With the laws uncoupled, it might be a least contradiction. We are far away from any other lithon, so the effects of the others will be quite small. It might work at that." He glanced at Delia, then looked down at his coinchanger and tugged the brandel around his neck. "And I might just as well while away the time with one puzzle as with the next. Yes, lead on. I will run through the formula once again."

Ponzar and the others turned and headed back toward the pit with the tablestone. Jemidon started to follow, then hesitated and looked back at Delia. She held her head downward, avoiding his glance. "Get out of the wind," he said thickly. "I will work on a seal when I am done with the alchemy."

Jemidon looked down at the pilot lying on the table-stone and tried to hide his revulsion. Both of the Sky-skirr's legs dangled over the edge of the rock like limp rags. The hands were folded across the stomach in a tangle of pliant fingers. The chest spread over the stone far wider than natural proportions would allow. Beneath the skin, Jemidon could see the weak throb of the heart. Crowded behind the pilot was the entire population of Ponzar's lithon. Manipulants, weavers, smiths, and scribes all waited respectfully to see Utothaz's last.

"How can he lay on his hands," Jemidon asked, "let alone work the pyramid to perform the decoupling?"

"A manipulant will assist," Ponzar said. "Signal when you are ready."

Jemidon checked off the materials at his feet. Ponzar had produced a larger flask of vinegar than before. Following Jemidon's instructions, he had even rummaged and found a purer sack of soda. Jemidon fingered the sharp piece of charcoal for writing the formula and brushed

318

his knuckles over a finely tanned hide on which to make the symbols. Mentally, he ran through the symbology just to make sure that it was all still fresh in his mind.

"Ready." He nodded to Ponzar. "When he has performed the decoupling, I will add the ingredients together."

Ponzar nodded to Utothaz, and the metamagician chittered instructions to the manipulant at his side. The fleshy fingers were pressed against the pyramid, and the vertices slowly turned. Jemidon felt an increase in tension, like a rope stretched by a great weight, and then a snapping release. He was adrift as before, feeling the wandering of the universe among the lattice of the laws. All eyes turned to him, expecting the flourish of the formula.

For a moment he hesitated, exploring in his mind the feeling that was no longer strange. He clutched the brandel about his neck, running his thumb and forefinger over the smooth surface. He visualized the mysterious box that spilled out secrets tipping on its side, the top flopping open, and all the contents pouring out to diffuse through the rest of his thoughts. He reached for the snaky tendrils as they floated past, fraying their strands into finer and finer threads, searching for the answer to the last of the puzzles. He grabbed at one knot of significance as it drifted past, some fact, some observation that was more important than the rest. But it squirmed from his grasp, hovering just out of reach with what he most wanted to know.

"The alchemy," Ponzar said softly in his ear. "You must hurry. Utothaz must also unlock for the succession testing, and there is very little time."

Jemidon coughed in response and wrinkled his nose. The smell was tangibly worse. He heard one or two of the others wheeze as well. He shook himself alert and carefully set aside the charcoal and leather. Cupping his hand, he dug into the sack of soda, snagging a nail on the burlap side. Again he dug, but stumped his fingertips against a solidified clump. When he retracted his arm, he lost half the load against the flap that fell in the way.

Jemidon reached for the flask with his other hand and frowned in annoyance. The stopper was stuck fast, even though he had tested it moments before. For an instant he fumbled; then one of the manipulants boldly reached from where he crouched and pulled the cork with a deft motion. Jemidon tipped his hand containing the soda toward the opening and watched most of the powder blow away, pushed by the wind. But before he could react, the manipulant plunged his arms into the sack and dumped two heaving portions into the flask. With a flourish, the Skyskirr pushed shut the seal.

Jemidon frowned, then shrugged as he saw the others paying no attention to his bumbling, but waiting instead for the scripting of the formula. He retrieved the small piece of charcoal between fingers suddenly numb and cold. Touching it to the hide, he started to draw the first swirl. Or was it a swirl? The second had a serif that curled into the third. The fourth was a simple triangle, or perhaps one with a dot where the altitudes crossed. Jemidon knitted his brow. This was nonsense. He had known it all just moments before. And success or failure did not matter. Utothaz would soon pass, conscious of pain or not. This was no examination for the master's robe. He gritted his teeth and tried to remember the formula. But with each passing second, it faded farther and farther away.

Jemidon closed his eyes and felt sweat form on his forehead. The icy wind cooled the droplets to become freezing pain. A chorus of chittering forced his attention back to the flask. He blinked at what he saw. At the last possible moment, he hurled it away to explode harmlessly downwind.

"It might not have succeeded anyhow," he said quickly before Ponzar could speak. "Perhaps some other contradiction forced it away."

The captain closed his eyes and did not respond. After a moment, he stood to full height in the wind and pounded the handle of his shovel for attention. He pointed at Utothaz, still managing to labor on the table, and motioned all the Skyskirr who were not manipulants to form into a line.

"We will use the decoupling instead for the testing." Ponzar turned to Jemidon and explained. "It is unfortu-

320

nate that the last moments of the pilot will not be without some pain." He paused and spoke in a whisper that Jemidon could barely hear. "And I think it is best that you try for possession of the key as well."

Jemidon shrugged and kicked at the sack of soda at his feet. "Why not?" he agreed. "I can perform none of my own domain's crafts. Perhaps my skill lies in the simple manipulation of the stones."

He said no more. In a foul mood, he pulled himself along the safety rope to the rear of the line. From the way the queue snaked around the uneven surface of the lithosoar, he had an unobstructed view of the tablestone. The procedure was simple enough. The first in line reverently swung down into the pit and listened to Utothaz's hoarse commands. Starting with brown cairngorm on predetermined marks, the Skyskirr moved the stones over calibrated trajectories chiseled into the rock and then he was done. For each one who tried, the sequence was slightly different. Some traced out hyperbolas, and others looped the stones in ellipses or circles about a common focus. But all apparently were able to do as directed. Ponzar indicated success by dipping his shovel after each had completed his task.

Finally Jemidon's turn came. He listened, puzzled, while Utothaz wheezed his instructions and then waited patiently for Ponzar to translate what had been said.

"Blue chrysocolla," the captain explained. "Two stones motionless a hand span apart. Move them together on a straight line. Accelerate their motion as they draw closer and collide."

Jemidon climbed down into the pit and reached into the scatter of stones. He coughed once and then shook with a spasm that made his eyes water and blurred his vision. With a feeling of sudden doubt, he closed his fingers around the nearest stone.

"No, not serpentine—chrysocolla," Ponzar said. "Two stones of the same type with a force that is to attract."

Jemidon squinted at his hands and saw that somehow he had picked up the wrong rocks. Staring at the tablestone, he closed on the proper targets and then looked at the carved inscriptions to see where they should be placed. A forest of crosses, squares, and tangled lines swarmed before his eyes. What had been so obvious standing on the edge of the pit was now a hopeless confusion. He stabbed blindly with his left hand and felt the stone jar on contact and slip from his cramped grip.

Jemidon hastily reached out to grab the free stone, but his sleeve swept across the table, knocking a dozen more off the surface to scatter into the pit. He bent forward to pick up what he had spilled and banged his head with a sharp crack against the side of the flat stone. He staggered to his feet, feeling suddenly dizzy, and fell backward, tripping over the telescope, which somehow had tangled between his legs.

One of Utothaz's manipulants, the one who had rushed to aid with the alchemy, slipped past Jemidon and moved the stones in the manner prescribed. The sense of drifting suddenly vanished. The last of the tests had been completed. The laws once more were in effect.

They all had succeeded in the simple exercise. All except Jemidon. Even the simple magics of Melizar's universe were beyond his ability to master.

He blinked aside the film that was forming in his eyes, searching his mind for what he should say next. He blinked again when he saw the captain bowing on one knee, his shovel dipped at his side.

Ponzar extended his right hand with the index finger pointing at Jemidon, thumb skyward and middle finger to the side. Jemidon whirled to look at the rest. They were all doing the same.

"By the grace of the great right hand, homage to the new pilot," Ponzar said. "Homage to the new pilot, or as he would say in his own tongue, homage to the meta-magician, master of all the laws."

"What do you mean?" Jemidon asked. "I failed. Of all of these, I was the only one who could not pass the simple test. If I cannot master the basic principles, what hope do I have of controlling the metalaws as well?"

"You are not Melizar's manipulant." Ponzar rose and pounded his shovel on the ground. "He would never have

322

sent a possible rival if he knew of that one's power. There is an instinctive distrust that grows as awareness unfolds. No, faraway one, the test has confirmed it. There can be no doubt. You are a metamagician. May the great right hand make you strong."

"Two metalaws," Jemidon protested. "Only two metalaws do I know."

"There is only one more," Ponzar said. "The Verity of Exclusion is the third."

"As Melizar indicated." Jemidon nodded. "After the battle in Plowblade Pass."

"Exactly so," Ponzar agreed. "The Verity of Exclusion, or, as the Skyskirr say, 'if skill with the key, then none with the stone.' You can be a mover of the stones or the one who uncouples, but not both. The great right hand does not permit such talent to reside all in one."

Jemidon gasped as the words hit him. The implication was staggering, if it were true. Manipulator of the laws or a practitioner, but not both. Talent in one excluded performance in the other. It was the answer to all his failures, bundled neatly in a single mass, coupled to a cause totally outside himself. He felt his lifelong burden suddenly release from his shoulders and sail away. Despite Melizar's twisting of the laws, despite the growing menace of the noxious air, his spirits soared. More swiftly than the fastest lithon, the feeling careened through his thoughts. There was nothing wrong with him. He was as worthy to hold his shoulders straight as the next. He was truly a man, able to return even a master's stare without looking away.

He reached out and grabbed Ponzar's arm. "I want to believe, Ponzar, most certainly I do. It would explain so much. The bumblings, the miscarriages—they would be tolerable to bear. I could not have become the thaumaturge's apprentice despite my sister's sacrifice, nor the magician's initiate, nor Farnel's tyro, nor any of the rest. It is a law, a metalaw, that prevented me all the while."

Jemidon managed to laugh. He almost jumped to click his heels, but remembered in time and grabbed onto the safety rope. He ran the facts through his mind; as they fell into place, one by one, his smile broadened. On Morgana, he could not work the simplest charms until after sorcery was no longer a law. He had fumbled through the ritual in Rosimar's guild, even though it was the simplest step. In the grotto, he could not grasp the rock-cutting sword. And even alchemy—when the domain was tightly coupled and the formula had no part of law, he remembered perfectly. But just now, when there was indeed a chance to effect its potency, he could not recall a thing. He was suited for no craft. No master's robe would he ever wear. It would be that of a metamagician instead, one whose skills transcended all laws. He could—

Jemidon stopped and frowned at Ponzar. "You say that there are only three metalaws, and now I know them all. The constraint of seven I understand and the manipulation of least contradictions as well. But the uncoupling." Jemidon shrugged. "I know nothing of the working of Melizar's cube or even Utothaz's pyramid."

"Those are only the crutches," Ponzar said. "The aids that help bring forth the powers the pilots possess inside. They are bound to the gradual awakenings, the growing understanding of the working of the laws. For each pilot, it is different, something unique to his own being, something that resonates with what molded him into the power that he is to be."

"But I have no such device," Jemidon said. "The only thing remotely resembling it would be this old coinchanger I carry and the puzzle that—"

Jemidon halted a second time. The thoughts were coming clear and fast. "Benedict's puzzle. Twenty-five coins," he mumbled. "The trick is to insert them in such a way that each column ends up with only one type. I have done the best I can, but have yet to come up with the solution. There is no way with twenty-five already in the chambers to set the initial state properly before I make any discharge. I would need something else, another from the outside. A twenty-sixth to have it right."

Jemidon's eyes blinked as it all rushed together in a flash. With trembling fingers, he removed the leather thong from around his neck and untied the knot. Slowly he slid the worn brandel from the loop. Holding his breath, he inserted it into the changer.

Jemidon heard it tinkle into the innards and paused a moment more. "Dranbots," he said, fingering the leftmost column. He pressed the lever and saw the glitter of five identical coins in his palm. "Galleons," he said more excitedly as he pushed the next. "Regals, coppers, and finally gold brandels, the last of all."

Jemidon pushed the final lever slowly, holding his lips in a tight line. He felt the strain of the stretched rope and then a sudden snap as the universe started to drift. Ponzar and the others resumed their reverent bows. It was true. Jemidon had decoupled the laws.

For a moment, no one spoke. Jemidon felt dazed from the staggering immensity of what he had learned. He was a metamagician, master of the three metalaws. At first he had thought he was pursuing a sixth magic, but now he understood that that concept was wrong. Although only seven could have power at one time, there were a countless number of magics, each governed by its own laws. Metamagic was something entirely different, with three metalaws of its own. And the metamagician was able to deactivate the underlying principles of a whole universe and replace them with others at his command.

Without thinking, Jemidon reached back to the table-stone and fiddled with the small rocks so that the laws would reengage. One of the manipulants scrambled forward and, with a slight bow, pushed aside his hand.

Jemidon frowned in puzzlement for a moment and then laughed. "Of course, I cannot perform the craft. It will take some getting used to. Um, black sphalerite, moving in a single line. Bring them to touching with increasing speed."

The manipulant looked back at Ponzar and heard the translation. Soon the laws were reestablished and Jemidon sagged to the table, the intense wash of emotion robbing the strength in his legs.

"The manipulants?" he asked Ponzar. "You said before that they must be attuned to the metamagician's power as well."

325

"As it is to be," Ponzar said. "The one who rushed forward has felt the urge more so than the rest. Perhaps because of our differences, he may be unique." Ponzar looked at Utothaz, still wheezing on the table, and up to the speck now more apparent in the sky. "But how many you have does not really matter. The transition has been accomplished. Utothaz may give his last in peace. I have done my duty as a captain. The great right hand will be pleased."

Ponzar turned to go, but Jemidon grabbed him by the shoulder and held him back. "Wait, I feel that there is still more. How does one select the manipulants? How do I know when we are well met?"

"Their dexterity is enhanced by a pilot's nearness. Like you, they have inherent skill. But close to your side, they are able to act far better than they could alone. You saw how well the one manipulated the flask and then the stones. The stronger the pilot, the more powerful are those who serve with him as well."

Jemidon's face brightened. "Not only the pushing of the stones, but any craft."

"Any of the laws," Ponzar said. "Why do you ask?"

Jemidon did not reply. Quickly he turned and scampered as fast as he could along the safety rope toward the entrance to the caverns.

"Delia," he called. "Delia! I know why you were able to receive so much aid from the rockbubbler and to say the glamours for Farnel with such little drill. At the very least, you are a sorcerer and a wizard. It is you who will find the pathway home."

Jemidon held his hands to his sides. He willed himself to take short swallows of air through his nose, but it did not help. The metallic smell was pervasive. The sulfur made him want to gag. Any deep draw only burned his lungs. His eyes watered, and he felt a tingling in his hands and feet. He looked at Delia, faithfully nurturing the flame to life for the dozenth time, and knew that she would not last much longer. Her eyes were nearly swollen shut. Her hands trembled as she manipulated the spark. Jemidon

326

wanted to grab the flint from her grasp, but restrained himself, because he knew it would do no good. Delia had to summon whatever devil she could. At best, he could only be near and watch.

He looked up the stairway leading outside to the reddish sky, now visibly dirty and gray. A fine ash swirled in the air, leaving a dark powder everywhere. Jemidon could hear the deep-throated hacks of a dozen of the Skyskirr, even though they were less affected than Delia and he. Two more had already submitted themselves for the feasting of the others. Jemidon had noticed a ruddy glow in the cheeks of those that remained, despite the foul air; their stomachs were distended from the offerings of their comrades. Occasionally they would look into Delia's chamber and smile encouragement, evidently assuming that, even near the end, their new pilot was trying to save them.

Delia coughed again, and her outrushing breath blew out the beginnings of a flame. She looked up at Jemidon with helpless eyes, but he managed a smile to encourage her to try again.

"Even if I start a blaze, it will be the smallest of imps," she rasped. "Without any powders, there is no way to summon a djinn."

"Relax and let whatever augmentation I bring mix efficiently with your own power," Jemidon said. "And if you are truly enhanced, a small devil might be enough to carry at least you back. And in benign air, you can conjure what is necessary to come after me. Besides, you are doing the best you can. The way you laid out the sticks in a row and had the flints ground to uniform size are things I would not have thought of. You are indeed a worthy manipulant."

A small smile tugged at the edges of Delia's mouth. She pulled her stringy hair out of the way and bent low to try again with the flame. Jemidon moved to cut out what flow of wind he could, but then tensed as he felt something begin to stir inside.

"Another unlocking," he muttered. "And somehow I feel that I must withstand this one." He grasped the changer with both hands and jammed his fingers under the levers to prevent their accidental release. But the strain built faster than he could resist. The laws uncoupled, and almost immediately he saw a distant flash of light.

Jemidon stood and peered outside. To the left, perpendicular to their direction of travel, he saw another flash that darkened the red to crimson and then a third. A sudden increase in pressure stabbed at his ears. The lithosoar shook and bobbed like a pebble churned by a wave.

A second pulse followed and then the last, each one more violent than the one before. And with the final wave of pressure, although it made no sense, the wind seemed to shift direction. Jemidon scrambled outside, looking around to reestablish his bearings. He saw the lithon to which they were rushing still directly ahead. They were close enough now that it was more than a mere dot in the sky. On a visible disk of blacks and browns, he could see dense clouds of smoke spewing forth to form a dirty halo around the sphere.

For a moment, he watched until he was sure. They were still flying to their fatal encounter. Nothing had changed their momentum, and yet the wind came from another direction. A swirl of debris caught his eye where he was sure there had been none before. It slammed into the lithosoar a little above his head, ricocheting off and then continuing on in the breeze. A circular eddy whipped past, and then another that tossed their boulder back and forth in a gut-wrenching jolt.

Ponzar appeared over the horizon, pulling quickly on the safety rope and motioning Jemidon to come to the tablestone.

"The laws have been changed again. I have felt it," Jemidon said as they met. He had to shout as the wind tore at his clothing and whistled around the rock.

"It is Melizar returning," Ponzar said. "The signal mirrors tell of it. Control of one 'hedron is not enough. His manipulants work some new art that whips the air into swirls. He plans to let none of the lithons soar as they choose until they have submitted to his will—until every pilot has broken his key and can manipulate the laws no more."

Ponzar started to say more, but gagged on the flux of foul air. He sank to one knee and let his shovel clatter on the hard ground. The stifling breeze pushed against the blade; in an instant, it was sailing away.

Another flash and shock wave shook the boulder. Jemidon felt his feet leave the ground. He reached out and snagged the safety rope in the crook of his elbow, just as he flew past. He twisted around to grip the line with his other hand and gradually hauled himself back onto the surface. Ponzar wrapped his legs around one of the stanchions and closed his eyes. He made the sign of the right hand and slumped to the surface of the rock.

"Follow the other metamagicians," he croaked. "As you gather strength, you will feel their presence more. Acting together, you might have a chance to stop Melizar as he tries to twist things farther away from the proper laws."

Jemidon looked up into the air and saw the turbulent winds rip at the bubbling brown gases from the other lithon. In great gouts of dirty cotton, the fumes exploded across the intervening distance, filling the sky.

"But the chance may be better back in my own universe," he shouted over the roaring wind. "There, wizardry and alchemy might provide some weapon better than attracting stones. I must help Delia conjure her passage back, to get to the archmage as we originally intended." He gagged and spat bitterness from his mouth, trying to shake the taste from his tongue.

"No, no, your duty is here." Ponzar shook his head. "You are the pilot and must act for the Skyskirr."

Jemidon tore himself free and pushed against the wind, back in the direction of Delia's cavern. His vision began to swim and his knees felt rubbery. He wanted to breathe deeply, but held his chest tight, hoping to reach the pocket before his senses slid away.

The roar of the air increased to a blistering intensity. The cold stung his lips. His knuckles turned white from their grip upon the rope. Hand over hand, in one strength-

329

draining tug after another, Jemidon pulled toward the opening that loomed just ahead. Deep browns enveloped him completely and made it hard to see more than a few feet in front of his face.

He shut his eyes to keep out the sting. From memory, he crawled the last few paces. With a gasp, he tumbled into the entrance and squinted open his eyes to see how Delia fared. She was curled in a tight ball in the far corner of the cavern. Her skin was pale and her breath came in short pants. He touched the coldness of her flesh and recoiled from the clammy feel. She smiled weakly and, with jerky movements, pointed across the chamber.

Jemidon saw a dance of light in the brown cloud that flowed in after him and sputtered in the last embers of a flame. A small, squeaky voice sounded somewhere above the roar.

"Better make it snappy, bub. I can only manage one, and my master said that it was to be you."

"No, you are to transport Delia," Jemidon choked.

"In another minute, it will be nobody at all," the imp squeaked. "I am not sure I can manage one of your size as it is, and that excuse for a flame doesn't give me much room to maneuver."

"Pilot, your duty," Jemidon heard Ponzar call from outside. "You will serve the Skyskirr, even if I must carry you to the table myself."

Jemidon looked at the darkening sky and back at Delia's crumpled form. He saw Ponzar enter the cavern with a drawn sword. "Delia and quickly," he commanded the imp.

"No, I said it is to be Jemidon," Delia managed to croak.

"I shall follow my master's orders, bub," the sprite said. "There is no other way. A gift, she said. A gift unfettered, with no obligation to repay. One free passage to the archmage in the domain of men. Now give me a finger and cut the chatter. It's going to be a tight squeeze."

CHAPTER EIGHTEEN

The Lord of Two Domains

THE passage through the flames was a confusion that
Jemidon could not understand. When they parted, he
struggled to pull his senses back into focus on patterns
that his mind comprehended. In the distance, he saw
morning-blue sky with pink on the horizon. To his right
stood rows of tents behind emblazoned standards; on the
left, squads of armored men were converging into formations. Directly in front, about a dozen startled men-at-
arms scrambled to their feet as he emerged from their
breakfast fire. Evidently he had arrived in the camp of
the archmage on a day of battle.

"Take me to the archmage and quickly," Jemidon said.
"He must send a large djinn to the place whence I came."
His heart raced with urgency. There was so little time.

"It looks human enough," the sergeant said to his men,
after a moment of shock. "And the little imp with him
has already disappeared. Surround him carefully. If he
resists, we will see if he is full of blood or green ichor."

"The archmage," Jemidon growled. "There is no time
for petty debate. What I have to tell him of Melizar will
be well worth his time."

Jemidon felt a sudden prick of pain at the nape of his
neck. He saw the drawn blades close in from all sides.

"Yes, the archmage it will be," the sergeant said. "He
has a standing order to report anything out of the ordinary,
even if it occurs just before the rebels attack."

One of the men brought forth hinged bracelets of iron
with a short chain in between. For a moment, Jemidon
tensed, but then he forcefully emptied his lungs. "Anything to speed the process," he said, thrusting out his

331

arms. "Travel behind the flame is but the least of what I have to tell."

In a moment, in the middle of a cluster of six, Jemidon was hurrying across the campground toward the group of silken tents with high pennons snapping in the morning breeze. He darted his eyes to either side as they trotted along. To his left, expanding almost as far as he could see, men-at-arms were dousing the last of their morning fires, slipping on their byrnies, and adjusting swords at their sides. Sergeants barked orders. Horse-borne pages waving standards called for where each group was to position itself in line. The faces of the men were grim. Tight-lipped, they did not engage in easy banter. When the eyes of their comrades were not watching, they cast furtive glances toward the hill to the north.

Jemidon looked out over the gently rising landscape. The foreground was empty. Cracked branches and trampled greenery indicated where the army must have marched the day before. Farther up the slopes was a motley of colors and glints of flashing metal that ran to the summit and stretched far to either side. It was the rebel army, packed shoulder to shoulder and marching in lockstep down the hillside. Jemidon tried to estimate the number, but gave up after he counted more than a dozen rows. He squinted to see the ragged end of the line on the east and saw that oceanside cliffs defined the other edge.

Behind the slowly moving wave, at the very top of the hill, were the smoldering ruins of Searoyal, a pile of jumbled rubble, where once had stood a walled city that could be seen leagues out to sea. Among the tumbled stones flapped the shabby canvas of the metamagician's tent. The sun glinted painfully from huge cubes of metal scattered to its left. Their covers gaped open into featureless interiors, like empty crates tipped on their sides. The tops of unneeded siegecraft were just visible over the crestline.

Jemidon glanced back at the men-at-arms. They all wore mail and carried shields of gleaming steel. Besides the standards of Arcadia, he saw the pennants of Procolon across the sea and even those of the southern kingdoms mingled with the rest. Barely two rows thick, the royal forces formed up, their thin line stretching to match the length of the one that approached.

On his right, Jemidon saw richly surcoated nobles emerge from their tents, testing the weight of their armor and slashing broadswords through the air. Squires tightened the girths on nervous horses and added the final polish to shiny helms. Behind the line of canvas, Jemidon could hear the pounding of the surf. He smelled the salt in the air. The royal forces were making a last stand; they had their backs to the sea.

In the center of the row, at the entrance to a modest tent beside the pavilion flying the royal colors of Arcadia, the sergeant pushed Jemidon's shoulder to duck and enter. Inside, along the opposite wall, had been erected a crude table of crates and planks. Along one side of the makeshift structure was a queue of pages that snaked through another opening at the rear. Seated behind the boards was a slight man in a robe of deep purple. His face was narrow and topped by fine yellow-brown hair. Wrinkles crept from the sides of eyes that had not known sleep for many hours. The furrows of concentration above the nose were no longer shallow with the smoothness of youth. Jemidon grunted as he looked at the robe. Along one sleeve were the logos of all five of the crafts.

"To Standall." The seated master set down his pen and ripped the parchment from the roll. "He is to use the ticklesprites only if lord Feston's elite guards falter. We call too much upon the demon world, as it is."

The page at the head of the line took the message and disappeared through the opening. As the rest moved up, the master thought a moment and then hastily began scribbling another note.

"Melthon should continue trying the formula," he said, "for the chance that alchemy might return. He is of no help otherwise, and the attempt cannot possibly hurt."

"Archmage Alodar," the sergeant said in reverent tones. "I realize that all of us must make the final preparations for battle, but something has transpired that I thought you should know." Alodar looked up from his writing as Jemidon was jostled forward. "He stepped from a flame just

333

as a demon would, although, as you can see, he is quite normal in form."

"Not wizardry as well!" Alodar muttered. "If this is a portent that it, too, withers away, then indeed we truly are lost. It is the only craft left that we can use."

"It remains unaltered as long as Melizar desires to conquer two universes," Jemidon said quickly. "He needs the means to travel between. And the laws do not just wither away. They are replaced abruptly by others. The Maxim of Perturbations instead of the Maxim of Persistence. The Rule of the Threshold rather than the Rule of Three."

Alodar looked at Jemidon and his eyes narrowed. "What babble is this? Neither magician nor sorcerer any more can ply his craft."

"In place of those arts, there are two others. By the perturbations, Melizar has brought down the walls of Searoyal. With animations, he has enslaved the rebels to his commands."

"Indeed, the minds of the people are clouded. That we have learned from the few who have been captured," Alodar said. "All our men are on guard to avoid any inducements that pull at their sight. And we abandoned the fortress and chose to fight on the plain, rather than be crushed by tumbling rock."

"With thaumaturgy and alchemy gone, Melizar probably will unleash even more strange forces against you," Jemidon said. "You should prepare for them as well. His powers come from understanding metamagic, the Postulate of Invariance, the Axiom of Least Contradiction, and the Verity of Exclusion."

Alodar's frown deepened. He rubbed his hand across his chin and, for a long moment, pondered what Jemidon had said. Then his eyes brightened; with a casual wave, he sent the pages away. "As good a course as any for the final preparations. Why not a gamble rather than filling chinks in a weak and tottering wall? Sergeant, release those fetters and be on your way. This man indeed might have things of value to tell us."

"Everything I will share," Jemidon said as the bracelets

fell away. "Everything that I have learned. But first I need a djinn. We must send one to Melizar's domain and save Delia from the fumes."

"A djinn? For your own personal use?" Alodar shook his head. "To save the life of one, when here thousands are in peril? You saw the forces arrayed against us outside. Wizards and demons will be our only hope to even the odds. And we have conjured all that we dare. Any more and the careful balance forged almost two decades ago might no longer be secure. It will do us no good to avoid one jeopardy, only to fall prey to another."

"Everyone knows full well how you became master of the five magics," Jemidon said. "That is not the issue here."

"You should understand that the battle today is no less important than the one on the Bardinian plain," Alodar replied. "This Melizar has swept all before him. The kingdom of Arcadia has crumbled. And with the moving pictures that twist the mind, devil-borne agents have stirred up the peoples of Procolon and the southern realms. The baronies are just barely able to keep order with all the troops they have. The one I hold dearest, Aeriel, strives to coordinate a defense across the sea. The balance is a precarious one. If Melizar wins here, the world will erupt in revolution. Everything will be his."

Alodar came around the table. "If you have something to offer, then help us defeat this strange one. Save the many. After victory, we will offer aid to the few."

Jemidon heard the sound of horns outside, the beat of drums, and the staccato march of men. How long had it already been? How much longer could Delia survive the fumes? He touched the changer at his waist and looked back into Alodar's unflinching eyes. It was clear the archmage's mind was set; he had a goal and would not be deterred.

"Very well." Jemidon sighed. "First the battle and then the djinn. As long as the one immediately follows the other. I will aid all I can." He squatted to the ground and began to speak quickly. "I was on Morgana when sorcery failed. It happened the night of the grand celebration."

335

"No, from the very beginning." Alodar glanced at the sand running from a glass as he reached for a pen. "Leave out no detail. The most insignificant might be important."

Jemidon sighed again. "My father wanted me to be a thaumaturge," he said. "He gave me his last gold brandel for the testing fee."

"And so mobilizing all the alchemists to manufacture sweetbalm in preparation for the battle was to our deterrent." Alodar paced around the confines of the tent, his hands behind his back. "They had to stop their normal productions to convert their facilities, and in the lull, when no formulas were being written, this Skyskirr changed the law. What you say is hard to accept, Jemidon, even if it explains what has come to pass better than the tale of any other."

"Exactly so," Jemidon said. He had wanted to rattle off everything at once. Each heartbeat seemed an eternity, but the archmage would not be rushed. He had asked questions about all aspects of Jemidon's quest, details from the very first, the apprenticeship to the alchemist, the initiates' examination at the inland guild, the graphical representation for the charmlets shown to Farnel. And with each answer, Alodar had grown more introspective, seemingly concerned with something else besides the working of the metalaws.

"And these uncouplings. You say that I cannot perform them." Alodar rubbed his sleeve with the logos. "The power has been awakened in you and no other of our kind."

"As it would appear," Jemidon said. "The Verity of Exclusion prevents a practitioner of the arts. And, by the random factors, I have tested its truth hard enough for myself."

Alodar nodded. "And now what do you propose?"

"Well, I would—" Jemidon paused. In the rush to save Delia, he had thought of nothing else. "I would challenge Melizar with manipulants of my own," he said after a moment. "I am a metamagician as much as he. I would bring about a decoupling. Direct the enactment of rituals, incantations, and formulas that are our own. Have the laws move in a direction that favors our cause rather than his."

"And which direction is that?" Alodar asked. "Have you studied the lattice? Are you sure it would not mean the end of wizardry instead?"

"If we could get a look, we would know," Jemidon answered quickly. "Perhaps by using a sprite to fly where Melizar has set up his camp and snatch the lattice away."

Alodar frowned. "From what you have said, Melizar proceeds methodically from a plan he has worked out in great detail. And for each perturbation, he pauses and carefully calculates the response that returns the rush of events to the course that he desires.

"This is no mere examination for a robe, Jemidon. Far more than that is at stake. How could what you propose have even the smallest of chances? Why would you succeed now when you have failed so often before?"

"But I am a metamagician." Jemidon scowled. Despite everything else, the anger and frustration began to bubble as before. The words of the archmage were familiar ones that he had tried for so long to dispel. "I am a metamagician. That is why I was unable, why I could not succeed, why I could not get the honor and respect. But now I understand what has to be done. Better than any other. Give me the means. I will show you. It may be your only chance."

"You state that you were prevented," Alodar said. "Because of something external, you were unequal to the task. And how convenient for you that is. Most of us do not have such luxury. We must look inside instead and understand what are our strengths and weaknesses."

"One cannot overwhelm a metalaw," Jemidon said. "It would be futile to try."

"And was it a metalaw that sent you after graphic abstractions instead of memory drill in Farnel's hut? Did a principle of the universe compel you not to list the simple incantations on paper before the thaumaturge's test? After the third failure with the alchemist's formula, what fundamental rule prevented you from assaying for purity?

337

How carefully did you plan your actions before the stumble in Rosimar's guild?

"And most important, consider this. You have shown a remarkable ability to deduce the underlying principle from the observed effects. With your skills, you have found three metalaws. But if that is indeed your talent, why did it take so long? Why so many years until a stranger hands you the clues? Why not suspect after your first failures that something else was wrong? Why were not they the key that opened this inner box of which you speak and tumbled out the answers?"

The archmage raised his index finger and held it poised in front of Jemidon's face. "Perhaps because the answers were not so clearly cut. Perhaps because, deep inside, you knew that you had not fully prepared, that you had become bored, and that you did not exercise discipline, focus, concentration, or the planning that every master must have. Perhaps because, metalaws aside, you knew in your innermost being that you had not put forth the effort necessary to wear the robe. You preferred instead to dabble at the next in the hopes it would be easier."

"The metalaw is true!" Jemidon shouted and backed off a step. "I have felt the uncoupling. It explains the dizziness, the lapses of memory, and all the rest."

"Not all the rest," Alodar said.

"Why are you telling me this?" Jemidon cried. "You are the archmage, ultimately responsible for all the crafts in the world. There is a battle about to begin outside this very tent, and you spend your time speculating about the weaknesses of someone you have barely met."

Jemidon's chest pounded. The words were too sharp. He did not want to face them after all that had happened. He was a metamagician, and the honor and respect would be his.

"I asked you what you would do," the archmage said. "But more important perhaps is why. Is it for the robe of the master?"

"Yes, yes, I have told you that."

"And anything else?"

Jemidon caught his breath. The archmage had been

striking at the old wounds that would not heal, and he had almost lost control. He squeezed his fists tight and looked Alodar steadily in the eye.

"And for Delia," he said. "Delia more than all." He paused a second and licked his lips. "We waste too much time. If you do not believe, I will continue on my own as best I can."

Alodar placed his hands behind his back and stared at Jemidon a long while in silence. Then he turned away and paced back and forth across the width of the tent with quick, precise steps while Jemidon seethed. The archmage stopped at the desk and fingered a magic ring that was now stone-cold. Finally he turned back and looked intently at Jemidon a second time. "I do believe you, Jemidon," he said. "I must. We have too few choices left. As staggering as the concepts are that you relate, they do explain all the puzzles with which we are beset.

"And so I have decided to give you command of the alchemists, magicians, sorcerers, and thaumaturges. Only the wizards must be withheld for their more critical tasks. What you submit has a kernel of merit. It will not hurt to add it to the feeble arsenal that we have.

"But there is more, more for you to be truly ready. If you are indeed to face Melizar, if, in the end, our fate does rest on your shoulders alone, then you must be a master of at least one thing—a master of yourself."

Alodar did not wait for Jemidon to say more. He went to the flap in the rear of the tent and ducked outside. Jemidon hesitated a moment and then hastened after. As he scrambled outside, he saw a shallow depression packed with men, probably more than a hundred robes crammed together with the implements of their nonfunctioning crafts. Near the far lip, a single squad of men-at-arms snapped to attention as they saw the archmage approach.

"You have all trusted my judgment in the past," Alodar said. "And there is little time to explain my decision now." He waved back at Jemidon. "Accept this one as your leader. Follow his commands as you would mine. He may send you into danger, but surely that is to be preferred to waiting passively for rebel blades to come slashing into your midst."

Jemidon squared his shoulders and stepped forward, but suddenly a great shout echoed from the plain. Trumpets blared an opening charge. "The archmage! Where is the archmage?" voices shouted. "Up on the hill behind their lines among the metal boxes! He must come and see. A circle of flame!"

Alodar did not wait for any reaction from the masters. He bolted around the side of his tent and headed for the battle line.

"I will show you my mettle," Jemidon shouted as the archmage disappeared from view. "I will prove the metamagician I can be."

Jemidon waited a moment for a reply, but heard none. It was up to him to prove himself one final time. Grimly he turned back to the masters.

"You with the flasks and powders. And over there, the sad-faced ones mumbling in the mirrors." He pushed his way to the center of the masters and whirled with arms outspread. "There is not time to worry about resonances. The archmage commands. All of you follow me. We will get as close to the fighting line as we can."

Jemidon ran out of the depression, not looking back to see if any would comply. But soon he heard the swish of robes and the clank of paraphernalia as he sprinted across the marshy ground around Alodar's tent. Apparently the word of the archmage carried enough authority that they followed without hesitation.

As he cleared the pavilions, Alodar was not to be seen. Instead, up the gentle slope, he saw the two angry lines close on each other and the battle begin. The grate of steel shrieked from a thousand collisions. Like a pair of mating snakes, the two armies writhed across the tilted plain. The men-at-arms with thick shields and shining mail slashed their swords right and left, cutting through leather and hacking off the blades of scythes. But onward the rebels came; mindless of the hurt, unflinching under the rain of blows, they whirled their flails and stabbed with their poles, borne forward by their comrades who pressed

340

from behind. In two or three places, the royal line thinned; and in one, a salient of brown broke through to circle from the rear.

Above the combatants' heads, the sky crackled and sparked. Pungent smells filled the air. Glowing sprites and tiny imps streaked down on bare heads, ripping away tufts of hair in their talons or dropping trails of itching powders in their turbulent wakes. Fox-sized devils sprayed their repulsive odors and radiated the feeling of unquenchable thirst and will-sapping pain.

Towering over them all, the larger demons roared in aerial combat against their brothers, who were commanded by Melizar's manipulant-wizard. Veinous wings of turgid green beat frantically for altitude, trying to elude glowing spheres of sputtering sparks which blackened on touch and sizzled away the pulpy flesh. From gnarled fingers shot bolts of piercing reds and violet that ripped the air into a hot incandescence.

Jemidon looked to the hill and saw on the rubble the circle of flame that had brought the page running to Alodar. Next to the tent, a huge djinn, far larger than the one that had carried Jemidon and Delia away, was twisted into an arch easily twice the height of a man. His cloven hooves and fingertips barely touched the ground. All along his scaly legs, his humped back with the furled wings, and his forehead and upper arms danced a deep crimson flame that shot high into the morning sky. Framed in the arch was the cloaked form of Melizar, the metamagician.

As he bounded over the terrain, Jemidon saw the royal flank farthest from the sea crumple and dissolve. A group of bondsmen swung with blades rather than with scythe and flail, trading the thrusts of the men-at-arms blow for blow. Because of their superior number, they had forced the corner back.

Jemidon frowned at what he saw. Most of the rebels' swords appeared to be made of wood. Only about one in ten was true steel. But all the weapons, metal or not, were clanging off the soldiers' shields as if they were of the finest temper. As Jemidon watched, one slipped underneath a slowly dropping guard and crashed against links of mail, popping ringlets and spewing blood.

"I would call the law something like 'same shape, same function,'" Jemidon shouted over his shoulder. "No doubt Melizar's replacement for thaumaturgy provides his minions with more than harvest tools." He glanced at another spot where the freetoilers had broken through and saw women and children behind the fighters, lofting blobs of a purple tar onto the backs of the men-at-arms. Everywhere it touched, the metal glowed red. Drops of molten iron sputtered to the ground. Burning sizzles mixed with howls of pain.

"Something to do with alchemy," Jemidon said as he signaled for a halt some twenty yards behind the struggling fighters. "Perhaps 'the base drives away the good.' No matter. I count no more than a score of each. Thaumaturges and alchemists, try examples of your craft. Work more of your magics than they. The others assist as best you can."

While the masters exercised their skills, Jemidon emptied the coins from the changer into his palm. Quickly he sorted through the collection and reinserted them in the slit in top. He held his breath as he fingered his old worn brandel last and saw it slip away. Working the five levers one by one, he emptied the sorted coins back into his hand.

Jemidon felt the familiar tension of the parting rope and imagined the creak of the fibers as they strained to breaking. For a moment, the line groaned and twisted, but then suddenly it was slack.

Jemidon frowned as he reloaded the changer. There was resistance. As Ponzar had said, metamagicians could struggle over the state of the coupling. Jemidon cast a hasty glance in the direction of the hilltop. It was too far to see more than the Skyskirr's outline, but he felt his presence nonetheless.

Jemidon grasped the changer tightly. He tried to visualize the rope again growing taut. Mentally, he tugged on the line, straining against a force he could not quite comprehend. He placed his feet wide apart and arched his back, swinging both fists to the side. Then he tried to bring himself erect, imagining the rope tied to his collar and tugging him from behind. His muscles tensed and then trembled from the effort. With eyes closed, oblivious to the noise and swirl of battle, he brought his arms forward and then his head. In his mind he saw the rope spring tight and, with a snap, burst in twain.

"Look at that!" a thaumaturge exclaimed. "The incantation works, the one that has failed ever since the craft went away. I feel the prick in my own arm, just as I have stabbed the doll."

"And sweetbalm," an alchemist said. "Only a trace, but the healer of wounds, nonetheless."

Jemidon turned to watch a wooden sword splinter on a downsweep. Farther away, a glob of tar solidified in midflight and bounced harmlessly from a shield. A great cry of confusion went up from the pressing rebels. The men-at-arms answered with a cheer. With tired arms, they held back the attack, for an instant stopping the onrushing momentum.

Jemidon smiled. "Perhaps we should try for the other two crafts as well," he said. "A simple ritual like the Neophyte's Cadence; and for sorcery we can use the Song of the Shifting Sands, just as Canthor did. Send someone back to the dunes and—"

Jemidon stopped and clutched the changer. He felt the hint of a tug and then a growing strain. He jammed his fingers under the levers, cradling the device close to his chest. A dull pain shot through his head. He closed his eyes and sank to his knees, curling into a ball. Walls of force around his mind seemed to ripple and tear apart into sinuous tendons. Like stubby fingers in massive gloves, they probed his thoughts, sending numbing jabs into deep recesses of his awareness. He felt his hands twitch on the changer and then, with an involuntary spasm, his left hand fell away, trembling with fatigue. In his mind he saw the coarse fingers surrounding him, fumbling with his own, prying them loose and pushing them aside.

Almost in helpless fascination, his other hand hurled free. A shower of coins tumbled into his lap. Simulta-

343

neously, he felt the laws decouple and accelerate away. With a rush, they sped to the next vertex in the lattice, back to where wooden swords and obnoxious tars held power, but they did not stop there. Like a peg counting score in a card game, the fabric of existence plowed onward, taking the laws several more steps away.

"Catapults," Jemidon heard someone suddenly yell. "They are using the siegecraft. Hurling missiles on friend and foe alike."

Jemidon shook himself out of a daze to see stones streaking across the sky. In a heavy shower of gravel, colorful pebbles and rocks cascaded down upon the line of fighting. Like hailstones hitting a slanted roof, they bounced from upraised shields and skittered across the ground. A few careened in Jemidon's direction and he saw the pale green of epidote crystals, not individual rocks, but conglomerates of smaller pebbles loosely held together by a sticky glue.

Jemidon felt the laws recouple. Instantly he realized what would happen next. "To cover," he yelled, "and stay away from the rock!" He glanced about quickly and dove for a small hummock that he hoped would be free and clear of the deadly rain. And as he did, in a series of loud pops all down the battle line, the grenades exploded into jagged shrapnel and high-velocity shot. Small missiles propelled apart from one another whistled through the air, tearing through flesh and ricocheting from metal that stood in its way. Men and maces, shields and swords, shirts of mail and leather vests, all danced along the ground, battered back and forth by the blows that struck from all sides. In an instant, the discipline of the fighting line vanished into a pool of wounded and dying men.

For a moment, the rebels in the rearmost rows were silent when they saw the carnage in front. But they quickly realized that now only a few remained to oppose them, isolated men who staggered dazedly among the bodies of their fallen comrades. With a triumphant yell, the rebels clambered over the bodies and headed for the wizards who still directed their imps with harassments from above.

Jemidon staggered to his feet. The battlefield was dissolving into a rout. Some of the wizards bravely stood their ground, concentrating on the demons they commanded, while others kicked over their fires and bolted back toward the sea. A flurry of pages exploded from the royal pavilion. Knocking shoulders, they jostled the king and the high prince on jeweled litters, tugging against one another which way to go.

Jemidon looked up the hill. Melizar was still framed in the arch of fire. But he saw others as well. Coming out of the red background beneath the demon's span were more Skyskirr with heads bowed and moving slowly toward the metal boxes.

"To the metamagician. He still is the key," Jemidon shouted. "Charge through the confusion of the rush. There is nothing left but to confront him as best we can."

Jemidon ran forward and picked up a shield from the ground. He ducked to the side to avoid the downswipe of a rebel racing past. Scrambling on hands and knees, he retrieved a sword. Just in time, he parried a blow that sent steel grating down his blade to the hilt. "Masters, rally to me," he yelled. "Men-at-arms, ready your weapons and coalesce the craftsmen into a group. Isolated, they are certain to fall."

Some of the masters hesitated. The rebels running through their midst cut two to the ground, despite widespread arms and empty palms. Most turned to run, but a few came forward, dodging blows and scrambling to Jemidon's side. The men-at-arms formed into a disciplined line, curving around Jemidon and the others. With swords drawn and shields locked, they began to run up the hill.

Up ahead, the onrushing rebels dissolved into an undisciplined mob. Like angry bees, they swarmed onto the isolated remnants of the royal forces, hacking away at those who still stood and charging after the ones who ran for the sea. A few saw Jemidon's sprinting squad and tried to re-form; but for most, their eyes were on the struggle around the royal pavilion and the glint of plundered jewels and gold. A few blows were struck in token resistance, and then the rebels backed off to attack more promising targets with smaller risks. Like a great ship

345

sailing out of harbor, Jemidon's wedge parted through the confusion of the battle and headed up the hill.

As they grew closer, Jemidon could see Melizar's own guard become alert. About twenty men in mail, all heavily armored, formed into a line to contest the advance. Behind them were two of Melizar's manipulants, staggering in drunken circles from the heat among the metal boxes, but still managing to stir pots of tar. A third chipped away at a boulder of orange-red realgar, dropping the shards into globular molds.

At the hillcrest, Jemidon saw Melizar accept the decoupling keys from other Skyskirr as they passed through the portal. With his tinkly laugh, the pilot directed them to the boxes and watched them crawl slowly inside the massive structures twice the height of a man.

Jemidon ran his wedge into the waiting warriors. With a slash of axe and blade, his squad began hacking at limbs and crashing into upraised shields. The two men on either side of Jemidon went down, and then another on his left. As Melizar's guards surged through the opening, Jemidon bolted into the gap with a pirouette, feeling the numbing jolt of blows against the shield as he squirted past. He ducked by the slow-moving manipulants and sprinted for the ring of flame. Flinging aside the sword and shield, he grasped the changer at his waist. With grim determination, he steeled himself for the confrontation. A magician and two alchemists managed to slip around the flanks and scrambled to his side.

Melizar slowly turned, while Jemidon tensed in readiness. The metamagician gestured to his manipulants and they stopped stirring the tar. One picked up a small pipe from the ground and whistled a short tune. Immediately, the air swirled into violent funnels. Jemidon heard strangled cries and turned to see each master spinning in a vortex, his feet off the ground and arms flung wide. Jemidon tentatively reached back to grab at one of the limbs as it spun past, but an outstretched palm slapped his own with a sting.

A bubble of panic began to form in Jemidon's stomach. He clutched at the changer and ground his teeth. Without someone to work the arts, he was powerless. Regardless of where he might shift the laws, it would do no good unless there was someone to exercise them when he was finished. He had done it again—rushed off to the confrontation without any semblance of a plan.

"So it is you." Melizar stepped back from where the djinn crackled and burned. "My misgivings were properly placed. You are far more than a bungler, one who merely adds grains of sand to the joints of my grand design. Far more than the likes of a Drandor, who gave even his skull to my other manipulants when I found him again." The Skyskirr laughed and waved his hands back toward the portal and then down to the plain. "Far more, and yet not enough. You were able to decouple the laws when my attention was distracted to my own 'hedron. But it was nothing to wrench control back from your grasp. And now it is almost finished."

Melizar pointed back at the portal. A cool breeze tainted with wisps of brown filtered through the opening. A high-frequency shriek bubbled from around the djinn's limbs. Jemidon saw the muscles twitch and tremble. Beads of dark sweat dripped onto the ground.

"A new use for the demons," Melizar said. "One that tries the strength of even the djinn. On his left side are the laws of your domain; on the right are those of mine. The shriek is their discord as they meet at the boundary in his scaly hide. But through the portal comes the refreshing breeze that allows my manipulants to shed the torpor of hibernation.

"Through it, I have received the other pilots, one by one. They tried in concert to move the laws from where I had locked them; but my sojourn here, where, except for you, there are no others, has made me strong. A mere step in the portal was enough to resist all they could try. And now, as I have commanded, they surrender their keys so their lithons might not be crashed together or stripped bare by the buffeting storms. I have conquered them all. And without the means to decouple, they are powerless. I can crush their bones and mix their marrow with common dust. They have no means to shield away

347

the disgrace. All except for Utothoz. His lithon, curiously, does not respond. But even now my manipulant is directing the window there. I will keep it open until he can step onto the rock. It cannot take long to search, and then I will have the last of the pilots' keys."

Through the opening, Jemidon saw Ponzar's lithon grow in size in a sea of brown. Tendrils of hazy vapor snaked through the portal. He began to gag on the smell that was growing stronger even in his own clean air. Behind him, down the slope, Jemidon saw the rebels in the row of tents, pulling away the silken panels and shouting with each discovery of hidden wealth. Here and there were pockets of resistance still, a few wizards about the archmage and a company of reserves standing their ground in the surf. But the outcome was clearly decided. The battle could last only a little more time.

The whirling behind Jemidon intensified. He saw the three masters flung on a puff of wind into the nearest of the open cubes, bouncing off the walls. Then suddenly strong gusts swept him from his own feet. He felt his changer rip from his belt with the slash of an airborne knife. With no way to control his motion, he jerked across the terrain, bobbing like a butterfly, but heading unerringly for the box. With a mighty billow from the rear, he slammed into one side, head pointed toward the ground.

He saw that the cube was mounted on a small platform with legs of unequal length that provided a level base on the slope. He grabbed at the bottom edge of the cube, trying to resist the blast of air pushing him toward the opening on top, but the wind increased to a roaring gale. Churning dust mingled with the stink of the Skyskirr vapors, blinding his sight. He was stretched into a painfully thin line, feet directly overhead. The muscles in his back and shoulders knotted from the strain. He tightened his grip as best he could; but, like bark pulled from a tree, his fingers slid from the smooth surface of the cube.

In a rush, he was hurled high in the air over the top of the container. Then the gale slowed almost as abruptly as it had begun. He plunged back earthward into the gaping opening now directly beneath him.

Jemidon saw the three masters scramble out of his way as he crashed into their midst, but he paid them little heed. He jumped and grabbed the upper edge of the box, frantically swinging his leg in a wide arc, attempting to find some purchase so that he could climb back out. But the top was too high. He could not hook his foot over the edge. In final desperation, he chinned himself and looked out on Melizar's smiling face.

"The cube is an excellent idea from the practitioners of your arts," the metamagician said. "Of course, your magic no longer works. My manipulants have had to build one based on the law I have moved into its place. And the device is not quite the same. The walls are as thin and light as bread, rather than built of thick metal that cannot be moved. Each contraction is less, a few arm lengths at most and not a halving. But it is as strong and sure as the original. In the end, the result will be the same. Think of it while I go for the first feast of my victory, the marrow of the one whom your kind label as king."

Melizar tipped back his head and laughed. With a flourish, he pointed to one of his manipulants, and the lid of the box suddenly rotated on its hinges. With a swoosh, it slammed onto Jemidon's head and began to push him down into the inside.

He looked about quickly, savoring the last sights, whatever they might be. The masters and men-at-arms who had followed him up the hill were all scattered in bloody disarray on the slope. Melizar was turning to march triumphantly down the hillside. The pillage continued in the royal tents. Manipulants were slumped to one side of the cube, exhausted from the heat. The portal on the other side opened onto Ponzar's lithon, and Delia was just a small distance away. Heavy brown vapors spewed through and contaminated the air.

With a gasp, Jemidon released his grip and fell to the bottom of the cube as the lid slammed shut. In the sudden darkness, he felt the vibration that meant the start of the contractions.

CHAPTER NINETEEN

Duel of the Metamagicians

JEMIDON'S thoughts exploded in tatters. All parts of his mind shrieked at once. The cube rumbled and shook, pushing against his back and thrusting him into the others. The cube, the cube! There was so little time before it would crush everything together. Nothing would be left, only a pulpy ooze that drained away in the end.

Think, he told himself. Reverse the spell. Escape.

Yes, escape from the box, but escape to what? Outside, victory was within Melizar's grasp. The archmage had been right. Merely having the power of a metamagician did not ensure success. He had failed again. Despite the boasts, he was not a serious threat at all. Melizar had brushed him aside as an unimportant perturbation to his plan.

The walls vibrated and contracted another step. Jemidon's forehead beaded with sweat. He bumped into one of the alchemists and smelled his fear. Jemidon had to get free of the cube and confront Melizar once again. And this time he would show him, this time would be different, this time he would—

Even in his panic, Jemidon's thoughts lumbered to a halt. He remembered what the archmage had said about how he would be tested. He recalled Delia's sharp words about rushing forward without any real idea of what he was to do.

Jemidon gritted his teeth and forced himself to draw a long, deep breath. Delia, he thought. She still had to be saved. And what did she care about struggling metamagicians in a stylistic battle that would be a tale for the sagas? By whatever means the rescue, she would not care.

Confronting Melizar on his own terms was not the way to do it. Jemidon did not have the aptitude, let alone the experience. He would have to use his strengths, rather than continue to flog away in a manner not really attuned to his innermost self. He must somehow pose the problem in a way that he could puzzle it out.

Puzzle! That was it! He must view the whole thing as just another puzzle. That was his strength, the solving of puzzles; that was his skill, the essence of his true interests and desires. He had the ability to deduce the underlying principle from observation, to jump to the answer from fragments of clues. He must use his natural capabilties to find the total solution, a solution beyond an escape from the cube, a solution that stretched all the way to the end. Savagely he pulled his arms around his chest and squeezed against the panic, forcing the chaos of his thoughts into a smaller volume.

The rumble of the cube bubbled and exploded against the barrier he began constructing in his mind. Methodically, one by one, he slowed his thoughts, just as they were about to break away, and brought them under control. Gradually, with steel bands of will, he caught and confined them all, pushing the terrors together and squeezing them out of existence.

He breathed again only when he was done. With a cold deliberateness, he examined the events that had led to his capture—all the images that surrounded Melizar in his camp upon the crest and each previous encounter that might give a clue how to proceed. He recalled all the detail of his last images before the lid slammed shut—Melizar walking down the hill, the manipulants, and the portal touching Ponzar's lithon. As he had done for so many puzzles before, he pondered them one by one.

The minutes passed, but still Jemidon willed himself to remain in his passive state. He felt an elbow push painfully into his side and heard the incoherent babble of the magician rise to a deafening wail. One alchemist repeatedly pounded the walls, and the other had retreated into a terrified silence. Despite the growing panic about him, Jemidon examined all the alternatives that his imag-

351

ination pumped into his awareness and made his decision. The chance of success was small. He did not know if it would really work, but at least it was calculated to the very end.

He shook himself out of his introspection and groped in the darkness for the crying magician. He slapped the master's face sharply and grabbed his cheeks.

"Listen closely," he said. "Your only hope now is to follow as I command. Remember the words of the archmage. To do otherwise is certain doom."

The magician stopped his babble and did not resist as Jemidon stood him up and placed him in line next to the silent alchemist. He boxed the remaining master in the ears to attract his attention, then laid a hand on the master's fist to stop the pounding.

"Now imitate me exactly," Jemidon said, "while the cube is the proper size for what we must do."

He crouched with his back against the wall. With a yell, he sprang across the volume and crashed into the metal plate near the lid. The cube shuddered from his impact and tipped slightly on the small platform that supported its base.

"All of us together! We can do it," Jemidon shouted. "If we can topple the cube, then we will have a chance."

The silent alchemist grunted, and then the other two masters nodded as well. With direction and hope, their own panic evidently began to dissolve away. As one, the four slammed into the side of the cube and felt it tumble forward onto the ground.

"And again," Jemidon yelled. "Before Melizar returns. Before his manipulants deduce what we are trying to do."

The masters squirmed and pressed together, shoulder to shoulder with Jemidon against the wall. Again they leaped to collide with the cube, rolling it forward another quarter turn.

"To what purpose?" the magician gasped. "We only make more unbearable the conditions at the end."

"Just follow my commands," Jemidon snapped back. "No, not that side. Now we have to change direction. There is need for explanation only if we succeed."

352

The box shrank again, leaving barely enough room for the masters to maneuver according to Jemidon's orders. They collided into the wall with a jolt that spun them over three times more.

As they struggled, the cube continued its contractions. They managed two additional rotations before it pinned their limbs in a tangle, so that they could no longer spring. One of the alchemists gasped with pain as the other tried to pull free a leg twisted to the side.

"Once more," Jemidon said. "Rock back and forth where you are. I think I can hear the whine."

Jemidon moved one foot from where it pushed against the magician's stomach until it rested high on the rear wall. Twisting his torso so that both hands were more or less angled forward, he oscillated his hips back and forth above the masters. He felt the box rock in response to his motions, as if balanced precariously over a slight irregularity in the slope. With a savage lurch that sent stabs of pain into contorted wrists, he tipped the cube over for a final time. He hoped his memory had been accurate. There would be no chance to maneuver again if he had misjudged the distance or orientation.

As the cube tumbled, Jemidon heard the walls vibrate with an ear-piercing grate. With a shudder, the box groaned and contracted. Like children wrapped in a blanket, none of the occupants could any longer move. With a bone-jolting crash, they came to rest against hard and solid ground.

The magician again began his incoherent babble. One of the alchemists added a mournful cry. Jemidon slowly twisted his head, gasping for air between sandaled feet that raked across his cheek. There was no time left. Either his assumptions indeed were correct, or the next contraction would be one of bone-crushing pain. Almost afraid to find out, he held his breath and began to extend his foot past a fleshy resistance, searching for the smoothness of a metal wall. Finally he made contact and pushed with what little leverage he could muster. For a moment, nothing happened. Then, with a pop, the structure fell away, allowing everyone to tumble out. Jemidon collapsed onto unyielding rock, barely able to see a hand span in front of his face because of the toxic brown vapor that swirled everywhere.

"Where are we? What has happened?" one of the masters managed to cough. "By what glorious accident are we set free?"

"We are in Melizar's universe, on Ponzar's lithon," Jemidon said. "And it is no accident that the box no longer works. See the red arch in the brown? There is the demon. We moved the cube through the opening. But more importantly, we moved it to where the law that contracts it does not have power. I could not be sure, but it was our only chance. Here it is a mere box of metal, unable to respond to the commands of Melizar's manipulant."

"Melizar's universe," the master gasped. "Then back through the arch and let us flee, before he returns and confines us again."

For a moment, Jemidon hesitated. He peered through the haze, trying to spot the opening to where Delia must be lying beneath the surface of the lithon. But then he clenched his fist and looked back toward the djinn. "No," he said, more to himself than to the others. "First it will be the tent," he commanded. "That is the pathway to the solution."

Jemidon did not waste any thought on how close had been his escape. He tugged at an alchemist's sleeve and whipped him through the portal. Like dazed sheep, the two other masters followed as he ran toward the flopping canvas.

When he drew close, Jemidon grabbed the faded panels in both hands. With a burst of strength, he ripped them away from the poles and rigging. Running around the structure, he exposed the contents to the air, kicking the tatters of cloth aside.

"Unpack all the crates and examine what they contain," he yelled. "Make ready to use whatever you find the most familiar."

Jemidon glanced at a realgar boulder and saw Melizar's three manipulants lounging sluggishly, awaiting the pilot's return. He looked down the slope over the bodies of the fallen masters and men-at-arms. He saw the metamagician and the remains of his retinue, about a dozen men-at-arms, all walking with majestic slowness to confront the Arcadian king.

"Duel!" Jemidon cupped his hands and shouted. "Duel of the metamagicians! Flee only if you are fearful of the outcome. Let us see the extent of your power, Melizar, when it is evenly contested."

Melizar stopped and slowly turned. He looked up the slope and waved his arms in annoyance. The warriors reversed their march. At a trot, they started back up the hill.

"Tambourines and knotted ropes," the magician called out from a nearby trunk. "Not like those for any ritual I know, but somehow similar, nonetheless."

"And potions and powders," an alchemist shouted. "Condensing columns, grimoires with arcane symbols, none like any I have ever seen."

"Get them all out and look for more," Jemidon called over his shoulder. "But do not manipulate any until I have given the command. Wait until Melizar begins his decoupling and I appear to resist. I am betting that he will try to handle things quickly with the realgar. He cannot ignore us while we are here. The threat is too great that I might attempt the same."

Jemidon nodded as he saw the metamagician reach for his decoupling cube and wave his arms to signal his manipulants. The pilot's followers stirred from their rest and began to move some of the smaller pieces of the rock in helical trajectories. Jemidon looked for the pile of keys that Melizar had collected from the other metamagicians when they passed through the portal to surrender. He saw the twisted remains of his changer lying on top. He ran over to where it lay and hefted the hunk of flattened metal that could hold coins no more.

And as he did, he felt the snapping jolt of a decoupling. While Melizar's men-at-arms rushed forward with swords drawn, the metamagician's laughter carried over their heads on the stirring of a breeze. Jemidon grabbed the battered changer and concentrated on resisting the un-

355

locking, but he never had a chance to start. He felt the fury of Melizar's power knocking his own feeble strength aside as if it were a leaf in the wind. The metamagician's rage, caused by his continual annoyance, bubbled in Jemidon's mind. The laws decoupled with a burst, not gradually drifting, but vibrating with the energy of the pilot's frustration.

"Now," Jemidon shouted to the magician. "As many elements of ritual as you can. Better and faster than you have ever enacted them before."

The magician reacted swiftly to Jemidon's words. He grabbed a tambourine and flung three cuttings of rope onto its flat surface, dancing them about with a tap of his hand. Immediately Jemidon felt the laws pause in mid-shudder and a gentle acceleration away from the node of the lattice.

"And now the alchemy," Jemidon shouted. "It does not matter what, as long as there is enough."

The alchemists responded by dumping a sackful of sparkling powder into an uncorked bottle of some fuming liquid. Sparks flew from the mixture, rising into the sky.

Jemidon looked at the manipulants struggling with the realgar. They still moved sluggishly, and their precise motions were not enough. The laws were drifting in a direction different from the one Melizar had intended. But the metamagician sensed what was happening as well. He waved his arms and his attendants quickened their pace, hurling showers of rocks simultaneously over the crest and down the slope in ragged sprays.

The laws kept drifting in the direction of the new magic and alchemy. Jemidon saw Melizar stop in his climb and huddle into a tight knot, the imp light above his head suddenly alive. For a moment, the drift continued uncontested, but then Melizar suddenly stood erect.

Jemidon felt the metamagician reassert his strength, this time attempting to relock the laws where they had just been anchored. The metamagician had decided that working with the magic and alchemy he had was better than giving them up, even in the hopes of activating the realgar. Again Jemidon offered resistance, grasping the changer and straining to force the fabric of existence farther from its mooring and increase the rate of drift.

But Melizar was far stronger. Jemidon felt the current begin to slow and then finally reverse direction, heading back to the node of the lattice from which it had sprung. He sensed the laws gaining momentum, tugged by Melizar's desire to complete the locking, overwhelming any tendency to wander away.

"Now, stop the ritual and the formula," Jemidon commanded. "Start others that are completely different. Use more exotic wares. Quickly, before Melizar completes the relocking!"

The magician dropped the tambourine and reached deep into another crate. He brought forth a collection of silken handkerchiefs and an empty tube into which he proceeded to stuff the squares, one by one. The alchemists broke the bottle of brewing chemicals, letting its purple stain soak into the ground. They began picking apart delicately preserved spider webs and pressing each of the strands onto some sticky paper that unwound from a bulky roll nearby.

The laws lurched again, heading in a new direction unlike the one before. Jemidon saw Melizar fidget with his cube, apparently puzzled by what his adversary was trying to do.

"Now again, the knots and mixing chemicals," Jemidon said. "Only this time, twice the activity of before."

The magician grabbed two tambourines, maneuvering one deftly in each hand. The alchemists scooped powder from the sack into a waiting row of vials. The laws spun, heading back in the direction they had been traveling, but with a speed twice what it was before.

"And again the silks and spider webs," Jemidon said. "More intensity. You must make it more."

The masters responded with precision. Like puppets with two sets of strings, they alternated between the rituals and formulas, sending the laws first one way and then the other, soaring past the original node with ever-increasing speed. And with each pass, the tug of Melizar's attempt to relock fed more energy into the system. The amplitudes of the oscillations became greater and greater.

Upward rushed Melizar's soldiers. Wider became the undulations. Jemidon felt the fabric of existence overshoot the next node of the lattice in one direction and then roar past two more as it came tearing back. He sensed Melizar exerting his maximum power to grab at the laws as they swung past, but the effort was not enough. The momentum could not be checked. With one final filling of the vials, the laws plowed through the lattice, past all the nodes that were recorded, into a region that Melizar had not explored before.

Jemidon saw the imp lights wink out, one by one, from around Melizar's hood. He turned to see that the arching djinn stood on the hillcrest no more.

"What have you done?" Melizar strained his voice above the trample of the onrushing men-at-arms. "The laws, the laws, they are new and strange. No one knows what their manipulations might be."

"It is as I planned," Jemidon shouted back. "Now the three who serve you will have no advantage over mine. We are equal in the crafts that we can comand."

For a moment Melizar was silent. With twitching spasms, he ran a hand over his cube. Impulsively he knelt, but then immediately stood again when there was no buzz of imps. He looked at his men-at-arms closing the distance to the crest and laughed.

"Yes, equal," he said, "equal for the moment. Soon the balance of manipulants will be three to none."

Jemidon did not reply. He turned back to look at the puzzled masters. "Vinegar and oil of vitrol, whatever you can find. Do not bother about the alchemy. Toss everything you can."

The masters hesitated and frowned. Jemidon ran into their midst and pointed to two flasks at random. One of the alchemists nodded. He mixed the contents and then hurled the containers at the men-at-arms. The first shattered harmlessly off an upraised shield, but the second hit the ground and brewed a minute longer before exploding into knifelets of glass. Two men yelled in surprise and tumbled to their knees with dozens of tiny cuts oozing blood.

The alchemists waved for the magician to join them. With inspired abandon, they concocted the remaining ingredients of the tent. Some became simple missiles that clattered off blade and mail; others, deadly grenades that cut into flesh. A bottle of oil, splattered against the middle of the advancing men, with a flaming torch thrown after, sent an explosion of fire along the line. One by one, the remaining soldiers went down, until only two were left.

Jemidon looped behind the masters. He tightened his grip on the changer. The outcome had to be exactly right for his plan to succeed. He looked among the tumbled crates for some more of the ingredients that had produced the smokiest reaction. Just as the warriors rushed upon the masters, he threw the chemicals into their midst.

One alchemist went down from the slash of a blade, but the other circled behind and felled the man-at-arms with a blow to the head. The smoke billowed from the mixing brew, dimming what anyone could see. Jemidon rushed into the opaqueness and aimed a swift kick where the soldier's groin should be. He heard a gasp of pain and then a dull thud as another of the alchemist's blows struck home.

Jemidon backed out of the smolder and saw the masters staggering after. He grabbed one by the collar of his robe and banged his head into the forehead of the other. Like sleeping Skyskirr, they slumped to the ground.

Jemidon took another step backward and held his breath, waiting for the reaction to run its course and the fumes to clear. When they had dissipated enough for him to see Melizar down the slope, he stepped slowly forward, shoulders slumped and with a dragging step.

For a moment, the metamagician did not react. He stood frozen, looking at Jemidon up the length of the slope. Then the pilot threw back his head and his laugh rang across the hillside, the loudest that Jemidon had ever heard.

"You did give me pause," the metamagician shouted. "A closer contest than I would have thought. But in the end, the result is the same. Your manipulants fall and you have no more resources, while I still have three in this universe and three more guiding the storms in the 'hedron beyond. It will take some time to probe and find where you have spun the laws, but you are powerless to stop my search. Eventually I will restore things to the way they were. You may as well come forward now and hand me your key as token of surrender. All you can do is wait and watch the enveloping of your fate."

Jemidon continued his cautious motion forward. He scanned down the hillside at the remains of the battle still in progress, but saw that Melizar took no notice. The metamagician had not moved. He waited with arms crossed, chuckling with his soft laughter.

Slowly Jemidon walked down the slope, moving with the gait of a man going to the gallows. With each step, he tightened his grip on the changer, holding it close to his chest, not wanting to give Melizar any reason to do other than stand and wait.

"Finally you caused a significant perturbation," Melizar said when Jemidon halted about ten feet away. "But it is a perturbation nonetheless. It still ends according to my plan."

"And perhaps according to mine as well," Jemidon said softly. "You are the keystone about which all else hangs. If you are felled, I can free the other pilots from the cubes that have now stopped contracting. Together, we can navigate to laws that will aid both our causes, coerce your manipulants to our bidding, reestablish the portal, and rescue Ponzar and the others on his lithon. And with no demons to oppose him, the archmage can summon enough devils of his own to escape from the battlefield. Without a leader, the passion of the rebels will dissipate into brawls for plunder. There will be no message across the sea to fan other rebellions. It will take some time, but order can be restored."

"You speak like a villain from one of your sagas," Melizar said, "telling all of his plan before he is thwarted. But as I have noted, there is a difference between your design and mine. I am the one who has succeeded, the

360

one who has brought his to full fruition. I still possess manipulants. I still have a basis of power, where you have none."

"There is more to my plan," Jemidon said. "It hinges on differences just as you speak. Differences indeed between you and me. Differences besides your greater experience, your well-thought-out plot, your strength that gives you the title of first pilot.

"Your whole existence has been one of metamagic," Jemidon continued, "one of living each day with the three metalaws, steeped with the reality of the Postulate of Invariance, the Axiom of Least Contradiction, and the Verity of Exclusion. But for me, it was different. I did not know of their existence. I struggled instead to master the manipulations, to work the crafts for myself, to mold my destiny with my own hands, rather than command the use of others."

"This prattle is of no consequence. Give me the key."

"I fully intend to," Jemidon said. "But first think of the meaning of the difference. To you, a metamagician without his manipulants is powerless. There is nothing he can do. You would let one approach within a few feet, confident that he must meekly wait until your base of power returns."

Jemidon lifted the changer in his hand. "But for me, the possibilities are not the same. You are without any crafts to command. For the next few moments, there are no rebels close enough to come to your aid. Think of it, Melizar. Our duel has just begun."

For a long moment, there was silence. Melizar eyed Jemidon's changer and then glanced over his shoulder. He took a cautious step backward. But Jemidon did not hesitate. With one swift motion, he flung the heavy mass of metal at the pilot, crashing it against the Skyskirr's skull with a bone-cracking snap. He watched the pilot crumple to the ground and grunted with satisfaction. As simply as that, it was over.

"And as a group, the other metamagicians were able to force a decoupling, using Melizar's cube," Jemidon said, "even though it was not as familiar as their own keys." Automatically, he touched his coinchanger, now restored through the efforts of the magicians and metalsmiths.

He looked around the assembled court and saw a mixture of expressions. The old king sat stone-faced, and the other nobles, clustered behind the makeshift throne, registered neither gratitude nor relief. Prince Wilmad's empty seat on the monarch's right was draped in black. The newer barons on the other side of the barn squirmed uncomfortably in their fine silks and linens, Canthor more than most. Jemilor, his equally new seneschal, had to keep reminding him not to slouch. Augusta smiled as Jemidon spoke, and even Farnel's stern visage was without some of its customary tightness.

Jemidon squeezed Delia's hand where she lay on the cot at his side. He smiled as she grasped his arm closer to her cheek. Her rescue had barely been in time, but the vapors which had spilled through the portal had lessened in density around Ponzar's lithon. The sweet air which drifted back in exchange was of benefit as well. With all the Skyskirr helping to rediscover wizardry and reopen the passage, they had been able to scoop her and the others away from the vapors before it was too late.

"And it is well they took the first pilot to the 'hedron before the opening was closed a second time," the archmage interrupted before Jemidon could continue. "For our universe, one metamagician is quite enough."

"If Melizar was so easily defeated, why did we waste precious arms and place our very presence in peril?" the old king rumbled. "This Jemidon struck him down unassisted, aided by neither sword nor master."

"With Melizar in control of the laws, there was no way you could reach him by the arts," Jemidon said. "And the rebel army kept away the men-at-arms. Indeed, when I rushed upon him in Trocolar's dungeon and he thought me a thief, he instinctively commanded the guards to effect my seizure. In the tent, after the battle of Plowblade Pass, he directed torporsand my way as he would to any errant manipulant. But when he saw me as another metamagician, one who worked his will through the direction of others, it did not cross his mind that I could carry any threat without attendants. He let me approach unhindered, calling no one to give him aid."

"Perhaps it is best we end all the threats while we are about it." The king looked at Jemidon through rheumy eyes. "We have seen ample evidence of what havoc can be wreaked by one with powers such as Melizar's." He turned his head stiffly in Alodar's direction. "And I think, archmage, that you will agree. Prudence dictates putting this one immediately to the sword."

Several of the nobles grunted agreement. Jemidon scowled, but Alodar waved the comment away.

"And then who will protect us from the next?" the archmage asked. "What if another comes from some other universe by stealth and attempts to move the laws away from where they have been restored? Who do you suggest to detect the unlocking, to struggle to keep the anchoring where it is?"

The old king frowned. He stroked his chin and stared at the archmage.

"I propose to add him to my retinue," Alodar continued. "His major task will be to keep the laws securely bound. If he does nothing else, it will be bargain enough." He paused and returned the king's stare. "Let me worry about what is best for those with talent in the arts. You will be busy enough rebuilding a kingdom from what is left."

"Selection of the new barons from those who fought against him was a wise first step," Canthor said. "Men who have sweated in the cages will much less likely subject others to them."

"And the vaultholders of Pluton are willing to make the loans that lubricate the reestablishment of order," Augusta said. "It is in peace that we prosper, not the anarchy of war."

"The masters of Morgana need the tranquility of their thoughts," Farnel added. "Without inner peace, no glamours of greatness can be cast. The possibility of losing our crafts again is not one we wish to consider."

363

The king turned his eyes back to Jemidon. "I am told that Melizar had a taste for exploration," he said. "If this one has the same talents, how would he be any different? Why should he be content with waiting to hold the laws firm against some future attack when he could send everything drifting instead?"

Jemidon cut off Alodar's reply. "I can speak in my own defense," he said. "No one here knows the drives of the metamagician more than I."

He paused and ran his tongue over his lips, frowning as he tried to put his feelings into words. "For me, the pursuit of the metalaws was like untangling the interlocking rings or removing the beads from a knotted rope."

"And now—" He waved his hands palms upward. Now it is solved. The mystery, the enticement, the allure, all are gone. Moving through the lattice only means boring repetition. The desires that pushed Melizar are not mine.

"And perhaps I have learned something more important than even the metalaws." Jemidon paused and looked at Alodar. "Raw talent alone does not guarantee success. My skills were puny besides those of Melizar, and yet I emerged the victor because of how I used them. For all of my quest, the lesson has been the same. Even without the Verity of Exclusion, I see now that it is doubtful that I would have won the robe with the effort I was willing to extend. I wanted it given because of superficial understanding, or a single dazzling insight, rather than in exchange for hard work and attention to detail."

"Then what is your desire?" the king asked. "How many brandels a year to bribe you from decoupling the laws?"

"My basic need has been satisfied," Jemidon smiled. "For all of my life, I have labored under the burden of trying to fit myself into the image that others would have of me. But the burden came entirely from within. The guilt, the quest for power and respect, tugged at me only because I let them." Jemidon took a deep breath. "They tug no longer. I am free. I quested for what I cannot have, but I gained that for which even the archmage cannot quest."

"Before the battle, I spoke of mastery of yourself," Alodar said. "And even in that, you have proved your mettle."

"Finally you came to your senses and planned before you acted," Delia joined in. "In the end, that made all the difference."

"I grant you, Delia, that there is merit in the way you approach problems." Jemidon's smile broadened. "But even in that, I am my own man. Yes, before I acted, I reasoned what it would take to open the cube and the manner in which Melizar finally must be confronted. But what if I had been properly cautious and calculating about all the risks and alternatives before I took the chance? If I had questioned whether the cube would roll though the demon arch onto Ponzar's lithon or merely to empty air? If I had debated whether the random fling of the laws would indeed send them where Melizar was unfamiliar and powerless? If I had needed to know for sure that the three remaining masters would exactly counterbalance a dozen men-at-arms, so that only Melizar and I would be left? Had I pondered all of that, I would still be calculating the outcome while pouring from the cube as a bloody ooze.

"I am what I am, Delia, strengths and flaws. I need apologize to no one for them. Others may mock me or throw gold brandels as they choose. I am satisfied with myself, and the rest does not matter."

"It is a wonder what saving the universe will do for one's self-esteem," Alodar said wryly. "But I do not plan to let you stay idle while you walk the garden paths of my retreat. You have the insight to construct the general from the particular. Even though you cannot work any of the crafts, I expect you to aid the masters in formulating extensions of their powers. You are unique among all the practitioners of the arts, Jemidon. As such, you of course become a master, entitled to the black robe. And even though you profess no longer to have a desire for fame, I suspect that it will come, nevertheless."

"And it was not one universe but two," Delia said. "The Skyskirr are as grateful as I am for Jemidon's gifts."

Gifts. The word resonated in Jemidon's mind. He remembered what Delia had done on the lithon. Without her, despite all his bold words, no success would have been possible. And she had done it not for the benefit of two universes, but for him alone. In the end, saving her had meant more than the robe.

Jemidon turned from Delia and looked at Augusta, just to make sure. Yes, even in that he had selected the right alternative. The vaultholder of Pluton would not lack for suitors, and there was only one with whom he wanted to share his destiny.

"And I expect you to teach Delia in those crafts as well," Jemidon said to the archmage. "She has shown talent in more than one and, close to me, her skills will prosper." He looked back down at Delia. "Perhaps I presume too much, but our pasts have been too intertwined for our futures to be far apart."

Delia rubbed the pale band of skin on her wrist where the bracelet had been. "You show some promise." She nodded. "I think I will keep you around."

About the Author

LYN HARDY became interested in fantasy while wandering through the fringes of fandom as an undergraduate at Caltech. In addition to reading and writing, he has sporadic bursts of enthusiasm for collecting stamps, comics, astronaut patches and playing cards. He currently lives with his wife and two daughters in Torrance, California.

Enchanting fantasies from

DEL REY BOOKS